A WEIGHT

OF

RECKONING

SEQUEL TO THE SEVEN WORDS

C. S. WACHTER

Shadowfall Publishing

A Weight of Reckoning
Sequel to: The Seven Words

Published by Shadowfall Publishing

Printed in the United States of America

Wachter, C. S.
    A Weight of Reckoning / C. S. Wachter
    Sequel to: The seven words
    ISBN: 978-1-7340591-0-6 (paperback)
    ISBN: 978-1-7340591-1-3 (ebook)

Cover Design by: Mountainview Books, LLC
Maps by: Nexgenstudio
Print formatting by: Mountainview Books, LLC

For Jesus.
Thank you for your continuous love, guidance, and blessings.

ACKNOWLEDGMENTS

Special thanks to Jan and Kelly.
The best critique partners a writer could want.

AMATHEA

Hebron

Providence River

Providence

Salem River

Port Ammon

Salem

Fox Hollow Farm

Bethel

Hope Farm

Ramon

West Branches

Jordan

Kishon Bay

Shilo Island

Jezabel Monastery

Uzziah River

Ferry Harbor

Port Dor

Kin Esdra Sea

7

ARISIMA

Great Desert

where the desert
drinks itself

Zuraya
Oasis

Aleppo
Monastry

Jadeth Sea

CORYLUS

Port Jervis

Loriann's Compound

Leclerville

Eschan

Kynian Forest

Highreach

River Road

Roaring River

James River

Sullivan's Edge

Aurum Sanctum

Sigmund's Estate

King's Highway

Westvale

Villagreed Southbury

Villagreed Willowdale

Cameron Sea

Shattered Continent

11

GLACIERIA

Frozen Wastes

Wataru Lands

Tetsuya's Village

Spirit Lands

Michi Lands

Roaring Mountain

Portal Station

Reeling Bowl

Khalon Lands

NEMORA

Balnard Province

Neth Province

Fort Gerard

Neth River

Inverness

Forgotten the Forgotten

Neth Forest

Heartfell Northland Blessed Hollow

High Hall

Vernoss River

Reinard

Derren Northern Province

Jervin

Amersby

Derren River

Derren Southern Province

Vern

Fort Milton

Falling River

Rockhall Province

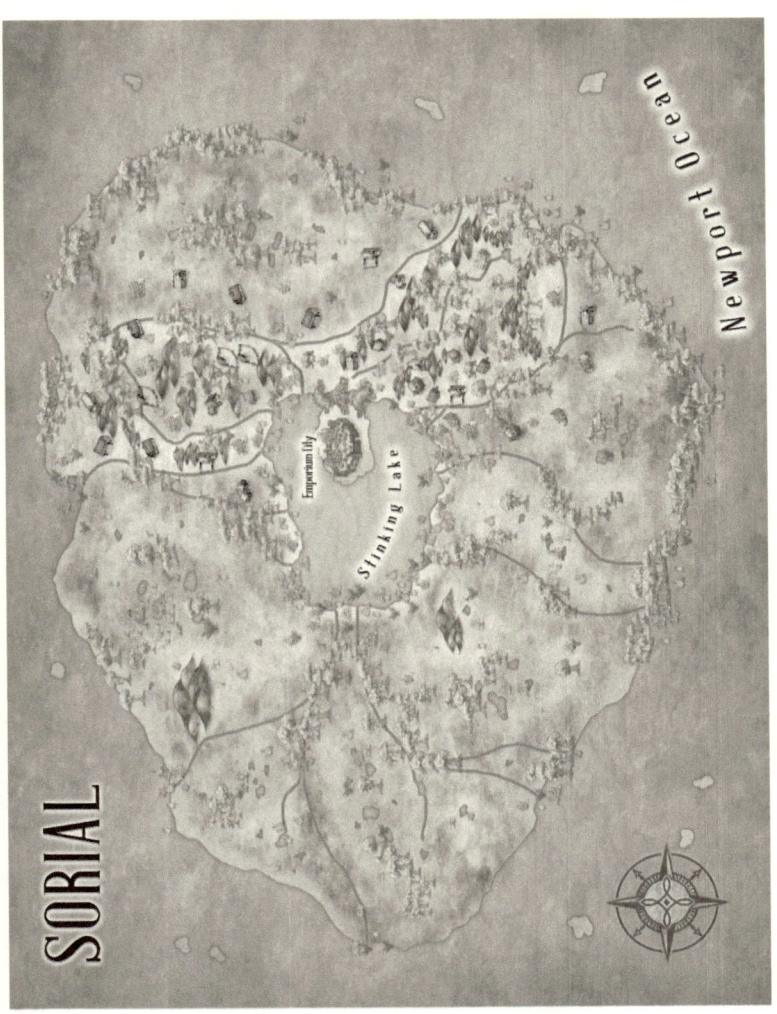

SORIAL

Newport Ocean

Emporium Ity

Stinking Lake

VERES

Nuant Gaerwyn – Headwaters of Gaerwyn Fall

Metal

Black River

Anderson Mine

Anderson Gaming Complex

Tiger River

Jallerian Mountains

Hart

Griffin Mine

Sharon Mine

Sharon River

Naameth Sea

SEVEN WORLDS OF THE OCHEN SYSTEM

AMATHEA:
Farming world magic deficit

ARISIMA:
Desert world; magic saturated

CORYLUS:
Royal world; home of Kierkengaard family line; magic saturated

GALCIERIA:
Ice world; magic saturated

NEMORA:
Woodland world; home of Kraftsmunn and Woodfield family lines; most magic saturated planet

SORIAL:
Merchant world; magic deficit

VERES:
Mining world; source of veredium; magic deficit

LIST OF CHARACTERS IN ORDER OF APPEARANCE

MITE—child-like ancient from Nemora; Rayne's friend

SETH HAMLIN—Prime Shepherd of the United Scrolls of Ochen church

DUCHESS CAILYN WOODFIELD—Rayne's aunt; Rowena's sister; Lady Mother for the USO church (Nemora)

ARNULF—Master of Sacrifices for the United Scrolls of Ochen (USO) church

HIGH GUARDIAN OF THE SCROLLS—HAD BEEN SIGMUND OF BAINARD—demon

RAYNE KIERKENGAARD—Crown Prince Rayne Nathan Samuel Kierkengaard of Corylus and the Ochen system; son of Theodor and Rowena; Chosen Light Bringer of the One

BOONE (LIGHTNING BOONE)—Rayne's dog

ANDREW—Rayne's page and close friend

CHEF CLEMENS—head chef at the Westvale Palace

SHALIMAR—Rayne's horse

BETHIE (ANNABETH)—young orphan girl from Amathea; adopted by Anne and Shaw

ELSIE—church cook; advisor and friend to all

LEXI (LADY ALEXIANNDRA) ERLAND—Duchess of Veres and daughter of Duke Justus Erland; Rayne's betrothed

DUKE JUSTUS ERLAND—Duke of Veres and father to Lexi; friend of King Theodor and Queen Rowena

DEREK FALKNOR—House of Falknor Representative (Sorial)

HARRISON STOCKEN—produce seller from Amathea

THEODOR KIERGENGAARD—King of Corylus and the Ochen system; Rayne's father

ROWENA KRAFTSMUNN KIERKENGAARD—Queen of Corylus and the Ochen system; originally from Nemora; Rayne's mother

CAPTAIN ANTON FONTAINE—Captain of Ochen Army

VARICK—personal representative of Duchess Cailyn (Nemora)

SERGEANT THEADA—guardsman of Duchess Cailyn (Nemora)

ETHAN—Second of Duke Justus Erland

SILAS—friend and employee of Duke Justus Erland

SEREN—Duke Justus Erland's cook; a healer

DANTON—advisor to King Theodor

THORVIN KRAFTSMUNN—Rayne's bodyguard; military advisor

STEVIE KASPER—twin to Sashi Kasper; friend of Rayne

CAPTAIN ELLIS—Ochen Army captain stationed on Arisima

SERGEANT NOAH REESE—Ochen Army sergeant stationed on Arisima under Captain Ellis; husband of Sashi; Rayne's friend

SASHI KASPER REESE—twin to Stevie; Rayne's friend; Noah's wife

ANNE PARSON RADINAJAN—healer; Rayne's oldest friend; Shaw's wife; Bethie, Warren, and Jonathan's mother

SHAW RADINAJAN—monk from Arisima; Rayne's friend; Anne's husband; Bethie, Warren, and Jonathan's father

BENNING—Ochen Army soldier originally from Nemora

OLIVER (OLLIE)—Ochen Army soldier originally from Nemora

GWYN THOMPSON—Senior Associate Shepherd of the
USO

CORALEA—shop owner; Rayne's friend on Sorial

MAYDA CREEDOFF—First Associate Shepherd Creedoff's daughter

VARTAN CREEDOFF—First Associate Shepherd of the
USO church; Mayda's father

ERIC AND JENS—members of the USO church; friends
of Vartan Creedoff

ASSOCIATE SHEPHERD OSGOOD AND DEACON
IDA—officers of the USO church

GILES—Rayne's cousin; betrayed Rayne to Sigmund; vanished on Binding Day

MARIUS—associate of Sigmund; vanished on Binding Day

BRAM—one-eyed prisoner of the USO

LORILEE AND SEBASTIAN—servants at Castle
Inverness

ELSPETH—Kindred healer

EAN—Kindred healer

FALLON—Kindred elder

NEAL—Kindred champion

1

And this is the judgment: the light has come into the world, and people loved the darkness rather than the light because their works were evil. John 3:19 ESV

"Know this, my beloved child, the light of my Spirit lives within you. It unites the lights of Ochen; the golden light of the Sun Sparrows, the blue light of Neth, and the red light of the desert. It will strengthen you and guide you. But beware, though the demonic darkness will be diminished, so long as individuals seek evil it will not be gone completely, just bound for a time. It will always strive to destroy the Light and the Words within you, but search it out and battle against it always, my beloved child." The One's words to Rayne on the Day of Binding.

Wind, massive and elemental, shrieked through the secluded hollow, tossing and churning the weighty branches of hoary oaks and long-needled pines as if they were kindling. The cloaked woman raised her hands, speaking words of power that were shredded and scattered by the tempest. Behind her, a similarly garbed figure stood watching. Silent. Approving.

Heavy magic, drawn to the glen by the commands, thickened the air above, building and swelling like rain-laden storm clouds, immune to the effects of the gale.

Only on Nemora. What strength. What power! You are strong indeed, my lady. Unexpected in one assumed to be weak of will and cowardly. If my need hadn't been so great, and your desire for revenge so consuming, who would have ever guessed the extent of your abilities? The man smiled and shifted his position to stand behind the woman as she continued summoning the potent energy of Nemora.

"Enough," he said, touching her shoulder. "You are marvelous, Lady Mother, to have gathered such an abundance of heavy magic in so short a time. Now, quickly. We must complete the sacrifices without delay before the energy dissipates."

Cupping her elbow with long, tapered fingers, the tall figure guided the woman to a stained, altar-like rock in the center of the hollow. He signaled for the offerings to be brought forward. Seven gifts, one for each ruined scroll of power, a necessary ransom to open the channel. A worthy sacrifice to restore the pride and glory of the worlds of Ochen.

"We're ready, Prime Shepherd Hamlin," a towering man said as his massive fingers drew a long, thin veredium knife from beneath his burnt sienna cloak.

"Excellent, Arnulf. Are you ready, Lady Mother?"

"I've been ready for three years, Seth. Get on with it."

Mite watched the activity of the cloaked strangers from a safe vantage point high up in an aged pine as he hummed a song of protection. Though the tree bounced, its upper branches heaving in the wind, the child-like ancient held on with little effort, trusting the resilient pine to withstand the testing.

Except for periodic meetings with his young friend Prince Rayne, the One's Light Bringer, Mite avoided crowds and cities as much as possible. At his age, solitude, time spent with his friends at the Camp of the Forgotten, or visits to the Kindred in Neth all held more attraction. But with the prince's wedding only a few weeks off, Mite had decided to travel to Westvale early. When he neared Inverness, a disturbing fluctuation of the energy levels prompted him to investigate the surrounding area. Heavy, dark magic impregnating the air around the site of ancient sacrifice drew him closer to the dark and pitted altar.

Now, from his high vantage, he muttered to himself. "Wrong. Wrong. Air too dark. Should not be. Mite must warn Ray-ray." As he watched, seven, bound, stumbling newcomers, with hoods tied over their heads, were led to the stone of sacrifice. "No. No. No. Not right, not right. Mite must stop. Bad. Bad. Very bad."

His heart thrummed a wild rhythm, and his hands shook. "Mite must do something!" His song of protection forgotten, the blue-haired ancient scrambled down the tree, mumbling to himself. By the time he was on the ground, the first victim had been forced onto the stone, kneeling, his head thrust forward like some poor, unsuspecting animal. With a smooth, swift motion, the knife sliced the victim's throat, sending droplets of blood arcing across the pitted surface of the stone. Hooded as he had been, the man never saw it coming. Mite cried in his spirit for the soul of the newcomer whose life blood now oozed over the flat rock, becoming one with the countless stains already impregnating the grisly altar.

"Creator Father, why? Mite must stop."

He sprinted down into the hollow as the bleeding body was summarily dumped from the altar and a woman, bound and hooded like the man, was forced to kneel in his place, her knees slipping on the bloody surface. Mite heard chanting, but it was just so much buzzing noise in his ears as he rushed forward, compelled to stop the slaughter. He was close, so close, when something knocked his legs out from under him. He landed face-down in the grass and in an instant, hands were on him, holding him down as he screamed his frustration and tears leaked from his gray eyes.

"Lookie what we have here," a high-pitched voice said. "Somebody's lost their kid. Must be a spy. Pretty little thing, too." Mite was tied and gagged, then forced to sit.

"Blood for blood; blood for power; blood for vengeance." The chanting burned in Mite's mind.

Scanning the cloaked figures scattered through the grove, the seriousness of his situation barreled through Mite. *So many newcomers. Stupid, stupid Mite.* In his horror at what he was witnessing, Mite had ignored his danger. He should never have run blindly forward; but he couldn't regret trying to stop the sacrifices.

Another bound figure was shoved up onto the flat surface, forced to kneel on the now slick and bloody slab, and the brutal knife set to work.

"No, no, no," Mite called out, his voice rough. "Stop. Oh, please stop. Newcomers must not summon darkness. Must not, must not."

Prayer rose in him and he gave vent. "Creator Father, please stop the darkness. Newcomers know not what they do. Help Mite, Creator Father. Help Mite now."

But no help came, only hands that grabbed Mite and stuffed a wadded-up piece of cloth into his mouth, before tying another around his head to hold the gag in place. Mite shuddered as the clammy material touched his skin. The cloth holding the gag must have been pulled from one of the victims; blood from it dribbled onto his shoulder.

The chant continued for a few more minutes. It stopped when Prime Shepherd Hamlin stepped up to the executioner. Hamlin lowered his hood revealing fine, aristocratic features and long silver hair. He smiled as all eyes focused on him. Mite's stomach revolted at the idea of this person smiling while newcomer blood ran off the stone behind him.

Taking the knife, Prime Shepherd Hamlin nodded, and another victim was wrestled into position on the altar. With a quick drawing motion, he slit the throat. Dropping the blade, he plunged his fingers into the blood on the altar and raised them over his head.

"By the blood shed here, we beseech thee great Guardian of the Scrolls, return from the void. I, Prime Shepherd of the United Scrolls of Ochen, seek your assistance. Come to me; show me what I must do to recover our scrolls of power. We are lost without their direction. Our people suffer. By the sacrifices offered here. By the efficacy of spilt blood. We open the channel to the void. Come to us; lead us."

The seventh victim was raised to the altar and forced to kneel.

"Seven blood sacrifices we offer, one for each stolen scroll." The prime shepherd's voice rebounded off the surrounding trees. "Come now. We call you forth to seek your command." With a swift motion, he lifted the knife and dragged it across the final victim's throat while the bulky executioner held the struggling sacrifice down.

"Blood for blood; blood for power; blood for vengeance." The chant continued.

Mite swallowed, the bile rising in his throat. His eyes watered as he watched the heavy magic of Nemora coalesce and spin over the sacrificial stone, churning, bubbling. Black streaks appeared in the gray, shifting and writhing. They grew in the funnel of energy until a dark form appeared in the center of the swirling mist.

"Why have you summoned me?"

Kneeling, the prime shepherd raised his hands in supplication. "O worthy Guardian of the Scrolls, we have called you forth from the void to seek your guidance. We would recover our Scrolls of Power."

"Blood for blood ... blood for power ... blood for vengeance. Yes, I like it." The figure spoke in a measured manner, his voice deep and pulsing with power. "There is a way. But you must not waver, human; to falter, to fail once you have begun, is to lose your soul to me for all eternity. Do you accept this bargain?"

"I will not fail, great Guardian of the Scrolls. Whatever you command, this will I do. Just return our pride and power. Restore to us the stolen scrolls."

"Listen well and obey. Seven sacrifices must you make. One human the first week on the Day of Binding, two humans the second week on the Day of Binding."

Mite moaned as the dark figure continued calling for blood sacrifices, increasing the number of offerings until he got to the seventh week.

"Seven humans the seventh week. All offered here at the stone of ancient power, and all performed on a Day of Binding."

"We will do this gladly," Prime Shepherd Hamlin said, his eyes eager.

"Do you think it will be that easy, little human? More! More is required!" The image in the funnel thundered. "Blood for blood; blood for power; blood for vengeance. So you proclaim, so shall it be. Potent blood must be shed. Costly blood. The light-infused blood of the Binder himself. It must be commingled with that of those sacrificed each Binding Day. Seven rites of sacrifice, seven weeks. For seven weeks, he must live in darkness and silence, and in darkness shall he die at the end. His life blood shall be the final sacrifice. This is the offering you must make to gain your scrolls. Only through blood and pain will their power be returned to Ochen. Do you understand little newcomer?"

"Yes, yes." The prime shepherd nodded. "We will do this. It is right and just. By his actions did the Binder destroy our pride and power, by his death shall they be restored."

Mite's skin pimpled as the figure in the funnel laughed. "Excellent. We eagerly await the final sacrifice."

The figure dissolved, and the funnel collapsed.

"We will begin the ritual of sacrifices on the next Binding Day," the prime shepherd announced. "You who have attended today, and all our fellow believers here on Nemora and flung across Ochen, are bidden to participate in the coming rites. Spread the word, the Binder will pay for his treachery and our scrolls will be restored to us."

As the worshipers dispersed, Mite was dragged to stand in front of the prime shepherd and the mysterious woman.

"A pretty child. We'll use him in one of the sacrifices."

"No. You will not," the Lady Mother said as she walked up to stand next to Prime Shepherd Hamlin.

The man crossed his arms over his chest and his eyebrows rose, sending deep furrows across his forehead. "Why ever not?"

"Because this creature is not human, Seth. He is an

ancient. But we cannot release him either. He's the prince's creature. If given the opportunity, the little ancient will run right to him. He would warn the accursed Binder and that we cannot allow. Keep him alive, for now. He might come in handy. But Seth, guard him carefully; the little one is tricky. We'll see what kind of leverage he can give us in the future, if needed."

The Lady Mother turned to face Mite. His heart froze, his eyes widened in horror, and his mouth opened and closed twice before he wailed. "No! Why? Why would you do this? Why?"

2

Soft tones of pearl gray and pale yellow were nothing more than a promise in the sky when Rayne blinked his eyes open. He lay, right arm flung across his chest, gazing out the open doors to his balcony. A light breeze fluttered the sheer white curtains, bringing with it a curious combination of scents; coming rain, the faint tang of salt from the Cameron Sea, and the fragrances of summer flowers. Rayne sighed, already missing Lexi. She had skipped off Corylus yesterday to spend two weeks with her father on Veres before returning to finalize plans for the wedding. *I'm getting married! Only six more weeks and two days!* He smiled at the thought.

Ever since he had seen Lexi in a dream before he reclaimed the Words of the One to Veres he knew he would marry the courageous girl with golden hair and eyes. And though the demons who sought to bring darkness to Ochen had been defeated on the Day of Binding, it seemed as if the time would never come when things were settled enough to allow Rayne and Lexi to marry. So much damage had been done to the political structure of Ochen by Sigmund's machinations. Only now, almost three years later, was Rayne's father,

King Theodor, finally able to set in motion the rulings to re-establish the Interplanetary Council and Interplanetary Court.

Several assassination attempts traced to pockets of scroll worshiping rebels had been made on Rayne's life. Then, six months ago, reports of scroll worshiper activity began to diminish and eventually fade out completely; It was as if the cult had vanished from Ochen. Rayne hoped the whole warped religion had finally faltered under the weighty truth that there was no real power in the physical scrolls themselves, and that scroll worship had been reduced to nothing more than a line in a history book.

He sighed. *Two weeks. It's only two weeks. Not long. Then she'll be back. It'll go by fast. She deserves this time alone with her father.*

He closed his eyes, turned on his side, and pulled the covers back above his head to no avail. He sighed again. *Well, I guess I'm wide awake now. Might as well get up.* Yawning, he stretched, threw off the blanket, and rising, walked out to the balcony. The air was already warm and sticky, a sure sign of late-day storms riding in off the Cameron Sea. Summer was just a couple weeks away and was already promising to be another hot one in Westvale.

Boone, always sensitive to Rayne's movements, rose and padded across the dense carpet in the sitting room where she had been sleeping near Andrew. Rayne heard the sound transition to nails clicking on polished wood as she entered the bedroom and walked out to stand at his side. Brushing against his leg, she stuck her wet nose up into the palm of his hand, seeking attention.

"Good morning, girl," Rayne whispered as he rubbed the rough fur on the top of her head. "Wanna go for a walk?"

Her tail thumped his leg in response. "Come on. Let's see if we can sneak out without waking Andrew."

After throwing on black, leather leggings; a silver, sleeveless tunic; and his black doeskin boots, Rayne crept through the sitting room. Andrew was still sunk deep in sleep, his breathing even, his mouth hanging open with a drizzle of drool at the corner. Rayne smiled at the slumbering page, eased open the door, and waved Boone through before closing it with a quiet snick.

The two descended the stairs with rapid steps and took a

few turns, before slipping through the kitchens, ducking assorted servants already preparing breakfast. After passing the ovens in the baking kitchen, Rayne grabbed an apple from a basket of fruit in the prep kitchen. He waved a thank you to the head cook, Clemens, who scowled at him, shaking his head.

"I know, I know," Rayne said, as he tossed the apple into the air and caught it. "Dogs aren't allowed in your kitchens, even if they belong to princes. We're just passing through."

"Of course, Sire," Clemens replied, bowing. "As long as you understand and don't bring that boisterous animal in here again."

It was a dialogue of routine. Every time Boone followed Rayne through the kitchens, the same words, or words of similar meaning were spoken. Everyone knew it was a form of greeting, nothing more. A ritual between the prince and the chef that had developed over the past few years. Not once in all that time had Boone strayed from following Rayne's heels, and her presence no longer upset Chef Clemens. The man often set aside roasted, meaty bones for the dog.

Rayne strode across the palace grounds to the stable, Boone running ahead then circling back to him, enjoying the activity. Rayne slowed as he entered the shadow-drenched stable, heading toward Shalimar's stall. The inky black, Arisimanian mare nickered in greeting as he approached. "Hey, girl."

She tossed her head and Rayne grinned. "I know. You want to run. Later, okay? I have a treat for you now. I promise we'll go for a run later."

The horse gently lipped the apple from Rayne's hand, and he was already on his way out the stable door as she crunched into the juicy fruit.

The young man and his dog jogged back across the grounds, now heading toward the cathedral, where they slipped in through one of the side doors. Rayne wanted to see how the finishing work was coming on the repaired building. His battle in the sanctuary with the Demon Master, Sigmund, and Brayden had damaged sections of the building's masonry and destroyed most of the stained-glass windows. Now, just in time for his wedding, the new replacement windows were being set, and Roboso, the artist who had painted a mural depicting the battle on the back wall, was adding final details.

Rayne slid into one of the shadowed pews to sit in the comforting quiet and pray. Already this morning, the craftsmen were at work on both projects. Boone whined to jump up next to him. "No, girl. Sit. Stay."

With a huff, she sat at his feet and Rayne closed his eyes. He calmed his spirit and focused on praying. He missed his early morning quiet time with Shaw, Anne, and Lexi. With Lexi gone and Anne due to give birth to her and Shaw's second child any day now, they had decided to forego study of the scrolls for the next few weeks. The wedding and honeymoon would push that back even further.

Rayne rolled his shoulders, absent-mindedly ran his finger down the thin scar that marred his right cheek, and wondered how Thorvin, his protector and mentor, was doing. He had hoped sparring with his old trainer would help him pass the time while Lexi was away. But, after assurances from Rayne that he would remain safely in Westvale until Thorvin returned, the big man had left a week ago to spend time working with the older students at Warren's Rest, the school and training facility that Rayne helped start.

When Rayne finished praying, he rose and whispered, "Come on, Boone. Let's go visit Elsie before I need to get back to the palace. Maybe she has some nice crispy bacon fried up and waiting for us."

He passed Shaw and Anne's cottage on his way to the church kitchen. It was dark and quiet. *The kids must be sleeping in. That's good. Anne needs the rest.* He took the path to Elsie's kitchen door.

"Stay Boone." Opening the door a crack, he peeked in. "Good morning."

Suddenly the door was yanked from his hand and flung open. "Yes! Yes!" Bethie shouted. He knelt to receive a hug from the little girl, but she ignored him, slipped past, and threw her arms around Boone's neck.

"Boonie, Boonie. Look NeNe Elsie, Boonie's here. Can she come in NeNe? Please, can Boonie come in? I'll watch her. You know she'll be a good girl."

Failing to hide her chuckle behind a flour coated hand, Elsie caught Rayne's eyes. "Now that was a fine greeting for you, wasn't it?"

"I guess I don't count when Boone's with me." Rayne suppressed a grin as Bethie stood in the doorway, hands folded in supplication, eyes wide, mouthing *please, please, please.* "At least I'm not the one who has to tell Bethie 'no'. I'm surprised to see her here at this hour."

Wiping the flour off her hands, Elsie gave Rayne a no-nonsense look. "Someone needed to give Shaw and Anne a break. Between Bethie, Little Warren, and another baby due any day now, those two are just exhausted."

"Yeah, I know. That's why we aren't meeting to study the scrolls until after we get back from Amathea."

"No," Elsie said to Bethie, who was still silently begging. "You can play with Boone another time, Bethie. What were you doing when Rayne came to the door?"

Bethie stopped pleading and looked down at her shoes, now scuffing the walkway. "Making bread?"

"Yes Bethie. You promised me you would help me bake this morning. I know you don't want to break a promise. Right?"

The little girl shook her head, still not meeting Elsie's eyes.

"Good. So, for now, you need to leave Boone out there, say a proper 'good morning' to Rayne, and come wash your hands. I'm sure Rayne will let you play with Boone later."

With a sigh, Bethie gave the black dog's head a final pat and scurried to the wash sink. "I'll play with you later Boonie. Okay?" she called over her shoulder as she lathered soap and rinsed her hands before wiping them dry. Then, with a giggle, she moved in front of Rayne and wrapped her arms around his waist. "Good morning, big brother Rayne. Can we play Seek with Boone later? You and me and Andrew?" She frowned. "Boonie always finds you first. How? Can we play in the King's Park again today? I like playing there." Without giving Rayne a chance to respond, Bethie moved right into her next topic. "I'm making bread with NeNe Elsie. Do you want to help? If you want to help, you'll have to wash your hands too."

Picking up the little girl, Rayne smiled and winked. "I don't think I'd be very good at making bread. But I am pretty good at eating it. I'm so hungry I'm about to collapse from lack of food. Do you think you and NeNe Elsie can give me some bread to eat?"

"NeNe Elsie, we need to give big brother bread and honey. He's soooo hungry."

She pushed out of Rayne's arms and ran to the table where a partially cut loaf of bread sat. "Can I cut it, please?"

Elsie moved to stand alongside Bethie and helped her hold the large, serrated knife and carve off two slices of bread. After the knife was placed carefully back on the table, Elsie turned to Rayne. "I'm sorry I don't have any bacon ready, but if you have the time, I can fry some up right now."

"Thank you, Elsie, but bread with honey will be fine. I need to get back to the palace soon anyway."

Elsie and Bethie took a few minutes to sit with Rayne before continuing their bread making. Rayne picked Bethie up and swung her around. "Thank you, little sister, for sharing Elsie's delicious bread and honey. Listen to NeNe Elsie, learn well, and soon I'll get to eat bread you have made yourself."

She wrapped her arms around his neck and snuggled her head under his chin. "You're the bestest big brother ever. I love you Rayne."

"I love you too, little one." He hugged Bethie, kissed her cheek, and set her down. "Thanks again for the bread, Elsie. See you later."

"Remember," Bethie shouted after him. "We're going to play Seek with Boone. You promised."

Rayne waved good-bye. "I didn't promise, but we'll see. Maybe later." Calling for Boone to follow, he headed back to his suite to bathe and dress. Seeing Elsie and Bethie helped him to focus on the good things he had rather than feeling sorry for himself while Lexi and Thorvin were away. He would keep busy and the time would go by quickly.

I think I'll even get in some archery practice this afternoon. Then, next time Noah and Sashi come home from Arisima I can challenge Sashi to a competition.

3

Catching her father's gaze, Lexi shook her head and rolled her eyes. A quick grin surfaced on her father's face, then twisted into a grimace before his expression became serious again. Lexi turned away to hide her own smirk. Derek Falknor, the representative sent to negotiate terms for the movement of goods through Sorial to Veres seemed oblivious to their frustration as he continued to drone on about the benefits of dealing with Falknor House.

After the downfall of Andersen House, the Falknor family had risen to fill the void. As head of the Shipping and Portal Guild, the family was now the most powerful of the merchant houses on Sorial. Derek continued speaking for another half hour as Lexi, Duke Justus, and Harrison Stocken, a produce seller from Amathea, ate.

Duke Erland had planned to meet with Harrison alone to discuss trade between the farming cooperative he represented and Veres—a barter of Amathean produce for veredium without any outside interference. That was why Lexi's father proposed meeting in Eleri rather than Emporium City.

The little restaurant where they now sat was one of Duke

Erland's favorite places to frequent when in Eleri. The food was always well prepared and the service discrete. The private room fronting on the quiet side street was pleasant, sunny, and comfortable with white tablecloths and well-padded chairs covered in a white and blue checked material.

Catching wind of the impending agreement, the Falknor Family insisted their representative be present. Now, Derek was extolling the benefits in having all the logistics of the transaction handled by the Falknors. They would oversee transport both ways through Emporium City, handle all necessary paperwork, and the inevitable tariffs and permits that would be levied by Sorial.

"As you can plainly see," he said, finally winding down, "it is beneficial for everyone concerned, to have the most powerful family on Sorial protecting your interests in this long-term arrangement." He sniffed and nodded, apparently satisfied with his monologue. Looking down at his plate of now-congealed gravy seeping out from his cold meat and potato pie, he scowled and motioned a waiter over. "This is cold. Take it and bring me a fresh, warm plate, immediately."

"I appreciate the points you have made." Duke Erland pushed his empty plate across the white tablecloth toward the center of the round table, where a waiter whisked it away.

"As the head family of the Shipping and Portal Guild, Falknor House's support would be quite valuable. However, I'm not certain your backing is worth the exorbitant fees you are proposing. In truth, the transportation of the goods can be handled by Mr. Stocken's co-op and our own people."

"Ah, my lord, but you've missed the point. The tariffs and charges for transportation through Sorial by unauthorized parties are quite steep. By retaining the Falknor family, it may appear that you are paying more for the shipping, but with the reduction of fees achieved by working through us, the cost for shipping is only slightly higher than what you would pay otherwise, and all the hassle is avoided."

"Yes, Mr. Falknor, you have made that point abundantly clear. For now, though, I would like to discuss the matter with Mr. Stocken and his co-op before any decision is made."

While the dialogue of negotiation proceeded between her father and Derek, with Harrison interjecting his opinion at points, Lexi stifled her frustration and gazed out the window, watching a young couple across the street. They were sitting together in a tiny alcove and her line of sight provided Lexi with a clear view.

She wondered what Rayne was doing while she was stuck waiting for this meeting to end. Her father had promised to spend the entire two weeks with her, but then agreed to this last-minute meeting, pushing off their departure by two days.

The couple were younger than Lexi and Rayne, probably about the age they had been when they first met three years ago. Though the boy was dressed in rough clothing—*maybe a mine worker?* The girl wore better-quality, stylish clothing—*a shopkeeper's daughter?*

As Lexi watched, the girl laughed, then with a fluid motion, flung her long, blonde braid over her shoulder. She tilted her chin up and gazed into the young man's eyes. *That's right. Lay it on. Keep his attention. That boy doesn't stand a chance. What a flirt. And right out in the street!*

After scanning the area, the young man leaned in and with a quick motion, kissed the now blushing girl. She bit the side of her lip, looking up at the boy. *How could they? What are they thinking? Where are their parents? I should go out there right now and set that hussy straight.*

Then it hit Lexi. *I'm jealous.* It was the only reason she could feel such venom toward a young woman she didn't even know, just because the stranger was with her sweetheart. She closed her eyes, drew in a deep breath, and pulled Rayne's image up in her mind, the way he had been when they first met. Still unsure, so much a boy, not a man, full of pain and determination. She chuckled under her breath, remembering how rough he had looked that day; wearing a bloody Andersen House vest and leggings, his hair chopped and a long braid still dangling at his temple.

And now? Well, now. He had grown so much. The unsure, slender youth was now a strong, well-built man, certain of his beliefs and his place in life. Though still on the slight side, his muscles had filled out and Lexi loved the way his strong shoulders narrowed to a firm waist and slim hips. He had taken to wearing his hair shorter, almost like his father's. Although Rayne's lack of care about his appearance usually meant it draped over his collar and shadowed his eyes before he got it cut again. And he was trying, with little success, to grow a beard.

With eyes still closed, and her chin nestled into the palms of her hands, Lexi brought to mind an image of Rayne working through a sword dance. It was two days ago. She sat next to Queen Rowena on one of the benches flanking the practice rings, observing his workout, mesmerized as always by his skill. His movements were fluid, precise, and quick. She had watched him with delight, pride filling her with the knowledge that he would be her husband in just a few weeks.

"Lexi ... Lexi, are you alright?" Her father's voice broke into her daydream. With a start, she realized she was blushing and chewing the side of her lip, just like the *hussy* across the street.

While Lexi had been engrossed in her memories, her father and the other men apparently concluded the business they were discussing. Lexi's cheeks grew even warmer. With her father still staring at her, concern written in the creases of his forehead, she mumbled, "I'm fine, just a little bored, I guess." She shrugged and smiled.

Harrison Stocken grinned. Understanding sparkled in his eyes as he rose and bowed to her. "I am sorry to have taken up so much of your special time. I know you were supposed to leave for the mountains yesterday. Please forgive us this interruption." He turned and bowed to the duke. "Thank you. I know the timing was inconvenient. However, I believe our time was well spent. Once we have the first shipment lined up, I'll send word to you both." He dipped his head to Duke Erland then to Derek Falknor before turning and leaving.

"Now," Duke Erland said, his focus on Derek. "What is this *other* business you needed to discuss with me?"

After pursing his lips and casting a quick glance at Lexi, Derek said, "Lady Genevieve, the current head of Falknor

House, has given me authority to present another service in the hope that you would be willing to act as an intermediary. The business arrangement I'm alluding to is to be offered by you to King Theodor. Due to circumstances, which I'm quite certain you understand, we can't present this directly to His Majesty."

"I see." Duke Erland stared at Derek for a minute, his brow creased in thought. "And what, exactly, is this *service* Lady Genevieve is offering to the king?"

"All of Ochen is tied together by skipping lines now regulated jointly by the Falknor family and the Corylus royals. Though King Theodor leaves the daily operations to us, he has control of the pricing structure. For the last three years, Falknor House, at Lady Genevieve's command, has kept close records of portal traffic. These records have given us insight into who and what is traveling where and when. In return for us supplying His Majesty with valuable information, he will return the right to set pricing for the lines to the Shipping and Portal Guild."

Duke Erland sat back, staring at Derek, his face a cold mask. "That is an unreasonable offer. His Majesty would never agree to such an arrangement. The guild's control of pricing would return us to a situation where most citizens could no longer afford to skip. King Theodor's lower pricing structure has benefitted everyone, including your family. More people skipping means more profits for Falknor House."

"To be sure, we do understand this. However, we would agree to His Majesty setting a cap on how much we can charge if he would allow us to control our own operation within those bounds.

"I have been authorized to pass on certain information as an example of the kind of assistance our amended relationship can provide His Majesty. Lady Genevieve is concerned that the current level of stability could be disrupted by the rise of a united scroll cult throughout Ochen. She fears instability will threaten our mutual interests. She is certain that it has come to the attention of Westvale that over the last six months, certain factions of the cult have disappeared, and their influence *appears* to have *diminished*. With the hope that this information will prove useful, she gives this one piece of advice to their Majesties. Take note of who has been skipping to Nemora."

Half-rising from his seat, Duke Erland growled, "And what is that supposed to mean?"

Derek inclined his head. "I've shared all I'm authorized to say." Rising, he bowed slightly to Lexi then her father. "I'll leave you now. Pass the offer on to King Theodor, or don't. It matters not to me. It is an olive branch from Lady Genevieve alone."

With that, he strode from the restaurant and sauntered toward the skipping line portals.

"What do you think he meant by all that?" Lexi asked.

Her father pulled in a deep breath and released it with a snort. "Probably nothing. Just the guild's attempt to manipulate Theodor." He snorted again. "But knowing the trouble those scroll worshiping fanatics have caused and keeping in mind the threats they've leveled against Rayne, I'll send a messenger to Theodor and Rowena."

Shifting in his seat, he looked full at Lexi and after releasing a sigh, smiled. "Well, daughter. Our time together has been cut into enough. Come, we'll head back to Kern House. Silas can go to Westvale, and you and I can prepare to leave for the Sharna River tomorrow morning." He rose and, taking her hand, helped her up.

"That sounds perfect." Lexi returned his smile. "No politics, no interruptions, no problems. Just my daddy and me enjoying the beauty of our hidden cabin. It'll be the first time we've gotten back there since Sigmund put that spike in you and Kern House was burned. One last opportunity before I marry into the royal line and get too bogged down in politics and social functions to have any time for myself."

Justus smirked. "Oh? And I'm supposed to believe that the handsome young man you are about to marry will have nothing to do with why you will no longer have time to spend with your dear old dad?"

"You may lie to yourself, but it's not politics that will be keeping you busy. You and Rayne have waited for three years to marry. That's a long time to wait. Between threats, political instability while Theo and Rowena worked to reestablish a stable rule after Brayden's machinations, and Rayne's efforts to spread the light, you two have put everyone else's needs before your own. Now, it's your time to be together. That is the real reason why this will be our last father-daughter outing. And that, my little girl, is how it should be."

Lexi smiled though unshed tears glistened in her eyes and slid her hand around her father's elbow. "Thank you, Daddy."

"You are most welcome. And I also thank *you*. I know how hard it was for you to leave Rayne and give me this one last chance to have you all to myself. Now, let's go enjoy it."

4

Andrew held a warm towel up as Rayne stepped out of his bath. Once he was dry, Andrew combed out his hair and then helped him into charcoal-gray, knee-length breeches and a light-weight white shirt with flouncy sleeves. A fitted, black vest with engraved silver buttons surrounded by an embroidered design of interwoven tree limbs in silver thread followed. Andrew had set out buckle shoes, but Rayne waved them off. With a slight groan of frustration, Andrew helped the prince into his black suede boots instead.

"They're going to be hot," Andrew mumbled as he leaned back on his heels, looking up at Rayne.

Getting up and stomping to shift his feet into better positions in the footwear, Rayne grinned down at Andrew. "Still, I prefer them to those ridiculous shoes."

Leaving Boone in Andrew's care, Rayne headed to the small audience chamber to join his parents in meeting with several informants and representatives from around Ochen.

Living in Westvale the last few years and accepting his dual roles as Crown Prince and Light Bringer had helped Rayne to gain the confidence he needed to converse easily with the ever-present nobles; he no longer avoided the main hallways. This morning, though, knowing his time was short, he just nodded quick greetings as he passed small gatherings of courtiers scattered around the pillars of the outer court, and strode toward the inner chambers with purpose.

Entering the small, informal audience chamber where he had first met the Reclamation Committee, Rayne saw his mother already seated in her normal place to the right of his father's chair, a cup of coffee set before her. His father stood at the sideboard where coffee and pastries were laid out, conversing with Captain Fontaine. Sun streamed in the windows along the east wall igniting dust motes and bathing the room in a golden warmth.

"Here he is now," Theodor said, as he turned to face Rayne. "Captain Fontaine was just informing me about the disappearance of scroll worshipers in Centerville. It seems the faction there has been disbanded by its followers. That's especially good news considering two of those assassination attempts on your life originated with the group in Centerville."

"Yes, good news indeed, Father. I hope it is a sign that the cult is dying out." Rayne poured himself a cup of coffee, breathing deeply of the fragrant aroma.

"It was only a matter of time," Captain Fontaine said, "until people began to realize there was no point in worshiping lifeless scrolls, especially after those *so-called* scrolls of power were destroyed. With the defeat of the living darkness and the continued spread of the message of forgiveness and faith in the One, how anybody could cling to such nonsense as scrolls of power is beyond me."

The three moved to the table while they were talking, and Rowena said, "You assume, Anton, that people are reasonable. In fact, most people tend to allow emotion to override reason. Only with the help of the One, is balance between the two achieved. And the fanatics seeking to restore the scrolls aren't known for balance. Or seeking the will of the One. They've mistakenly sought revenge against Rayne for destroying their precious scrolls when it's a well-known fact Sigmund, not Rayne, incinerated the original scrolls."

"Well then, my dear," Theodor said, taking his seat at the head of the table. "Let us trust that the One has brought reason and balance to those foolish, misguided scroll worshipers, and that we are now witnessing the demise of their abominable cult."

As Theodor was speaking, one of the guards opened the door to announce the arrival of representatives from Arisima.

"Good," Theodor said. "Let's get started. I want to wrap up these interviews before lunch."

For the next three hours, Rayne, his parents, and Captain Fontaine listened to a series of representatives from all seven worlds report on a variety of topics including the disappearance of scroll worshipers.

"We are unaware of any current activity of the Scroll of Power cult on Nemora," Duchess Cailyn's personal representative, Varick, reported when asked about residual activity on his world. "In fact, Her Grace specifically asked me to allay any fears you may still harbor in regard to the various factions on Nemora. There are none. The situation is well in hand.

"In addition, Her Grace sends personal greetings to King Theodor, Queen Rowena, and especially her nephew, Crown Prince Rayne. Know that you are always in her thoughts. Her Grace hopes you will all find time to visit her at Castle Inverness soon."

"Please return our greetings and well wishes," Rowena said. "I am certain she is still suffering from the sudden loss of Miles. If you will consent to linger a few hours before returning to Inverness, I would ask you to deliver a correspondence from me to my sister."

Varick bowed. "I would be honored, Your Majesty."

Though Theodor had hoped to finish the meetings before lunch, they didn't conclude the final interview until well into the afternoon. When Rayne finally returned to his suite after grabbing a quick lunch, Andrew and Boone were gone. *Looks like I'm going to get that chance to practice archery.*

He changed into basic brown leather leggings, a simple sleeveless beige tunic, and his serviceable black leather boots. Grabbing his bow and a quiver filled with arrows he had crafted himself, he headed toward the archery fields beyond the practice rings.

Though he could have stopped at the barracks to request a boy to help return arrows, after the morning's meetings, Rayne not only felt the need for action, he desired the quiet of solitude. He'd retrieve his own arrows.

The rich, warm scent of freshly harvested hay sweetened the air as bees buzzed, zipping past him while summer birds called to each other in the woods around the deserted archery fields. With the temperature rising, Rayne found himself alone in the far field this afternoon. *Excellent. An undisturbed place to practice and think.*

He had been shooting for over an hour and despite his sweat-dampened shirt and hair, felt quite pleased with himself. Entertaining visions of defeating Sashi in their next match, he startled when an unknown voice called his name. Nerves sent him spinning toward the threat, sighting down his arrow.

Varick, the messenger from Nemora, stumbled to a stop, his eyes wide. A second man, dressed in the royal blue uniform of a Castle Inverness guard, moved to Varick's side. A seasoned soldier by the look of him. His hair cropped short in the military style favored on Nemora, spotless uniform, and stiff posture all spoke of confidence.

The man reminded Rayne of Thorvin.

"Ho there, Your Highness," Varick shouted. "Hold your arrow. It's me, Varick. Remember ... from this morning? I need to speak to you."

Rayne lowered his bow, loosened his arrow and slipped it into his quiver as he watched the two men approach, curious as to their purpose. "Sorry Varick. You startled me. What is it?"

"A message came for you from Nemora." Varick waved the soldier forward. "Report to His Highness what you told me."

The soldier squinted at Rayne, and Rayne had the uncomfortable feeling he was being judged and found wanting, but then the man bowed. "The ancient called Mite arrived at Castle Inverness in a troubled state late last night. Duchess Cailyn has been with him since. This morning, Her Grace tasked me with the mission to bring you to Castle Inverness in all haste."

Rayne looked up into the man's deep-set brown eyes. "This doesn't make sense. Why didn't Mite just come to talk with me here. If he's already in Inverness, it's an easy thing to skip to Westvale."

The soldier drew his shoulders back as if insulted, pulling his uniform taut across his large chest, and met Rayne's gaze with a determined focus. "What I know is that Duchess Cailyn ordered me to bring you quickly and guard you with my life. I do not question her orders."

Rayne huffed out a deep breath as he scanned the practice field, wishing Thorvin was around. He knew going off-world alone was reckless, but if Mite needed him, he would go. And Aunt Cailyn's guard seemed quite capable.

The last three years had been a time of peace and recovery after Sigmund and the Demon Master almost plunged all Ochen into darkness. Rayne's recent trips to Nemora had been without incident. And after the meetings this morning, he was comfortable that whatever remained of militant scroll worshipers no longer offer any threat.

Besides, I'll get to spend some time with Aunt Cailyn while I'm there. She hasn't been herself since Uncle Miles died. It's just to Castle Inverness. What could go wrong?

Rayne turned back to the soldier. "Mite must have his reasons for asking me to meet with him in Inverness rather than here. Since you've committed to guarding me with your life, why don't you tell me your name."

"Theada, Sire. Sergeant Theada. Guardsman to Her Grace, Duchess Cailyn of Inverness."

"Well, Sergeant Theada, the sooner we leave, the sooner we can return. I just need to make a quick stop at my suite. I can't appear before Aunt Cailyn like this." Rayne waved a hand down the front of his sweaty tunic.

"Of course, Sire." Theada paused. "If … you … wish."

The sergeant's hesitation and manner set a shaft of concern through Rayne and he pulled in a hiss of breath. "What are you not saying?"

The man's eyes flicked to Varrick then back to Rayne. "Well, Sire. I wasn't supposed to say anything, but ... well, I got the impression the ancient might be dying even as we speak. It seems he got involved with something dangerous and took the worst of a beating. Of course, that's just my perception."

"Why didn't you tell me this first?" Rayne growled as he bounced on his toes then sprinted toward the Great Square. "Let's go." He dropped his bow and quiver of arrows in one of the sword barrels scattered through the practice fields.

"Hold up a second," Varick said as he came alongside Rayne, panting, and threw a cloak over Rayne's shoulders.

"What's this for? I'm already too hot." Rayne reached up to slip off the cloak.

Varick's hand settled over Rayne's, holding it in place. "Just a precaution, Sire. Though the scroll cult is on the decline, I believe you would be safer if your identity was not advertised when we skip."

"It would be a justifiable precaution, Sire," Sergeant Theada added as he reached over and drew the hood up to cover Rayne's midnight black hair. "Come, Sire, we must hurry. I promise you'll be safe with me. And I've arranged for a dozen men to meet us once we're in Inverness."

Rayne slowed then pulled to a stop, glancing back toward the palace. "I should leave word for my parents. Let them know I'm going to meet Aunt Cailyn so they don't worry."

"Leave it to me, Your Highness," Varick said. "I'm meeting with Her Majesty shortly to receive her missive to Duchess Cailyn. I'll tell her that you've been summoned to Inverness and will be back within a few hours. Please allow me the pleasure of serving you in this way."

Rayne grimaced, wondering if he was doing the right thing, but anxiety for Mite outweighed any other concerns. He released a huff of air and began jogging. He picked up speed as he loped into the Great Square with Sergeant Theada following, while Varick turned toward the palace. *Varick will explain what happened to Mother. She'll understand.*

When they arrived at the Westvale Portal Station, Rayne

moved in the direction of the ticket sellers to arrange for passes, but Theada stopped him. "No need. I have passes."

The two navigated around pockets of travelers scattered in front of the various portals and slipped through the one for Nemora without notice. The momentary sensation of sinking passed, and Rayne stepped out into the Inverness Portal Station. As always, he was impressed by the beauty of the Nemora station. Built to mimic a cathedral, its benches were designed to look like pews and stained-glass windows allowed in ample light in shafts of blue, purple, and green.

Sergeant Theada grabbed Rayne's arm, propelling him through the crowded station and out into a murky, drizzle. "Come, Sire, we must hurry."

The thick, magic laden atmosphere pressed down on him. His senses shifted to high alert at the level of dark energy. "What the … the energy … way too heavy … and wrong. Something's wrong." He slowed and stopped, pulling his arm from Sergeant Theada's grip.

"Her Grace will explain everything, Sire." The soldier growled deep in his throat and shoved Rayne forward. "Keep moving. This way." Rayne was herded into a narrow alley that brought back memories of the day Sigmund had taken his body, forcing his spirit into that of a sickly old man.

"No. No. This isn't right." Rayne skidded to a stop, forcing Theada to pull up behind him. Rayne pushed back his hood, certain now that something was wrong. *Stupid. Stupid.* He shifted, scanned the murky alley then turned to tell Sergeant Theada he was going back.

The sound of shuffling and movement in the shadows on his right claimed his attention. As he threw up his arm to ward off the threat, something crashed into the back of his head and his world went black.

5

Andrew, breathing hard from his run with Boone, stumbled into Prince Rayne's suite. He laughed, and Boone jumped up on him, still excited from the activity.

"Your Highness? Rayne? Are you here?" Andrew called. "That's strange. I thought Rayne would be back by now."

While Andrew checked the balcony, Boone sniffed at the small writing desk in the sitting room. Andrew startled when the dog raised up on her hind legs, set her front paws on the desk, and growled deep in her throat.

"What's the matter, girl? Something got you upset?" He walked over to the desk as Boone sat and whined. "A note? Who would be leaving a note here?" Andrew picked up the stationary and read the broad, scrawling handwriting that looked nothing like Rayne's normally tight script.

Dear Mother and Father,

I am certain you are concerned at my unannounced departure. I have left this note to ease your anxiety. This afternoon I received a missive from Lady Alexianndra and Duke Erland inviting me to join them on Veres for the next two weeks. My feelings for the lady have incited me to respond to the invite in an immediate and spontaneous manner; I am on my way to Eleri City. Look for my return with the lady and her father in two-weeks' time.

Rayne

Andrew read the note through several times. The unusual wording and the sudden departure left him with mouth hanging agape.

"That idiot," he mumbled. "Her Majesty is not going to be happy when she learns he's gone. He was supposed to help her with wedding stuff while Lexi was away. I guess planning a wedding isn't nearly as exciting as skipping to Veres and having an adventure with Lexi and the duke." Andrew's brows drew down. "But then again, this isn't like him; just leaving a note like this." He gazed at Boone. "Well, they say love makes people do strange things, Boone. It's stupid if you ask me, but I guess that's what's happening to our prince. It's just you and me for now. I don't suppose you'd like to come with me to report this to the queen?"

Boone whined as if she understood.

"No? I didn't think so. You know, Boone, for a smart person, your master can be a total nitwit at times."

After getting Boone food and water, Andrew left her in the suite and headed toward the public areas of the palace. "Is Her Majesty here?" he asked a royal guardsman stationed outside a small receiving room the queen often frequented when she was holding audiences without the king.

"Her Majesty is meeting with the representative from Nemora before he leaves for Inverness. Do you need me to announce you?"

Andrew hesitated for a moment, considering his options, then nodded. "Yes, Whinston, I think I need to see her right now."

He was pleased when Whinston slipped back out the door a minute later, holding it open behind him. "She says you may enter."

Andrew stepped into the dim room. The smallest of the

receiving rooms, it was usually filled with shadows, having only two tiny windows set high up near the vaulted ceiling. Heavy, flocked paper covered the walls in shades of teal blue and deep green. An immense, hand tied rug in complementary tones laced with images of flying birds in gold and pale yellow softened the somber hues on the walls. More formal than the other audience chambers, the room was rarely used for meetings. But Andrew knew the queen liked to spend time in the tranquil place when she sought solitude and quiet in the midst of a hectic schedule. She sat there now, on a gilded throne of modest proportions, set with teal cushions. A man Andrew did not recognize stood facing her.

"It was quite unexpected, to say the least," he was saying. "The young prince was so excited, I myself was profoundly moved. It's most obvious that he loves Lady Alexianndra deeply. I felt his joy and, indeed, felt quite privileged when he asked me to convey the message regarding his abrupt departure to you and His Majesty."

Rowena's gaze shifted to Andrew standing at the door and she waved him forward. He approached and knelt.

"You may rise, Andrew." She cast a fond smile at the young page. "Your timing is impeccable. Varick here is a representative from Duchess Cailyn. He has just conveyed a message from my apparently truant son. You wouldn't know anything of his current whereabouts, would you?"

"I do, Your Majesty. In fact, that's the reason I've come to see you."

"Explain."

"When I returned to the prince's suite a short while ago, I expected to find His Highness there. Instead, I found this note on his writing desk."

Rowena waved for Andrew to bring the note to her. She unfolded the paper and scanned it with pursed lips. After a few minutes, she looked up at Andrew and Varick. "Well, it seems as though this note corroborates your story. Though this sudden departure is unlike my son, I do know love can cause irresponsible behavior in young people. However, I find the current situation disturbing."

Rowena's eyes narrowed as she focused on Varick. "Why would my son ask you to deliver a message if he had already left a note?"

Varick inclined his head, his gaze dropping to the floor. "Your Majesty, the young prince was quite … ah … distracted. Anything more, I can't say."

Setting aside a vague feeling of disquiet, Rowena reached to her right and picked up a sealed missive. She motioned Varick forward. "I thank you for the service you have given my son. Your patience while I composed this does you credit. Please deliver it to Duchess Cailyn, with my best regards. You are dismissed."

Varick bowed deeply and, tucking the paper into an inner pocket of his doublet, stalked out the door with rapid steps.

When the door closed behind him, Rowena said, "Now, Andrew, what do *you* make of this?"

"Please excuse me Your Majesty, but I don't know anything except that I found the note when I returned to His Highness' suite. I didn't hear what the man from Nemora told you. Do you think something happened to Rayne?"

Sighing, Rowena's gaze dropped to her restless hands. She shook her head. "No, I suppose not, Andrew. But I think I just learned that even someone as responsible as my son, can make mistakes and allow his emotions to prompt him into unwise actions without regard for others or his own safety.

"He could at least have taken the time to meet with me before skipping off to Veres. He didn't even think to take a guard with him." Her eyes swiveled back to catch Andrew's. "Thank you, Andrew, for bringing this note to my attention. You are dismissed."

After Andrew left, Rowena sat in silence for several minutes, allowing her spirit to calm and center. "Something's not right," she murmured into the empty air. "I don't know what; but whatever it is, I feel a shadow upon my heart."

Releasing a huff, she formed a sense tendril and searched

for Rayne. Not locating his presence in the palace or the city, she sighed and drummed her fingers on the arm of her chair, deep in thought. *I guess he did skip to Veres ... and yet.*

She rang a small silver bell set on the table to her right, summoning her guard.

"Yes, Your Majesty?" Sergeant Whinston asked in a hushed voice, upon entering.

"Send a page up to His Majesty with a request that he join me here as soon as possible."

"Yes, Your Majesty, it shall be done."

"And have someone come in here and light the lamps. It has grown dark."

6

The setting sun stretched shimmering fingers of amber beams that pierced through breaking clouds, lighting the study where Lexi sat treasuring the golden warmth. She and her father had returned from Eleri in the late afternoon and planned to leave for the cabin the next morning. Her father was going over last-minute instructions with Ethan when Silas walked in.

"Any questions?" Duke Erland asked Ethan.

"No, my lord. Don't worry about anything. Just go and have a good time with Lexi. We'll take care of everything here."

"You've been practically running things yourself for the past six months, Ethan, and doing a fine job," Justus said. "Profits from the mines are up, and the workers all seem content with the wages we've been paying. I am certain things will continue to run smoothly for the next two weeks as well."

Ethan nodded.

"Are you ready?" Duke Erland looked up at Silas.

"As ready as I'm gonna be, my lord."

Justus rose from the table where he had been going over accounts with Ethan, walked to a small desk, and picked up a sealed envelope. His eyebrows scrunched together in thought, he tapped the envelope against the knuckles of his left hand. "I know Lady Genevieve suspects something is happening on Nemora, something to do with the disappearance of scroll worshipers on other worlds. But right now, all she has is supposition. So, before you skip to Corylus, spend a few days in Eleri; talk to the people there, especially any that are in town from outlying areas where that cult has had more influence. Feel them out. If you can gather additional information to take to King Theodor so he can make a more informed decision about dealing with whatever is happening, it will be worth waiting a couple extra days to give him this."

Justus shook his head. "Scroll worshipers are normally vocal about everything they do, and though we didn't have many here on Veres, their current absence is unsettling. I've got a bad feeling something's brewing. Just a couple days, Silas, then deliver the message and anything else you learn to the king and queen before returning here."

Shivering at the loss of warmth as she moved from the square of sunlight, Lexi rose and walked to Silas, pulling an envelope from her skirt pocket. "And while you're in Westvale, would you please give this to Prince Rayne?"

"Oh! What's this I see?" her father said, failing to stifle the grin working its way across his face. "You've been apart what, not quite two days? And already you are sending love notes? Perhaps we should cancel this father-daughter outing and return you to Westvale tonight."

"Father!" Lexi groaned. "Don't be so ... absurd. It's not a *love* note ... exactly. I just wrote to let Rayne know we're heading to our cabin on the Sharna River tomorrow. And ... I just wanted to ... tell him ... I wish he was here. That's all. Why must men always read more into things than are there?"

Justus, Ethan, and Silas chuckled lightly as Lexi harrumphed, her face warming.

"There's no need for you to get upset or deny the truth that you are thinking about Rayne," Justus said. "It's perfectly normal to miss your sweetheart when you are apart. You and Rayne have not had an easy time of things and I'm grateful you are finally getting married. The bond you two share is strong and unique; it's had to be. Never be ashamed to admit your love."

"Oh, Father, I could never be ashamed of my love for Rayne. It's just that my note is not a confession of *love*. It's just a little way of saying 'hi'. You referring to it as a *love* note is not strictly truthful, and it made me uncomfortable."

"I am sorry if I caused you any discomfort, my dear. I didn't mean to. Will you forgive me?"

"Of course, Father." She walked to him and wrapped her arms around his waist. "And I'm sorry I got upset with you. Please don't think I want to return to Westvale before we've had this time together; I don't. I've been looking forward to this trip with you for weeks and I wouldn't trade it for anything."

He smiled down at her and rubbed his hand up and down her back. "Good. I'm glad to hear that. Now I'm going out with Silas and Ethan for a few minutes. By the time I come back, Seren should have the evening meal ready."

After the men left, Lexi called for a servant to light a fire in the study. With autumn coming on, evenings at Kern House were getting colder. Once the fire was blazing, banishing the growing shadows to the far corners of the room, Lexi asked the man to check with Seren about the evening meal. As she waited for a response, she lit a lamp and sat at the table where her father had been going over books with Ethan, scanning the figures they had been discussing.

I wonder what Father is worried about. He's right. The mines are doing well. So much for needing a slave labor force to keep profits up. She smiled at the thought.

When King Theodor outlawed slavery on all seven worlds of Ochen, there had been many who opposed the measure, mostly the Sorial merchants. They had grown accustomed to making easy profits buying and selling kidnapped victims of the slave traders, especially the pirates on Arisima. Though slavery was still not completely eradicated, King Theodor had done much in the last couple years to hunt down and punish those who continued to benefit from the illegal trade.

Lexi even joined Rayne a few times, leading rescue efforts and freeing groups of captured innocents bound for the secret slave markets. They worked closely with Captain Ellis, who had taken over command of the interplanetary troops stationed on Arisima, and Noah, who was now a sergeant and assistant to Captain Ellis. Noah had specifically requested the post in Zoraya, the capital of Arisima, with a desire to continue working with Captain Ellis to put an end to the pirates and their slave trade. When Noah and Sashi wed nearly two years ago, she joined him there.

Though Rayne had kept his anger under control when they confronted the slavers, Lexi knew the effort it took. Having been raised a slave, the prince knew first-hand the horrors of slavery and his fury at those who traded in human misery always hovered just beneath the surface. Over the last three years, he had worked tirelessly with his father and Captain Ellis to ferret out and bring an end to the hidden slave markets still operating on Arisima and Sorial.

Lexi shivered as disturbing images from their last trip to Arisima rose in her mind. She had skipped with Rayne, Thorvin, and nearly fifty soldiers from Westvale, to join Captain Ellis, Noah and a contingent of their soldiers in Zoraya. They were acting on information King Theodor received about the current location of a mobile slave market they had been trying to locate for months. But the whole thing was a sham, a trap set by the Vagrants of the Scroll to kill Rayne, whom they now called the Binder.

The fighting had been brutal. Lexi shook her head, remembering. The sheer number of vagrants who attacked them was unexpected and if not for the vagrant's lack of skill in arms, Rayne, Lexi, and many others would not have survived the trap.

Lexi shivered, recalling how pale Rayne had been when he fought the effects of a poisoned arrow.

"Lexi," her father's voice, seasoned with alarm, seeped into her consciousness. "Are you alright? You're trembling, and you look as pale as a ghost. What's wrong?"

Lexi shivered once again, as a cold tendril of fear traced

up her spine like an icy finger. Justus stepped next to her, wrapping an arm around her shoulders.

"Oh, Daddy. It's nothing. I was just remembering something that happened a while ago, and it made me afraid for Rayne. Why do so many people want to harm someone as good and caring as he is? If he hadn't stopped Sigmund and that horrible Demon Master, I can't even imagine what our lives would be like now. Will it never end? All the threats, all the violence. Those ignorant scroll worshipers. I abhor them! I wish they were all dead."

"Lexi, Lexi, you don't really mean that. Even Rayne understands those people are to be pitied not hated. They've been deceived and are caught up in something they can't escape. They need our prayers, not our hatred."

"I don't think I can do that—pray for them. I've tried, but it's all too raw yet. Sometimes I feel like a momma bear and Rayne is my cub. When he's threatened, I just want to rip those responsible for his pain to pieces. I'm not strong like he is. I can't forgive so easily.

"When you walked in, just now. I was thinking about the last time we went to Arisima. Rayne nearly died because the whole thing was an elaborate trap." She pulled in a deep breath and wrapped a hand around her father's forearm, staring off, seeing nothing except memories. "Even then, once those Vagrants of the Scroll were rounded up and taken prisoner, Rayne spoke to them about the love and forgiveness of the One. He told them about the gift of the Son. And even while they were still cursing him, he prayed for them.

"I've seen him do the same thing with slavers. And I know how he feels about slavery. Still, he speaks of forgiveness. To those we've rescued *and* to those we've apprehended. I can't do that. I can't." She shook her head. "How does he do it?"

Pulling a chair next to Lexi's, Justus sighed as he lowered into it. "I can't explain *how* he does it, but I think I know what makes him *able* to do it."

He paused for a moment, concentration lines deepening between his brows. "Because the One called Rayne to be his Light Bringer, he gave Rayne certain gifts to enable him to do what he's been called to do. In other words, the One didn't just call Rayne, he also equipped him for that calling. And that task centers around bringing light into dark places. I don't think Rayne can *not* forgive. Forgiveness is part of his makeup; how the One created and forged him to be.

"That doesn't mean he approves of people like those slavers going free, he understands there are consequences to our actions. And yet, even in prison, people can find the spiritual freedom of forgiveness the One offers. You, more than anyone else, must understand how he still, after everything that's happened, wrestles with his past. Aware of his own bloody actions, he believes he is unworthy to condemn anyone who is willing to seek the One. And that, my dear, is his strength.

"My strength, however, is waning though," Justus said, winking at Lexi. "Let's see if that can be remedied with food." Standing, he reached down and helped Lexi to her feet. "We need to be well fed, and get a good night's sleep, if we plan to leave early tomorrow."

Lexi linked her arm through her father's. "Thank you. You are a very wise man, Father."

As the two were walking into the dining room, Lexi suddenly cried out, pulling away from her father and wrapping both arms around her torso.

"Lexi? What's wrong?"

Tears pooled in her eyes and she shook her head, gasping in deep breaths until the pain in her chest eased. Seeing the concern written in her father's face, Lexi said, "It's okay. I'm okay now."

"What just happened?" Justus asked as Seren hurried over and the two helped Lexi into a chair.

Lexi shook her head. "I don't know. It suddenly felt as if my heart was being ripped in two. I could see nothing, and I was filled with terror for Rayne. But it's passed. I'm fine now. I hope he's alright."

"He's safe enough in Westvale." Justus patted Lexi's arm. "From what you've said, he wasn't planning to go anywhere until after the wedding. Right?"

Lexi smiled up at her father and Seren. "That's right. Thorvin made Rayne promise he wouldn't leave the capital while he was at Warren's Rest. Rayne promised; he'll keep his word."

With Lexi insisting that her strange attack had passed, and she was well, Seren got the table set. When all was ready, Justus, Lexi, Ethan, Silas, and Seren sat and discussed plans for leaving in the morning as they enjoyed Seren's grilled fish, mashed sweet potatoes, and mixed greens salad. A dessert of peach cobbler rounded out the meal. The peaches were a rare treat given to Duke Erland by Harrison Stocken as a thank you for meeting earlier in the day.

Although Lexi had convinced her father and Seren that she was fine, she lay awake in her bed for a long time. Unsettled emotions swirled in her. *Something's not right. Please, blessed One, keep Rayne safe. I don't want to disappoint Father, but I feel such anxiety for Rayne. All I can do for now is trust that you are in control.*

7

Rayne blinked sticky eyelids open. Impenetrable, inky darkness pressed down on him, drawing up deep-seated terror. Old and familiar, it coursed through him. His head throbbed, and a sickly-sweet coating on his tongue triggered his gag reflex. Eyes flicking down, Rayne sought the ever-present radiance that hovered at his scarred wrists and gasped. The glow he had carried in his body for the last three years was gone, not a glimmer of light could be seen in the absolute dark.

No! No! Please no. Not happening. Not possible. He held trembling hands before his face, stabbed by the loss. *Can't see anything. Blind? Am I blind?* He tried to calm his rising panic, find his center, and release the light; but heavy, stifling magic filled the air—smothering, oppressive. His mind spun in circles and he couldn't concentrate. *Can't breathe.*

He attempted to focus his magic and form sensing tendrils. Over the last few years, he had perfected the skill and came close to matching his mother in strength. But spikes of hot pain shot through his skull with the effort. He shook his head in frustration, but then grabbed his temples, gritted his teeth, and collapsed onto a hard, cold floor as the agonizing spikes ignited, burning holes in his brain.

When the searing pain subsided, he pressed up onto his feet. "Okay. It's going to be okay; I just need to get my bearings." The need to hear something other than the sound of his breathing in the stifling silence, drove him to speak aloud.

Reaching out, his fingers brushed a hard surface in front of him. Smooth, cold, solid. He shivered. Taking a step forward he reached up, running his hands over the glass-like surface as high as he could feel, then down until his fingers found the floor. The floor and wall were smooth, polished stone, curved like the inside of a ball. Moving to his right, he continued feeling his way along the wall, seeking a corner. The wall curved and curved; he found no corner. The curving rock continued. *Did I walk in a circle? Come back to where I started? How big is this place?*

He backed up into the wall. Pulling in a deep breath he squelched his fear of the unknown and stepped into the black void. Counting. *One. Two. Three. Four. Five.* His outstretched hand hit the wall before him. The room—*cave?*—was five steps across. He moved along the wall a couple paces, once again placing it at his back, and stepped out. *One. Two. Three. Four. Five. Yeah! I'm in a small, stone room, five paces across ... and ... no door!* Panic seized his chest in a crushing grip. *No door! How can there be no door?*

Turning back into the wall, Rayne ran his hands over the surface and stepped sideways, examining the slick rock face with his fingers. *It's all the same. I don't even know where I started.* He continued his search, though he was certain that he must have circled the room already. *Nothing. Again.*

He spent what felt like hours examining the stone face of the circular room, unwilling to admit that he had circumnavigated the chamber countless times. *If there's no door, how did I get here? Magic? Dark magic? And where is here?*

Fear and anxiety soured his stomach like a bitter brew. He sank to the floor in the center of the room, pulled his knees to his chest, and wrapped his arms around them. *What now?*

"Hello!" he shouted. Rising again, he licked the residue of

sweet sticky substance off his lips, ignoring the nausea the taste summoned. "Can anyone hear me? Is anybody there?" His shouts died in the thick atmosphere of the silent black that enveloped him.

Returning to his position on the floor, Rayne prayed aloud. "Blessed One, I'm lost. And I've lost the light. Why? Why would it be gone now when I need it so much? I don't even know where I am or how I got here. And, my Lord, it's so dark. Darker than the darkest night. Please, help me. I don't know what to do."

Once again, he strove to find balance at his center, but with no success. He shivered. Awareness that he wore nothing more than rough-woven, sagging trousers, not his own, loose and tied at his waist, blossomed in him. His clothes and boots were gone, and the chamber was cold and damp. He ran his hands up and down his upper arms trying to find some warmth in the motion.

Lord, where are you? Are you still with me?

A gentle warmth ignited deep within, and Rayne heard the voice. It was muffled as if the One spoke through a heavy blanket, but he felt it within his spirit. *Do you trust me my son?*

Yes, my Lord. I trust you.

Even now I am with you, my precious child. Be strong. I am always with you. Cling to that truth in the darkness to come. Remember, you are never alone.

After a bit, Rayne's heavy eyelids drooped, and he slept. When he woke, he rejoiced to see a faint glow highlighting the scars on his wrists. His light was returning.

A deep, heavy rumble vibrated through the floor and walls, and a gray rectangle appeared in the solid black before him. A door. Silent, cloaked figures filed into the room. Without a word, two grabbed Rayne's arms and flung him onto his back, pressing him into the floor.

"Who are you?" Rayne ground out through gritted teeth as he struggled against his attackers. "What are you doing? What do you want?"

Two more joined the first, entrapping his hands and lower arms, while another larger figure secured his legs. A sixth moved to his head, immobilizing it between feet placed on either side. He tried to struggle, but it was useless, he was pinned to the stone like a bug on display. Highlighted by the faint light pouring in the doorway, two other forms slipped into the cramped chamber. One, petite, stopped just inside the doorway. The man at Rayne's head dropped to kneel, now trapping Rayne's head between his knees. He seized Rayne's chin and forced his mouth open. The last man leaned forward, and Rayne sensed more than saw the movement of the tall stranger's arm reaching toward his face.

"No!" Rayne's protest emerged as a choked grunt. Heat rose in him in waves of frustration and fruitless anger. He banged his head into the knees trapping it, arched his back, and beat his heels against the floor; all to no avail. "Who are you? Why are you doing this?"

The unrelenting fingers once again pried his mouth open and the man standing above his head bowed in closer. With a quick motion, he poured thick liquid into Rayne's mouth. The fingers shifted, and two strong hands now covered Rayne's mouth and nose, closing off his air. Tears leaked from the corners of his eyes as he swallowed the liquid. It tasted like the residue he had licked from his lips earlier. Once Rayne swallowed, the hands lifted. Everyone filed out. Not one word had been spoken. Except for Rayne's outbursts, and some grunts, the silence had been complete.

Within less than a minute, a numbness settled on Rayne and his light flickered out. Once again, he was surrounded by total, impenetrable black. Bile rose in his throat, and he shifted to sit against the wall, attempting to heave up the honey-like concoction, but it wouldn't come. All he managed were dry heaves. Sick. Cold. Alone. The darkness and silence were like a living presence suffocating him.

He tried to pray, but the burning spikes returned, boring fiery holes in his skull, and he cried out at the agony. Moving back to the center of the floor, he lay on his side and curled into a ball. Memories of Sigmund's cage rose. How many times had he fallen asleep there in the same balled-up position?

He had no idea how long he slept. When he woke, all was

as before. He relieved himself against the wall wondering if he would be kept in this prison for much longer. Time passed, though the reality of it seemed nothing more than an illusion. Rayne prayed. He recited extensive passages from the Words of the One from memory, speaking aloud just to hear the sound. Thirst became unbearable and his stomach grumbled its empty state.

When glimmers of light began to appear on Rayne's arms again, the room rumbled, and his silent enemies entered through the gray door. As before, they surrounded him, the same positions taken, the same brew forced into his mouth. After swallowing, he was allowed to sit, and a mug of tepid water was pressed into his hands. He took a sip, then downed the full mug. After he finished the water, he was given a chunk of coarse bread.

He stuffed the whole chunk into his mouth then chewed it with slow purpose. A groan slipped through his lips as the taste and texture flooded his senses. *Food. Wonderful food.* The men pulled Rayne to his feet and bound his hands in front of him, leaving a long, loose lead dangling on the floor. His eyes went wide and he swallowed the partially chewed bread with haste as they stuffed a wad of cloth in his mouth. Another cloth was wrapped around his head, holding the gag in place. He was blindfolded, a bag was pulled over his head, then a cloak was thrown on, covering all.

Conserving his strength in the hope that a chance of escape would present itself, Rayne stumbled behind as he was pulled along.

A short distance and a steep incline later, the soft caress of a gentle breeze alerted Rayne to the fact that he was outside. *I was underground.* The fresh scents of wet earth and pine overwhelmed his senses after the close, dank air of his prison. Insects trilled, and the hushed night rustlings of small creatures sounded over loud—it was incredible.

They walked for almost an hour, Rayne stumbling in his blindness and weakness, yet relishing every breath and step. Each time he tripped, someone grabbed his arms and pulled him back to his feet. Still no one spoke. Rayne tried to pray, but as before, spikes of pain, like burning shards of glass, drove the prayer out.

They slowed. Tree limbs rustling gave way to voices chanting. The chanting grew louder, the utterances clearer, as they approached what must have been a large group of people.

"Blood for blood; blood for power; blood for vengeance." The words pounded against Rayne's mind. Voices surrounded him, chanting, droning, repeating, "Blood for blood; blood for power; blood for vengeance."

He was pushed down to his knees, the hood and blindfold removed. He blinked. The meager light of the twin moons shafting through a thin layer of clouds seared his eyes. *Two moons, I'm still on Nemora.*

Squinting, his eyes leaking tears, Rayne recognized where he was. The ancient sacrifice stone was the same altar Brayden had brought him to sixteen years ago when he was five. *I'm close to Castle Inverness. If I can just get away, I can make it to the castle. To Aunt Cailyn.*

Sounds of muffled cursing drew his eyes to a struggle taking place at the flat-topped stone. A shirtless, well-muscled man with a hood tied over his head like the one Rayne had been wearing was wrestling against two men who were attempting to force him onto the altar stone. Though bound and blinded, the man was still putting up a fight.

I should help him, Rayne's fuzzy brain insisted. He had no idea what he could do to help, but as he attempted to rise, four men lifted the resisting prisoner onto the rock while heavy hands pushed Rayne back to his knees. Rayne's eyes wandered across the area again. Scores of cloaked men and women crowded the hollow, hoods covering their heads, shielding their features, swaying as they chanted. *There must be over five-hundred people here.*

As one, the voices stopped. The only sound in the night was the sighing of wind in the trees as a tall, thin man and a slight womanly form approached the sacrificial stone. Another man, immense and imposing in his cloak, clutching a dark, long bladed, veredium knife, approached the other side of the altar.

The tall, thin man raised his arms. "Blood for blood; blood

for power; blood for vengeance. Mighty Guardian of the Scrolls, we offer this sacrifice now according to your words. First day, first sacrifice. One human and the blood of the Binder. As you have commanded, so will it be. Seven sacrifices, seven weeks." He turned, looking back to where Rayne was kneeling and after a moment, nodded. Rayne was pulled to his feet and thrust forward to the stone. He was forced to kneel again, pushed down against the rough altar, next to the blind-folded man who was now being held on his hands and knees.

As soon as Rayne was in position, the man with the knife slit the throat of the victim, allowing his blood to run down onto the stained and pitted surface. Rayne's eyes were drawn to the huge hands of the executioner and he stared without thinking. The chanting began again, "Blood for blood. Blood for power. Blood for vengeance." The knife wielder turned to Rayne and with the sharp point of his blade, pierced Rayne's neck. A slight, shallow cut. Hands forced Rayne's head forward until droplets of his blood fell and mingled with the blood already pooling in and running out of a bowl-like depression in the stone.

Lifting her arms, the woman, now standing alongside the leader, called out, "Blood for the spilled blood of our dead."

The crowd of worshipers echoed their response.

"Blood for the returned power of our people."

Again, the crowd raised voices like a surging of the sea against a wall of stone, repeating her call.

"Blood for vengeance on those who have caused our immeasurable pain."

The final words sighed through the crowd as if they were all in a trance.

"So shall it be."

The woman's voice sounded familiar, but Rayne's brain was so fog-filled, he couldn't grab hold of the speaker's identity.

The tall leader spoke again. "As you have commanded, so has it been accomplished. Blood of a human and blood of the Binder. We beseech you, mighty Guardian of the Scrolls, accept this our first offering."

Stunned and sickened at what he had just been part of, Rayne struggled to control the tremors seizing his body. Heavy hands pressed into his shoulders and held him on his knees. His hair was pulled, yanking his head back, allowing a fresh flow of blood to dribble from the nick in his throat. *I'm next! They're going to slit my throat too!* His heart thumped into a rapid rhythm as the fear swelled within him, but the gag was pulled out and the sweet potion filled his mouth. He swallowed.

Hauled to his feet, he fought to remain upright on legs turned to mush. Losing his balance, he dropped back onto his knees. The gag and blindfold were replaced. Once again yanked up onto his feet, he was dragged forward by the rope tied at his wrists. By the time he scrambled out of the glen, his stomach climbed his throat. Choking behind his gag, he swallowed the burning bile. He stumbled, fell. Shadows swam in his mind and hands were pulling at him. He knew nothing more.

8

The twelfth day after Rayne's unexpected departure, Rowena, her hair pulled up into a mass of blue-black curls at the crown of her head, wearing a simple, cotton charmeuse gown of cobalt blue, was going over plans for the formal wedding dinner with Chef Clemens. She had already approved the decorations for the Great Square, with an eye to creating a mountain meadow in honor of Lady Alexianndra's homeland of Veres. She had also fixed the menu for the food stands that would be situated around the square for the citizens of Westvale, keeping the fare simple but plentiful. Hand pies and skewered meats were crowd favorites, as well as wraps with different fillings. Food people could hold while walking and socializing. Though she put on a mask of calm, she was finding it more difficult each day to keep moving forward. With Rayne gone and the wedding less than four weeks away, she needed help.

Danton, one of Theodor's chief advisors stepped in, lending his assistance and relieving a good amount of stress. But a strange sense of disquiet pervaded Rowena's spirit at unexpected moments, laying claim to her attention and distressing her. She would be talking and suddenly cry out, certain she was falling into a dark hole. Whomever she was speaking to would panic and reach out to her, pulling her back to reality. The frequency of her blackouts was increasing, and Theodor had called twice for the healers to examine her. Each time, they found nothing physically wrong.

"That sets the appetizers and main course, but we need ..." Rowena's focus blurred, and her stomach clenched as she plunged downward into the chill of an endless black hole, cutting her words mid-sentence. Deep darkness and silence assailed her. She cried out as terror sent her heart into an irregular rhythm. For a fraction of a second, she thought she sensed Rayne and the distinctive odor of blood, but then the seizure was over.

Rowena raised her head and blinked, clearing the cobwebs from her mind. Clemens stood over her, his eyes wide and fearful. She had collapsed onto the table and he was fanning her as he shouted for the healers.

"Please, no," she mumbled. "I'm fine now, Chef Clemens. Really."

He stopped calling but kept waving his hands. "But, Your Majesty, you called out and ... then you went still and quiet. I thought ... oh, my. I thought you had died."

"I'm fine now." Rowena pushed up onto her feet, holding onto the table to steady herself before straightening. "I don't wish to alarm anyone needlessly." Standing tall, and in complete control despite the pebbling of sweat on her brow, she said, "I fear I must cut our discussion short; I'm due to meet His Majesty. I trust your opinion regarding the rest of the meal. If you have any other concerns, talk to Danton."

"Of course, Your Majesty. If you're quite sure, Your Majesty."

Though outwardly cool and composed, inside her spirit quailed at a residual sense of loss; a pressing need to speak with Theodor drove her onward despite several people calling out to her. She approached the audience chamber where Theodor had scheduled several appointments for the afternoon and pausing, pulled in a deep breath to calm her inner quaking. One of the guardsmen saw her coming and with a deep bow opened the door.

Rowena had hoped to find Theodor between meetings, but upon entering the room, allowed a slight smile to surface when she saw Silas, one of Duke Erland's people from Veres.

She swept in before him and as he bowed to her, held out her hand. "Welcome my friend. Have you skipped here with Prince Rayne and Lady Alexianndra? I thought they surely would be enjoying their time away for a few more days yet."

Silas missed her proffered hand as an expression of equal parts shock and confusion suffused his features. "Excuse me, please, Your Majesty, but why would His Highness be with Lexi? She's still with her father at their cabin near the Sharna River."

Rowena's heart stuttered as she stumbled to the small, throne-like chair next to Theodor's.

Theodor rose, took her elbow and guided her to the chair, then turned his attention to Silas. "I was led to believe my son skipped to Veres to join Lady Alexianndra and her father not twenty-four hours after she had left Westvale for Veres. Now, you tell me this isn't so. If he's not here and he's not on Veres—Where. Is. My. Son?"

11

Thorvin growled deep in his throat as he approached Westvale. A deep disquiet had been churning within him the last few days and he even rode through the night knowing that, had he stopped at an inn, he would not have been able to sleep. He mistrusted internal promptings; they belonged to people like Rayne and Shaw, not seasoned warriors like Thorvin.

His time at Warren's Rest had been well spent. Most of the ten oldest, original students would be ready to enter the military in the fall and those who weren't, would probably be ready next spring. Two would never make warriors, but Thorvin and Rayne had already spoken to Theodor with the idea of putting them into other positions at the palace. Warren's Rest was proving to be the wise investment Rayne hoped it would be when he first approached his parents with the project five years ago.

Now, with the heat of a hazy afternoon rising around him in a listless, breezeless air, and storm clouds building out over the Cameron Sea, Thorvin rode through the King's Highway gate into Westvale. He waved distractedly at the guards on duty, his mind fixed on settling in, then finding Rayne, the prince he had dedicated his life to protecting.

After leaving his horse at the stables and cleaning up in his quarters, Thorvin strode to the palace, his pace quick and purposeful. The heavy air left a coating of moisture on his bare arms and his bristled, dark brown hair. The first rumbles of distant thunder could be heard as sunlight dimmed with a yellowish cast around him. He planned to grab a quick bite in the dining hall before searching out his charge. *Let's see. At this hour, he's either at the training rings or out riding that black horse of his. Well, if he's riding, he'll be heading in now. I'll check his suite once I've grabbed a bite.*

Thorvin breathed in the delicious aromas drifting from the dining hall, his stomach rumbling in response. As he started into the large room, scanning the raised dais with the hope that Rayne would be sitting there, one of the king's royal guardsmen called out to him.

"Lord Kraftsmunn, Lord Kraftsmunn. I was just on my way to your quarters. His Majesty sent me to see if you had returned from Warren's Rest and bring you along if you were back."

Thorvin's stomach dropped and his disquiet rose a notch. "It's Prince Rayne, isn't it?" His voice sounded a deep rumble as if echoing the thunder building in the distance. His eyes once again scanned the table reserved for the royal family, confirming its empty state. "Something's happened to the prince."

"I'm sure I don't know, my lord." The man motioned for Thorvin to follow him. "What I can tell you is there's a visitor from Veres with a message from Duke Erland and soon after his arrival I was sent to find you."

"Is Prince Rayne with the king and queen?"

"No, my lord. The prince left Westvale days ago. They say he went to Veres."

"Went to Veres?! What would have prompted him to go

to Veres?" Thorvin paused as a growl worked its way up through his throat. "Lexi, that's what—who—whatever. And you say this messenger is from Veres?"

"Yes, Sir."

"Idiot boy!" Thorvin mumbled to himself as he followed the guardsman to one of the smaller audience chambers.

"Ah, Lord Kraftsmunn, I see you've decided to grace us with your presence." Theodor stopped what must have been agitated pacing in mid-stride, anger rolling off him like steam from a boiling kettle, as he glowered at Thorvin. "We have a situation. I can't believe I'm forced to say this again, but Rayne is missing."

Thorvin stared at Theodor for a full minute before grinding out, "What happened?"

"Please, Theodor, Thorvin, and you too Silas, sit down. Let's discuss this reasonably. Pacing and accusing isn't going to help the situation." Rowena waved everyone over to several wing-back, green leather chairs set in a grouping in front of a red brick fireplace at the back of the room, behind the throne-like chairs.

Theodor and Thorvin stomped over and sat like a pair of enraged lions forced to inaction, while Silas slinked over, a guilty, uncertain look on his face. Once the men were sitting, Rowena took the remaining chair. "Now, gentlemen, I'm going to start at the beginning with what I know so we can move forward on common ground.

"Twelve days ago, a representative from Cailyn met with me to receive my response to a letter from Cailyn. When he arrived, the man informed me that he had seen Rayne just a few minutes earlier. He said that the prince asked him to relay a message. Basically, he said that Rayne received an unexpected invitation to join Lady Alexianndra and her father for their father-daughter outing. Though I thought it odd that Lexi would send an invitation after having planned to spend time alone with her father; and equally strange that Rayne would not only leave without seeing me, but that he would send such an important message to me through a stranger. My concerns were soon put to rest, however. As I was speaking with the Nemorian,

Andrew asked to see me. Apparently, Rayne had left him a note explaining that he was going to join Duke Erland and Lady Alexianndra on Veres. Andrew's note verified what I had been told, so I assumed that Rayne acted impulsively in response to Lexi's request."

"But Rayne never went to Veres, did he Silas?" King Theodor stormed, bounding from his chair to begin pacing again.

"No, Sire. Not that I know of," Silas said, his voice soft and uneasy. A bright flash of lightning lit the room, leaving after-images on Thorvin's eyes, as heavy thunder vibrated the palace.

Thorvin ran his hands over his short, bristly hair and groaned. "I knew it. I just knew something wasn't right. I should have returned days ago."

"And what would you have done?" Theodor ground out, rounding on his friend in anger. "Oh, yes, that's right. You would have *protected* my son, just as you promised. By the seven, Thor, you should have been here when Rayne left, not off training some wannabe soldiers. Rayne was your responsibility. You gave me your word you would protect him. Well, Thorvin Kraftsmunn, where is my son?"

"Please, Theodor, yelling at Thorvin isn't going to help. You know Rayne insisted Thor go to Warren's Rest and we all agreed it was a good idea. Rayne also gave his word not to leave Westvale while Thor was gone. What's more important now is, if Rayne didn't go to Veres, we need to determine where he *did* go."

Theodor turned to Silas, his brown eyes flashing. "Tell me, Silas, did Justus or Alexianndra send word to Rayne asking him to join them on Veres?"

"No, Your Highness. When I left Kern House Lady Alexianndra and Duke Erland were planning to leave for the cabin on the Sharna River the next morning. There was no mention of the prince joining them. In fact, I'm carrying a letter from Lady Alexianndra for the prince. She asked me to deliver it to Rayne while I was here in Westvale."

"Let me see the letter," Rowena said.

Silas pulled a sealed envelope from an inside pocket of his vest and handed it to the queen. She broke the seal, unfolded the parchment from within, and read quietly. "It's as Silas said. Lexi had no intention of inviting Rayne to join them. She was missing him but wished him well planning the wedding without her. She said she would bring him back something from Veres to remind him of past times there."

Rowena stopped speaking and looked up, catching Theodor's eyes. "Someone planned this well. Our son has been gone for almost two weeks and we were duped into thinking he's been on Veres with Lexi. Now, we have no idea where he went, and the delay has allowed the trail to grow cold."

Silas cleared his throat, pulling attention back to himself. "Um, Your Majesty—I mean—Your Majesties, I also have a message from Duke Erland. Perhaps there's something in his letter that might clear things up."

Theodor motioned for Silas to give him the letter. He broke the seal and read it. Rising, he handed the parchment to Rowena. Running his fingers through his trim, brown beard, he chewed his mustache while giving Rowena a chance to read. "Well, Rowena, there's a common denominator here isn't there?"

"Yes," she replied, meeting his gaze, "It seems all paths lead to Nemora."

9

It took Lexi and her father two days to travel to their small cabin in a secluded hollow on the Sharna River. They had traveled at a casual pace, crossing the Eleri River in Eleri and then letting their ponies meander down the mountain path toward the Sharna River crossing. The hardwoods, dyed in vibrant shades of orange, yellow, and red, stood out among the dark green firs; the air, brisk and clear, smelled of pine and old oak leaves. They talked about things from their past and shared hopes for the future.

The Sharna River crossing passed without incident; the water was early autumn sluggish, and the trip took less than an hour. Lexi and her father pushed the ponies a bit more after the river, hoping to have enough time to set up a camp if they couldn't stay in the cabin. It proved to be a prudent plan. This was the first time they had visited the cabin since Justus's injury, and when they arrived, they groaned at the amount of work needed to make it livable again. The front door sagged on rotted hinges, the roof had a hole in it, there was a family of racoons living under the porch, and leaf litter filled the rooms.

"Perhaps we should just continue sleeping in our tent for the duration of this trip," Justus said with an apologetic grin as he and Lexi scanned the dwelling, their heads poked in the front door. "I'm sorry Lexi. I should have sent a crew here to fix the place before we came." He stepped away from the door, turning to glance back at the woods, and released a sigh. Well... as long as the weather cooperates, we should be fine."

Lexi giggled. "You mean like when I was seven and insisted coming here didn't count as a vacation unless we slept in a tent and it rained for three days straight?"

Justus chuckled. "I forgot about that." His golden eyes twinkled. "Yes, daughter, just like when you were seven."

That first evening, Lexi scoured the area for firewood, which proved to be quite abundant. In no time, she gathered a large pile. Justus repaired their old fire pit, rolling over new rocks to set around it. Finding the remains of an ancient fallen oak, he hauled over two large branches to provide seating.

While her father built a fire in the pit, Lexi claimed one of the branches for her own the moment she saw it. Justus smiled. "I knew you would like it. The thing reminds me of the tree you used to climb."

Lexi returned his warm smile. "I don't know how you dragged this here. It must weigh a ton." She juggled the limb until two smaller branches shot out like the arms of a chair, then sitting on the main trunk, she leaned back and rested her arms on the angled limbs. "It's perfect. Just like a real chair. Thank you, Daddy."

"You're welcome, daughter. Enjoy it."

Old memories of times spent at the cabin kept the two reminiscing through the days that followed. Busy mornings were devoted to cleaning and fixing the cabin, but leisurely afternoons were set aside for relaxation, swimming or hiking, and talking the way only a father and a daughter could.

Justus set a small net trap in the river the second day there and fish became the mainstay of their meals. By the following evening, the door to the cabin hung straight and the family of racoons had been displaced. Though the cabin now offered shelter, Lexi and her father chose to continue sleeping under the stars as the evenings were too perfect to waste indoors. The two weeks passed in what seemed like the blink of an eye, and if not for Lexi missing Rayne, she would have asked her father to stay another week.

"The fire should be okay for a bit," Justus said as he rose and brushed wood splinters from his pants. "I'm going to see what we've caught for our final supper and pack up my trap. I shouldn't be long."

Soon after her father left, Lexi yawned and stretched, her eyes felt like sandpaper and her eyelids drooped. The fire crackled a soothing lullaby. Lethargy, like a warm, comforting blanket, enveloped her. Unable to resist, she shifted on her log, laid her head down on her arms, and dropped into a deep sleep. And Lexi dreamed.

Lexi ran. It seemed as if she had been running for a long time, swathed in a penetrating, dark mist. Unable to see anything through the cocoon of black that enveloped her, she stretched her hands in front of her face as she ran. The surrounding gloom was so complete, she couldn't even see them. Fear surged. *I'm blind.* She tried to stop running, stumbling with the effort as the dark void sucked her forward. Leaning back, she fought the relentless pull of the oblivion that drew her. *No!*

Light, soft and hesitant, flickered around her for a second before it vanished in the dark. *No. No. Please don't leave me alone in the dark.* The light sputtered again, shimmering faintly around her, dispelling the fear of blindness.

Then she was falling. She screamed.

She was in a small space, just a few feet across. She couldn't breathe. Everything was close, too close, and blacker then the deepest night. Terror erupted, hot and compelling; she sucked at the dense air, pulling it into lungs that seemed constricted by the irresistible dark.

Pain seared her chest as if her heart was being ripped from her. *Rayne!?* She felt him there in the dark. His panic sent her reeling.

"Rayne," she shouted. She whimpered as powerful terror, pain, and confusion assailed her, flinging her back. The need to comfort him overshadowed all else. "Rayne, you're not blind. Rayne? Can you hear me? I'm here. You're not alone, I'm here. I'm here."

She heard the voice of the One. *Be strong. I am with you.*

"Rayne! Please answer me, Rayne!"

"Lexi, Lexi, wake up. Wake up!" Her father's voice, anxious and overflowing with concern, pierced the cocoon of darkness, and Lexi bolted upright.

She clutched at her father with shaking hands. A hot lump she couldn't speak past, lodged in her throat. She gasped and swallowed hard. "Oh, Daddy. It's Rayne. He's in danger and he's so scared. Daddy, we have to go to Westvale. We have to go to Westvale now."

11

Lexi chafed at the delays that seemed to beset her at every turn. Cold, heavy rain moved in during the night. The rain turned into a windswept deluge as she and her father broke camp, hampering their efforts to move with any speed on the slick, muddy mountain paths that became rushing streams within hours. The journey to the ferry crossing that had taken them less than a day coming, took two days returning. Then, with river running high and rough, they were forced to wait another three days before the ferryman would risk the crossing.

When they finally arrived at Kern House, Lexi, frustrated and anxious, packed and had already requested another pony be saddled for her, when Justus told her she needed to wait until morning to leave for Eleri.

"If something has already happened, you can't change it, and I'll not allow you to travel alone if there's any kind of threat. Besides, it's Binding Day and you're exhausted. We will attend the evening service, then get a full night's sleep in a bed. It will do us good. You'll just have to wait, daughter."

The worship service grated on Lexi's jumpy nerves and she found sleep as elusive as a phantom. She tossed and flung her covers off only to pull them back on. She was beset by night terrors and was certain she could hear a vast crowd of people chanting for blood and sacrifice. She wanted to sleep and dream, hoping to connect with Rayne. Though the thought of experiencing Rayne's fear and pain again scared her, if she allowed the dream to come, perhaps she could learn something of what was happening to her beloved. Finally, sometime during the wee hours of the night, she slipped into a dreamless sleep.

The next morning, eight days after her dream, Lexi jumped from her pony, tossing her reins at one of the guards who had accompanied her father and her to Eleri. It had rained again last night, and water spattered, catching the sun's rays in glistening arcs, as she landed in a puddle. But she didn't notice, her thoughts were focused on getting through the portal and back to Westvale.

The rain which had continued for days finally stopped, and this morning the sun had risen in a clear, rain-washed sky. She squinted against the sparkles, her eyes blinking at the sudden flashes. Once again, she felt Rayne, knew he was in a dark place, knew he was losing himself in a lonely pit of despair. Her heart throbbed as if it was being shredded by razors.

"Hang in there Rayne. I'm coming. I'm coming," she mumbled as she sprinted past the two large freight portals and pushed through the door into the simple building that housed the small individual portal. She didn't even stop to purchase a pass, leaving her father to deal with the portal attendant who yelled for her to stop. Without hesitation, she jumped in front of a man waiting his turn to skip and barreled into the portal.

Heat, humidity, the reek of unwashed bodies, and the stench that was Emporium City didn't even register for Lexi. She sprinted across the square, dodging vendors' stalls, to the Corylus portal. Waving broadly behind her, she ran toward the line of travelers waiting to skip. "My father's coming. He'll pay for my pass," she shouted.

She thought she heard a voice calling her name, but ignoring it, bounced into the portal, cutting off a rather large-built, red headed woman with an umbrella who huffed angrily at her, sounding like a submerged swimmer bursting up out of the water.

Stumbling into the noisy Westvale station, Lexi pulled to

a stop, catching her breath, startled by the level of activity and clamor surrounding her. *Why are there so many soldiers?*

"I'm here," she mumbled again. She glanced back at the portal wondering how long it would take for her father to follow. "Sorry, Daddy. I'll see you at the palace."

Heavy, humid air slapped her in the face as she skipped down the steps of the Westvale Portal Station, cut across the crowded and noisy Portal Square, and sprinted toward the Great Square and the palace. Moisture pooled on her exposed skin and turned her hair into golden red frizz, baking her back in the intense sunlight. She was grateful she had chosen to dress for the heat and humidity of early summer in Westvale, wearing a light, cotton print shirt in shades of turquoise and gray over a gray leather split riding skirt and calf-high black boots. With a huff, she pulled the heavy mass of her hair up, exposing her neck to the fitful breeze coming off the Cameron Sea.

"Lady Alexianndra! Hey, Lexi, wait up!" The voice she had been half-hearing since Veres, penetrated her thoughts at last; she stood for a second before turning to scan the square. *I know that voice.*

"Finally, whew. Where are you running to?"

"Stevie?" Confusion speared through her racing emotions. "Where did you come from?"

"Ummm, how about from right behind you. I thought you cut in front of me at the Veres portal on purpose. That you knew it was me."

Her mouth forming a circle, Lexi said, "That was you? I'm so sorry. I didn't even see you."

"I can tell." Stevie shook his head his mouth twisted in disgust. "As if it isn't bad enough that Emma broke up with me, now my *friend* decides to see right through me. Oh, that's right, you're nobility. I guess they don't notice little things like commoners waiting in line before them."

"No, no. It's nothing like that; you know better. It's Rayne. Come on we can talk while we're walking." She started jogging toward the palace.

"Hold up," Stevie said frowning and holding up his

palms. "You're heading for the palace. I'm going the other direction. I need to get back to our shop in the merchant's quarter."

"I think Rayne's in trouble, and it's taken me forever to get here. The pressure to make certain he's okay is pushing me to rush. Please, will you come with me to the palace?"

"What do you mean 'in trouble'?

"I don't know." Lexi moaned. "I can't be sure of anything now, except I dreamed that something bad happened to Rayne. I hope I'm being overly dramatic and it's nothing serious. But, come on, Stevie, please. Can't you run any faster."

She broke into a sprint, Stevie shrugged and raced after her. Reaching the front gate of the palace grounds, Lexi pulled up short with Stevie stumbling to a stop behind her. "Oh, no," she groaned. "Something must have happened. They never close this gate."

"Yeah, you're right. I don't remember the last time I saw this closed," Stevie agreed as the two strode to the front of the guard shack.

A guard Lexi recognized approached them, and she strove to remember the man's name.

"Lady Alexianndra!" the man said, his eyes widening. "I thought you was supposed to be back days ago. If we'd known you was comin' now, we would have arranged for a carriage to meet you at the station. Please, give me a minute, my lady, and I'll get this gate open for you."

"Don't bother. We can go in through the wicket if you'll unlock it for us."

"Thanks, Carlen," Stevie said as the guard walked toward the small entry set into the large door that flanked the massive veredium gate. "Why is the main gate locked anyway?"

"I'm sure I don't know. But I'll tell you this. There's been one big hubbub going on in the palace. People coming and going. They've called back troops from Arisima, Sorial, and Amathea. Keeping it on the down low. And, from what I hear, the line to Nemora ain't working. Haven't checked it out myself, but I heard that no one's been able to skip there for the last few weeks. Where've you been Stevie? I thought with your ..."

"And Prince Rayne?" Lexi interrupted. "Is he involved in this *hubbub?*"

"Now that's an interesting question, my lady because nobody's seen His Highness for the better part of three weeks. We all figured he was doing some kind of religious purification ritual before the wedding. But then Thorvin comes back two days ago and he's been storming around like an angry wasp. Whatever's happening, the royals and them that work inside the palace ain't talking about it."

He had unlocked the wicket while he was talking and pulled it open. "There you go my lady. Sorry for any inconvenience."

Lexi and Stevie sprinted across the lawn and into a side door of the palace. Cutting through several small halls, they reached a main hallway where they passed guards who averted their eyes. Crisscrossing hallways that usually bustled with noise and activity were empty and quiet.

"They're probably in one of the audience chambers," Lexi whispered as if afraid to break the resounding silence as the sound of their passage echoed off the walls. "If they're meeting with military leaders, they need a place with privacy and room for everyone."

She led Stevie through several turns before entering the section of the palace where the king and queen met with petitioners. Lexi began to get anxious as they proceeded and saw no sign of anyone. Her concern at not being able to find the room in which the royal couple were meeting, dissolved when she rounded a corner and saw Andrew pacing near a closed door. Two guardsmen flanking the door, stood at attention. Boone, who had been sitting near the wall jumped up, and with tail wagging, bounded toward Lexi and Stevie.

One of the soldiers acknowledged Lexi with a small smile of recognition and opened the heavy wooden door, waving her in. After a short rub behind the ears to Boone and shooting Andrew a quick smile, Lexi strode into the chamber with Stevie on her heels.

The scene that met her eyes was unexpected. Walls of heavy stone in shades of sienna and burnt umber rose from a floor covered by well-worn, pitted, terracotta tiles. There wasn't a single window. Three lit candelabras marched down the center of a massive, age worn, oak table that sat atop a hand-tied rug in shades of green and umber. Detailed maps of all seven worlds covered the walls. Lampstands, molded to look like oak trees with finely wrought branches reaching toward the ceiling, stood in the four corners. A dozen prismatic lanterns hung from each. Lexi recognized the room from descriptions she had heard. This was the Kierkengaard family war room.

Her eyes scanned the people sitting on carved oak chairs around the table. She took note of several empty seats. As the door closed behind Stevie, heads turned. Rowena stood, and with a smile of encouragement, opened her arms, beckoning Lexi forward.

It took every ounce of control Lexi possessed to not run into Rowena's arms. Remembering her position, she walked with as much regal poise as she could muster. By the time she reached the queen, however, any reserve she had was depleted, and with a cry she fell into Rowena's arms and wept.

"I know, I know my dear." Rowena's embrace warmed Lexi. "We'll figure this all out. It's going to be alright." Rowena rubbed Lexi's back and gave her a few minutes to calm. "There is more happening here than Rayne's disappearance. Would you like to take the seat next to your father's and join us in this session? As the duke's heir, you are entitled. And as he has not yet arrived, your input as representative of Veres is important."

Lexi sniffed once, then composed herself. "He's on his way right now. I just couldn't wait so I ran ahead."

"Very good," Theodor said. "I'm glad to hear that. I value your father's opinion and was concerned when he hadn't come yet."

"We just returned to Kern House last night and left first thing this morning for Westvale. I … had a dream. But it kept raining and … we couldn't get back."

"We'll talk more after, my dear," Rowena said. "For now, please take the seat next to Silas. When your father arrives, he can take Silas's place."

Lexi took the seat Rowena indicated. Looking around the

table, she recognized several of those in attendance. Theodor sat on a large, throne-like chair at the head of the table, with Rowena to his right. The chair to Theodor's left, across from the queen, was empty, probably meant for Rayne. The position next to Rowena, usually reserved for the representative of the Interplanetary Council also sat open. Captain Fontaine sat next, with the subsequent two chairs vacant. Derek Falknor occupied the next position, a soldier wearing the uniform of an Interplanetary Captain beside him. Lexi smiled to see Silas sitting in the chair before her own, acting as her father's representative.

On the opposite side of the table, after Rayne's chair, Thorvin sat in what would normally be the chair occupied by a representative of the Interplanetary Court, followed by Captain Ellis and the representative from Arisima. The final four seats were occupied by men Lexi didn't recognize. Probably the representatives from Amathea and Glacieria.

"Stevie Kasper, as you have seen fit to enter here, why don't you go back out and retrieve that wayward page from the hallway. I know you are both concerned for my son. You may take seats along the wall, there," Theodor said, suppressing a grin.

Nodding, Stevie left for a moment and returned with Andrew and Boone trailing.

"Your Majesty, are you certain it's advisable to allow two unauthorized youth to be present while we discuss such weighty matters?" Derek Falknor protested. "And a dog? Really, this is highly unorthodox."

"Unorthodox maybe, but then again, this whole situation is unorthodox. I will vouch for both these young men. They are close friends of my son; I would trust them with my life, I know Rayne has. And since his disappearance seems to be at the center of this situation, I'll allow them to stay." Turning his focus on Stevie and Andrew, he added. "I expect you understand the gravity of what we are discussing here?"

Stevie and Andrew nodded.

"Then you must know, divulging anything you are privy to during this meeting will be considered treason, and if you are caught doing so, you will be severely punished."

"Yes, Your Majesty," Stevie and Andrew said in unison.

Lexi gave the two an encouraging smile before they turned to take seats along the wall next to Noah.

"Now, my choice would be to immediately proceed with this meeting," Theodor said scanning the faces around the table. "However, since Duke Erland is on his way, I propose we call a break. Rowena, would you please see that some light fare is set in the adjoining room? We will reconvene once Duke Erland arrives and everyone has been refreshed."

With a slight wave of her hand, Rowena summoned a page from the shadows by the dark fireplace at the front of the room. She whispered to him briefly, and the boy left in a rush. Those in attendance stood, stretching, and moving about. Stevie, Noah, and Andrew were already caught up in an animated conversation, so Lexi looked at Rowena, who nodded for Lexi to approach.

"Come with me, my dear. We need some time to talk in private." Rowena took Lexi's arm.

10

Rowena led Lexi into a small receiving room two doors down from the war room. It was an unusually dark space for the palace, with two tiny, lead-paned windows set up high in the walls directly beneath the vaulted ceiling. Shadows hugged the corners of the room even after Rowena lit a Caarwyn Rill lantern, its prismatic light seeking to banish the gloom. But Lexi didn't feel any danger in them, like the shadows before Rayne had bound the living darkness, just a comforting peace as Rowena walked past the small throne. It was a formal room, more so than any of the other audience rooms Lexi had seen. Rowena ran her hand over the back of the throne, caressing the age-worn wood.

"I have always felt a certain peace in this chamber," she said. "It is a sanctuary for me on busy days when I need a quiet place to sit and think, and, above all else, pray. I have spent many hours here in prayer these last couple weeks. Even before I learned my son was missing.

"Tell me, Lexi, you've felt it too, haven't you? This spiritual malaise? It's like something evil is seeking to drag me down into a hole of dark despair. Please, tell me you've felt it and I'm not alone."

She turned back to Lexi, her face pale; and Lexi noticed what she hadn't seen earlier, the dark circles under the queen's eyes. Stilling the quivering in her hands, Lexi nodded.

Rowena pulled in a deep breath before continuing. "At first, I discounted the sensation, thinking it was a result of the stress of planning the wedding without Rayne's help. But then the blackouts started. Two days ago, Silas gave me the letter you sent to Rayne, exposing the lie. You never invited him to join you on Veres. I knew what my spirit had been trying to tell me for days, something terrible has happened to my son."

Lexi drew to the distraught queen's side. "I wish I had asked him to join us. Then this wouldn't be happening."

"You've felt his terror too, haven't you, Lexi? The fear? The pain? And the consuming darkness?"

The lump at the back of Lexi's throat grew, hot and pressing, stealing her breath, as Rowena wrapped her in a hug and the two clung to each other. There was no need to speak; the shared fear bound them in a way nothing else could. They stood together for many minutes, shrouded in the silence of the chamber, allowing the grief to hold sway. But then, as if they had come to a mutual agreement, they pulled back, settling their emotions and seeking the calm they needed to face the situation.

Setting her face into a cold mask and straightening her shoulders, Lexi said, "please, Your Majesty, tell me what you know."

"Come, my child, sit with me." Rowena was, once again, the self-controlled queen of Corylus and all Ochen. She led Lexi to one of the four small chairs in front of the throne, before settling in another herself, and telling Lexi about the man from Nemora. How he lied.

"He was here as my sister's representative. If he lied about Rayne, how do I know he didn't lie about Cailyn. I'm worried something has happened to her. Ever since Brayden's death and Miles's suicide, I've been apprehensive about her emotional state. She's prone to hold things in, and then collapse under the pressure. Cailyn has always been sensitive, afraid of confrontation, weak. If someone has taken advantage of that, there's no telling what she might do.

"I wanted to skip to Nemora immediately after talking to Silas. But we discovered that the skipping lines to Nemora were closed to inbound traffic soon after Varick left. The Shipping and Portal Guild kept the situation quiet to avoid any scandal. From the manifests Derek Falknor showed us, the lines from Corylus to Nemora haven't reopened, and those from Sorial have only been open on days prior to Binding Days. Theodor and I are convinced Rayne is on Nemora. We plan to send several people there next Binding Day eve. After considering our alternatives, we came to the conclusion soldiers traveling through the portal would alert our enemies of our suspicions. Instead we decided to send just a few individuals disguised as scroll worshipers.

"I am insisting I be included in the number who skip. Not only will I be able to make certain my sister is safe, I'm also the only one with strong enough magic to handle the energy on Nemora. I know Theodor isn't happy about it, but no matter what he says, I'm going. You and I know something is happening to Rayne, and I worry that harm has come to Cailyn as well. I would never forgive myself if I could have helped either of them and didn't. But because our skipping to Nemora could put both of them at risk, it's important that our identities remain unknown."

"I'm going with you." Lexi's jaw set at a stubborn incline. "Rayne's fear was so intense and crushing. I can't live with myself if I sit here in Westvale, safe, while he's in danger."

Rowena smiled at Lexi. "Together then." A look of concern crossed her face. "We'll have to convince Theodor that it is not only a wise decision to send us rather than soldiers, but the best decision. He is not happy that I'm insisting I go. So … you and I must stick together. If we don't, he'll just use his power to forbid us from leaving Westvale."

Returning with Queen Rowena to the alcove of the war room where a selection of foods had been set out, Lexi was relieved to see her father talking with King Theodor. As she walked up to him, he turned. A frown flitted across his face, only to be replaced with a smile. "Here she is now. The impulsive daughter who left her father behind to face two very angry portal attendants and make his way to the palace alone."

Lexi lowered her gaze to the floor. "I'm sorry Father. I

couldn't wait any longer to see Rayne." But then, meeting Justus's eyes, her voice rose, tears pooled in her eyes, and her words raced. "It's as I feared, Daddy. He's not here. Something terrible must have happened to him. They thought he was with us on Veres. Her Majesty has been having blackouts and feeling the same sense of fear and darkness that I've been feeling. The king and queen believe he was lured to Nemora where we can't go because the portal's closed. But Her Majesty plans to go there and rescue him just as soon as she can. I'm going with her. You will let me go, Father, won't you? Oh, you must, you just must."

"We will see, my daughter." Justus wrapped his arms around Lexi, pulling her into a gentle hug. "Nothing has been decided yet. That's part of what this meeting is about. His Majesty will have a say in who goes to Nemora. And, my dear, from what he has told me, nothing can be done for several days yet."

The next half hour went by in a haze for Lexi, as arguments broke out over what was more important.

"I would think that discovering what the scroll cults are doing on Nemora would be the more pressing issue," Derek Falknor said. "I appreciate your concern for your son, but as king and queen of all Ochen, your responsibility to your subjects should take precedence over your personal feelings."

The representative from Arisima nodded. "Lord Falknor is right. Though we sympathize with your concern, how can you be certain the prince has been kidnapped, rather than responding to a call as Light Bringer. And even if we were certain he's been taken against his will, how can you be sure he's on Nemora? Determining the purpose behind the scroll worshipers gathering in the kind of numbers we have seen on the reports needs to be your top priority. Not an add-on to tracking down His Highness."

"He's been taken." Thorvin pounded the table. "He wouldn't have left Westvale without telling anyone where he was going. He wouldn't have reneged on his promise to me, unless he was taken against his will."

"Isn't it true that a note was left?" Derek raised his eyebrows, letting the question sit on the air.

"A fake. A misdirect." Thorvin shot to his feet, his hand reaching for a sword that wasn't on his hip.

"Of the two issues, the massive gathering of scroll worshipers is the more important." Derek Falknor glared at Thorvin. "Lady Genevieve sent me here purposefully to push for an investigation into the issue. She's not the only noble concerned about this issue."

"Prince Rayne's disappearance is more than just a family problem. He is the crown prince and royal heir. That's got to count for something." Thorvin's face resembled a storm cloud.

"Without any other evidence, how can we even be sure he was taken against his will. Perhaps he went willingly with some friend and will turn up here in a couple days. You're too close to the situation to think rationally where the prince is concerned." The Arisimanian representative speared Thorvin with a cold look.

The arguments continued, and tensions rose. Lexi looked toward Rowena, expecting her to say something, build a case for finding Rayne. The queen sat, quiet, composed, and staring forward. Even Theodor said little, and Lexi couldn't get a read on what he was thinking. His face was a mask of calm. She glanced at her father and he winked, causing her to wrinkle her brow in confusion. "Just wait," he mouthed.

A short while later, when the discussion wound down, Theodor rose and looked around the table, meeting each person's eyes. "I have heard your arguments and understand the positions you have all taken regarding what should be done. And I have made my decisions.

"Her Majesty and I believe our son's abduction and the closing of Nemora are related. In any case, the situation in Inverness must be investigated. The queen is concerned for her sister and we are both troubled about the substantial number of individuals who have skipped to that world in the last six months. Ever since the activities of the scroll cults began to diminish on every other world." Theodor paused for a moment, giving those sitting around the table a chance to register his words.

"As the situation currently stands, the Nemorian portal is

closed to traffic from Corylus and only open to inbound traffic on a periodic basis from Sorial. Sending in an armed force of soldiers is not only impossible given the skipping line situation, it could result in the line being shut down completely.

"Therefore, I have asked Lord Kraftsmunn to lead a small band of hand-picked individuals. Thorvin and his companions will travel in disguise and blend in with the scroll worshipers skipping to Nemora. Their first duty is to determine why the scroll worshipers are congregating there. I've also asked him to ascertain if they pose a threat to Ochen. While on Nemora, they are to contact Duchess Cailyn and verify that she is in no danger. If possible, they are to enlist her aid in reopening the portal to travel from Corylus. While there, in addition to investigating the scroll cult activity, this party is to search out information regarding the location of Prince Rayne.

"Considering our options, and the concerns of all involved, I trust this plan will be a good first step in dealing with the scroll cults and finding my son. Lord Kraftsmunn is familiar with Nemora and has dealt with scroll worshipers in the past. Are there any questions?"

Lexi stood, squared her shoulders, and faced King Theodor with fixed determination. "This isn't a question and it isn't a request. It is simply a statement of fact. I will be going to Nemora with Lord Kraftsmunn." She sat down, arms crossed in front of her chest, mouth set in a line that allowed for no discussion.

Theodor pursed his lips and considered for a moment before saying, "I leave the final decisions regarding his companions to Lord Kraftsmunn. If he is willing, I won't gainsay him."

With a rustle of silk fabric, Rowena rose. She didn't even glance at Theodor, but instead focused directly on Thorvin. "You know you need me, Thor. I'm the only one here who can wield the heavy magic of Nemora. And, if that is not enough, no one—and I mean *no one*—can stop me from going to Nemora to search for my son."

His face screwed up as if he had just sucked on a lemon, Thorvin nodded. "If the schedule remains the same as it has the last few weeks, the Sorial line to Nemora should be open again in six days. I will be contacting the rest of those I plan to take with me before then."

The meeting ended, and Lexi and her father joined Silas, Noah, Stevie, and Andrew at the back of the room.

"Well, Silas," Justus said. "It's good to see you. It seems your arrival was most timely. His Majesty told me Lady Genevieve's information about the skipping patterns for Nemora was instrumental in their checking into the portal closure. Also, your report of scroll worshipers from Veres moving to Nemora helped Theodor understand some of what is happening. If not for that, they would not have discovered the connection between the lack of the cult's activity throughout Ochen, and the considerable number of people skipping to Nemora these last six months. I am sorry that the time you spent in Eleri before coming here kept the king and queen from learning of the prince's disappearance earlier. If they made the connection with Nemora sooner, a party could have been sent to investigate days ago."

"Yes, sir." Silas ducked his head.

"Daughter." Justus turned to face Lexi. "'A statement of fact?' You *will* be going to Nemora with Lord Kraftsmunn? I know you can be headstrong, however, as your father, I must insist you remain here in Westvale. Lord Kraftsmunn will have enough on his hands without needing to watch over you."

"And I must insist she be allowed to accompany us to Nemora," Queen Rowena said as she and Thorvin approached the group. "My future daughter-in-law and I have already made a pact to support each other and search for Rayne together. We have shared our feelings and our fears. We are quite determined to skip to Nemora as soon as possible, even if we must go alone. I give you my word, Justus, I will watch over your daughter with utmost care." She walked to Lexi's side, settling her arm around Lexi's smaller shoulders with confidence.

"I agree. Lexi should come with us," Thorvin rumbled as he stepped between Justus and Lexi. "I've traveled with her before and I know that she's capable. Also, if—no, when—we find Prince Rayne, he'll want to see her.

"In fact, since King Theodor has left it to me to decide

who will go, and because we're not supposed to do anything more than gather information, I've decided to take the prince's friends. Their commitment is certain, and I know I can trust them to do all they can to bring His Highness back safely, even though our official purpose is to gather intelligence."

Thorvin turned his focus on Noah and Stevie. "Noah, as a member of the Corylus military, I've already requested you be assigned to me for this trip. Captain Ellis agreed. What do you think, Stevie, are you interested?"

"You couldn't leave without me. Rayne's my friend. And if I know my sister, she's going to want to go too."

"He's right," Noah said. "There's no way we could go off world looking for Rayne and leave Sashi behind. Especially if Lexi is going. You know Sashi; she'd find some way to follow."

Thorvin arranged for everyone skipping to Nemora to meet in the dining hall of the palace early in the morning on the sixth day after the meeting. The day before Binding Day. Lexi was sitting at the royal table with her father, King Theodor, and Queen Rowena, when Thorvin walked in. Lexi's eyes rounded and her jaw went slack at Thorvin's choice of companions, but when she thought about what he said the day of the meeting, his decisions made sense.

Stevie, Sashi, and Noah walked in together, all dressed for travel. Lexi had been concerned she would be the only woman wearing leather trousers, and grinned to see that Sashi was wearing them as well. Like Noah, Sashi wore a military-style jacket in deep blue over a white shirt. With her red hair pulled up under a cap, she looked like she was ready for anything.

Lexi excused herself to meet with the other travelers. As she scurried down the four steps to the main floor, her eyes caught on two people she didn't expect to see this morning. *No way. Three people, two adults and ... an infant. No, Shaw and Anne are just here to let us see the baby before we skip. That's it.* "Anne." Lexi held out her hand in greeting. "Oh my gosh! You have the baby. A little boy, right? What's his name?"

Within seconds, Anne was the center of attention as Lexi, Sashi, Noah, Stevie, and Thorvin came to stand around her, staring at the tiny form sleeping in the folds of a cloth draped across Anne's chest. Even Queen Rowena and King Theodor came down to greet Anne and see the baby.

"Yes, another boy." Anne lowered her gaze to the infant, her smile radiant. "Bethie and Warren now have a little baby brother and his name is Jonathan."

Gently touching the tiny hand, Lexi said, "He's beautiful; and the name is perfect. I'm so glad we are getting to see him before we leave."

"Oh?" Anne's eyebrows arched. "I guess you don't know. You'll be getting to see a lot of him. He's coming with us. Elsie is watching Bethie and Warren, but Jonathan is too young to leave behind. He needs me to feed him and my *brother* needs me as well."

"You can't mean to travel to Nemora with a newborn." Lexi's eyes grew wide. "You just gave birth. Don't you need to … recover?"

Anne laughed. "No, I don't need to recover. I'm perfectly healthy and able to travel to Nemora with you. And, like you, I refuse to be left behind. As soon as we heard that Rayne was in trouble, Shaw and I knew we would be part of whatever was done to find him. Besides, if any of you need a healer, you'll appreciate me being part of this band. Shaw and I discussed this fully with Thorvin over the last few days. We're part of your disguise. How better to blend in than to have a couple with a baby traveling with you? Don't think for a minute, Lady Alexianndra, that you are the only stubborn person allowed to claim a place on this trip."

Lexi stared as awe washed over her. She had never seen Anne look so beautiful before; healthy, glowing, full of spirit and energy as she argued her cause. Her hair was loosely pulled into one long wheat-blonde braid that fell over her shoulder down to her waist. She was dressed in a simple green button-front shirt over a chestnut colored leather split riding skirt. The baby was resting comfortably in the cloth sling, leaving Anne's arms free.

"I did leave the decision of who would be part of this team to Thorvin," Theodor said with a sigh. "If he says Anne is going, I think you need to accept that, Lexi."

While they were talking, two young men, one tall, blonde, and muscular, the other dark and slight, entered and walked over.

"Good, you're here," Thorvin said. "Let me introduce the last two members of our company. The tall, blonde is Benning and the shorter dark guy is Oliver."

"Ollie, Sir," the young man said, his dark chestnut eyes earnest. "Please, sir, I prefer Ollie."

"Sure," Thorvin ground out giving the young soldier a surprised look. "Ollie. Captain Fontaine recommended taking these two soldiers with us to Nemora. Benning's originally from Rockhall Province and *Ollie's* from Neth.

"So, that's it. We're all here. Let's grab some breakfast, review final plans, and then head right over to the Portal Station."

When everyone had eaten, Thorvin stood and picked up a bulky sack from the table. He pulled out a dusky brown, hooded cloak, shook it out. "Everyone, take one of these. Remember, we need to blend in so put your cloaks on as soon as we get to Emporium City. I know it's going to be hot, but we'll have to put up with the heat for a short while. If all goes well, we should be able to skip to Nemora within the next couple hours."

11

Seth Hamlin stood at the bank of mullioned casement windows overlooking the park-like grounds of Castle Inverness. Morning fog shrouded the hickories and oaks below him, muting their greens into shades of grayed-green, while the fir trees near the wall stood like sentinel ghosts, marking the edge of the forest beyond in the murky light.

He took a deep breath, wrinkling his nose at the earthy smells that wafted up from the damp foliage below. He pulled the glass pane shut and turned to walk back into the warm room. Contentment softened the lines on his face as he sipped a steaming cup of coffee. As was his habit, he wore a freshly laundered sienna United Scrolls of Ochen cloak over a beige robe with USO embroidered over his heart in gold thread. His waist-length silver hair was gathered in a loose braid down his back.

A brisk fire flickered to his right warming the early morning chill and casting a glittering light on two large gemstone rings adorning his first and third fingers. If he turned his hand just right, the flare intensified. He smiled. "Not bad for a shopkeeper's son, eh Father?"

Turning, he set the now empty cup and saucer on an

elegant white table with fine, spindly legs, next to the remains of his breakfast. A soft rain began spattering the window sill and he sighed. He detested the weather on Nemora. Once the United Scrolls of Ochen grew powerful enough to banish One worship and claim territory on all seven worlds, he would move to Arisima. The desert planet suited him, with its beautiful oases and warm breezes.

But for now, he was needed in Inverness, close to the sacrifice stone. He would not neglect his duty. *Soon. We will observe the fourth sacrificial rites tomorrow night. In three-weeks' time, all the worlds of Ochen will recognize my authority. They will finally deny the deceiving myths of the One and acknowledge the supremacy of the scrolls. They will have no choice. With the Light Bringer dead and his deceit revealed, all will bow to us.*

A quiet knock on the door pulled Seth from his musings.

"Prime Shepherd Hamlin, Senior Associate Shepherd Gwyn Thompson is here as you requested."

"Very good. Send him in."

Seth shifted to stand in front of the fire as he turned to face Gwyn. "Good fortune and welcome, Gwyn," Seth said as a portly, balding man with an overgrown brown mustache and large muscular arms entered. He was a couple years younger than Seth and though he wore a maroon United Scrolls of Ochen cloak, it was crumpled as if he had slept in it. Seth stifled a sigh at the man's appearance.

"Humph," Gwyn snorted. "It's me, Seth. You ain't got no need to be all formal with me. We've known each other too long for that."

A stiff smile flowed onto Seth's face. "True, true, Gwyn. We've know each other for many years now." Seth sniffed. "So, is it done?"

Gwyn scowled. "Jus' like you wanted. No one's gonna get onto Nemora this week. I sent out the word to our people. They'll wait for next Binding Day eve. How did you know King Theodor was sending spies here this week?"

"I have my ways, Gwyn."

"Well, if that's all your wantin', I'll be headin' back to the camp."

"No, Gwyn. Stay. We need to talk." Seth walked to the door and sent the young guard to the kitchen for more coffee and something to eat. "Sit down, Gwyn. The coffee will be here shortly."

Gwyn eyed one of the upholstered, lion footed chairs in front of the fireplace. He settled on the white and pink material, an uneasy look flitting across his face. With the firelight glinting in his eyes, he sat without saying a word.

After the coffee and a tray of pastries arrived, the two men began nursing the warm, fragrant brew. Seth watched Gwyn through lidded eyes for several minutes before clearing his throat. "I won't beat about the bush here, Gwyn. Word has come to me that you are openly questioning the doctrines of our faith. Your position as Senior Associate Shepherd, and my strongest ally, has kept you safe so far. I have withheld judgment and given you time to disprove these lies. But I will not condone spreading discord among the faithful. Tell me, old friend. There's no truth to those stories, is there?"

Gwyn frowned and looked down into his coffee, his lips firm, forehead puckered. "You know I always backed you, Seth. No matter what. From the time we was young, I was there for you. Remember back when you first told me about the scrolls and we went to fight on Glacieria? We believed in what we was fightin' for; we believed in the scrolls. It seemed right and good. We was helping all of Ochen by protectin' the scrolls, working to stop the return of One worship. Together we listened to the High Guardian of the Scrolls speak words of power, and the fire burned in us.

"But Seth, I ain't so sure anymore. These sacrifices we're doin', this thing with the prince, what you promised to that *creature* in the hollow, it don't feel right. None of it feels right." He paused, chewed on his ragged mustache. "Seth, have you ever read one of those scrolls, wondered what they say?"

Seth's eyes narrowed and his back stiffened. His friend's words were dangerous, and Seth erected a wall of ice against his deep feelings for the man. "What? What nonsense are you spouting? Read the scrolls? You're talking blasphemy! Gwyn, I can't—no—I won't listen to this. Do you even realize the position you put me in by speaking of this? By the seven, I'm the Prime Shepherd, and you've just confessed to a violation of our law that's punishable by death! You know the scrolls were never meant to be *read*! They are to be worshipped and reverenced! *Read?* Never! That's what the One worshipers do, and that's what's led them into their perverted faith. That's what the accursed Binder preached!"

"Seth, listen to me." Gwyn chewed his mustache and shook his head. "I been readin' one of them copies of the scrolls. I picked it up the last time I was in Westvale. The Words of the One to Corylus. Seth, I asked myself, why would there even be words written on the scrolls, if they're not to be read?"

Seth rose and paced before the windows as light rain spattered on the glass. Even in the fire-warmed room, a chill wormed through him at his friend's question. He wanted Gwyn to stop talking, stop incriminating himself and putting Seth at risk. He had worked hard to gain the position of prime shepherd, he'd done unspeakable things that even Gwyn didn't know about. He would not risk his position, not even for his oldest friend.

"Seth." Gwyn spread his arms, pleading. "Please, just listen to me. The Words I read ... they made me think. And the more I read, the more I wanted to read. It's like they're fillin' some kind of hole inside me. They've spoken to my heart and..."

"Enough!" Seth exploded. He stalked over to stand between Gwyn and the fire. "Stop talking. Just stop talking. I refuse to listen to this. The only reason I haven't called the guard and had you thrown in a cell is because we've been friends for so long. You're my right hand, second in the faith. But I will not tolerate this contempt of our laws. If you don't confess your blasphemy and turn from this course right now, I'll see your blood mingling with the blood of the Binder at the next sacrifice. Do you understand, Gwyn? Don't force me to choose between my friendship with you and my faith! Admit your mistake and repent for even thinking to read one of those tainted copies. Because, if you don't, I'll be forced to do something we'll both regret."

"Seth, I can't do this anymore." Gwyn shook his head and huffed as he pressed up onto his feet. He set his cup on the table and removed his crumpled cloak, dropping it on the floor at Seth's feet. "I won't bother you anymore with my questions. Though I wish you would ask some yourself. If you'd just consider it, we could try to find where the truth really lies ... together.

"Seth, I'm leavin'. I won't be a part of this any longer. It's wrong. What we're doin' is wrong. The Bindin' didn't take our power, it freed us from the darkness that was enslavin' us. And what you're doin' with these sacrifices is puttin' us right back into that slavery. I see that now, Seth. I'm walking out of here; you can either call for the guard or let me go. The choice is yours."

Seth cursed and grabbed Gwyn's arm as he tried to pass. "Don't. Your walking away now will raise too many questions among the faithful and I can't allow that. Gwyn, I'm asking you now as your friend, as your *brother* in all things, stay by my side, at least until the sacrifices are over. You can do that for me, can't you? Just a few more weeks. You've felt it, haven't you? The swelling of energy in the glade each time we've completed a ritual? It's working! By the seven, we're close to reclaiming our lost scrolls."

"Have you even heard a word I've said?" Pain laced Gwyn's voice. "You have to stop this. What you're feelin' ain't the scrolls, it's whatever was defeated by the prince when he bound the livin' darkness."

"Where did you hear that?"

"I read it, Seth. It's written in the Words of the One to Corylus."

Potent fury seized Seth, coursing through his veins, overriding any sense of reason. He clutched Gwyn's arm tighter and hurled him back toward the fireplace. Gwyn stumbled over the stone hearth, crashing down onto the unyielding stone. In that instant, Seth grabbed the veredium poker and smashed it over Gwyn's head. He groaned and reached his hand up to the side of his head where blood was flowing freely down onto his shirt.

"You will not destroy what we have built," Seth snarled.

"I won't let you. You have betrayed me and all we fought for. You have betrayed Ochen.

"Is that what you want Gwyn? To be a filthy One worshiper? Fine. Die with your new hero for your false faith. I give you the privilege of being the last human to shed his blood before I finally spill every remaining drop from that false light bringer who deceived all Ochen with his myths of a One."

Turning to the door, Seth spoke to the guard. "Get some help, chains, and a gag. Chain this traitor and put him with the other prisoners. He has betrayed us. Gag him until he's locked in a cell where he can't spread his blasphemous poison to any of the faithful."

12

Mite must wait. Creator-Father says Mite must wait. Why must Mite wait?" Mite grumbled as he scraped at the crumbling mortar between two rocks in the wall of his cell. "Creator-Father says wait. Wait. Wait. And Mite waits. But nothing happens. Heavy magic grows strong; darkness comes. Mite fears for friends. Mite fears for Ray-ray. How much longer must Mite wait?"

Be patient, my servant, the voice of the One spoke into Mite's agitated spirit. *Pray. The young Light Bringer needs your prayers, Mite.*

"But Mite wants to do more. Help friend Ray-ray, not just pray."

Mite, you are helping your friends when you pray. Prayer comforts those lost in dark places. Be patient, trust. Soon you will meet someone I have sent to help.

"Creator-Father, please. Let Mite bear the darkness for young Ray-ray. Please. Mite's heart is breaking. Please, Creator Father, let Mite bear the darkness for his friend."

Your love for my Light Bringer does you justice, Mite. But he must walk his path just as you must walk the path set for you.

Two more days went by. Mite marked them with a piece

of coal on a smooth-faced stone near his sleeping pallet. He had hidden the coal and a tiny knife in a small inner pocket of his jacket when he went to investigate what was happening in the ancient hollow. He counted one mark for each sunrise. Thirty-four marks now adorned the smooth gray stone.

Keeping track of the days helped Mite remember to worship the One each Binding Day. Tomorrow would be the fifth Binding Day he had spent locked in this cell.

Each Binding Day eve also brought turmoil to the prison. The victims chosen for the sacrifice were forced to drink a mind-numbing potion before being bound, blindfolded, and led out to the altar. Knowing Ray-ray's blood was also shed as part of the ritual, Mite covered his ears during the herding of the sacrifices, closing his mind to the truth of what was happening, then praying even harder for the One to stop the evil.

Mite's eyes flashed, and he bared his teeth when a man he recognized as one of the leaders of the United Scrolls of Ochen was thrown into his cell. The man had stood with Prime Shepherd Hamlin and the Lady Mother, overseeing as past sacrifices were prepared to be taken to the hollow and now, he himself was sitting on the floor of Mite's cell, a bloody cut still dribbling a red stream down the side of his head.

Mite backed into the wall, keeping his distance from the bleeding man, saying nothing. Suspicion leaked from his pores as he watched the man probe his wounded head with thick fingers.

A look of regret creased already deep lines around the man's eyes and mouth. He swiveled his glance away from Mite then back. "Hello again, little one. Never thought you'd see me in here with you, did you?"

Mite stared for a moment without moving, his gray eyes squinting. Mistrust of the situation drove him to softly chant an ancient hymn of protection as his back touched the wall and he slid down into a sitting position.

The man groaned, pulled himself upright, and scanned the small, shadow-drenched cell. "Only one sleepin' mat, eh? I guess this serves me right, thinkin' Seth would listen to reason.

"What's that you're mumblin'? Is it prayer? I've read in the

Words of the One to Corylus that those who believe in him should pray."

Hissing with a swift intake of breath, Mite growled. "Lies, lies, lies. Scroll worshipers always lie. Lie to others. Lie to self. Just like darkness lovers, you do not read the Words of the One."

Shifting his stocky body to a more comfortable position, and leaning forward on stout arms, the man said, "Would you believe me if I told you I have read the Words of the One to Corylus and that's why I'm in here with you now, rather than outside preparin' for tomorrow's sacrifice?"

Mite mumbled a few choice words, then turned to look toward the tiny barred window high up on the wall. Morning was half gone. He glanced back at the man. "What is the scroll worshiper's name?"

"Gwyn, my name is Gwyn Thompson. And what are you called, little ancient?"

Mite debated whether to tell his name or not but decided it didn't matter if the man knew. "Mite. My name is Mite." He looked out the window again before glaring at Gwyn. "Will scroll worshipers sacrifice at stroke of morning like before?"

Sitting up, Gwyn twined his fingers and looked down at his hands as he blew out a puff of air. "Yes. Tomorrow, after the day changes at midnight, will be the fifth sacrifice. The blood of five prisoners will blend with the blood of the Binder, as commanded." Gwyn continued staring at his hands for a minute before raising watery eyes up to Mite. "I'm sorry. I'm so sorry. I know now that what we're doin' is wrong. I tried to tell Seth, Prime Shepherd Hamlin, but he won't listen. He thinks I've been poisoned 'cause I've read the Words. Our doctrine forbids readin' the scrolls. It's punishable by death." He released a sigh that ended in a groan. "He was my friend."

"Scroll worshiper feels sorrow for friend?"

"Yes, Mite." Gwyn nodded then grimaced as he reached up to the cut on his head. "I feel sorrow for my friend."

"Mite feels pain for friend, too. Light Bringer good friend, special friend. Will Gwyn tell Mite if friend Ray-ray is okay?"

Shame flitted across Gwyn's face before he looked away.

Mite rose and moved to stand next to Gwyn, he bent his head to catch the man's eyes. "Ray-ray's bad hurt, isn't he? Mite remembers what he heard. 'For seven weeks, he will live in darkness and silence, and in darkness shall he die at the end.'

"Mite felt Ray-ray's pain and fear. But no more, no more. Why? Why can Mite no longer feel his friend? Why?"

Gwyn groaned as he pushed up off the floor. He walked to stand under the window, looking up at the small square of light filtering into the cell. Mite watched him closely and when the silence grew, asked again, "Why? Answer me, scroll worshiper."

Gwyn turned back to face Mite. "You are a prisoner, too. How is it you worry more for your friend than for yourself?"

Mite shook his head. "Scroll worshiper does not understand. He says he read the Words but did not listen with his heart."

"Ah, yes." Gwyn nodded. "The Words speak much of love. That we are to love others. This puzzles me; it is not the way of scroll worshipers. We are commanded to pursue power and control. Only with the scrolls of power can Ochen be returned to her former glory. To love others is seen as weakness."

"Wrong. Wrong. To love is not weak. The One loves with much power. His love called the Light Bringer to banish the darkness and save Ochen. Demons gone. Good! But newcomers still seek evil. Bad. Bad."

Gwyn's brow crinkled in thought. "But the Binder destroyed our scrolls. If he truly wanted to save Ochen, he wouldn't have ruined our source of power." Gwyn paused, his eyes scanning the empty air before him. "But they were just parchment, weren't they? Nothing more."

"Yes, yes, yes. Scrolls just parchment. Words of the scrolls point to Creator-Father ... the One ... he is true power. Scrolls not power, just parchment and ink."

Gwyn moved back to Mite and sat facing him. "Can you teach me more?"

Mite huffed. "What Gwyn want to know?"

13

Lexi wanted to hit something. Anything. Frustration battered her spirit like storm-tossed waves of the Cameron Sea as she stood behind a furious Queen Rowena and listened to Thorvin argue with the Sorial portal attendant who informed them that the skipping line to Nemora was closed.

"I'm sorry, sir," the portal attendant said for what must have been the fiftieth time. "I just sell passes, I don't control the lines."

"Is there a problem here?" A tall, thin man wearing a Falknor House uniform asked as he positioned himself in front of the portal attendant's counter to face Thorvin. Lexi could hear Queen Rowena's intake of breath. *Oh no! She's going to say something and ruin our disguise.*

"Please, we're so sorry to be an inconvenience," Anne's soft voice came from behind Lexi as Anne moved to stand next to Thorvin. She smiled up at the man. "It's all my fault, you see." She ran her hand over baby Jonathan's head. "They were trying to get me to Nemora. My mother and father already moved there and they still haven't seen my baby. My friends ... well, they got a little excited. As long as the portal will be open next week, I guess we'll just have to wait until then. It will be open next Binding Day eve, won't it?"

The man looked down at the sleeping baby and a brief smile crossed his face. "Oh, so you're moving to Nemora, too?"

Anne nodded.

The man's eyes scanned the area and then he bent over Anne. "USO, right?"

She nodded again, biting her lip.

His smile returned and grew larger. "Me too. I also planned to skip this week but something big was happening on Nemora. Didn't you get the message?"

A rueful grin appeared on Anne's face. "No. That would be my fault as well. With the baby and all..." She shrugged.

"Well, not to worry. Prime Shepherd Hamlin promised that all those who were unable skip this week would be made welcome next week. He knows many have been traveling to Nemora for the sacrifices and he's prepared a place for us all to stay until we're settled. If you want, I can arrange for accommodations here in Emporium City for you and your friends until next Binding Day eve."

Anne glanced back at Thorvin who gave a slight shake of his head.

"Thank you, sir," Anne said. "But we have friends we can stay with." She paused and smiled again. "I do, however, look forward to seeing you in Inverness."

"As do I. It pleases me to see young scroll worshipers like yourself preparing to bring up the next generation honoring the scrolls. Given time, we'll show those One worshipers the error of their ways. Then we'll have a truly united Ochen."

The man bowed to Anne, scanned everyone else, then strode away.

"Anne," Lexi whispered. "That was incredible."

"Yeah." Thorvin huffed out a breath. "Quick thinking."

"Thank you, Anne," Rowena said, her voice subdued. "I almost did something stupid. I'm not used to hearing 'no.'"

"Come on. We'd better get out of here before we draw any

more attention," Thorvin grumbled. He took Rowena's arm and guided the company away from the portal square.

"Where are you taking us?" Rowena asked.

"We can't go back to Westvale now. Too many people saw us and with these cloaks on, it would raise questions. Rayne's friend Coralea has a shop not far from here. I know she'll help us."

Thorvin led them through several markets and alleys before heading to Coralea's shop. Along the way they passed numerous groups wearing robes similar to theirs; some ignored them when they passed, but most greeted them and asked if they were also United Scrolls of Ochen members trapped here on Sorial for the week. A couple larger companies offered them shelter.

"I see you have a little one too," a cloaked lady carrying a toddler said to Anne. "Isn't it wonderful that we're going to have a home world of our own where we can raise our children to honor the power of the scrolls. Why don't you join us? We've set up a camp a short distance from the lake. It's not so bad there."

Anne smiled. "Thank you, but we have friends here. Perhaps we'll see you on Nemora."

When they were close to Coralea's shop, Thorvin stopped the group. "Her Majesty and I will go in. The rest of you wait for us here."

Rowena hissed. "Thor, you're as bad as I am at this. Remember, Rowena, just Rowena."

He grumbled but nodded as the two moved into Coralea's Cloths of the Worlds shop.

Lexi rubbed her hands up and down her arms under her cloak. She wasn't cold; far from it, beads of sweat pimpled her forehead and her upper lip. It was more a feeling of someone watching that brought gooseflesh to her arms. *Am I the only one? Imagining things?* But then she caught Stevie's eyes scanning the street in the direction from which they had just come.

"You feel it too, don't you?" she asked Stevie in a quiet voice. "Someone's been following us."

Everybody crowded closer, nodding. "Yeah," Stevie said. "It's kinda hard to miss."

Andrew grabbed Boone's collar and crouched back behind the side of the poorly constructed building he had just scooted around. *No! They didn't just see me. They couldn't.*

Boone's tail thumped a couple times and Andrew whispered, "Quiet Boone. We're never going to get to Nemora if they find us following them."

He peeked around the corner again and released a sigh. The eight sets of eyes that had been trained in his direction moments before were now focused on each other. If he listened hard, he could make out Stevie's words. "Thorvin knew. I could tell."

Andrew pulled back as Lexi's eyes shifted from Stevie back toward him. *Too close.* "Come on, Boone. Let's move back a little."

"What are you doing?" a girl's voice asked from behind Andrew. He jumped and spun in a circle while Boone wagged her tail. *Not a threat. Boone would know.* He faced a girl who looked to be about his own age wearing a cloak similar to the one he wore.

"What are you doing?" she asked again. "You're spying on those people, aren't you? I've been watching you since you left the portal square. Pretty suspicious if you ask me."

She gave him a level look, her light brown eyes full of accusation and question, her hands on her hips.

"W ... wa ... what's it to you?" Andrew managed to huff out with some measure of self-assurance.

"It's nothing to me." The girl lifted a pert, freckled nose into the air while flinging a long brown braid over her shoulder. "I was bored, and you were ... interesting. At least more interesting than sitting in the camp with my father for another week waiting to skip to Nemora.

"What's your name? Mine's Mayda, Mayda Creedoff. You skipped in from Corylus, didn't you? I watched. That group of people you were following was very interesting. They're wearing scroll worshiper cloaks, but their cloaks are old, just like yours. Didn't you get the new cloaks? See." She pointed to her left shoulder. Embroidered on her burnt sienna cloak were the letters USO in gold thread. "We're all supposed to be wearing the new colors when we skip to Nemora. It's to show that we're all united now. Anyway, are you avoiding my question? Are you going to tell me your name or not?"

Andrew held up his hands, palms out. "Ah ... ah... Well, if you would stop talking for a minute and give me a chance, maybe I could. Sheesh! You sure can talk a lot."

Mayda glared at Andrew. "You're rude. Do you know that? What a rude..."

"Andrew. My name's Andrew Overton." Andrew breathed a sigh of relief when Mayda's mouth snapped shut. He looked up in time to catch Stevie's back disappearing into the Cloths of the Worlds. "No!" he moaned.

Mayda spun on her heels and looked toward the shop before rounding on Andrew. "Well, are you gonna tell me or what?"

Andrew's mouth dropped open. "I don't know you. Why would I tell you anything?"

Mayda grinned, stepped up to Andrew, and flicked the edge of his robe. "Because we're both part of the United Scrolls of Ochen so that makes us friends. I have to tell you, there aren't too many our age." She looked down and kicked the cobbles. "And it would be nice to have a friend."

Andrew lifted eyes to the front of the shop where his friends had disappeared and then looked back at Mayda. *She does like to talk. Maybe I'll learn more this way. I can always catch up to the others when we skip. Yeah, they're not going anywhere in the meantime.* Andrew smiled at Mayda.

"That sounds good. I'm tired of always being left out because I'm only fourteen." She looked away and huffed then drawing her mouth into a stiff line, said, "Well ... almost fourteen."

Three days later, Andrew was sitting with Mayda outside a tent at a camp filled with USO cloaks, a short walk away from Emporium City Island.

"Are you going into the city to check on those people

again today?" Mayda asked. "You still haven't told me who they are and why you're following them."

Andrew shrugged and reached over to rub Boone's head. "I'm sorry. I can't tell you about that. I mean ... I do like talking to you, you're ... well ... you're nice; but I have to keep track of those people, so I know where they are when it's time to skip to Nemora. I have to see where they go when we get to Inverness. It's real important."

Mayda looked across the hodgepodge of temporary dwellings, her expression more serious than Andrew had seen it before. "I could help you. I've been to Inverness before."

"You have? You didn't tell me that."

Mayda chewed her lower lip. "Yeah. Twice. My pop took me to the last two sacrifices."

Andrew's eyes went wide. "Sacrifices? I didn't know scroll worshipers believed in sacrifices. *Human* sacrifices?"

Mayda's gaze dropped to Andrew's face, her eyebrows drawn down. "Yeah, sacrifices. You know. At least, you're supposed to know. All USO believers know. Andrew, tell me the truth. You aren't a believer, are you? If you were, you would know about the High Guardian's command for the seven weeks of sacrifices. Who are you really?"

Andrew swallowed. "I ... I can't tell you. But you have to believe me that I must get to Nemora, and the only people skipping there now are scroll worshipers."

"Are you a spy for the Church of the One?"

"No, Mayda. I'm not a spy." Andrew gulped, his eyes went wide, and he flapped his hands. *Please let her believe me.* "I just need to find a ... a ... friend who's already on Nemora. It's a matter of life and death. Are you going to tell your Pop?"

Mayda got up and turned her back to Andrew. "It was really awful."

"What?"

"Those stupid sacrifices! I was glad that we couldn't skip to Nemora this week. I don't want to go to another! But Pop's really involved. He's our local Shepherd. If I don't go with him, people will wonder." She turned back to Andrew, tears hanging on her eyelashes. "I've worshiped the scrolls my whole life and always believed their power was for the good of all the seven worlds. My Pop says, if everyone joins the United Scrolls of Ochen we'll have peace on every world. But, Andrew, they're ... killing people at these sacrifices. It's bloody and horrible. And this last time, the air got really thick and hard to breathe. I tried to talk to Pop, but he won't listen to me. He's quit his job with the Falknor Family and he says when we skip this next time, we're staying there. Prime Shepherd Hamlin offered him a prominent position."

"Mayda, this is important," Andrew asked, his voice a gentle whisper. "Tell me about the sacrifices. Please, I need to know; my friend could be in big trouble. Who are they sacrificing?"

Mayda's eyes focused over Andrew's shoulder and grew large. "Pop! I didn't expect you back so soon."

14

Andrew turned. Seeing the look in Mayda's father's eyes, he took a step back and bumped into Mayda.

"What were you tellin' him, girl?" Mayda's father glared, his gaze bouncing from Mayda to Andrew then back again.

"Nothing Pop. Nothing important."

"You was talkin' about the sacrifices, weren't you? You know you ain't supposed to talk to strangers about them until we're on Nemora."

Mayda pursed her lips. "Aw, come on Pop, you know everybody knows about the sacrifices by the time they get here. It's got to be the worst kept secret on the seven. He's one of us and I didn't do anything wrong."

Mayda's father took a step toward Andrew. Boone growled at the man, sending him back again. "You muzzle that mutt or I'll kill it."

"Boone. Quiet. Sit."

"That's better," the man huffed. "You got family here, boy?"

"No, sir."

"Ain't you skippin' with any adults?"

"No, sir. It's just me and Boone."

"What's your name?"

"Andrew."

"Well, Andrew. You come to the right place. My name's Vartan. Vartan Creedoff. You remember it, kid. Prime Shepherd Hamlin just named me his First Associate Shepherd. Next to him, I'm the most powerful man in the United Scrolls of Ochen. All the other officers now have to report to me."

Vartan strutted in front of Andrew, his chest puffed out. "You were askin' Mayda about the sacrifices, weren't you? Want to see one yourself, don't you, Andrew? 'Course you do. Everybody wants to be part of what's happenin'. It's the most important ritual of the church right now. But not everybody gets invited, only those who are worthy. Well, what if I told you I could get you special permission to attend the next sacrifice? You'd like that, wouldn't you?

"Mayda, girl, get us some food. I'm powerful hungry and I bet your friend is too. We men need to talk. You go make us somethin' tasty. Go, girl. And don't you give me none of your lip."

Mayda looked at Andrew as if he was something she wanted to crush under her boot. All he could do was shrug and mouth, "I'm sorry."

Before she turned toward the communal cooking fire, she pointed at Andrew and shook her head. "We need to talk," she mouthed back.

"So, tell me, young man," Vartan said. "What world are you from and how long have you been worshipin' the scrolls?"

Andrew settled onto the same spot where he had been sitting while talking to Mayda and lifted a prayer to the One. "Boone, come. Sit.

"Well, sir, I came from Centerville on Corylus."

"Oh, yes. Centerville. Good city. Lots of worshipers have come from Centerville. The church there was well established even before the Bindin' took place."

"I know, sir. Centerville ... the Church of the One ... their bishop tried to ... exterminate our church there. The old bishop. Bishop Hedrick."

"Yes, boy, you're right. Were you involved in that at all?"

For the next few minutes Andrew danced around Vartan's questions but then the man began to talk about himself and his rise in the USO. After listening for almost an hour, Andrew swallowed and broached the topic of the sacrifices.

"Mayda told me she's been to two sacrifices on Nemora. I've been on my own, traveling, ever since I heard the USO was … relocating to Nemora. I don't know anything about these sacrifices."

"There's not much to tell," Mayda's icy voice broke in as she walked toward them carrying a heavy pot.

Andrew hopped up, causing Boone to jump up and skitter around. "Here, let me help you," Andrew said to Mayda.

She glared at him. "I can do it myself."

The meal was bland and Vartan dominated the conversation, talking about the USO and how the prior Associate Shepherd had committed blasphemy by actually reading the Corylus Scroll. Soon after he finished eating, he grabbed a jacket from their tent.

"Stay with us, Andrew. When we skip to Nemora, I'll introduce you to Prime Shepherd Hamlin. He's always looking for young men like yourself who believe and want to be more involved with what's happening." He gave Mayda a peck on the cheek. "Be nice to our young friend, girl. I'm going to spend the evening with the lesser officers and I won't be back until late. You kids behave."

After Vartan left, Andrew watched Mayda's back. It was stiff and foreboding. After a few minutes, she let out an exasperated huff and crossing her arms, turned to face Andrew. "I lied to my Pop for you, so you owe me. Well, are you going to tell me what you're after?"

"I told you, Mayda, I just need to get to Nemora when my friends do."

Mayda's eyes flashed with barely suppressed anger. "First, those people aren't your friends. If they were, you would be with them, not sneaking around following them. Second, you're a liar. You used me to get next to my father so you could get to Nemora. You want to see a sacrifice, don't you? Well, fine and good, liar boy. You succeeded. I hope you're happy. Now I'll have to go too. I told you they were horrible and I didn't want to have to go again. And here I am, talking to someone my own age that I hoped would be my friend and he turns out to be just another blood-loving idiot like the people who deceived my Pop. I'll bet you even believe that thing they summoned will bring the scrolls back. Well, I've got news for you. The scrolls are gone. Destroyed. They can't come back no matter how many people we kill or how often we mix their blood with the Binder's blood. It's just not going to happen."

Andrew's heart missed a beat. "What? What did you say about Rayne?"

Mayda pulled up short. Her eyes flashed wide and her mouth turned down at the edges. "I knew it. You *are* here to spy on us. If you do anything to hurt my Pop..."

"No. I'm not here to hurt anybody. But I am here to help my friend. My friend just ... happens to be ... Prince Rayne. The Light Bringer. The person you call the Binder."

Mayda's eyes screwed into slits. "You lied to us! Get out of here. Now! Go!"

"Mayda ..."

"No! My Pop may be wrong about some things, but he's my Pop and I won't let you hurt him. Just go!"

Andrew held out his hands, palms forward. "Please, calm down, Mayda. Just listen to me. Okay? Just a minute. That's all I'm asking."

Mayda stared at Andrew for several heartbeats before relenting. "Why? Why does it have to be this way? I thought we were friends I enjoyed talking to you and spending time with you. But you're a One worshiper, aren't you? From the time I was little, the One worshipers hated us. The Binder destroyed our sacred scrolls." She focused on her hands as she twisted them in front of her torso, braiding the fingers then releasing them. "But we should be better than them. That's what Mama always said."

"Where's your Mama now?" Andrew asked as he motioned for Boone to come to him.

"She was ... one of those..." Mayda's voice cracked. "She

was one of those who never woke up on Binding Day. I hate the Binder. It was all his fault."

"Hate is a terrible thing," Andrew offered.

Mayda nodded. "I've heard people talking—One worshipers. They say that the Binder saved Ochen from something evil. My Pop says the Binder himself brought the evil to Ochen when he banished the High Guardian and destroyed the scrolls. That's what I always believed. But since coming to Sorial, I've listened. In the markets, I follow people and listen. Like what I was doing when I met you. People like you—One worshipers—say that the Binder brought the light and defeated the darkness and that's why they celebrate Binding Day.

"Andrew, I want to know the truth. I've never been so confused before. I love my Pop, but somehow I know in my heart that these sacrifices are wrong ... and so my Pop is wrong, too."

She turned away, still twining and untwining her fingers. "Before coming here, I never met a One worshiper. I grew up believing they were all the enemy, hateful and cruel." She shook her head. "But that's not true; I know that now."

Mayda sank down onto a small stool near the tent flap, staring at the ground. "All I know for sure is that when the sacrifices were happening last time, I was scared. Like there was something I couldn't see and it ... it was ... I felt its loathing for life and light. The air was hard to breathe. I was used to the energy on Arisima, but this was different. Andrew, I love my Pop but I hate what he's doing."

Mayda took a deep breath and looked up at Andrew, dark brown bangs falling in her milk chocolate eyes. She sniffled. "Tell me, Andrew. Was it all a lie?" She shook her head and looked away with a frown. "Did you lie about wanting to be my friend?"

"No." Andrew's soft voice pierced the heavy air between them. "I do want to be your friend. I think you're nice, and special. But ... I need you to understand that I *am* a One worshiper. I think scroll worship is wrong. And..." Mayda opened her mouth to speak but Andrew held up a hand, stopping her. "And I will do anything to help Rayne. He's not what you've been told. How about if I tell you what I know about the Light Bringer? Maybe then you won't be so confused."

Mayda screwed her face up as though she was going to scream at Andrew again, but then she relented and after releasing a sigh that sounded more like a moan, she said, "Please don't hurt my Pop and please don't lie to me again."

Andrew swallowed the lump that had taken up residence in his throat and nodded. "Okay." Mayda raised her almond shaped eyes to Andrew and a feeling he couldn't explain washed through him. *Gosh, she sure is pretty. Get a grip Andrew, she might be the only way to find Rayne.*

15

ᚾ

Coralea left the care of her shop to her assistant and hustled the companions out a rear entrance. "Come, this way." With hurried steps, she led everyone through several back alleyways and over a small footbridge onto the mainland. "I'm sorry but this is the long way around. I didn't think you would want to go back through the center of Emporium City right now. With the Nemora skipping line closed, there are just so many scroll worshipers loitering around the city."

They skirted the edge of the sulfurous lake for almost five miles, and Coralea was breathing hard when a series of old warehouses came into view. "This way. We're almost there."

A short distance farther, she crossed a small stream of water flowing into the lake. "Here it is. Just ahead now, that old warehouse. This is where we used to meet when One worship was against the law on Sorial. It was here that I first met His Highness."

A few minutes later, Thorvin and Noah lit lanterns and they descended heavy wooden stairs into a lower level of the building. It was dusty with the remains of furniture scattered about, but it was cool and the smell from the lake wasn't oppressive. Coralea vanished through a door at the back of the room.

"Good. Good," she said, her voice carrying through the open door. "There are still supplies here. Tomorrow I'll have my nephew bring you more food. Since you don't want to draw any attention to your group, I thought this would be the best place to lay low for the week. Let me know if there is anything else you need. I'll do my best to get it for you."

"Coralea, thank you." Rowena hugged the portly woman. "We'll be just fine. If we need anything else, one or two of us can go out without raising suspicion. Don't bother your nephew. You've done enough."

Coralea huffed. "Not nearly enough. If I'd known Prince Rayne had come through here against his will, I would have tried to help him."

"We still don't know if it was against his will or not," Rowena said. "He might have come willingly for some reason. We just … don't … know."

Lexi walked over to stand next to Rowena. "Thank you, Coralea. Right now, I think the best thing you can do is pray for Rayne."

Coralea hugged Lexi. "Of course." She glanced over at Rowena while still keeping an arm around Lexi's shoulders. "If it's all right with you, Your Majesty, I'd like to tell Pastor Zeb what's happened. We'll be meeting tomorrow morning for Binding Day service and I'm certain he'll want to let everyone know what's happened to the young prince. I wouldn't be surprised if he asks for a day of prayer for the prince's safe return."

Rowena nodded. "Prayer would be most welcome. Just make certain everyone understands the need for discretion. We can't afford to have our presence on Sorial discovered."

"Not to worry, my dear. If there's one thing we know how to do here on Sorial, it's how to keep our mouths closed. We kept our very existence a secret for years."

After Coralea left, the companions settled in. Anne and Lexi swept the large room while Noah and Sashi cleaned the kitchen. Thorvin took Benning and Ollie with him to purchase additional food items. Shaw and Stevie searched among the remains of wrecked furniture to locate anything they could use. Within a few hours, the group was sitting around on a motley mix of wooden crates, a couple chairs, and the floor, enjoying a filling meal of chunks of chicken cooked in a sauce and served over rice. It wasn't fancy, but what Anne and Lexi had learned from Elsie's cooking lessons helped make it flavorful.

The next day passed without incident. Everyone except Rowena spent time in the marketplace, listening, paying attention to snippets of conversations, seeking out information as to what the scroll worshipers were doing on Nemora. Lexi went out with Noah, Sashi, and Stevie. When Stevie looked at Lexi with a question written in his eyes, she shook her head. "No, I don't feel it today. Whoever was following us yesterday isn't here today. What about you, do you feel anything?"

"No." Stevie rubbed his hand over the back of his neck. "No prickles of eyes on me."

Lexi pulled the weighty scroll worshiper robe away from her body, flapping the hem to allow air to circulate around her sweaty legs as the twin suns drew droplets of moisture to her brow and upper lip. When they passed a weapons stall, Stevie, Noah, and Sashi were all drawn in. Lexi sighed. *If Rayne were here, we would be just as excited as the twins and Noah. Without him, it all seems so pointless.*

The four continued to wander through several markets and were on their way back when Stevie reached out to grab Lexi's arm. "Feel that?"

She nodded. The hairs on the back of her neck rose in response to unseen eyes watching them. She scanned one side of the market while Stevie scanned the other. Stevie sent Noah and Sashi ahead while Lexi and he ducked behind a bookseller's stall. But when several minutes passed and they couldn't identify anyone as the person following, the two joined Noah and Sashi at the entrance to the next square.

"Are you two sure someone was watching us and you weren't imagining things?" Sashi asked.

Stevie huffed and Lexi said, "Well, I can't be certain, but

I think it was real. Let's head back before we pick up our tail again."

The air in the basement of the warehouse brushed cool against Lexi's skin as she slipped the heavy cloak from her shoulders. "I don't know how the scroll worshipers manage wearing these cloaks all the time. I mean, it would be great on Glacieria, but it's pretty awful here."

Noah and Sashi volunteered to make the evening meal with supplies they had picked up in a produce market while they had been out.

Several hours later, after a hearty meal, Shaw suggested they form a circle and pray.

"Thank you, Shaw," Rowena said, as everyone came together. "I know we've all been praying individually and that's a good thing. But there's power in coming together in prayer. I don't know why we didn't do this before."

Shaw nodded. "We were all so wrapped up in our own thoughts and fears, I think we just forgot the support we can be to each other." He looked over at Thorvin who leaned against the wall with arms folded across his chest. "You picked us for this mission for a reason, right Thorvin? I think the One prompted you to choose this group for his purposes. He led you to bring all of us to Nemora with you so we could be spiritually strong together. Well, what are you waiting for? Come, join the circle."

Thorvin grunted and scowled at Shaw. "I guess you're right. But don't expect me to pray so everyone can hear in this circle thing. I don't pray aloud."

Ollie slipped in between Lexi and Sashi, giving each a shy smile, but Benning scanned the circle and took a step back. "I believe in the One. But this whole praying in a group thing. Well, I'm more like Thorvin. I was raised to believe prayer is a private thing between me and the One. You all go ahead, but if you don't mind, I'll just stay here and pray quietly by myself."

Shaw nodded. "Of course, if you feel more comfortable that way."

Jonathan slept through the prayer time in a wooden crate Anne had lined with a blanket. As Shaw was wrapping up the prayer, the baby began fussing, his cries sounding loud as they echoed through the room.

"Well," Anne said as she comforted the fretting baby. "As always, the One's timing is perfect. And we do need to remember that. Though this delay has left us all frustrated, we need to remember that the One is in control."

In the wee hours of the morning as the lantern they had left burning low was flickering, Lexi sprang up from her bedroll. "Rayne?" she screamed out into the emptiness of the basement. "What ... Where are you?" *I feel him. But he's so weak.* "Please answer me." She pulled in a deep breath and scanned the darkness around her. She wasn't the only one awake. Rowena's whispered pleas brought unshed tears to Lexi's eyes.

"Where are you my son? Please ... let me help you. Try, please try to send me a tendril so I can connect with you." In the half-light, Rowena's moisture-laden eyes mirrored the flickering lantern light as she turned toward Lexi. "You feel it too, don't you? Like before? But ... now ..." Rowena sobbed. "We're losing him."

Lexi rose to comfort Rowena. "I still feel his fear, but it's muted." She tried to sneak past Sashi without disturbing her, but as she passed, Sashi reached out and grabbed her hand.

"What does it mean?"

"It means Rayne is getting weaker," Anne said from where she sat along the wall feeding Jonathan.

"Let's pray." Anne shifted Jonathan and rose. The four ladies gathered together and for a second time that night, prayed.

The early sun had risen a few hours ago and the later sun would add its heat to the already sweltering day in another hour. Lexi, Rowena, Anne and baby Jonathan, Shaw, Stevie, Noah, Sashi, Ollie, and Benning stood in a line stretching from the Nemora portal, across the square and down one of the main thorough-fares of Emporium City. It was Binding Day eve on Sorial, and the markets and squares were busy as usual, but the cloaked people standing in line were given a wide berth.

Thorvin strode toward them from the portals, his hood low over his face, and Rowena asked, "Well, are we skipping?"

Thorvin nodded. "It's late morning on Nemora and the line will be opening in the next few minutes."

Lexi realized she had been holding her breath as her lungs forced her to suck in a deep gulp of air. They had wasted a week stuck in Emporium City, but now, at last, they were on their way to Inverness. Lexi shook her hands out to relieve some of the stress building in her shoulders. She glanced behind her. Anne stood next in line with Shaw close behind her. Benning was speaking with Noah, Stevie, and Sashi in quiet tones beyond Shaw. Lexi's eyes caught on a familiar face, but then it was gone, vanished into the shifting crowd beyond.

"Did you see that?" she asked no one in particular.

"What?" Thorvin scanned the area, his voice tense as both he and Ollie took a step closer to Rowena.

Lexi shook her head. "I must have been mistaken."

Thorvin shifted to stand next to Lexi. "What? What did you *think* you saw?"

Lexi half turned back to Thorvin and looked up with a frown. "Andrew. I thought I saw Andrew."

"Benning, you know what Prince Rayne's squire looks like, right?" Thorvin's eyes roamed over the shifting line behind them. "Take a quick look around. That idiot had better not have followed us."

"If he did that would explain what we felt, Lexi," Stevie said, as Benning sprinted toward the end of the line.

"Yeah," Lexi said, tension melting from between her shoulder blades at the realization that the cause of her discom-fort could have been nothing more than Andrew. "If Andrew is following us, he's probably been watching us the whole time."

The line was already moving, and the companions were approaching the Nemora portal when Benning returned. He shook his head. "No. I didn't see Andrew. I checked the whole end of the line and the surrounding market. Nothing."

Lexi turned to look behind one last time, then she stepped into the portal.

16

The sense of home hit Rowena as she stepped out of the portal in Inverness behind Thorvin and Benning. Though Nemora hadn't been her home for many years, her connection to this world was still strong. She scanned the cathedral-like portal station, the stained-glass windows and benches built to resemble church pews calling forth memories, while the rest of their group stepped through the portal.

Thorvin herded them to a quiet corner at the far side of the portal station. "Okay. For now, we'll just keep moving forward with these scroll worshipers to the camp they've been talking about and see where we land. Everyone keep your eyes and ears open. We don't know what we're walking into."

Rowena touched his arm and shook her head. "You go ahead. I'll catch up to you later. With so many people heading to the camp I'm confident I'll find it easily. I need to go to Castle Inverness and check on Cailyn before I do anything else."

Thorvin frowned and growled deep in his throat. "Why don't you just use that sensing thing you do? Now that you're on Nemora you can sense your sister, right?"

"I could, but I want to see her in person. So I'm going to the castle."

"That's not what we agreed on. You promised we would stick together, and that you would listen to me."

"Well, I lied." Rowena sent him a cold smile. "Thor, you know me. How could you think I wouldn't check on Cailyn before leaving Inverness?"

Thorvin ground his teeth. "Yeah, you're right. I knew you would pull this." He turned to Noah. "Just like we planned. You, Sashi, and Benning go with Her Majesty. You'd better go too, Stevie." His eyes roamed over the others. "The rest of you come with me. "Noah. I'm entrusting the queen's care to you. Bring her to that camp safe. Got it?"

"Yes, sir."

Rowena glared at Thorvin. "And what if I refuse this *protection*?"

"Remember Theo's words, Row, I'm the one in charge while we're on this mission. No matter what you say, I have the final word here."

Rowena nodded. "If you insist. I'll meet you at the camp later. You be careful."

"You, too."

"Well, are you three coming with me, or are you just going to keep standing here waiting for an order from Thorvin." Rowena marched out of the station, making a direct beeline for Castle Inverness, Benning keeping step right behind her. Noah and Sashi trailed, their eyes scanning.

When they reached the castle gate, two guards dressed in uniforms Rowena didn't recognize, stepped forward and crossed lances. The taller of the two said, "By what right do you seek entry here? No one is admitted onto castle grounds without invitation."

Rowena threw back her hood and scanned their liveries with pursed lips. "By what right do you attempt to block me? You will announce the arrival of Her Royal Majesty, Queen Rowena, to Duchess Cailyn at once. I'll need several maids and two serving men to report to the royal suite as soon as can be arranged."

Without hesitation, Rowena strode up to the heavy oak doors and tapped a rhythm with her toes as the guards scrambled to open the entryway while bowing to her.

"Nemora's moons," Sashi said. "I thought we were supposed to be in disguise."

"Not here," Rowena replied. "Even if I tried to hide my identity here, too many people know me. It's best to just take advantage of that. We will not need to wait long for Cailyn to appear."

With a rapid stride, Rowena led the others through an open courtyard, up a set of immense stone stairs, past several gawking guards, and into the castle proper. Her brow furrowed as they entered the chilly stone building. *Heavy magic? Here? Something is definitely wrong. What's going on?*

Within minutes they ascended the curved central staircase and entered the double doors to the large royal suite that was always kept vacant and ready in case Theodor and Rowena chose to visit without notice. Already, several maids were pulling coverings from the red and gold furnishings and two men were building a fire.

"Your ministrations are no longer needed here." The servants stopped their work and stared past Rowena. "Leave now."

Rowena turned to see Cailyn standing in the doorway. "Cai. Thank goodness. I was so worried. Are you all right?" Rowena started toward her sister. Cailyn waved her back, a cold look of haughty disdain in her eyes.

"Cailyn?"

Cailyn entered with a stiff, measured tread, followed by a servant carrying a tea set and pastries on a silver platter. "How wonderful. My loving sister has come for a visit. I can't imagine what has brought you here when you haven't come to see me in so long. How good of you to finally come."

Cailyn waved for the girl to put the tea service on a sideboard. "Though it is early for afternoon tea, what better way to receive you than to sit and chat while enjoying a warm cup of tea. Don't you agree, Ro?" Cailyn turned to the serving girl. "Serve the tea, child. Everyone, please come and seat yourselves.

Ro, you sit here next to me. You must sample my special brew. I'm longing to hear what you think. Don't be shy. It's an excellent new blend I created myself."

After serving the tea and setting the baked goods on several small tables with gold-leaf designs on the corners, the girl bowed out, leaving the room to Cailyn, Rowena, Noah, Sashi, and Benning.

Once the serving girl closed the door behind her, Rowena approached Cailyn who patted the pink cushion next to her once again. "Cailyn? You're scaring me. What's gotten into you? You're acting so strange. Does it have anything to do with the increase in heavy energy? Cailyn, what's going on here?"

"Tell me, Sister, how is my nephew?" Cailyn's cold eyes focused on Rowena who settled in the offered place, a cup of tea in her hands. "I suppose he must be quite busy preparing for his upcoming wedding."

Silence ensued for several seconds. *Keep calm, Row. If you push Cai now, she'll only retreat. That's how she copes. Help me holy One.* Rowena let a heavy sigh slip from her lips. "Cai, Rayne's disappeared. We think he might be here on Nemora. That is one of the reasons I am here now. Cai, talk to me. We haven't received word from you since Varick left and I was afraid something happened. Please, sister, tell me what is going on here. Why have you cut Nemora off from the rest of Ochen? Why are all these scroll worshipers congregating here?" *Why am I reading increased levels of heavy magic?*

"So many questions, Sister, so many questions. Calm yourself; take a few minutes now to relax and enjoy the tea. Your answers will come in due time."

Why wasn't Cai surprised when I told her Rayne was missing? Due time? I'd better cooperate otherwise I'll be sitting here until midnight.

After tasting the tea, Rowena grimaced, set her cup and saucer on a table, and faced Cailyn, "Thank you for your hospitality, Sister. That truly is a unique blend of tea, quite too sweet for my taste, but your tastes have always run sweeter than mine." She settled her hands on her lap. "I am relieved to see you well, Cailyn. As I said before, I have been worried about you."

Cailyn's light lavender eyes pierced Rowena's deeper amethyst ones; her lips pursed. She raised her chin and said, "Sister, come now, admit it; you haven't given my tea a fair trial. You disappoint me. Please, try some more. I am quite certain you will find it grows on you after a few sips." She picked up Rowena's cup and pressed it into Rowena's hands. "Here, dear sister, try some more. For me? I worked so hard to make this special."

Taking the cup, Rowena wondered what Cailyn was up to now, but she took several sips, allowing the sickeningly sweet tea to trickle down her throat.

Cailyn nodded. "That's right. Thank you." A smile crossed Cailyn's face and she released a light chuckle. "Seth thought it would take you longer to make the skip, but I knew you'd come before the sacrifices ended." Cailyn stood and moved to the fireplace where flames were flickering through the logs. She wiped her fingers over the white mantle and then brushed the tips across each other as if she was looking for dust.

"Have to watch these servants, you know, Sister…"

"Cailyn," Rowena breathed out, her eyes narrowing. "What … sacrifices? I don't understand you. You're not acting like yourself at all."

Cailyn choked, a high-pitched, hysterical sound. "Not myself? Oh, sister, you are quite wrong. For the first time, I am, finally, myself. Watch."

Heavy magic began to coalesce in the room. *What is she talking about? Sacrifices, heavy magic? Dear Lord, no.* Alarm shot through Rowena, settling in the pit of her stomach, as Cailyn closed her eyes and pulled even more heavy magic into the room turning the air dense with energy. Within seconds she had a small flame resting on her upturned palm. She opened her eyes and smiled. "See, sister. See how strong I am."

"Yes, Cailyn. You are strong. I've never doubted that." *Stay calm and keep her talking.* "Come, sit with me and enjoy some more of your excellent tea. We can talk and you can tell me what's been happening here on Nemora. Ever since you lost Miles, Theodor and I have been so worried about you."

Cailyn settled herself primly on the ornate pink and gold loveseat next to Rowena. She didn't touch her teacup but sat with folded hands resting on her lap as if she was mirroring Rowena. Rowena smiled at her sister. "This is nice Cailyn, why don't you drink some more tea and we can chat, just like old times."

"Old times?" Cailyn whispered. "Old times?" Her voice grew in volume and her face hardened. "That's just like you, Row. Let's talk about *old times* and ignore the present." She jolted up from the loveseat and moved to stand near the open door. "You expect me to ignore my son's death. Overlook the fact that your son betrayed and murdered him. And then Miles ..." She breathed in a gasp of breath. "Miles ... Miles is dead. He may have taken his own life, but that inhuman assassin you birthed is to blame for that as well. If he hadn't killed Brayden, I would still have both my son and my husband. But I'm making it all right. Everything will be right again. Soon. Soon. A couple more weeks and it will all be over."

"Cailyn," Rowena struggled to reel in her rapidly swelling fear. "What have you done? Where is Rayne?"

"She has done that which needed to be done in order to return Ochen to her proper glory and power."

Rowena's gaze was drawn to the man who spoke. There was something about him that spoke of power and control, something mesmerizing. He walked in with casual self-assurance and a smile. Very tall with silver hair flowing loose around his shoulders, his hazel eyes sparked with confidence. But what caught Rowena's attention were his long, tapered fingers which he held to his chest, framing a USO emblem embroidered in golden threads on the reddish-brown cloak.

Noah, Benning, and Sashi rose to stand between Rowena and the man while Stevie positioned himself behind the queen. He chuckled. "Come now, we're all friends here. Right, Lady Mother?"

Cailyn glided across the room with a graceful movement to stand next to the stranger. He held out his elbow and she wrapped her fingers around it. "Rowena, I'd like to introduce Seth Hamlin, Prime Shepherd of the United Scrolls of Ochen Church. He is a good friend. I've waited for a long time to introduce him to you. Your son knows him well."

"Enough, my dear." Seth patted Cailyn's hand. "We wouldn't want to spoil the surprise."

Cailyn gazed up at Seth, her eyes glittering. "Is it time?"

Seth smiled down on Cailyn. "I believe it is, Lady Mother. Your people await your presence to select those chosen to participate this week. Have our guests enjoyed their tea?"

"Yes. It should be producing the desired results any time now."

"Marvelous. Soon we shall let them join the others awaiting the sacrifices. I am in total agreement with your earlier suggestion. I think they would make an excellent audience for the seventh sacrifice. It does seem fitting."

"Yes," Cailyn purred. "Your ambition and my revenge fulfilled at the same moment, Seth. Very fitting."

Seth waved to the men standing at the door. "Escort our *guests* to the holding cells."

"No way," Noah growled, drawing his sword. Benning and Sashi stepped in to either side of Noah, their swords at center. Rowena began to pull heavy magic from the air but before she could accomplish anything a strange lethargy overcame her and she collapsed. The last thing she saw was Noah, Sashi, and Benning also crumbling to the floor. *Stupid! Stupid! Bloody sweet tea. Ferris Root!*

17

Andrew and Mayda talked long and often in the days prior to skipping to Nemora. One afternoon, as Andrew helped Mayda chop potatoes and carrots for a stew, a small girl with dark-brown pigtails skipped up to Mayda and handed her a package wrapped in brown paper. She glanced shyly at Andrew and murmured, "It's from Mama, she said you were waiting." A bright grin lit the girl's face and she skipped off.

"Tell your mother thanks for me!" Mayda waved after the girl as she disappeared around the side of a tent.

Andrew glanced at Mayda, curiosity wrinkling his brow. "What's in the package that made you so happy?"

Pursing her lips, Mayda shook her head while moving the package around behind her back. "None of your business, fancy boy."

"Is that right, tough girl?" Andrew feinted to the right, then went left behind Mayda and grabbed the package with a triumphant smile. He waved it around and pretended he was about to drop it into a pail of water.

"No!" Mayda yelled. "No, no. Please don't do that."

"Then tell me what it is." Andrew ran his hands over the

package, feeling the shape of what was inside. "No, wait, I've figured it out. It's a book, isn't it?"

"Yeah. So what about it? I like books. Is that a crime, spoiled Westvale brat?"

Andrew got serious. "No, it's not. I just never took you for a book kind of person."

"Well now you know, so give me the book."

After handing Mayda the book, Andrew said, "The truth is, I like books too. So, if you want, when this is all over, I can take you to the King's Library in Westvale ... I mean if you'd like that."

Mayda's eyes grew large. "For real? You promise? I've only ever been to small book stores or borrowed books from other scroll worshipers. Mom taught me to read, but Pop never thought much of girls reading. He did let me buy a book of my own once. I read it so much, it fell apart."

"What do you like to read?"

"Adventures!" Mayda exclaimed without hesitation, prompting an ongoing discussion about their favorite adventure stories.

As the week went by, although she still defended her father to Andrew, Mayda agreed to keep the truth of why Andrew wanted to get to Inverness a secret.

"I've known Prince Rayne for almost six years now. I've seen the lights of Ochen glow around him. I was there when he returned to Westvale, trapped in the old body, but still fighting against the darkness. I can't believe you didn't notice the changes after the demons were bound and sent away."

"We were told the changes were something to resist. An evil sent to weaken us as a church when the Binder destroyed our sacred scrolls and banished the High Guardian."

"Rayne didn't actually banish the thing you call the High Guardian; the One did. But he was no guardian, he was a demon who deceived people and tried to enslave all Ochen. And the truth is, that so-called High Guardian actually destroyed the scrolls himself with dark fire."

"So ... if what you've been telling me is true, everything I thought I knew about the Binder was a lie." She shook her head. "And if that's so, Pop is wrong. But he'd never listen to me. Maybe, if things change, he'll change too."

The next day Andrew discovered the benefits of skipping with Mayda and her father. Associate Shepherd Vartan and his party had the authority to cut to the front of the long line of scroll worshipers waiting to skip. Andrew traced the column of people hoping to catch sight of the group from Westvale, but he didn't see them. *They'll probably go to the camp. I'll look for them there.* He scanned the square one last time as he followed Vartan into the portal, clutching Boone's leash, while Mayda brought up the rear.

Vartan was in good spirits as they left the Inverness Portal Station with three other officers of the United Scrolls of Ochen church. A misty rain was falling in the first hour of an early autumn afternoon. The sun's light muted by a gray-blue haze. Two men in burnt umber USO cloaks were waiting outside the station. Vartan and the officers greeted them with a lot of back-slapping and good humor.

"This the young man?" one of the two asked Vartan.

"It's him." Vartan motioned Andrew forward. "I'd like you to meet a couple good guys, Andrew. Eric and Jens. They know what we're tryin' to accomplish here. You can trust them." The man introduced as Jens smiled and held out a new cloak. "Here you go son. If you're gonna participate in the sacrifice tonight, you have to look the part. Besides, in this weather, you'll appreciate the heavier weave. Yours looks like it's seen better days."

Eric moved in behind Andrew reaching to remove his old cloak, but Boone's hackles rose and she growled. "Whoa," Eric said. "Hey, kid, call your dog off. We were just tryin' to do you a good turn here. Ain't no need to let the beast get all snippy with me."

"Sorry," Andrew mumbled. "Boone. Boone. Sit. It's okay, girl."

Boone sat at Andrew's side, but continued to rumble deep in her throat.

"When we get to camp, you're gonna have ta' keep that mutt tied up. She's gonna make a lot of people nervous," Jens said.

"Yes, sir." Andrew slipped out of his old cloak and handed it to Mayda who watched the whole exchange with narrowed eyes. He reached for the cloak Jens held and flung it around his shoulders.

"Nice," Vartan said. "Now you look like one of us instead of just some wannabe."

The three officers who had skipped with Vartan said their good-byes joking about seeing each other near midnight in the hollow.

"Yeah, it should be a good one." Vartan said with a smile as the three rode off. "I hated missin' the last one but I'm lookin' forward to tonight." He turned to Jens and Eric, rubbing his hands together. "Five enemies bleedin' out and the Binder sliced again. I heard the air was gettin' real heavy the last sacrifice. We're doin' it. We're finally doin' it. Just a couple weeks and the Binder will die. We'll have our scrolls and the High Guardian back. Come on, Andrew, join us for a few drinks before we go to the camp. It's a dusty ride there." Vartan laughed at his joke as Andrew wiped a rivulet of moisture from his cheek.

"Pop, no," Mayda said. "Don't you have better things to do than take Andrew and get drunk?"

"Lighten up, girl," Vartan said. "We ain't got to be back in camp until supper." He turned to Eric. "I think Mayda's sweet on the boy." The men laughed. "Don't worry. I'll take good care of your boy. You be a dutiful daughter now and take the dog to camp. Make sure you tie him up good. We'll meet you there in a little while. Now, go. Skedaddle."

Andrew shrugged and handed Boone's leash to Mayda who scowled at her father. "You just better not get there drunk. And if you get Andrew drunk, I'll … I'll put stuff in your food to make you spend tonight in the latrines instead of at the sacrifice."

Jens laughed, his belly rolling with his mirth. "That's some girl you got there. Lots a spunk." He slapped Vartan on the back.

"Yeah, ain't it the truth." Vartan's frown morphed into a crooked smile. "I'll see we're back at camp by mealtime; and I'll make sure your sweetheart ain't drunk."

"Pop!" Mayda protested as Vartan snaked his arm around Andrew's shoulders and propelled him into a side street. Eric and Jens trailed, laughing.

Nearly four hours later, the roles were reversed. Andrew supported a rather unstable Vartan as they followed Eric and Jens to the United Scrolls of Ochen camp. Shadows were lengthening as evening set in and though the drizzle had stopped, their cloaks smelled like damp sheep. They crested a rise overlooking the vast camp just as the setting sun tinged everything a curious shade of purple-blue. Andrew stumbled to a stop stunned by the sheer size of the site as he blinked in the Nemorian sunlight.

"How many people are here?" he asked Jens as the man paused to look back.

"Oh, I can't say fer sure, but what I hear is close to twenty thousand believers have moved to Nemora. Most of them decided to remain here until the sacrifices are complete and the High Guardian returns. Prime Shepherd Hamlin has done a wondrous thing gathering everyone here."

Vartan pulled his arm off Andrew's shoulders and staggered upright. "Tonight, in the first hour of Binding Day, we celebrate the fifth sacrifice. After the seventh sacrifice is completed, we'll be on our way to our new homes. Tonight, you are one of us, Andrew. After we eat, I'll introduce you to the prime shepherd himself. Wait until you meet him. He's something special, he is."

Andrew grimaced as he followed the others down the incline and into the camp proper. He didn't care if he never met Prime Shepherd Hamlin. After listening to Vartan, Eric, and Jens for the last few hours, Andrew battled against an overwhelming fear for Rayne. Eric had explained about the seven weeks of sacrifices and how Rayne's blood was mixed with the blood of those sacrificed each time. But what really sent Andrew's stomach up into his throat was the repeated phrase, 'For seven weeks, he will live in darkness and silence, and in darkness shall he die at the end.'

Andrew recalled Queen Rowena's fainting spells and the rising fear of darkness. He realized now, she had been feeling Rayne's fear and pain.

Andrew found it hard to sit through the meal. He kept hopping up and then sitting back down. When he sat for any length of time, first one leg would bounce and then the other. Mayda kept giving him questioning looks.

"What's wrong with you?" she finally whispered when they had a moment alone.

"Did you know about this *seven weeks of darkness and silence* thing?" he hissed.

Mayda looked away, avoiding eye contact. "Yes."

"Why didn't you tell me?"

"You were upset enough already, and I figured you'd learn about it soon enough."

"You should have told me, warned me." Andrew shook his head. "What did I get myself into? This is too big for me. And twenty thousand people! There are almost twenty thousand scroll worshipers? When did they get so big?"

Mayda sent Andrew a look of pure disgust. "What did you think? That just because the Church of the One was so big and powerful, we'd just up and fade away? Well, I can see how that worked for you." Her eyes flicked to the right then back to Andrew.

"Hush, Pop's coming back."

Vartan strode over to the smoldering fire, pointing up at the sky. "Look, a good omen. The sky has cleared. It's going to be a grand night for a sacrifice. Prime Shepherd Hamlin told me the heavy magic should be exceptionally strong tonight. Come Andrew. Mayda. He's waiting to meet us before we leave for the glade."

18

Lexi stumbled to a standstill, her mouth gaping as she glimpsed the camp of the scroll worshipers, trying to wrap her mind around the sheer numbers.

"By the seven," Ollie mumbled. "Who would have ever thought there'd be so many."

Thorvin growled, his mouth turning down at the corners. "Doesn't matter how many. They're still going to fall. Come on, let's get down there and do what we came to do; get the information King Theodor needs and find Rayne."

He glanced over his shoulder. "You alright, Anne? Want me to carry Jonathan for a bit?"

"I'm fine, Thorvin. Shaw can take him if I need a break."

They worked their way back into the line of people streaming from the portal station and followed the leaders into an open area where a man stood on a raised platform waving the new arrivals forward. Lexi figured close to four hundred people must have skipped from Sorial that morning and were now gathering in a semicircle around the speaker.

"Come on, keep moving in so you can all hear me." The man's voice boomed over the heads of the assembling crowd.

When the whole group had filled in around him, he continued. "Welcome, fellow believers. I am Associate Shepherd Osgood and your liaison to the church authority. Prime Shepherd Hamlin has personally asked me to greet you this afternoon. I won't keep you out in this weather for long, but there are a few camp regulations you need to be aware of before I release you to your regional deacons who will help you find accommodations."

Despite his promise to not keep them long, Osgood went on at length about the glory that would soon be returned to Ochen because of the efforts of men like the prime shepherd and himself. Lexi's mind wandered as she scanned the camp around them. The misty rain had stopped while Osgood spoke, and streams of blue-tinged light broke through the shredding cloud cover. The air smelled after-rain fresh with a hint of pine and Lexi shivered at the chill it held. Here on Nemora, autumn was well underway.

Osgood's words drew Lexi's attention back to the man.

"I have one final announcement to make before I dismiss you. As I am sure you are all keenly aware, we have suffered oppression by those currently in power throughout Ochen."

A smattering of angry words and hisses spread through the people.

"It is true that we have banded together on Nemora to learn more from the wise words of our prime shepherd, and to fellowship with others who believe as we do. But that is only the beginning; we have also united here to raise an army. In time the militia of the United Scrolls of Ochen will spread the truth of the power of the scrolls to the people who are being misled by the current leaders. We will defend our beliefs and our way of life."

Noisy agreement and cheering broke out and Lexi wished she could cover her ears against the clamor. After several minutes, Osgood raised his arms to signal for quiet. "After giving you two days to settle in, we expect all of you to assemble at the practice field when the first morning bell sounds. At that time, we will determine your abilities and assign you to the unit you will serve with. Anyone who has skill with manipulating magic energies will be expected to test for qualification to special units.

"Remember, my fellow believers, we are in a war for freedom and freedom doesn't come without sacrifice. Everyone who has arrived today will report for militia duty and any who refuse will be banished. You are dismissed."

A dour-faced woman, who identified herself as Deacon Ida, gathered together about fifty people, including Lexi and her friends, and herded them to one of the outlying areas where several unoccupied tents were set.

"This will be your camp within the larger camp." She waved toward the tents. "You will be responsible for keeping it clean and making your own meals. Unless given special permission, you will remain in your assigned area after dark. Supplies can be purchased at one of the supply tents scattered throughout the valley. Ask. Anyone who has been here for any length of time will be able to direct you to the closest.

"Get acquainted with the other people in your sub-camp. Not only will they be part of your militia unit, when we leave here to establish communities these will be the people you will live with. Prime Shepherd Hamlin thanks you for joining us in this momentous undertaking. As Junior Shepherd Osgood suggested, you should take the next couple days to settle in and acclimate before beginning training."

Deacon Ida turned to go but Lexi sprinted to her and grabbed her arm. "I have a question."

Ida stared down at Lexi's hand on her arm, her eyebrows climbing her forehead as her mouth flattened into a sharp line. Lexi released her. "Sorry. I just wanted to stop you, so I could ask some questions before you go."

"I have no time for questions now, young lady." She glanced at Lexi's robe and then lifted her eyes, taking note of Thorvin and the others who had moved in behind Lexi. Deacon Ida huffed. "You don't even wear the proper attire. Not one of you. Where exactly have you come from?"

"We've come from Corylus but have been out of touch for a while," Shaw said, his voice calm and soft. "I apologize for our impertinence. It's just that, because we have been in seclusion due to oppression by the Church of the One, we have many questions." He offered a small, hesitant smile.

"Your apology is accepted." Deacon Ida frowned at Lexi. "You, child, need to learn manners." She scanned the companions again. "And you all need to purchase proper robes. We are united now, not individual churches. As members of the United Scrolls of Ochen you must dress the same as everyone else."

She sighed and shook her head. "Okay, I see you need help. I can't spare the time now with the sacrifice scheduled for midnight, but I promise to come by early tomorrow afternoon and assist you in settling in."

"Sacrifice?" Lexi asked.

Ida rolled her eyes. "They'll let anyone in these days. Don't you know anything, child?"

Lexi shook her head.

Ida pursed her lips. "Tomorrow. I know I'll regret this, but I promise to explain all about the camp, our militia units, and the ritual of sacrifices tomorrow. For now, get yourselves set up with a meal, relax, then get some sleep. You all look like you need it. I'll be back tomorrow."

Once her raw-boned frame disappeared beyond the tents, Thorvin said, "You all stay here. I'm going to roam the camp for a bit and see what I can learn about this militia, and these sacrifices."

"I'm going with you." Lexi's voice was firm and her eyes unyielding.

Thorvin shook his head. "Not this time, Lexi."

"Take her with you," Anne said. "We'll be fine here, and you'll draw less attention if she's with you."

He growled but relented. With a nod, he waved for Lexi to follow in the direction Deacon Ida had taken. They wormed their way past other groupings of tents, also set in circles around central cookfires. Thorvin pressed toward the heart of the camp proper until they heard weapons clashing.

"This way," Thorvin changed direction, heading toward the sound of veridium on veridium. After maneuvering around several more groups of tents, their view opened onto a field where the valley ended and a series of foothills led into higher mountains. Several hundred men and women were practicing in pairs with swords and staffs while groups of twenty to twenty-five practiced unit maneuvers.

Lexi's stomach dropped at the sight. "This is what His Majesty feared, isn't it Thorvin? There are so many."

"Look around." Thorvin grunted. "This is just one group. Let's get to that higher ground and see if we can get a better idea of how many people are actually here."

The two skirted around the practice field toward a forested hill beyond. Using the cover of a dense stand of pines, they scanned the valley. Thorvin swore under his breath. "There's got to be close to twenty thousand scroll worshipers here. Theodor needs to know. Let's head back to the others. I just hope Rowena is there."

"On the way, let's find out what we can about the sacrifices," Lexi said. "I didn't think the scroll worshipers had any rituals."

Coming across a gathering where people were talking openly, the two moved into positions that allowed them to overhear the conversation without drawing attention to themselves. After listening for a few minutes, Thorvin walked up and asked if they could join those sitting around the fire.

"We skipped today and we're just so thrilled to meet so many other believers." Lexi forced out a stiff, wide smile.

"Welcome and well met, fellow believers," a gray-haired man with a well-creased face said.

As they settled in, the conversation continued to center around the two main topics they had heard discussed at various campfires they had passed throughout the camp; the establishment of the USO as the primary religion of Nemora and the fall of Associate Shepherd Thompson.

"What I hear is that he went crazy. Actually read a copy of the Corylus scroll," one man said, shaking his head as he broke a small stick and threw the pieces into the fire in front of him. "Blasphemy. Pure blasphemy. He should have known better."

"Bad business, that," a man with a massive red beard mumbled from across the fire.

"What happened?" Thorvin asked, sitting next to the first man. Lexi peered around Thorvin waiting for the man's answer.

"Just what you'd expect. Prime Shepherd Hamlin confronted him and now Gwyn Thompson is locked up with those destined for sacrifice. He broke our law, committed sacrilege in reading a scroll. Now he's going to pay the price."

"Serves him right," the bearded man said, spitting into the grass at his feet. "The traitor gets just what he deserves."

"It's a shame, though," a woman sitting next to Lexi said. "I liked Associate Shepherd Thompson. He talked to us like we were important, not like some of those others who act like we're no better than dirt."

"Just goes to show how deceitful those One worshipers can be. One of them must have gotten to Thompson and corrupted him. Otherwise he'd never have betrayed Prime Shepherd Hamlin. I heard they'd been together from the beginning," the bearded man grumbled. "I say a curse on all One worshipers. I guess Thompson'll be one of the five bleeding out tonight."

At the reference to the coming sacrifice, Lexi's stomach knotted. As she and Thorvin had meandered through the camp they heard quite a few references to seven weeks of sacrifices and a chant everyone participated in after midnight.

"Have any of you witnessed a sacrifice?" Lexi asked, focusing on the fire. She could feel Thorvin's eyes on her, knew he was concerned she asked the question outright instead of waiting for information to be offered.

The bearded man huffed. "Stupid question. Do any of us look like we're officers? Only officers and a select few are invited to the sacrifices."

"Except the last one, two weeks from tonight," the first man said. "Everyone goes to the last sacrifice. In the meantime, we all participate in the chant. You'll see. It's amazing to be a part of something so important. Tonight, just before midnight, you'll hear the call to worship. We gather in our sub-camps and then, when the day changes, we all chant together, our voices rising with those physically present at the sacrifice. The last couple Binding Days, we all felt the change in the atmosphere. The High Guardian is returning for sure."

"Blood for blood. Blood for power. Blood for vengeance," the bearded man chanted. Soon all those around the fire joined in and several others walked over and chimed in as well, while Lexi swallowed her fear, closed her eyes, and prayed to the One.

"I don't like this," Thorvin rumbled as they headed back to their sub-camp. "Militia units that look like they're preparing for war; this whole blood for blood, blood for power, and blood for vengeance thing." He shook his head. "Prime Shepherd Hamlin is planning something big and Rayne's right in the middle of it. After Sigmund's binding, and three years of peace, I hoped my job as Bodyguard to His Royal Highness was finally coming to an end. Looks like I was wrong."

"The scroll worshipers never forgave Rayne for the destruction of the scrolls even though Sigmund did that himself. You remember when we were on Arisima two years ago and he got that scar. And again, last year, when they sprang that trap and poisoned him. If that pirate hadn't given us the antidote, he'd be dead now." She huffed, hatred for all scroll worshipers squeezing her heart.

"I was hoping that was the end of it; that with their numbers and influence decreasing, the threat was past."

Lexi's eyes wandered toward the hill they had climbed earlier, unable to meet Thorvin's gaze. "I guess we all hoped that was the case. We were wrong. The episodes Her Majesty and I have been having are connected to Rayne, to things he's experiencing. If the scroll worshipers already ... sacrificed ... Rayne, he'd be dead. But as of the last Binding Day, we both still felt his fear and pain." She paused and chewed her lower lip. "And yet, this time was different. The sense of Rayne was so weak. We need to get to tonight's sacrifice."

Thorvin nodded. "Yeah. Then we need to get word to Theodor about what's happening. This prime shepherd is using the United Scrolls of Ochen to bring together all the separate individual groups from all the worlds into one strong unit. If they aren't stopped soon, there's no telling how powerful they might grow."

When they returned to their sub-camp, they found Anne, Shaw, and Ollie sitting apart from the others.

"Jonathan's crying and Anne's need for privacy give us perfect excuses to separate from the rest of our camp mates," Shaw said. "We volunteered to set up a small fire away from the others and nobody argued."

"What did you find out?"

While Shaw and Anne dished out bowls of a bland meal of beans, Lexi and Thorvin told the others what they had learned. Lexi couldn't sit still and ate little. Needing to do something, she volunteered to clean the dishes. Ollie helped her, carting everything to the small stream and back again. By the time they returned, Thorvin had taken her place, pacing with nervous energy.

"Rowena should have been here by now." Thorvin said.

"Perhaps she lost track of the time catching up with her sister? Or, more likely, couldn't find us in all these campsites," Anne said.

Thorvin shook his head. "Yeah ... maybe." He shook his head again. "I don't like it. This whole situation is going from bad to worse."

The clouds had all but dissipated and Nemora's blue sun was setting in vibrant shades of violet and maroon when Thorvin rose from where he had been sitting, whittling a chunk of wood. "I need to check on something. You all stay here. If I'm not back by tomorrow night, do your best to fit in. Then, when you get the chance, slip away and head back to Inverness. If you can't reach Rowena, get to Corylus. I don't think you'll have any problems skipping off Nemora. Tell His Majesty about Rowena, these sacrifices, and that the United Scrolls of Ochen church is raising an army."

Anne looked up from Jonathan who was noisily enjoying a meal. "Where are you going?"

Shaw, Ollie, and Lexi all stood, and Lexi said, "We're not letting you disappear. If you're going, take someone with you at least."

"Not this time." Thorvin shook his head. "Ollie, you take care of them. That's an order."

"Yes, sir."

Lexi let out a huff of protest, screwed up her eyes, and

shook her head, but before she could say a word, Thorvin cut her off. "Not this time." He strode into the growing dusk.

Lexi sat back down, frustration and concern churning in her gut.

"It'll be okay, Lexi," Anne said. "Thorvin knows what he's doing and if he insisted on going alone, he had his reasons. Here, you need something to do and Jonathan needs burping. Come take him. Help me."

Lexi sighed but smiled lightly as she rose and took Jonathan. Her smile broadened as she looked down on the baby who was struggling to focus on her face while waving a tiny hand in the air. "Okay, my dear. Up on my shoulder. Let's see if you can get a couple good burps out."

She lifted him up as Anne slipped a burp cloth over her shoulder. Patting Jonathan's back with firm but gentle pats, Lexi paced, humming a song to soothe the baby.

Jonathan was sleeping soundly, Anne and Shaw talking quietly, while Ollie and Lexi were taking turns pacing when Thorvin, stepping with the quiet tread of a mountain cat, emerged out of the dark night. Without a word, he walked to the fire and held his hands out to the warmth.

"Well," Lexi said. "What did you find out?"

Thorvin's eyes flashed as he turned to her, his mouth a flat, angry line. "I hoped I was wrong. I wasn't. There are guards stationed around the perimeter of the whole camp. When they say we need to stay here, they mean it. No one is allowed to leave except those who are officers or have special duties with the militia. If we want to find out what's happening at these sacrifices, we'll have to sneak out after the prime shepherd and his buddies leave and follow them. It's going to be tricky and dangerous." He paused, his breathing heavy.

"Anne. Shaw. I'm changing the plans. You need to sneak away to Inverness and find Rowena. Don't get caught; but if you do, use some excuse like you needed something for the baby. Ollie. You stay with them; keep them safe. Be careful!" He turned to Lexi and shook his head. "I don't like it, but I can't have you following me. So, I guess you'll have to come with me."

Lexi nodded.

"But don't think I'm happy about this. You *will* listen to me. When I say jump, you jump. If you can't agree to that, then I'll tie you up and have Ollie untie you when I'm long gone."

"I'll listen. You won't regret bringing me."

Thorvin glared at Lexi. "I should have my head examined. I said once long ago that you and Rayne lack sense when you are together. If we find him tonight, keep your head and remember, you promised to listen to me."

Lexi nodded as she rested her hand on the hilt of one of the short swords hidden under her robe.

19

Rayne awoke. His head throbbed in time with the wound on his neck, and the now familiar sweet taste of the drug they kept giving him coated his tongue. His mouth felt vile, as if some fuzzy animal had taken up residence there.

Visions of the last offering assailed him. *Did those things happen or were they some vivid nightmare?* He sat up and his doubts vanished like morning fog on a sunny day. *Real. Very real.* He wrapped his arms around his bruised ribs and reached tentative fingers up to feel the sticky residue of blood where it had dribbled down onto his shoulder. His probing found the newest slice, puffy and tender, just beneath his left ear.

If not for his prayers, whole segments of the Words of the One that he quoted aloud, and the periodic warmth of the One's presence, Rayne would be lost. Days blended into weeks and together into nothingness in the pit of endless, silent night. His past rose up, bloody and haunting. Faces of his victims begging for life, or scowling and cursing him, plunged him into an abyss of self-loathing. The line between reality and fantasy thinned and blurred.

Every time the light within him began to swell, its

unblemished glow flickering through the scars on his hands and wrists, he would be forced to drink the numbing tincture. In his isolation, he started longing for those moments. Desire for the deadening effects of the sweet potion grew in him. When his captors entered, rather than fight them, he now reached out for the tiny bottle, drinking every drop and licking the remains. The pain and fear would retreat as the tonic spread through him.

Time passed until, once again, Rayne was taken to the ancient sacrificial stone. Four victims were slaughtered before he was forced to kneel at the altar and his blood was added to theirs. The tall, thin man with the long silver hair spoke. "As you have commanded, so has it been accomplished. The blood of four humans and the blood of the Binder shed for you. We beseech you, mighty Guardian of the Scrolls, accept this our fourth offering."

As before, Rayne was drugged at the stone. This time, though he was weaker, he was forced to stumble the entire way back. He collapsed in his dark prison and retched as the stench pervading the cell replaced the fresh, night air. Not long after, another silent, cloaked figure came with a bucket and motioned for Rayne to clean his cell. In the dark room, with nothing more than a cleaning rag and bucket containing a thin layer of water at the bottom, the task was absurd. If not for the faint gray light seeping through the doorway, it would have been impossible. By the time he was done crawling on his hands and knees, attempting to clean in the dark, he felt vile beyond bearing.

"Please." His harsh whisper broke the silence. "Please, help me. Please. At least let me wash. Anything. Just say something." The figure took the bucket and left without a word, plunging the damp stone chamber into black silence once again. Rayne curled into a ball and, for the first time since this imprisonment began, tears streamed to the floor from the corners of his eyes and he gave vent to his grief, allowing unrestrained sobs to shudder to the surface.

"I can't," he mumbled into the dark silence. "Father One, how long? How long must I wait? I'm losing my mind. I'm dying. Didn't I do that once before in obedience to you? Why don't you save me? I've been your servant, done all you've asked. Why won't you help me now?"

My beloved child know that I am with you. I am always with you. The voice was so faint and the warmth so weak, Rayne wondered if it was real or a figment of his shattered mind. He paced, counted his steps. Always the same, they were always the same. *Five by five. Five by five.* He screamed. He cried. He forgot to pray and could no longer remember passages from the Words.

Wild thoughts assailed him. He was fourteen, back at Sigmund's manor, still a slave, and everything that had happened since then was nothing more than a dream. Soon he would wake up and find himself in the cage with Sigmund's colleagues surrounding him, laughing that he had believed the dream was real. He saw their faces in the oppressive darkness and heard Sigmund's voice. *Soon my rebellious little bird, soon.*

Master, please, make it stop. I'll behave. I promise. Whatever you want. I'll do whatever you command.

When the time of sacrifice arrived again, Rayne's legs refused to cooperate. With a groan, he dropped back to his knees. Sickness, hunger, and the effects of the potion he had ingested countless times left him weak and incapable of standing on his own. He needed the honey-like tincture now, grabbed the offered bottle with unsteady fingers, and downed its contents as the sensation of stupor washed over him, deadening the pervasive physical and psychological pain. The knife wounds on his neck refused to heal, they festered, oozing pus and pain. Fever raged through his body. Still they gagged and blindfolded him and dragged his unresisting form up into the nighttime air.

His captors lifted him on a horse, tied him to a saddle, and led him to the stone. When the time came, they dragged him off and removed his blindfold. He groaned at the searing brightness. Though this night only a sliver of Ledia's blue light filtered through the trees into the hollow, it was too much, and he squeezed his eyes shut as tears leaked past the lids. He trembled as they held him on his knees and cut his neck before forcing his head forward so his blood flowed onto the altar, joining the blood of the five others sacrificed there.

The chanting seemed to go on longer this time and even in his current state, Rayne's spirit quailed at the strong malevolence spawning in the heavy magic of the glade. He wanted to warn the fools surrounding him of the danger they were summoning. But he couldn't seem to remember why he should warn them or why the darkness caused him terror. His mind was a jumbled mess of disjointed thoughts. After the ritual, he drank the sweet liquid before being tied again on the horse. Within minutes, he lost consciousness.

11

'You know I always backed you, Seth. Whatever you chose to do, from the time we was young, I was there for you. Together we listened to the High Guardian of the Scrolls speak words of power and the fire burned in us.

But Seth, I ain't so sure anymore. These sacrifices we're doin', it don't feel right. None of it feels right.'

Gwyn's words pricked Seth's psyche like a horde of stinging insects, and he growled as he watched his large and formidable Master of the Sacrifice, Arnulf, slice the necks of the five sacrificial victims. After the fifth succumbed to his knife, two lesser officers brought the Binder forward. The words rippled through Seth again. *'These sacrifices we're doin', this thing with the prince, it don't feel right ...'*

Seth ground his teeth. *You're wrong, Gwyn. It feels right. It is right! The power grows stronger with every sacrifice. It's presence here at the altar tonight is real, sparking the air, lending us strength. You should be sharing this moment with me; we should be doing this together like we always planned, bringing the High Guardian of the Scrolls back, returning the true power to Ochen.*

Seth's rage at Gwyn's betrayal coursed through the prime shepherd like a potent poison as spiraling fingers of heavy magic spread into every inch of the glade, frosting the trees and people with shadows. His eyes locked onto the slight form of the Binder now kneeling next to the altar stone, head thrust forward as Arnulf set his knife. Seth ground his teeth. *You! It's all because of you. Everything. You banished the High Guardian. You deceived the people with phony copies of the scrolls, insisting that everyone should read those spurious books. Now your blood will make right what you have set wrong. Gwyn, you should have been stronger.*

"Blood for blood. Blood for power. Blood for vengeance." The chant grew in volume, stirring the magic-laden air as Arnulf bled the Binder and his rich, light-infused blood, now darkened by the effects of Ferris Weed, dribbled downward to join the blue-tinged puddle.

Seth glanced to his right where the Lady Mother, Duchess Woodfield of Inverness, stood, erect and unmoving, her face an indecipherable mask. The Binder was, after all, her nephew, and at every sacrifice Seth watched her closely for any sign that her compassion would override her need for vengeance. He squinted. Apprehension over her state of mind after just imprisoning her sister turned his stomach into a congealed mass of fearful concern. Without the duchess calling forth the heavy energy in the air, the sacrifices would be insufficient to open the barrier that separated Ochen from the realm where the High Guardian and his colleagues had been exiled.

He set his fears aside when his eyes were drawn to the dark shadows bubbling and roiling over the altar stone. A self-satisfied smile bloomed across his elegant features as he watched the coalescing shadows merge into a more solid form. "Can you see it, my lady, feel what is coming? Our righteous will has brought this to pass, yours and mine. Each week the power grows stronger and the shade more solid. As the Binder weakens, so too does the barrier that holds back the return of our sacred scrolls. In two weeks, at the final offering, when the life blood of the false light bringer flows over the stone, our High Guardian of the Scrolls and the very Scrolls of Power themselves will be free to return to us. True light will again shine on the worlds of Ochen."

When Cailyn made no response, Seth's gaze flicked back to the powerful woman at his side. "Are you not pleased, my lady?"

After another moment of silence Cailyn responded, her

voice soft and faltering. "My vengeance … screamed out within me." She pulled in a breath and huffed it out. "'Make him pay for your baby … for your husband … for all he took from you'." She waved a hand toward Rayne and the men dragging his inert form to the waiting horse and shook her head. "'He must suffer as I have suffered.' The voice in my head demanded my compliance. Look at him, Seth. What have I done?"

Alarm swirled through Seth's gut like an unholy brew and words tumbled out. "Do not question your resolve, my lady, or the righteousness of your anger against our enemy. Remember why you chose this path, how you brought your need to me. Yes, you are right. We need to look at him my lady." Seth pointed at Rayne now being lifted onto the horse. "Look closely and remind yourself that this *sacrificial offering* is no longer your nephew; he is the Binder. The foe who slaughtered your only child without remorse and caused your husband so much pain he had no recourse but to take his life. Stir up again your fierce need to get justice for your dead loved ones, your longing to have his agony match your own. Cling fast to that desire now when we are so close to achieving our ultimate goals."

Arnulf's signal caught Seth's eye. "Please think no more on this for now, Lady Mother. We will discuss it later. Now I must address our people."

"As always, you are right, Seth." Cailyn wrapped a hand around his elbow and walked with him to the small platform set near the altar stone.

20

Seth had been speaking for almost an hour when Arnulf sprinted up to the dais and waved for Seth's attention, the Master of the Sacrifices' large face a curious shade of gray as he shifted from foot to foot. Seth nodded his recognition and started the chanting once again, then he stepped down from the platform to stand next to Cailyn.

"Arnulf, you had better have a good reason for interrupting me." Seth's eyes pinned Arnulf like twin daggers.

"He's gone." Arnulf spread his hands in supplication. "The Binder. He's been taken."

"What?" Heat flooded Seth's face and set a storm brewing in his stomach. He balled his hands into shaking fists, attempting to block the fury rising in him. He looked up at Arnulf. "What do you mean? How is this possible?"

"He had help. The guards were attacked by two masked assailants and knocked out on their way back to the castle. Those men must have taken the horses and rode off with the Binder. As soon as the guards regained consciousness, and realized the prisoner was gone, they came to me and reported what happened."

Seth closed his eyes and reined in his escalating fury. He needed to think with a clear head. Murmurs rose around him as Arnulf's news began to filter through the crowd.

"I can find him." Cailyn's words penetrated Seth's wall of frustration. "I will send out sense tendrils; he can't escape me." She reached out to grasp Seth's shoulder and he opened his eyes. "Seth. If we are to succeed, we must move now."

"You can do this? Even with a fresh dose of Ferris Weed in him?"

"Trust me."

Seth breathed in through his nose then released the air through bared teeth with a hiss, cleansing his system of doubt. "Yes, Lady Mother." Turning back to Arnulf, he began to bark orders. "Arnulf. Choose two men and bring horses. You will accompany the Lady Mother and me. We will pick up the trail while it's fresh."

With a stiff nod, the large Master of the Sacrifice turned and sprinted through the crowd.

"Associate Shepherd Osgood." Seth caught his subordinate's eyes. "I leave command of the camp to you until my return. Coordinate with Captain Theada; he'll give you any support you need."

Turning to his military commander, Seth placed a hand on the grizzled old warrior's shoulder. "Captain Theada, prepare the militia and tighten your control of the portal station. If my suspicions are correct, King Theodor is behind what's happened. He will attempt to use this distraction to infiltrate Nemora." Seth paused, his brow creasing into deep fissures as he considered how to best regain control of the situation. "Though skipping off world without authorization is unfeasible, the Binder's rescuers will most likely attempt to ferret him off Nemora as soon as possible. If they try to skip, kill the others but capture the Binder. It is imperative he be taken alive. Without his blood, the sacrifices can't be completed, and if the pact isn't fulfilled, we will..." A tremor ran through him as he recalled the words spoken by the High Guardian and the pact he had made. "At all costs, he must be found. We cannot fail.

"First Associate Shepherd Creedoff, return to ... First

Associate Shepherd … First Associate Shepherd Creedoff?"
Seth's eyes scanned the group surrounding him.

Vartan ran up, huffing as he stepped through the circle
surrounding the prime shepherd. Seth waved him forward.
"Come, my friend. We have no time to waste."

"My … my … daughter…" Vartan stuttered.

Seth glared at his Second. "Is there a problem, Vartan?"

The man's mouth opened and closed a few times and he
swallowed hard before he spoke. "No, Prime Shepherd, no
problem."

"Good, Vartan. Quickly. Return to camp with Captain
Theada. Round up volunteers from the First Company, about
fifty men you trust." He paused, his thoughts tumbling over
each other. "And supplies, whatever you can gather within the
next hour or two. Return here and follow the trail we will leave
for you. Catch up to us with all haste."

Seth turned to Cailyn as Vartan and Captain Theada jogged
toward their horses. She pulled her hood back up over her head
and closed her eyes. All doubt, cast aside, Cailyn began to
gather the potent magic-laden energies still filling the glen, summoning them back to her. *He can't be far.* She formed a searching tendril and sent it out in a series of waves. Like the
widening ripples on a pond after a stone had been thrown, it
moved outward, through the surrounding air. *Focus. Focus. I'll
show Ro. She isn't the only strong one. There. Faint but certain. Interesting. West.* Confidence and assurance filling her, she murmured
into the dark, heavy air, "You thought to escape nephew?" She
clicked her tongue. "You're so like your mother, underestimat-
ing me." Flinging back her hood, she tossed her head and
smiled at Seth. "I have him." She strode toward the horses,
chanting under her breath, "blood for blood, blood for power,
blood for vengeance."

Rayne clawed his way up from a well of oblivion. Something was different. Water splashed over rocks nearby. Chuckling and enticing. *So thirsty.* Soft ground—not smooth hard stone—lay beneath him. Someone was pulling the sack from his head.

"Rayne?"

"Is he awake?"

"I don't know. I think he's in bad shape."

Voices? So ... familiar. Voices from his past. But he couldn't think through the numbed chaos of his broken mind. "Lexi? Lexi?"

"Rayne?" The first voice penetrated Rayne's confusion. "Hey, Rayne. It's me, Giles. Can you hear me? Come on, cousin. Don't you die on me now."

"We have to get him off Nemora," the other said.

Giles pulled the blindfold free and started working on the gag. With it off, he asked again, "Rayne, can you hear me? Can you talk?"

Giles? Who? Cousin? Betrayer! A shiver ran through Rayne. *Why ... Who ... is he?* Rayne startled as a wave of dread surged through him. In his weakened state, all he managed to accomplish was to fling his hand in the direction of the voice. *Not bound. Untied? Giles? Can't trust him!* "Lexi," he called again, weakly. "Lexi." He battered at the darkness.

"Whoa," Giles took hold of Rayne's flailing hand. "Just settle. I've got you. I've got you now."

Rayne inhaled great gulps of air, struggling against old fear, weakly swinging his other arm as his heart beat a rapid cadence, sending his blood drumming in his ears.

"This isn't working," Giles said. "I can't help you unless you stop fighting me. I know you have no reason to trust me, but just do it for now. Okay, cousin? Just trust me for now. I'm on your side. Marius is with me. A lot has happened since you saw us last. We're here to help you, okay?"

Rayne cracked his eyes open and immediately squeezed them shut against the pain. The quick look confirmed what he knew. The voice belonged to Giles, the cousin who had betrayed him to Sigmund and was responsible for Rayne's spirit being imprisoned in the body of a dying old man almost four years ago.

"Rayne. You have to trust us. I know you'll find this hard to believe, but we want to help you."

"Giles?" Rayne's voice rasped. He swallowed against the burning lump wedged in his throat. "When?"

"Yes, yes, it's Giles. I'm here to help you this time."

Rayne cracked open one eye to squint up at Giles again. "Giles?"

Giles nodded. "I'm glad you're still with us."

"Well, he won't be for long." Marius scanned the area then dropped his gaze to Giles and Rayne, his mouth turned down at the corners. "At least he won't be if we don't get him away from here and off Nemora. Soon. Although I don't see how we can skip with that witch's guards watching the portal station. And we can't stay here much longer. We need to move. Those religious fanatics are probably already on our trail."

"Yeah, I know." Giles's focus shifted back to Rayne. "I know you're hurting, cousin, but we have to move you now. Once those blood-thirsty scroll worshipers realize you're missing, they'll be coming after us. Probably mad as a swarm of bees whose honey's been taken. I guess Marius and I aren't very good at this rescue thing. We may have stolen you for the moment, but I have no idea what we're going to do with you. Like Marius said, there's no way we can get you safely off Nemora. The portals are under United Scrolls of Ochen control."

"South," Rayne whispered with the last of his energy. "Take me ... to Neth. To the Kindred. They'll know ... what ... to do."

21

Andrew swallowed the bile rising hot and demanding as he watched the sacrifices. Five victims had been forced to kneel on the bloody altar. Five times the thin, dark knife slit through a throat and the blood streamed. Andrew was past ready to turn away and run as far as he could from the accursed place where the dense air hindered breathing and he struggled to swallow past the burning, choking lump in his throat. Mayda's small, warm hand wrapped around his icy fingers. He looked down at her in question.

"They're bringing him now." Her voice was a soft, pained whisper.

Andrew caught the sorrow in her eyes before she looked away, and sniffed his own runny nose. Straightening his shoulders, he turned back to face the stone as the chanting around him rose in volume. Then he saw the figure being dragged to the altar. *Oh, my Lord. Rayne! No. No. No.*

One of the men tugging Rayne forward plucked off the hood and Andrew drew in a sharp breath. Only Mayda yanking his hand saved him from screaming his horror and fury. Instead, covered by the dark night and sound of chanting, Andrew moaned and pulled his fingers into tight fists.

"Stop," Mayda hissed. "You're crushing my hand."

Not trusting his voice, Andrew just nodded as he loosened his grip, his eyes fixed on Rayne. *Why, mighty One? Why are they doing this?* He shuddered as Rayne was forced to his knees, not on the stone as the others had been, but next to it. Andrew nearly jumped out of his skin when the knife nicked the side of Rayne's throat. Silent revulsion rose in him as Rayne's head was forced down and forward until his blood dribbled onto the crimson pool already saturating the stone surface. Still the chanting droned on. Andrew's skin prickled as a dark shadowy form coalesced above the altar before shredding into remnants that hovered over the chanting worshipers.

Rayne's head was pulled back and one of the men who had come with him poured a vial of something into his mouth. After that, his hood was replaced, he was dragged back to the horse, and his limp body was tied to the saddle. The two men who brought him mounted and, pulling his horse behind, moved off in the direction from which they had come.

Prime Shepherd Hamlin and a woman whose face was hidden in a deep cowl approached the sacrificial altar.

"I have to go," Andrew whispered to Mayda as he turned toward the departing figures. "I have to go. I … I have to help him."

"What do you think you're doing? You can't follow horses on foot, especially in the dark," Mayda hissed.

"Boone. I'll go back for Boone. She could track Rayne anywhere."

"I'm coming with you." A sharp edge of conviction turned Mayda's whisper rough.

"No. It's too dangerous."

"It's more dangerous for you if I don't come. Most of the officers know I'm Associate Shepherd Creedoff's daughter. I can help you if we get stopped. Come on. We can sneak away while Prime Shepherd Hamlin and the Lady Mother are speaking. She doesn't talk much, but he'll talk for a long time."

The two slipped back into the thicker shadows beneath

the trees then ran, Mayda leading the way. They moved out of the glen at a full run, but once they reached the thicker trees of the woods, their sprint slowed to a jog.

The walk to the altar stone from camp had taken over an hour and Andrew wrestled with worry over the time they were losing by going back for Boone. But he also knew that without her, he could never track Rayne.

Guides had been stationed at points with lanterns revealing tripping hazards when they came this way earlier. Now, screened by a canopy of immense branches and a rising mist, the narrow path was dark and treacherous in Rem's weak light. From time to time, when the sky opened to them, Andrew glimpsed Rem's form like a silvery blue eye watching from above, reflecting in the puddles that lined the path. Old tree roots and young suckers seemed to turn into grasping hands that reached out from the leaf-strewn, rocky trail with purpose, tripping the two. Rocks that in the daylight would be easily avoided, slowed their progress even more. Frequently they were forced to stop so Mayda could find the trail after losing it in the gloom.

Andrew struggled against a mounting fear that they had fallen prey to an evil spell and would never reach the camp. It seemed as if he had been running for an eternity. Twice he stopped to vomit in the leaf litter on the side of the trail and more than once he needed to wipe tears off his chin. Finally, Andrew pulled in a full breath of relief when he followed Mayda into an open field. She stopped, bent over with her hands on her knees, and breathed hard. Before them was the rise marking the edge of the USO camp, the murky sky above reflecting the glow of numerous campfires.

Andrew hunched as well, gulping in the dense, magic laden air. After a couple deep breaths, he caught Mayda's eye and she nodded. He groaned as he straightened, then, jogging up the incline, wondered where they were in relation to Boone and how much farther they would need to go. Distracted and huffing, Andrew crested the rise and plowed into a large, cloaked figure.

Lexi shifted her shoulders, repositioning the pack hidden under her cloak, as she followed Thorvin's erratic movements, like threading her way through a maze. Every shift of direction was a direct result of the movements of guards around the camp. *Why do they have so many guards here? To protect their people? Or keep them in?* Her thoughts were disrupted when Thorvin snorted, waved for her to follow, and picked up his pace as they scrambled up the hill beyond the ring of torches and guards.

She was following close on Thorvin's heels, sprinting toward the top of the rise, when he grunted and came to an abrupt halt. Lexi twisted, momentum pushing her a few steps beyond Thorvin before she came to a stop and turned back. Two slight, shadowy figures stood before the big man, one staggering as if he had stumbled.

"I'm sorry," the stumbling form mumbled. "Sorry. Didn't see you there. Excuse us."

Recognition sparked through Lexi's jumbled thoughts. "Andrew? Is that you, Andrew?"

"Lexi?"

"Andrew? What are you doing here?" Lexi whispered.

"No time for a reunion," Thorvin rumbled. "Were you heading in or out?"

"In," Andrew said. "We need to get Boone."

Thorvin scanned the lighted area behind them. "Let's go. Now." He led the way back into camp. No one spoke until he pulled up in the shadow of a large tent. He rounded on Andrew, his eyes sparking in the light from a nearby torch. "Explain yourself, boy. By the seven, what are you doing here?"

Andrew swallowed hard but flattened his mouth and returned Thorvin's glare. "I followed you. But that's not what's important. We know where Rayne is … or at least where he was. We came back to get Boone so she can track him. But we've wasted too much time already. They're on horses and way ahead of us now. We need to hurry. Please, Thorvin. I can explain things later. You can join us if you want; but whether you agree or not, Mayda and I are getting Boone and going back for Rayne."

"You saw him?" Lexi's voice ghosted from her in a pained whisper. "Is he okay? Where is he?"

Andrew shook his head; his mouth worked but no words came.

"If you want to help your friend," Mayda said, "we need to get the dog and get out of here before someone stops us. My father may be the Associate Shepherd, but the guards will question where we're going at this hour."

"Andrew." Thorvin drew his sword and pointed it at Mayda. "Tell me. Can we trust her? She's one of them."

Mayda's eyes went wide but Andrew stepped between the tip of Thorvin's blade and Mayda. "Yes, we can trust her. Please Thorvin, she's not our enemy."

Thorvin flicked his eyes to Lexi. She fought down the urge to draw her own weapons and take the life of this enemy, but instead she nodded. He sheathed his sword and waved for Mayda to lead the way. After casting a quick glance around, the girl sprinted toward the center of camp. It took another half-hour to work their way past gathered knots of people and get to Boone. When she saw them, her back end began to swivel as her tail swung, and she whined her delight.

"Down, Boone!" Andrew said as she jumped on him while he leaned over to grab her leather leash and exchange it for the lead she was wearing.

While Andrew got Boone, Mayda ducked into the tent and came out with a pack. "Got our stuff, Andrew." She positioned the straps on her shoulders.

Within minutes they were on their way out of the camp, Boone straining on the leash, towing Andrew. Mayda followed with Lexi on her heels and Thorvin bringing up the rear.

"We'll need horses." Thorvin waved toward the picket line they were passing, one of several scattered around the edges of the large camp.

"The guards will notice pretty fast if horses disappear." Mayda glanced up at Thorvin.

Thorvin grinned at Lexi and she mirrored his expression.

"Yeah." She nodded. "Set the whole line loose, startle them, and let them run through the camp. It'll feel good to cause a little havoc among these barbaric scroll lunatics."

Seeing the look of hurt on Mayda's face, Lexi shrugged and turned her back on the girl. She couldn't care less if she hurt the scroll worshiper's feelings. What was she doing with Andrew anyway?

"Andrew, you and Mayda wait here." Thorvin winked at Lexi. "You remember how to be stealthy, don't you?"

Lexi flashed Thorvin a grim smile. "Hoped I wouldn't need these skills again, but yeah, I remember."

Following Thorvin's lead, Lexi crouched and ghosted through the wavering shadows to the mist-dampened picket line. When they were in position, Thorvin signaled and Lexi untied the horses from the near end of the line while he did the same on the farther side. Within minutes all the horses except the four Thorvin and Lexi held onto were loose. Thorvin pulled his horses forward toward Lexi, waving his free hand, sending the remaining horses charging off in various directions.

Thorvin, Lexi, Andrew, and Mayda were just moving away from the lights, leading their horses, when the camp came to life like a kicked hornet's nest. Voices clamored and several of the loose horses ran past.

A man's deep voice penetrated the darkness. "Guards! Guards! To me! Prime Shepherd Hamlin needs every able-bodied man! Now!"

Shouting continued and grew in volume as people scrambled to catch the spooked horses and alarm spread through the camp.

"It sounds like a bigger problem than a few horses." Thorvin drew to a halt, scanning the space between them and the outer ring of torches. "Keep going. Take it slow, easy. Make like we belong and keep your ears open."

The deep voice called out again above the uproar to Lexi's right. "Prime Shepherd Hamlin sent me to round up soldiers to join him and the Lady Mother while Captain Theada takes a contingent of soldiers and secures the portal station."

"No."

Lexi turned at Mayda's gasp. "What?"

"That's my father. Why is he here now? He's supposed to be with Prime Shepherd Hamlin. Something really big must have happened."

Mayda's father cursed. "Who let these horses loose? Eric, gather soldiers from the first company. Jens round up enough horses for us. Otherwise Theada'll take them. We need to get back to the prime shepherd immediately."

"What's wrong, Vartan?"

"What's wrong, Jens? I'll tell you what's wrong. The Binder's been taken."

"How's that even possible?"

"Oh, it's possible alright, because somebody did it. Arnulf is tracking them. Prime Shepherd Hamlin and the Lady Mother are following. We're supposed to bring soldiers and catch up to them in all haste." Vartan paused for a moment, then said in a hushed voice, "I'll tell you this, though, if we don't get the Binder back and finish the sacrifices, I don't want to be around to find out what that High Guardian is going to do. Move."

His voice faded as he sprinted away calling out more orders.

Lexi froze, paralysis locking her knees at the man's words. *Binder! Sacrifices? High Guardian? Sigmund? No. No. No. It can't be.*

Thorvin grabbed her arm and propelled her toward the edge of camp. Once they were beyond the lights, he whispered, "Everyone mount up. Andrew, get Boone to ride with you. We need to get out of here before we're spotted. Mayda, you know where we're going?"

"Yes."

"Okay, you lead."

Lexi shifted to flank Andrew and Mayda, glaring at the two even though she knew they couldn't see her expression in the dark. "Once we've put some distance between us and that camp, we need to talk. And when we do, you *will* tell me everything you know about Rayne and what's happened to him."

22

He's passed out again," Giles said, gritting his teeth and wondering why he ever committed to this foolish course of action. "What do you think? Should we try for Neth?"

Marius snorted a breath out his nose. "I don't know. Maybe. Before, when he was that old man, those ancients in Neth kept him alive, helped him get stronger." He paused, listening, scanning. His eyes flicked back down to focus on Rayne and Giles. "It's certain we're not getting him off Nemora anytime soon. Might as well try Neth. Those cursed scroll lovers won't expect us to head south."

Giles's lips flattened as he looked down at his cousin's ashen, scruffy face. "He looks really bad. He smells awful too, like infection."

"That slob of a scroll worshiper we met at The Flying Pig Tavern in Inverness was so into his cups and proud of what they were accomplishing. After you left, he was more than happy to tell me all about the seven sacrifices requiring human blood and the blood of the Binder. But he also mentioned the Binder being condemned to live his days in darkness and die in darkness. He laughed about it. 'A righteous punishment for the enemy who destroyed our Scrolls of power', he said."

Giles let loose a puff of frustration. "Idiots. He's probably been kept in the dark for weeks now. That explains his reaction to even Ledia's dim light.

"Thanks for putting up with that slimy drunk as long as you did. I couldn't stomach spending another minute with the self-righteous slob. But if we hadn't met him, we'd never have learned how much the United Scrolls of Ochen have grown or that they were offering human sacrifices to the banished demons at that old altar stone. Knowing Sigmund and what he put in place, I guess it was to be expected."

Giles paused, his mind spinning. "Five sacrifices tonight." He considered the implications. "So, if this was the fifth week and Rayne's blood was needed at each offering, he had to have been a prisoner for at least five weeks. And there's no way to know how long he was *condemned to live his days in darkness* before the weekly rituals started. That explains a lot; weeks of no light and all those cuts from that dirty, wicked knife. No wonder he's burning up with fever, Marius."

"Yeah." Marius agreed. He ran his hand along the lathered neck of his horse, then shook his head, a sour look on his face. "I'll bet that was Ferris Weed tincture they gave him after they sliced him tonight. That stuff messes with the mind. It's used to block magic and make the user docile. It's also highly addictive. I've seen users dependent on it … it's not pretty. If they've been giving that to him all those weeks, he's going to be hurting without it."

Both men got silent, focused, as sounds of rustling and noisy voices penetrated the underbrush in the direction from which they had come.

With guarded steps, Marius joined Giles at Rayne's side. "Get on the horse," he whispered. "I'll help Rayne up to you. Head due south. I'll take the other two horses and once I've led whoever's following on a false trail, I'll find you."

Giles mounted and, leaning over, helped Marius lift Rayne up in front of him. Wrapping arms around the limp body, Giles nudged the horse and moved off trusting Marius to cover their tracks.

Giles rode easily for the next couple hours, not pushing

the horse, but not stopping for a break. The night had turned dark under a heavy cloud cover and rain spit fitfully from time to time. Rayne's body threw off heat, warming Giles's chest. Every so often Rayne would mumble incomprehensible words, but he didn't wake out of the drugged stupor.

"What did you get yourself into this time?" Giles asked, remembering Rayne's troubled history. "Why on the seven would you go anywhere without a guard? Where's Thorvin, huh?" Giles paused as Rayne moaned and shifted. "Hey, none of that now. I can't have you falling. You're already pretty pathetic as it is. For someone as keen on bathing as you are, I must say; right now, you stink like a privy. I guess they wouldn't bring you a tub whenever you requested one, would they, Your Highness?"

They rode in silence until the sky began to brighten. Shades of gray streaked with pearlescent pink and lavender appeared as rays from the rising sun reflected off the bottoms of the breaking cloud cover and set droplets scattered on leaves to sparkling. Rayne started moaning and struggling weakly as the light intensified.

"Yeah, I hear you," Giles said. "We'll stop in the next patch of heavy woods."

It was nearly a half-hour later before they reached a dense copse of oak trees with some spruce scattered through, their damp scent filling the air. By that time, Rayne was wrestling with Giles, struggling to cover his eyes. "Please make it stop," he pleaded. "My eyes. It hurts."

"Almost there," Giles said. "Just hang on a bit longer."

When they reached a patch of deeper shade, Giles swung off the horse. Turning, he helped Rayne down, pulling his arm over a shoulder and guiding him to a soft patch of moss. Rayne kept his hands over his eyes as Giles lowered him to the ground.

"Be right back." Giles ran back to tether the horse and grab his bags. When he returned, Rayne was lying on his side, both arms wrapped around his head, doing his best to block the light. Giles pulled the cloth blindfold from his pack. "Move your hands. Let me put this on for you. For now, I think it'll help."

After wrapping the blindfold in place, Giles pulled the hood back over Rayne's head. "You're doing good cousin. Doing good. Did that help?"

"Giles?" Rayne whispered; his voice gritty as sandpaper.

"Yeah, Rayne, it's Giles."

"I thought I was dreaming." Rayne shifted, reached up to touch the hood covering his head. "Am I dreaming? The light... it's gone."

"No," Giles said. "The light will come again. You will bring the light again. It's part of who you are."

"Who I am?"

"Yes, who you are. And who you are right now is a man who needs water. Stay put, I'm not going far, just to the creek. I'll be right back."

Giles grabbed the water skin and sprinted to the stream they had been following for the last several miles. He knelt by a deeper pool, submerged the skin, and watched the air bubbles rising to the surface as it filled. He shook his head, gazed out into the mist shrouded trees, and remembered the night Rayne and he played King of the Hill back on Amathea.

"You were right, cousin," he whispered into the sun-kissed morning air around him as tiny midges danced in the beams. "I gave up too easily back then, always did. I should have been stronger, listened to you. Instead I just followed Brayden and Sigmund because it was easy. Then Marius and I ran away the day you defeated the darkness. We should have stayed. You would have pardoned us; I know that now. You always saw the best in me, didn't you? Marius too. I hope you still do. I pray they haven't bled that from you."

He pulled the dripping water skin from the stream, corked it, and hurried back to where he had left Rayne. Coming over the slight rise, Giles stopped. Rayne was struggling to pull the hood off his head.

"Wait," Giles hissed as he sprinted over and knelt next to Rayne. "It's going to be bright, the sun is melting the haze. But if you want, let me help you."

Rayne sucked in a breath and pushed back, away from Giles. "Who are you? Did Sigmund send you?"

"It's me. Giles. Your cousin. Sigmund's gone. He's been gone for three years now. You're with me on Nemora. Remember the USO, the sacrifices? The rescue? I went to get water but now I'm back. Here," Giles pushed the water skin into Rayne's hand. "Water. You need to drink."

"No!" Rayne shouted and flung the bag back at Giles. "It's poison. I know it's poison." He tried to stand, but fell to his knees, his hands grappling with the hood. "I'm blind. It's Sigmund's punishment. No ... no ... wait." He sucked in several deep breaths. "No ... I know what this is. It's the One's punishment. My penalty for all the blood I spilled. Do you see it? Dripping from me. It's always there. Blood and death. Blood and death."

He fell to his side and curled into a ball. "Five paces. Five paces. Blacker than night. Never changes ... five paces by five paces. Nobody speaks. Nothing but silence. Not a word. I'm not here. Just another shadow. Why won't you talk to me? Say something?"

Giles stared at his babbling cousin, uncertain if he should speak or just let Rayne ramble. When Rayne finally settled, Giles spoke in a soothing voice as he reached over to remove the hood.

As soon as his hands touched Rayne, though, he tried to sit up and reached out, grasping at Giles's shirt. "The tincture. Give me the tincture. Make the glow go away. Nothing hurts then. Please."

Pity shot through Giles at Rayne's words. Marius was right; Rayne needed the tincture and Giles had nothing to give to help him through the pain. Instead Giles did what he could; he removed the hood while keeping the blindfold in place. Helping Rayne into a more upright position, Giles encouraged him to drink water, handing him back the skin every time he pushed it away. When Rayne refused to drink anymore, Giles gently lowered his head onto his lap, crooning soft words until Rayne's breathing evened and Giles knew he slept.

Rayne's body threw off heat like the inside of an oven, he shivered frequently, and mumbled in his sleep. Checking the side of his neck and seeing the oozing, festering wounds left from the sacrifices, Giles pulled a small knife from his boot and cut off a corner of the United Scrolls of Ochen cloak he was wearing. Wetting it with water from the skin, he washed the wounds and then rung out the cloth to bathe Rayne's face and arms.

"Marius, where are you?" Giles scanned the trees around him, listening to the quiet rustlings of small animals and intermittent bird songs. Morning bled into afternoon and Rayne continued in his fever-riddled sleep. "I can't do this alone, Marius. Come on; what's taking you so long?"

23

Rayne's eyes refused to cooperate. Something weighed on the lids, holding them closed. He inched fingers up his face to find a cloth wrapped around his head and he pushed it up onto his forehead. The soft, blue-tinted light of a Nemorian sunset stabbed at him. He grimaced at the pain that flooded his eyes and sent impulses of throbbing agony into his brain. He blinked. Tears came, washing the grit from his eyes and dribbling down his cheeks. He started to pull in a deep draught of forest fresh air.

Where am I? Augh! Rayne's deep breath morphed into a shallow pull of air as pain seized him and nausea roiled his gut. He blinked again, forcing his watery eyes to adjust to the soft light. *So sick!* He raised a hand to the side of his neck where he probed the oozing wounds left by the sacrificial knife, his fingertips discovering a sticky, slimy mess. He groaned again before the stench of his own body hit him and dry heaves clenched his abdomen, bringing more pain. When his stomach settled a bit, he called, "Giles?"

Was that real? Giles ... the rescue? Or ... did I imagine ... dream the whole thing?

He wrapped his arms around his torso and tried to make sense of where he was and how he had gotten there. But his mind folded in on itself, jumbling thoughts and memories until he didn't know what was real or imagined.

Cracking open his still leaking eyes, Rayne scanned the area. He was alone in a tiny clearing surrounded by large oak trees, their branches stretching out in a leafy canopy over him. His gaze caught on his bare arms where a soft, golden glow flickered before disappearing. Blinking again, he stared at his hands as he drew them from around his waist and brought them up to his face, close. *I'm glowing. How long? The tincture ... stops the light. How long since I've had it?* He groaned.

Voices drew his eyes to the underbrush on his right. "... half the night ... day ... almost night again. Where have you been, Marius?"

"Hey don't blame me. It took me a lot longer than I expected to lose those crazy fanatics."

Fear and panic surged. With an effort of will, Rayne stumbled to his feet, swaying, eyes locked on the portion of woods from which the voices came. He tried to lock his knees, but they gave out and the world began to spin.

Giles's shout reached him as if from the bottom of a deep well. "Rayne! Don't ... I'm coming..."

The blackness took Rayne again. He was floating ... dark silence surrounded him. Then strong arms were upholding him, and he sank into the comfort and peace of that presence. Time lost meaning and Rayne slept. He woke, the arms still encompassing him as a faint glow sparked around him and a song of rest permeated the air. Then the voice he knew so well spoke. *Be still, my child. I am with you. I have prepared a way. Go to Neth; there you will find help. Though the Ferris Weed will call to you, cling to me and I will strengthen you.*

Rayne blinked. Time returned to normal as gravity's unrelenting force pulled him downward. Giles ran toward him, a sheet of panic blanketing his face. "...I'm coming."

Giles caught Rayne as he pitched forward. "Steady. You shouldn't have gotten up. I'm sorry I wasn't here. I went to get more water, then Marius showed up."

Marius walked up to stand over Giles and Rayne. He dipped his head. "Your Highness." Then turning to Giles, he continued. "Why did you wait for me? I told you to go. I may have lost those idiots for now, but they can't be far behind. They must have a good tracker with them."

Rayne strove to focus on Giles and Marius but trying to concentrate was like trying to scoop up water with a net. Random thoughts and memories shifted and blurred, refusing to coalesce into anything of substance in his pain riddled brain. He blinked again. Giles shifted around to help Rayne sit. "Here, I brought you some more water. Drink. It'll be good for you."

Rayne's hands shook as he reached for the water skin and his stomach clenched at the thought of drinking, but he forced himself to take a few small sips before lifting the skin back to Giles. "I-I n-n-need … tinc-tincture. It hurts … bad. Please." Rayne rubbed his hands up and down his arms as he clenched his teeth against the searing pain building in his head.

Marius cursed. "What did I tell you, Giles? I knew it. They've been feeding him Ferris Weed. He's gonna keep asking for it and unless we get him some, it's only gonna get worse."

Giles, still focused on Rayne, shook his head. "We don't have that stuff, Rayne, and we can't get it. We're in the middle of nowhere, heading to Neth, just like you asked. They can help you there, right?"

Rayne closed his eyes, swallowed and nodded, immediately regretting the action. "Neth. Yeah, Neth. Must get to Neth. Be okay. Marius … Marius is right … let's go." He grabbed the arm Giles held out and allowed his cousin to pull him to his feet. Giles and Marius each took one of Rayne's arms, drew them over their shoulders and helped him stagger to the waiting horses.

Once Rayne was settled, Giles hopped up behind him. "You okay? I'm here; I won't let you fall."

Pulling up next to them, Marius nodded then scanned the woods to the north. Without a word, he turned his horse's nose south and set the animal in motion.

The following days blended into a mix of painful waking hours riding with Giles, and restless, nightmare-infected sleep.

Whenever they stopped, Giles or Marius tried to get Rayne to drink and eat before continuing. Most times, he would push them away, refusing food and drink.

The fourth night, they set a cold camp. "They're close," Marius said when he returned after scouting the trail behind. "It's a good thing we didn't light a fire."

Rayne thrashed and mumbled in sleep. "No ... no, all lies... dark. Please..."

"How much farther to Neth?" Giles asked, bathing Rayne's hot face and arms with a cool, damp cloth. "He's getting worse. If we don't do something for the infection soon, I'm ... I don't know if he'll make it."

Marius's forehead furrowed. "We should reach the outer edge of the forest by late tomorrow." He walked over to where Giles sat with Rayne's head resting on his lap. "I'm gonna get some more water."

Giles nodded. Marius huffed then scuffed over to their packs and pulled a piece of waybread and a water skin from his pack and tossed them to Giles. He started walking away, the other water skin in his hand, turned back with an oath. "What are we doing Giles? I mean, really? This all seemed like a good idea before; but now? They're gonna catch us and when they do, guess who's going to be part of the next sacrifice?"

Marius flung the water skin about and shook his head. "No. I'm not dying for him, not when we can turn this around. It wasn't so bad when Sigmund was here, remember? We had power, position, wealth? Maybe those scroll worshipers are right. All we have to do is give them Rayne. He's dying anyway; you said so. If they can open the portal for Sigmund to return, he'll reward us. We won't have to continue wandering around the seven, looking for piddling jobs just to stay alive, avoiding soldiers and officials everywhere we go.

"We can tell them we're old associates of the High Shepherd ... that we tracked and killed those who helped the Binder escape ... that we want to join them, be part of bringing the High Shepherd back."

Giles stared at Marius, his mouth moved, forming unspoken words, until he said, "No ... no! For three years we talked about how we could make things right. For three years! Was it all a lie? You said you regretted not helping Rayne before. We agreed! We talked this over before making the decision to rescue him. You know what he is; what he's done. By the seven, how could you even think to return him to what they've got planned?" He shifted Rayne's head and slid out from beneath him, pushed to his feet, and stalked over to stand nose to nose with Marius, his hands curled into tight fists. "Tell me where this is coming from." Giles paused, searching Marius's eyes. "You're afraid." He huffed out an aborted laugh. "Well, I am too. But I won't give in to the fear. For once, I refuse to take the easy way out.

"If you want to betray Rayne, I can't stop you, you're stronger than I am and a trained fighter; but I won't go with you either. Do what you must, and I'll do what I need to. If you leave now though, we're through. Go, join the scroll worshipers if inviting Sigmund and his colleagues back is what you really want. Invite the darkness to return to Ochen. I don't have the skill or strength to stop you, but you'll have to kill me to get Rayne."

Marius cursed, his face twisting into a look of pure disgust. "Why do you have to make this so hard, Giles? Why continue this course when he's dying anyway?" Marius waved at Rayne. "At least this way, we won't die with him. Open your eyes! He'll never make it to Neth."

"No."

Giles's heart jumped into his throat when he heard Rayne behind him, stumbling toward them, the blanket Giles had wrapped him in dragging behind.

"Kill me now. Kill me and save yourselves." He stopped, stood with planted feet, his face a mask of sheer determination under a sheen of sweat. He shook his head, staggering with the effort before righting himself. "Won't let them use me ... I'd rather die ... now." He nodded. "Do ... it!"

His eyes pierced Giles, drawing up old memories of when the two had played King of the Mountain a lifetime ago. *Why am I thinking of that now?* The truth hit Giles like a punch to his gut. Rayne never gave up; he would do anything in his power to stop what the scroll worshipers were trying to accomplish. Even if it meant his own death.

Marius pushed past Giles, barreling into Rayne, knocking him to the ground. He stood over Rayne, his chest rising and falling as he drew in heavy breaths, his face a mix of anger and pain. "You're an idiot, you know that? From the first moment I laid eyes on you, when you were trapped in that old man and still put yourself out there to save those kids, I knew it. Why? Why do you have to be like this? I can't be like you. I tried." Marius crashed to his knees next to Rayne, his breath whistling as he drew in gulps of air. "On Arisima. You knew then. You knew and still took me to Westvale with you. Why? I don't understand. Tell me—why."

Giles leaped forward and grabbed Marius's arm. "Stop. What are you doing? Leave him alone."

"No." Rayne's voice, hollow and soft, pulled Giles up short. "He needs ... to know." Rayne's eyes worked to focus on Marius. "The One called you. Even then ... he said ... I needed to ... take you."

Giles reached to catch Rayne as he lost consciousness, but Marius was already there, cupping the back of the prince's head and pulling it into his chest. "I'm sorry. I'm so sorry." Giles heard him mumble into the top of Rayne's head. "You're as frustrating as ever. A fool. And I'm an idiot for believing in you."

Giles grabbed two blankets, threw one over Marius's shoulders and the other over Rayne, before wrapping a third around his shoulders and settling in to sleep. When he woke, the first rays of the blue-tinged Nemorian sun were daggers of light piercing the foggy haze that had risen around the stream. Rayne was still sleeping soundly, his head resting on Marius's folded blanket. Marius was gone.

24

Rowena stared up at an unfamiliar ceiling as the odors of moldy straw and unwashed bodies tickled her nose. A sticky, sweet substance coating her tongue triggered a gag reflex, but she choked it down and forced herself to swallow. *Oh, my, but that's awful. Where…* She blinked, closing her eyes for a moment before opening them again as she fought to make sense of what had happened and where she was. Reality seeped into her fuzzy thoughts, and she groaned. "Oh, Cailyn, what have you done?"

"Thank the One, you're awake."

"Sashi?"

"Yes, Your Majesty, it's me. Nemora's moons, Your Majesty, I know the duchess is your sister and all, but right now I'd like to strangle the witch. Ferris Root. She dosed us with Ferris Root. When I get out of here…"

"Here?" Rowena tried to sit up and Sashi wrapped an arm around her back to support her. "Where is here? I don't remember anything after … Rayne. By the seven, she's involved in Rayne's disappearance."

"Like I said, sister or not, that witch deserves to be boiled in her own Ferris Weed tincture."

Rowena's eyes roamed the cell. "Where we are?"

"Sorry, I just woke up a short while ago myself and I haven't a clue. Noah and Benning are in the cell next to us. That's all I know."

"I think we might still be in the castle. Help me up."

Sashi gave Rowena her elbow and stabilized the queen until her legs strengthened beneath her. After a few deep breaths, Rowena walked the couple steps to the door made of heavy veredium bars, rested her head against two, and peeked out. "Noah?"

"Here, Your Majesty. Benning, Stevie, and I are here. I'm sorry. I was supposed to protect you and I failed."

"You couldn't know. How could you? Even I didn't suspect my sister would betray me like this."

"Ray-ray's mother?" A small voice called from the cell opposite Rowena's. "Yes. Yes. It is Ray-ray's mother. Why?"

"Mite?" Confusion drew Rowena's brows downward as she caught sight of the diminutive ancient staring at her through the bars across the hall. "I could ask the same of you."

"Stupid, stupid, Mite. Mite let dark-loving scroll people catch him."

Rowena released a mirthless chuckle. "Well, if Mite was stupid, then so was I. It seems we're in the same predicament." She checked the hallway in both directions and asked, "Have you come up with a way out of here yet?"

Mite's face wilted and he shook his head. "No. No. No. No way." His face brightened. "Unless ... Ray-ray's mother can use the energy?"

Rowena's brow puckered. "I don't know. Ferris Weed blocks magic, and it seems that my loving sister just dosed me with it."

"Ferris Weed bad, bad, bad. Magic won't work. Energy no good. Scroll people make Mite drink too. Yes, yes, yes."

"But they didn't today." A heavy-set balding man moved to stand behind Mite. "Something's happened. Something major. The senior guards all ran out after that messenger arrived in the wee hours and the remaining guards are on edge."

"Have we met?" Rowena studied the stranger.

He ducked his head and studied the floor. "No, Your Majesty."

"Scroll man right." Mite closed his eyes and screwed his face up, wrinkling his pert nose, then opened his eyes and smiled. "Mite feels it, feels the energy. If Ray-ray's mother can help, Mite can trick the guards. Get us all out, out. Yes, he can."

"No." Rowena clenched her fists as her mouth flattened into a stern line. "I'm through playing games. And there is no way anyone is getting near me with Ferris Weed again. My ability to draw energy is already reviving. Mite, give me a little time to flush the Ferris Weed, then I'm going to pull power from you. I haven't achieved the status of Master Mage without reason." She drew in a deep breath and released it slowly, her face turning cold. "Get ready, Sister. It's my turn. And if you've harmed my son, all of Nemora will not be large enough to protect you from me."

She turned to Sashi. "I'm going to rest for one hour. Do not let me sleep longer than that." Rowena turned back to the door and spoke into the hallway. "Mite, Noah, Benning, prepare yourselves. In one hour, we're getting out of here."

Queen Rowena moved with quiet dignity to the small straw tick in the corner, settled on her side, her back to the room, and prayed. *Blessed One. You called my son and now he's in danger. I need your strength to save him. Help me to rest now and in one hour's time, give me the ability to pull energy from this heavy air. Guide my steps. Give me wisdom to escape this place, find Rayne, and face Cai.*

She pulled what energy she could from the surrounding atmosphere and set in motion the magic needed to purge the Ferris Weed from her body.

ᚭ

Her strength almost back to normal, Rowena rose from the scratchy tick, flexing her fingers and loosening her shoulders.

"Your Majesty. I was just about to wake you. How did you know an hour had passed?" Sashi stared, her eyes widened with wonder.

Ignoring the baffled girl, Rowena strode to the locked door and sent a sense tendril into the locking mechanism. "Just as I thought," she murmured under her breath. Raising a hand, she focused a pulse of energy into the opening where a key would fit and with a quick twist, unlocked the door. It swung open on squeaky hinges.

With a purposeful stride, the queen set off down the narrow hall, Sashi at her heels. When she reached the small room at the end, the lone guard sprang onto his feet, jostling the table where he had been playing with a deck of cards, flinging the cards onto the floor. He stumbled back as Rowena advanced, her palms open toward him.

"Keys." Rowena spoke the word with cold authority.

The man's mouth opened and closed several times before he pointed to a shelf where a large veredium ring of keys hung on a hook.

"Sashi. Take those and release our friends." Rowena nodded toward the keys. After Sashi sprinted out the doorway with the keys, Rowena ground out, "Now, young man, if you desire to live through this day, you will answer me. And you will answer me honestly. Where are the other guards?"

"There … there ain't any. They been … been called away."

"Where is my sister?"

The man shook his head, backing away. "I don't know."

"Wrong answer." Rowena sent a pulse of energy into the man. He screamed, stumbled over his feet, and fell to the floor, sobbing.

"Please … please, my lady. I don't know. Please … don't hurt me."

Rowena growled and released a second pulse. The man screamed as Mite entered, supporting the heavy-set man from his cell.

"Your Majesty, he isn't lying. The guards don't know where the duchess is."

Rowena turned, clamping down on the fury burning within her, to face the stranger, her face set like stone. "And how would you know this if you have been a prisoner? Tell me. And if you lie to me, I promise you will feel worse pain than this idiot groveling on the floor."

"He is speaking the truth. The Binder escaped after last night's sacrifice and the Lady Mother went with Prime Shepherd Hamlin to find him."

"Don't call him Binder! His name is Rayne." Rowena clenched her fists and with an effort of will calmed enough to speak. "I assume Prime Shepherd Hamlin is the man who has been uniting the scroll worshipers?"

The man nodded.

"Tell me, who is this Lady Mother and what are these ... sacrifices you refer to?"

"Her Grace, Duchess Cailyn, is the Lady Mother. And ... the sacrifices ... we ... should talk about them after we've gotten away from here."

Rowena ground her teeth. "What have you done Sister?" She shook her head. "There is much I need to learn, and time is now my enemy. Is there a place where we can talk safely?"

"Your Majesty." Noah jogged in. "There's a common cell at the end of the hallway and there must be over two dozen people in there. Do you want me to release those prisoners?"

Rowena chewed her lower lip. "No, not yet. Not until I know what's going on."

"Your Majesty." Mite's cellmate gazed at her, sorrow creasing the skin around his eyes. "If you leave them, you condemn them to death. They have been imprisoned as future sacrifices."

"Please, please, Ray-ray's Mother. Must help others. Must. Must." Mite squirmed under the weight of the man he was supporting.

"Benning, help Mite. Noah, take Sashi with you, release any others who are imprisoned, and bring them here. Quickly!" Rowena turned back to the other prisoner while Noah and Sashi sprinted from the room. "What is your name?"

"Gwyn Thompson, Your Majesty."

"You appear to know much of what is happening here, Gwyn Thompson. Am I correct in thinking we are still in Castle Inverness?"

"Yes."

"I thought so. Cai and I used to play hide and seek in the abandoned dungeons. I see she's found a new use for them."

She turned to the guard cringing on the floor. "You will come with us. I'm not finished with you yet and I'm not leaving you here to sound an alarm."

Several minutes passed before Rowena heard the noise of a group moving toward them. Pulling in a sharp breath, she squared her shoulders and prepared to address the freed prisoners. A ragged looking group of individuals filed into the room.

"My people have released you. Are you willing to follow me, or would you prefer to seek freedom on your own?"

A large man with a patch over one eye grimaced. "And who be you?"

Noah glared at the man. "That's Her Majesty, Queen Rowena. So show some respect."

"Noah!" Sashi hissed.

"Sashi, it's all right. Whatever secrecy I might have had is gone now." Rowena faced the one-eyed man. "I am Rowena, Queen of Corylus and all Ochen. But what is more important right now, is that I'm the woman who is planning to escape from here and open the portals to Corylus. I need to know; will you follow me?"

With a rustle of clothing and suspicious eyes, the prisoners spread in front of the doorway, staring, quiet. The man with the eyepatch seemed to be their leader; the others kept looking to him.

Rowena maintained a cool eye contact with the man. "What's your name?"

Rather than answer her, the man spit, then asked his own question in a voice that sounded like grinding boulders. "So, you be the real queen or are you somethin' else?"

Without a word, Rowena pulled heavy magic to herself and created a tiny ball of sparking energy on her palm. The man's one eye widened and Rowena allowed a satisfied smirk to light her face. "I am Queen. And I am a Master Mage. Now, we will all fare better if we stick together."

After glancing at his companions, he returned his attention to Rowena. "My name be Bram and we be with you."

Rowena turned her focus to Noah. "Check for weapons. And hurry. Despite what this guard said, I suspect we won't be alone much longer."

Within minutes, Noah, Sashi, and Benning had located and distributed weapons among the prisoners. Although not everyone was armed, most now carried short swords, staffs, or short spears. Noah and Sashi both chose swords while Benning and Stevie wielded spears.

Rowena nodded her approval. "Noah, keep an eye on our prisoner. Mite, lead us somewhere we will be undisturbed while I try to figure out what to do next."

Mite conferred with Gwyn and within minutes was leading the group out through a side door. They hadn't gone far when they ran across a pair of guards, but Bram was quick to join Noah and Sashi in dispatching them.

"Try not to kill next time," Rowena whispered. "These are my people and I would prefer to save them if I can."

Bram's one eye glared at the queen. "Your people or no, you haven't seen what I've seen."

25

Rowena pulled the hood of her cloak down further over her face. Once they were beyond the castle walls, Mite set a rapid pace. All twenty-seven of the prisoners from the large cell followed, strung out behind Rowena, Sashi, Noah, Benning, and Gwyn as Mite led them down a hidden path in the woods behind Castle Inverness. Bram brought up the rear, angry and violent. Despite Rowena's request that they not take lives if possible, the man had killed several more guards as they made their way out of the castle. The sun had crossed its zenith and was lowering behind the massive evergreen trees that dominated the woods around Inverness, tinging the air with Nemora's distinctive blue light.

Rowena's breath caught in her throat when she realized where Mite was leading. The cottage was even more dilapidated than it was three years ago when Rayne led her and Theodor to this very place and explained how he woke up there after Sigmund forced his spirit into an old, frail body.

After Rayne accepted his calling as the One's Light Bringer, the demon planned to control him by placing his spirit within that sickly frame. But Sigmund failed. Rayne confronted him in the great Westvale Cathedral and, with the power of the One, bound Sigmund, the Demon Master, and their colleagues, banishing them from the worlds of Ochen.

Now, they were dealing with the aftermath of Sigmund's machinations. Labeling himself the High Guardian of the Scrolls, he had introduced the false religion of scroll worship onto all seven worlds, and despite the demon's defeat, the cult continued to flourish. Only now did Rowena realize how much.

Rowena's shoulders bunched when she entered the cottage. Taking note of the changes, she looked around in wonder. Though the outside of the building remained rundown, the interior was neat, clean, and well furnished with white-washed walls and heavy drapes covering the window. Several lanterns sat on three tables placed around the room. Gwyn sent Benning to fetch a flint from the fireplace mantel and light them.

"Mite leads right. He does. He does." The little ancient looked up to Gwyn with a huge smile.

"Yes, he does." Gwyn nodded. He turned to Rowena and gave a short bow. "It will be a little tight with everyone in here, but it will be safe for now."

"What is this place?" Rowena mumbled.

"It used to belong to some old man. I guess he died." Gwyn scanned the room.

"I know that." Rowena bristled. "Probably know more about that than you do. I mean, what is it used for now?"

"It is a place where many who work at the castle come to worship the One and read his Words in peace."

While Gwyn was speaking a rumble sounded beneath Rowena's feet, vibrating the floorboards. As she watched, a tingle running up her arms, a trap door in the floor opened and a middle-aged woman peeked out. Her eyes grew round as she caught sight of the group, she let out a squeak, and attempted to drop the door. Noah was quicker and grabbed the woman's arm, dragging her up into the cottage. The flustered woman took one look at Rowena and dropped to her knees. "Your Majesty! Oh, Your Majesty. It's true. You are here. We were praying you would come."

"Who are you?" Rowena took in the apron and clothing as she stepped back to allow the woman room. "You work in the castle, don't you?"

Several other voices sounded from the open trap door and a man's head, haloed with a frizz of white hair, appeared. "Lorilee, Lorilee are you all—" The man's eyes rounded in a mirror image of Lorilee's a moment earlier.

"Sebastian?" Rowena released a small portion of the tension squeezing her chest. "Oh, thank the One. Someone with sense. Get up here Sebastian and tell me what is happening here."

Noah reached down and helped the elderly man up into the room. A young man who looked to be about twenty followed and with a quick movement slipped in front of Sebastian saying, "Leave my grandfather alone. He knows nothing."

Ignoring him, Noah scanned the opening. "There's a group of people down there, Your Majesty. What do you want me to do?"

Rowena pursed her lips and considered for a moment. "Go down and ask them to wait, Noah. I need to talk to Sebastian."

Sebastian grabbed the young man's arm, pulling his attention away from Rowena. "Relax, my boy. These are not enemies; this is the queen." He moved to kneel, but Rowena stopped him with a frown and a wave of her hand.

"We don't have time for formalities." Rowena motioned to a chair at one of the tables. Groaning her frustration with the whole situation, she glared at the others crowded into the small dwelling. "All of you, find a place to sit and settle for the moment. After I've talked with Sebastian, I want to hear your stories."

Bram bristled, releasing a loud huff through clenched teeth as the others squeezed into places on the floor. "This is a waste of time. I'm leaving."

Stevie moved to block the man as Rowena said, "No. You're staying right where you are. Until I know more about what is going on here, no one is leaving." Though her words were spoken in a soft tone, their authority rang through the room. With a snarl, Bram lowered himself to the ground. Benning, tall and threatening, hovered near the man, one hand gripping the spear he had taken, the other pushing the captured guard down to a sitting position next to Bram.

Once everyone was settled, Rowena glanced at Gwyn and Mite. "Mite, bring your friend and come join us."

With a curse Bram jumped up. "This man is a scroll worshiper. One of them that came to choose who was gonna be sacrificed." He pointed at Gwyn.

"No. No. No." Mite spread his hands, palms out in a pacifying gesture. "Scroll man not scroll man any longer. He now worships the One. He does. He does. Scroll man was to be offered to darkness. Now he helps Mite. He does."

Bram reached for his sword, but Benning raised his spear, blocking the move. "Her Majesty told you to sit. Please?" Benning stared at the man, his face cool and unthreatening, yet there must have been something in his eyes because Bram took a step back and sat.

Interesting. Rowena looked at the young soldier with new respect. "Thank you, Benning.

"Bram, I promise we will get to the bottom of this. Just be patient. Now, let's get started." Rowena pulled in a deep breath and prepared herself to set aside her motherly fear until she gained the information Theodor would need to address the issue surrounding the scroll worshipers. But, before she could begin, Noah emerged from the trap door and made his way around the people scattered on the floor. "Your Majesty, the people below are all servants from the castle. They claim they need to get back to their duties before they are missed."

She glanced at Sebastian who nodded. "Your man speaks the truth, if we do not return soon, our absence will be noticed."

Her brow crinkling, Rowena thought for a few seconds. "Is there anyone who can stay to answer my questions?"

A smile split Sebastian's face as he nodded. "I can, Your Majesty. I'm old now and don't have many duties. Please if you let the others return to Castle Inverness, I'll be most happy to answer any questions you have."

"Noah." Rowena's focus shifted back. "Go down and tell them they can leave. But make certain they understand that they are to speak to no one about what they've seen here. Tell them it's my specific order. Then, have them come up in ones and twos and leave the cottage." Shifting her gaze to Sashi. "Sashi, You're in charge of the door. See to it that only one or two leave at a time."

The servants filtered out the trap door and through the cottage while Rowena continued conducting her investigation. Forty minutes later she shook her head at what she was learning.

Not quite two years ago, within weeks of Miles's suicide, Prime Shepherd Seth Hamlin of the United Scrolls of Ochen met with Duchess Cailyn for the first time. Over the next year, he returned several times, bringing small numbers of scroll worshipers with him. Almost ten months ago, he moved into the castle. In the last six-months, cult members began skipping to Nemora in the hundreds and Duchess Cailyn declared that scroll worship would be the only religion recognized at the castle. Anybody still worshiping the One would be banished. Several weeks later, Duchess Cailyn made the announcement that the United Scrolls of Ochen was the official religion of Nemora.

Though the scroll worshipers set up a camp outside Inverness early on, by the time Seth Hamlin moved into the castle, many had already scattered throughout Nemora. Rowena's anxiety spiked another notch when she learned that the United Scrolls of Ochen now boasted an army numbering near three thousand currently training at the Inverness camp. *What are they planning? I need to get word to Theo. Now! We knew they were up to something, but this? Beyond what we could imagine.*

But fear and a growing sense of Rayne's peril sent a shiver through Rowena's spirit when Sebastian mentioned human sacrifices.

"We were led to believe the scroll worshipers didn't believe in sacrifices," Rowena whispered, fear squeezing her throat. "What changed?"

"Well, we don't rightly know," Sebastian said. "Almost

two months ago, the United Scrolls of Ochen claimed control of the skipping lines. That's when people started disappearing."

"That's when we called into the void for the High Guardian of the Scrolls." Gwyn's voice was soft and burdened with remorse. He shook his head. "Oh, what have we done?"

Ice gathered in Rowena's veins as she lifted her eyes to the ex-scroll worshiper. "Yes. Tell me, what have you done? And what does this have to do with my son?"

Mite reached across the table and rested his small hand on Gwyn's thick, blocky fingers. "Gwyn must tell Ray-ray's mother. Must tell all. He must. He must."

Rowena watched the exchange, already preparing. Every instinct within her screamed out that it was going to be bad and she swallowed hard, steeling her emotions. "Tell me everything."

Gwyn met her eyes for a second before lowering his gaze to the table where he scratched at the rough wood with a broken nail. "You already heard how large groups began coming to Nemora about six months ago. But Seth's—Prime Shepherd Hamlin's—plans started long before then. Seth and I had been friends for, oh my," he sighed, "almost forty years. When he first accepted scroll worship as the true religion of Ochen, I followed without hesitation. He's that kind of person, you know. Someone you admire without even thinking about it; a natural leader. I won't lie to you. You need to know I was his second in command, Senior Associate Shepherd, so you'll understand I was a part of all that happened."

Bram released a hiss and started to rise but Rowena stopped him with a wave of her hand and a commanding glance. "Stay. I need to hear this."

Gwyn met Rowena's gaze as her eyes caught hold of his, and he nodded. "I know. That's not what you want to hear." He cleared his throat, his eyes drawn down to his hands again. He pulled in a deep breath and released it in a slow huff.

"In the last year, Seth changed. We were together on Arisima when he got the idea for the first sacrifice. A sacrifice made to call out to the High Guardian of the Scrolls. He had already formed the United Scrolls of Ochen and said this was the next step in reclaiming the true scrolls. I don't know where he learned that he could reach into the void and communicate with the High Guardian, but he had very specific instructions. At that time, I, like every other scroll worshiper, believed the Binder—I'm sorry, Prince Rayne—had imprisoned our High Guardian in the void as an attack on us so we couldn't threaten the Church of the One.

"Seth said we needed to gather on Nemora because the Stone of Sacrifice is here. By that time Duchess Cailyn had become a follower and she was willing to do whatever Seth asked."

Gwyn hesitated, his mouth twisting as if he had just eaten something bitter, his hands trembling with nervous energy. He raised watery eyes to Rowena. "She hates the prince. Filled with anger for the deaths of her son and husband. She was pleased to cooperate with the kidnapping and his ... ongoing sacrifice."

"My sister? She knows where Rayne is? Was involved in what's happened to him?"

Gwyn nodded.

Rowena closed her eyes, pain stabbing her heart. "Okay. Cai's in this with Prime Shepherd Hamlin. So, tell me about this ... ongoing sacrifice. What is that?"

"The first sacrifice was successful. The High Guardian appeared and Seth spoke with him. He told us there was a way to recover our lost scrolls, but it involved seven weeks of sacrifices. Each week, on Binding Day, a sacrifice must be offered; one human the first week, two the second, up to the seventh week when seven humans would be sacrificed as the final offering."

"How does Rayne figure into this?" Rowena's voice came out in a strained whisper.

Gwyn shook his head, breathing hard. "The words spoken by the High Guardian were ... they were ... 'Blood for blood; blood for power; blood for vengeance. So you proclaim, so shall it be. Potent blood must be shed. Costly blood. The light-infused blood of the Binder himself. It must be commingled with that of those sacrificed each Binding Day. Seven rites of sacrifice, seven weeks. For seven weeks, he must live in darkness and silence, and in darkness shall he die at the end. His life-blood shall be the final sacrifice. This is the offering you must make to gain your scrolls. Only through blood and pain will their power be returned to Ochen.'"

Gwyn shuddered and went quiet.

Rowena's world shrank into a pinprick of pain that then exploded through her spirit, leaving her shattered and numb. No one spoke for several minutes until with a gasp and a cry Rowena stood. "We must put a stop this. Where is my son?"

"He's gone." The bound guard's voice sounded from his position on the floor as his eyes met Rowena's, a look of pure misery on his face. "That's what all the commotion was about. Why there was only a couple of us left to watch you. We was so close, only two more sacrifices and then this had to happen. Why can't you One worshipers just leave us alone?"

Loathing set Rowena's blood to boiling, drawing her lips taut and her eyebrows down in anger. "We leave you alone? My son is hurt and missing because you didn't leave him alone. How dare you! How dare you! You're lucky I don't just let Bram loose on you right now."

She took a step toward the man and bent to meet his eyes. "In fact, you will tell me everything you know, or I will leave you and Bram alone in this cottage until he tells me you're ready to talk to me. Do you understand?"

The man's face went white, but with a snarl, he spit at Rowena's feet. Bram let a curse fly and pushed up while Noah and Benning both pulled weapons.

"Okay, okay," the man called out, cowering at Rowena's feet. "We was at the sacrifice night before last, the one after that traitor left us." He pointed at Gwyn, glaring despite his position on the floor. "All was goin' just like Prime Shepherd Hamlin said. We could feel the air get heavy and we knew the High Guardian was close. It was a good sacrifice, just like the High Guardian asked. Five humans and the blood of the Binder. After it was done, the guards took the Binder, just like always. But then while Prime Shepherd Hamlin was talkin' Arnulf came runnin' back sayin' somebody took the Binder. Prime Shepherd Hamlin went red to bust a gut and started shoutin' for things to happen. He ordered Captain Theada to lead a bunch of soldiers to secure the portal. Then told Associate Shepherd Creedoff to gather men; said he and the Lady Mother were going to go with Arnulf and Associate Shepherd Creedoff was to follow. If we lost the Binder, we wouldn't be able to free the High Guardian of the scrolls.

"It's his fault we lost our scrolls in the first place. He needs to pay." The guard's eyes grew glassy. "Blood for blood. Blood for power. Blood for vengeance." His chant started out soft but as it increased in volume, Bram roared and jumped on the man, punching his face again and again until Benning and Noah pulled him off.

26

Lexi bit back the impatience that threatened to rub her nerves raw. The impulse to pull up and scream for Mayda and Andrew to tell her what they knew flooded her. She swallowed the scream. The need to keep moving overrode her need for information; only speed would help find Rayne now. But she wanted answers from Andrew and his little, scroll-loving friend in the worst way. Even with the need to move quickly pressing down on them, the dark forest hemming in the path they followed slowed their progress. Lexi ground her teeth as their trot was slowed to a walk once again.

"How much farther?" she called out to Mayda.

"We're almost to the Sacrifice Stone," the girl hissed back.

"What then, Thorvin?" Lexi's eyes went to the dark form riding before her.

The barely visible head shook from side to side. "We try to pick up the trail. I hope you're right Andrew, and that hound can track Rayne even if he's on horseback."

"She can do it," Andrew said, rubbing his eyes. "We used to play this game back in the King's Park, Seek with Boone. No matter where Rayne hid—and sometimes he'd even sneak back into the palace—how long we waited to seek, or what horse he rode, Boone always found him. I don't know how she does it; I guess they just have a special bond."

Ledia emerged from the cloud cover as they approached the altar, large, purple, and almost full, tinging everything with her blue rays, while Rem's softer silver presence angled beams across the tops of trees. Lexi shivered. She jumped from her horse and approached the stone. Her stomach attempted an upward revolt as she moved through the energy-laden air, her feet leaving prints in the dew-wet grass. Thorvin's strong presence next to her grounded her in reality as her eyes took in the still glistening, bloody Sacrifice Stone. She thought she heard Rayne calling and her skin pimpled. She opened her mouth to answer, but the sensation of Rayne's presence vanished. She swallowed down her call.

"Is that ... Rayne's blood?" Soft as a gentle breeze her question was whispered on a puff of breath.

Andrew came up on Lexi's other side. "Yeah." His whisper matched Lexi's in airy dismay. "At least some of it is."

Boone ran around the base of the altar, her nose low, skimming the trampled grass and blood. She began whining, a pitiful sound that drew a burning lump up Lexi's throat.

"We can't waste time here." Even Thorvin's gravelly voice sounded thick in the shadowy air. "Get Boone to follow Rayne, Andrew. Do what you need to. Make her 'seek'."

"Just give her a few minutes," Andrew said as his eyes tracked the circling dog.

"Tell me, please, while Boone is ... tell me. Rayne ... how bad is it?" Lexi turned to face Andrew. The blood, there was so much. Her visions of Rayne and the darkness almost drove her to her knees.

Andrew just shook his head and his lack of words drove the knife of fear deeper into Lexi's heart.

"He was part of the sacrifice," Mayda's soft voice broke the silence. "Supposed to live in darkness and add his blood to each of the sacrifices until the seventh and last one. Then he was supposed to die which would open the way for the High Guardian of the Scrolls to return with the true scrolls of power.

But it was wrong. Whatever that thing is my pa and the others were calling, it was wrong, dark, terrifying."

Lexi saw the look of fear overtake Mayda's face. But Mayda continued speaking, her voice soft and breaking with sorrow. "He's alive. They had to keep him alive until the end. That was part of the deal. But he's sick now, weak, and they've been giving him Ferris Weed so he can't glow or anything."

Lexi's knees gave out and she sank into the damp grass just as Boone lifted her head and voiced a mournful howl. Then Boone raced into the surrounding trees.

Thorvin reached out to Lexi, pulling her to her feet. "Horses. Now."

They scrambled to mount and took off following the swift shadowy form that raced after her master. Boone moved like an arrow in flight across the glen and into the woods.

"Andrew," Thorvin called. "You have to get Boone to slow down. We can't follow her through these trees in the dark at this pace. We'll lose her."

Andrew whistled to the dog and after several tries, she bounded back to him, whining and barking. "I know, Boone, I know. But we can't follow you like this." He dismounted and clipped the leather lead onto Boone's collar. "I'll hold onto her. We won't be as fast, but we won't lose her this way."

The word 'seek' was barely out of Andrew's mouth when Boone took off, dragging the boy behind.

Two hours later, Boone slowed and circled in a spot by a stream where lush, green moss was matted down and hoof prints had torn up the soft soil and small plants. Thorvin dismounted with Lexi and Mayda following. Lexi took the reins to Thorvin's horse and tramped behind Mayda who led her horse and Andrew's to the water for a drink.

Boone seemed to find what she was looking for and began pulling Andrew, but he tugged her to the water. "Come on Boone, we need to take a break. We'll keep going. I promise."

The dog turned her soft eyes up at the boy and whined, but then trotted into the stream and began lapping water. Mayda opened her pack and pulled out a packet of dried meat. She handed a few strips to Andrew who gave a piece to Boone.

"Lexi," she touched Lexi's arm. Lexi pulled her arm back and scowled at the girl before turning her attention back to Thorvin who was stooping, studying the moss and broken ground, his expression intense.

Her brow darkening, Mayda thrust the dried meat forward again. "Here. You need to eat."

Lexi shook her head.

"Don't be stupid," Mayda said. "You can't keep going without eating.

Lexi's cold eyes met Mayda's and she shook her head again, then walked to Thorvin. "What do you see?"

"There were two or three horses here first. Two bodies laid down here in the moss." He pointed at two slight depressions in the damp growth. "At least I think so. Other horses' hooves have trampled the area. One horse went that way." He pointed downstream, to the south. "Two went that way." He pointed upstream. "The three that followed must be Prime Shepherd Hamlin, the Lady Mother, and their people ... hum ... it looks like they started to go south, but something turned them around." He moved up the stream a short distance. "Yeah, they followed the two horses north."

He paced back and forth a few times, then said, "If Boone is right, and Rayne headed south, we might be able to catch up to him before Hamlin figures out his mistake and turns around." He nodded as if he came to a decision. "Lexi, Mayda's right. Take some of that jerky. You can eat it in the saddle." He reached out to Mayda who handed him several strips, then he said, "Andrew, you and Boone ready to go again or do you need to rest more? Sun'll be rising soon."

Boone yipped when she heard her name and strained against the lead, pulling south. "Well, I don't know about me," Andrew said. "But Boone is ready."

Mayda again offered Lexi some of the dried beef. Lexi sighed but took a couple leathery strips. As she moved to mount, once again she felt Rayne's presence. It was so soft and weak, but it was as certain as the blue streamers of Ledia's light now skimming through the trees and blending with the silver light of Rem. "I'm coming, Rayne," She murmured into the night air.

Lexi chewed her lip as she filled their water skins at yet another tree-shrouded brook. The water sparkled like silver jewels in filtered beams of sunlight while a cool morning breeze caught the branches of a weeping willow that shadowed the stream causing the sparkles to disappear and reappear. She would have thought how beautiful it was if she wasn't so exhausted. Their path had continued almost due south for the last three days and though they had all expected to catch up to Rayne by now, they still trailed behind. Close but distant. His presence within her wavered, coming and going like the shimmers on the stream.

Raising her eyes, she caught sight of Andrew and Mayda, each holding a small net, trying to catch some fish. The supply of jerky was almost gone, and they had run out of travel cakes yesterday. Though they rebelled at losing the time, the horses needed to rest and eat, and so did they. Thorvin had vanished nearly a half-hour ago, stalking off and grumbling about finding game to hunt.

"We're on the border of Neth here. Once we enter those woods, there will be no hunting," he said after insisting they take this time to rest and eat before entering the infamous forest.

Boone lay with her eyes fixed to the south as she licked her paws. Andrew had tied her to a tree; if he hadn't, she would keep going. Even now, Lexi could see the tension in her muscles and the focus of her unwavering eyes.

27

Oliver and Benning waited, like deeper shades within shadows, beneath the overhang of an old brownstone inn a block from the Inverness Portal Station. They scanned the line of United Scrolls of Ochen soldiers standing guard, questioning those who entered the station. Any who wandered too close to the line of nervous scroll worshipers were harassed and sent away. The two soldiers huddled against the rough exterior seeking shelter from a misty rain as they studied the guards.

Intermittent drops of collected moisture dribbled from the overhang above the large window Rowena watched through as she sat at a well-polished table in the Blue Moon Tavern. Her eyes flicked back and forth between Benning and Oliver and the soldiers. Shaw's voice pulled her attention back to Anne and Shaw sitting across from her. She couldn't suppress the smile that surfaced as Little Jonathan waved a hand at his mother's face.

"We never imagined we would find you here in town," Anne said as she wiggled her thumb for Jonathan's chubby little fingers to wrap around. "We thought for sure you were still at the castle."

"I was wondering how I would ever find you in that massive camp when Benning pointed you out coming toward us." Rowena's gaze wandered back out the window to observe Mite approach Benning and Oliver.

"Thorvin told us to find you if he didn't return last night. We almost waited another day; I'm glad we didn't," Shaw said. "It was providential that Oliver and Benning saw each other when they did, otherwise we would have continued up to Castle Inverness and missed you."

"If you went to the castle, the servants would have let you know where I was. I planned to send Sebastian to find you tomorrow, but I couldn't wait any longer to send word to Theodor. Are you certain you're comfortable with this plan?"

Shaw turned to Anne. "Are you?"

She nodded. "We will be fine. No one will suspect us as long as we have Little Jonathan. But ... are you confident you and Mite will be able to switch the Corylus portal to inbound exactly forty-eight hours after we skip to Sorial?"

Rowena sighed. "If all goes as planned, yes. Both Mite and I are fully recovered from the Ferris Weed. With how potent the energy is here now, I should have no problem pulling enough to me and funneling it to Mite so he can construct an illusion. It will be a tight window, but once Theodor and the soldiers begin to skip in, we can release the illusion magic. They can overcome the guards and keep the portal open. I just hope Theo has enough soldiers in Westvale to pull this off in two days."

"He was keeping a large contingent available in Westvale in case they were needed, wasn't he?" Shaw asked, shifting his focus from his son to Rowena.

"Yes, but we never expected the number of scroll worshipers here to be so great. Or, that they would be building an army. But at this point, we have no other option except a show of force. I pray they choose to surrender rather than fight. The thought of our people killing each other because of this cult sickens me. Discovering the truth that these scroll worshipers have already been using human sacrifices to summon the bound demons back to Ochen horrifies me even more."

Shaw looked away and sniffed. "You haven't asked if we learned anything about Rayne."

Anne shook her head at Shaw and Rowena caught the expression of censure on her face. "Don't ... you don't have to hide anything from me. I heard enough to know he's been part of these sacrifices. But I also know he's still alive. When Theo arrives, we'll go after him. I hate waiting; with every hour that passes I feel him getting farther from me, and my ability to sustain my composure weakens. As queen of Ochen I have no choice. I pray for my son continually, a nonstop litany to the One. And yet my duty compels me to remain here for now."

"We have prayed and will continue to pray as well, Your Majesty," Anne said, her voice soft with compassion.

Mite slipped onto the bench next to Rowena. "Benning sent Mite. It is time. Scroll people guard is changing." He focused his bright gray eyes on Shaw and Anne. "Friends ready? Must go now. Take Little Jonathan and go now, now, now. Go to Westvale."

Rowena shut out the growing pain in her heart as they left the Blue Moon Tavern. She turned to Anne and took the baby from her arms, kissed him, and with a smile that tore at the edges of her heart, she blinked back threatening tears. She handed Jonathan to Shaw and hugged Anne close.

Shaw gave Jonathan to Anne. Rowena hugged Shaw, stepped away, and nodded. "Be safe."

"We will. We'll be just fine. A quick skip to Sorial then on to Corylus." Shaw nodded, blinking back his own tears.

"You'll find him," Anne whispered, meeting Rowena's eyes. "I know you'll find Rayne. Then we'll celebrate with Rayne and Lexi's long-awaited wedding. Trust, Rowena. It will happen."

They said goodbye to Mite then moved toward the shifting line of USO soldiers and the portal station. After allowing some distance between, Rowena and Mite followed. They had no plans to interfere with Shaw and Anne's skip unless they got into trouble. And, as they listened from a position across the street from Benning and Oliver, the guard waved Shaw and

Anne into the station. Their story that Anne's mother was sick worked. Soon now, Anne, Shaw, and little baby Jonathan would be back on Corylus. Things would be set in motion.

Only two days. Just two days and your father and I will come for you my son. Rowena swiped at the tears that tracked down her cheeks after Anne and Shaw disappeared through the doorway into the station. "Be safe," she whispered. She looked down at Mite. "Are you ready for the next phase?"

"Mite's ready. Always ready to help Ray-ray and Ray-ray's mother."

Rowena signaled to Benning with a shift of her head, then, sticking to the shadows, headed back toward the castle with Mite, Benning, and Oliver following.

The burden of her anxiety pressed down on Rowena. Like a heavy, coiling serpent it rested deep inside, slowing her, turning her muscles to lead weights. With deep breaths she continued to set one foot in front of the other. *Please, keep Anne, Shaw, and Jonathan safe. And please bring Theo through in time.*

Bram jumped up the moment Rowena walked through the door to the small cottage. "Well, did they make it? Is help coming?"

Rowena sighed. The man was annoying. She wasn't certain if his words were said with mocking disdain or real hope and she wished for a task she could send him to complete. She dreaded the next two days, trapped in this room with the impatient, irritating man. Then it hit her; Bram's plan to destroy the scroll worshipers' weapons, if synced with Theodor's arrival would be the perfect distraction. She balked at the thought of Bram, worrying her lower lip as she considered her options. *Bram's strength and knowledge would be needed to pull it off; but who to send with him? Should I go myself?* She shook her head. *Mite and I can aid ... no. We must conserve our strength to take over the portal station for Theo's arrival.*

"Benning," Rowena called. She hesitated then called Bram as well. Walking to the far corner of the room where they wouldn't be interrupted, Rowena eyed the two men, still questioning her decision to include Bram. He was so unpredictable and violent. Once again, she sighed and resigned herself to the fact that he was what she had to work with. But Benning would keep the man from unnecessary violence, as long as he followed orders. And she'd send Stevie as well. He had developed a good relationship with Benning.

"Bram. I instructed you several times to avoid killing whenever possible. You have disregarded that order. If I send you on a mission with the direct command to obey Benning and follow his orders, will you control your impulses?"

Bram's one eye glinted and he clenched his jaw. "It depends, *Your Highness*. What might ye be askin'?"

Laying her doubts aside, Rowena said, "Benning, Bram, how do you feel about destroying the USO's weapons supply before King Theodor arrives?"

"What do you have in mind, Your Majesty?" Benning asked, a crooked grin lighting his face.

"Bram. You said you know the layout of the scroll worshiper's camp. How accessible is this weapons' stash you planned to destroy before you were caught?"

A sly smile surfaced on Bram's face and he nodded. "Ye be clever asking me this. It's been a dream I've tended for weeks now. Just let me confer with me friends and we'll take good care o that. I had a good plan in place and it won't take much to put it back in motion."

A stern look flattened Rowena's lips and she stared at Bram for several long seconds before releasing a huff and saying, "I, by the power that rests in me as Queen of all Ochen, do hereby press you into my service until such time as your assistance is no longer required."

Bram snorted, and the muscles of his jaw bunched, but Rowena ignored his discomfort. "You will work with Benning and Stevie ... and ... you will obey Benning without question or I will personally see you punished for disobedience. Now, collect your friends and wait outside. Benning will join you shortly."

Bram stormed across the room to where the group from the cells sat. He pointed at two men and one woman who then followed him out the door.

Rowena turned her attention back to Benning, once again

sizing up the young soldier. "You can keep a lid on him, can't you?"

He nodded.

"Good. Take Oliver and Stevie with you. I need this completed before we go to the station in two days. We must be there when King Theodor skips. Mite and I need to set the illusion and open the skipping line. If the weapons can't be destroyed in the allotted time, forget them and return here. Allowing King Theodor access to Nemora is my number one priority. Destruction of those weapons is a worthless goal if our army can't take advantage of it."

"Yes, very good, Your Majesty." Benning bowed, then waving for Oliver and Stevie to follow, left the cottage.

"This is a difficult decision for you, to remain here while your son is in danger." Gwyn stepped to Rowena before lowering his eyes to the floor. "Please tell me what I can do to help you. I need a task to distract me from my guilt."

Rowena turned cold eyes on the man. "What makes you think I would do anything to assuage your guilt. If you want to do something, kneel and pray for forgiveness. And stay away from me."

Mite had come up to Rowena unnoticed and reached for her hand, wrapping his small fingers around hers. A shiver ran up her spine as memories of Rayne's fingers laced in hers surfaced. He had been so young and trusting. Her own guilt rose, sending ribbons of remorse to tighten her throat and bring tears to her eyes. How could she condemn Gwyn when she had allowed Brayden to abuse Rayne for years? *I'm no different.* She swallowed a rising sob.

"It's okay," Mite murmured. "Ray-ray forgave the past long, long ago."

Her choked sob turned into a full cry. "How? How could you know what I was thinking?"

"Mite feels things. Feels Ray-ray's mother's pain. Do not be afraid. Creator-Father holds his Light Bringer near." Mite patted Rowena's hand. "Creator-Father always with Light Bringer. Ray-ray never alone. Mother will see. Yes, she will … she … will. Mite too. Mite must trust though it is hard. It is. It is."

226

Rowena nodded, pulling in a deep breath, stilling her rampaging emotions. "Thank you, Mite. I guess we both need to be reminded to trust." She turned to Gwyn. "I know you are sorry for your past actions. I know this. But letting go of my anger ... that doesn't come easily. It will take time. Tell me how you came to be a scroll worshiper. Perhaps that will help me to understand why all these people have turned to this false religion."

28

Falling. Panic shot through Rayne and he bolted upright, flinging his arms out, his eyes snapping open with force. A groan rose, seeking to burst through parched lips, but he clamped his mouth shut, trapping it inside. He blinked, burning, crusty eyes wandering. *Where am I?* Blue-tinged light filtered in past white curtains rustling in a soft breeze at a window. *So familiar. Safe.* Releasing his tenuous hold on consciousness, he collapsed back onto the soft bed.

Voices flitted through the fog of Rayne's mind. *Past? Present?* He didn't know. Couldn't seem to find any solid place to settle his thoughts. Need, vast and demanding flooded through him. *The tincture.* The hold it had on him terrified Rayne, but the insistent pain coursing through him wouldn't let go. He needed the relief of oblivion.

The voices returned. There was something so familiar about them. *Who?* They weren't dark and full of menace like the voices that had haunted him in the black pit. *Where am I?* He groaned and struggled to pry open eyelids that resisted the effort as if they had been glued together.

"... still can't believe we made it."

Giles?

"We are most gladdened thou hast come. The young Light Bringer is dear to our hearts here. To think anyone would harm him so, sets my blood to boiling."

"Elspeth?" Rayne croaked the name as peace flooded through him. He was in Neth. He was with friends.

"Thou art awake." Elspeth's round, compassion-filled face hovered over Rayne. "My heart is gladdened to see thee."

Rayne reached up and ran the tips of his fingers over her cheek as he blinked back burning tears.

"Rayne." Giles's face came into view followed by Ean's. "I was worried. You wouldn't wake up. Even when Fallon and his people insisted they carry you into Neth, and we let the horse go, you slept like you were dead."

"We have been praying most earnestly for thee," Ean said, a smile lighting up his round face as he placed a very familiar tray on the small table to Rayne's right.

Rayne nodded. "It hurts." A soft sob broke through his reserve.

"I know, my young friend." Elspeth's face wrinkled with sorrow as she patted his arm. "Try to rest easy now. Ean and I have brewed up a tea laced with herbs to help thee cope with the pain. Ferris Weed is most addictive but not impossible to leech from the system. T'would be best to sleep through the pain and the tea will make thee drowsy."

With Giles's assistance, Ean fluffed a couple pillows, set them behind Rayne's back, and helped him into an upright position so he could drink. Despite the bone-aching pain, Rayne relaxed into the warm comfort of the soft pillows and the safety of being among his friends in Neth.

As conversation ebbed and flowed around him, Rayne let his mind drift back to the last time he had seen Giles; the day the One bound the living darkness using Rayne as his conduit of power. Giles had stood with Brayden at that final confrontation, siding with Sigmund and the Demon Master before disappearing. An enemy. Now he stood by the open window, here in the Kindred's House of Healing, speaking with Elspeth and Ean in low voices. A friend.

What do I do with that? And Marius ... Do I have to forgive them too, Lord?

Deep warmth of the One's presence flooded Rayne. His eyelids grew too heavy to hold up any longer. He succumbed to the unrelenting call of sleep.

When Rayne awoke, night had fallen and other than the sounds of insects and the rustling of leaves outside his window, all was silent. A slight breeze set the white curtains at the window to billowing inward, bringing with it the scent of pine needles and the earthy smell of mushrooms.

Rayne sighed and stretched, his back, arm, and leg muscles contracting then releasing, eliciting a deeper sigh. He pulled in a gasp of air. Every movement was free of pain and easy. He blinked his eyes open. Though a haze seemed to blanket his sight, the crusty residue left by the Ferris Weed and weeks in darkness was gone. A stiff bulk at his neck drew his fingers up to explore the edges of a thick, wide bandage before scratching at the fabric.

Wide awake, he pushed to a full sitting position, swung his legs over the side of the bed, and planted his feet on the smooth wood floor. Drawing in a slow breath, he pushed upright. A muted chuckle slipped past his lips as he walked to the window, his body strong, a soft, multi-hued glow radiating from his arms illuminating the darkness around him. He brushed aside the dancing curtains and drew in another deep breath of sweet, fresh air. He released it through an open mouth then just stood without thought or motion. The blue-tinged light of Nemora's moon nourished his spirit and he breathed out a groan at the joy filling him.

The need to be under the open sky mingled with an internal pressure to pray prompted him to turn and scan the room, eyes searching for clothing. Nothing. Running his hands down the front of the simple, white sleeping gown, he chuckled. "I've dressed in worse," he murmured into the quiet.

Moving with cat-like grace, he padded down the hallway and out the front door into the beckoning moonlight. Skirting the building, Rayne picked his way down to the edge of the lake, where he stood for a moment, scrutinizing the surrounding woods.

Tendrils of anger slipped through his mind. The One had not been in that dark hole with Rayne as he grew sicker and weaker. His internal battle sought release through words whispered into the wisps of fog rising from the lake. "Why?" Rayne swallowed hard. "Why didn't you stop what was happening? I know how strong you are. You could have stopped what they did to me, how they used my blood in their summoning sacrifices. By the seven, they're actually trying to bring Sigmund back. Where were you? Why did you leave me?"

In the distance, a bullfrog rumbled. The breeze ruffled the surface of the lake setting the moonlight to dancing in flickering sparkles. Rayne stood silent for a minute, two, waiting. Nothing. He pulled in a deep breath, a scream hovering. He closed his mouth, then his eyes. Like a sigh, the whisper rode his breath through his lips. "You didn't leave me, though, did you? You were with me the whole time."

Warmth flooded Rayne's spirit and, the wordless voice within him spoke. *I promised I would never leave you or forsake you. Do you believe this?*

"Yes ... yes." Rayne's gaze drifted over the lake as a sob died in his chest. "I believe you always keep your promises. But ... I felt so alone. Why?"

For an instant, Rayne was back in the small, chill-inducing room, staring down at his own form, curled on the hard floor. But he wasn't alone, around his shivering body hovered a glowing presence.

Do you believe? the voice whispered within Rayne.

"How?"

You closed yourself to me when you embraced the effects of the Ferris Weed, my child. But even then, I held you.

The present flooded back around Rayne and he stumbled at the sudden shift. Unable to speak, he nodded. Soft night sounds filled the air, insects, leaves rustling, the lake lapping. Rayne dropped to his knees, praying. When he again opened his eyes, the first rays of sunlight were skimming the now mirror-like surface of the lake. He shuddered at the thought of what the One was asking of him, but rising, he squared his shoulders and returned to his room in the House of Healing.

"You want to what?" Giles sputtered, droplets of tea scattering in the air before him. For a moment his eyes went wide, then they narrowed in anger. "Marius was right. You are insane. I risked my life to get you away from those lunatic scroll lovers and you want to go back? No. No. I didn't save you only to help you get yourself killed. You must have misunderstood. There has to be another way."

Rayne met Fallon's eyes before lowering his gaze to the table while the fingers of his right hand traced the fine scar on his cheek. He knew what Giles was saying made sense ... from a human perspective. He needed to give Giles time to vent. And Fallon's thoughts were a mystery. The Kindred hadn't yet spoken his opinion.

"Tell me again," Giles said. "Tell me just what it is the One expects you to do."

Rayne raised his focus to impale Giles's angry eyes. "Go for a walk."

"What?"

"You heard me, Giles. Go for a walk and cool down. When you are ready to listen, then we can talk. Until then, my words will make no sense to you."

"At your command, *Your Highness*." Giles snapped out the words as he rose and gave a mocking bow then stormed out the door.

A half-smile lifted one side of Rayne's mouth. "He has grown some backbone."

"Perhaps he is correct," Fallon mused, his eyes pinning Rayne. "Thou wast close to death when we found thee. Is it truly wise to expose thyself to capture once again?"

Rayne dropped his face into his hands, then ran his fingers back through his midnight black hair as he released a quiet sigh. "Perhaps not, Fallon, but I will not disobey the Creator–Father." He lifted his head and met Fallon's gaze. "Believe me, I was angry and terrified last night when he told me to go preach to the Scroll Worshipers. I wanted to tell him no, I can't do it. Facing them again is the last thing I want to do."

Rayne's gaze shifted away, his eyes unfocused. "But I won't deny his calling on my life. He reminded me in no uncertain terms that I am to bring light into dark places and right now those Scroll Worshipers are living in the darkness Sigmund planted years ago. They need to be set free. I've done it before …"

The memory drew the fingers of his right hand back up to the thin scar he had earned with a prior attempt to preach on Arisima. He shook his head and allowed the sour repugnance inhabiting him to twist his mouth in disgust. "But now … after … those horrible sacrifices, the black hole, Ferris Weed …" His voice faded to a faint whisper. "I'm just so tired of fighting."

Fallon sat without speaking as Rayne dropped his head into his hands and the minutes dragged by. Fallon's voice, when he spoke, was soft. "It is time, my young friend, for me to be strong for thee. Just as thou wast strong for me. Dost thou remember how thou spoke to Wife Neci and me when thou first sat at my hearth?"

Rayne looked up, and Fallon, his face calm and set, nodded before continuing. "Yea. I well remember the words spoken by thee when I quailed at the thought of the coming darkness.

"'This body, my prison, is dying. But I refuse to give up. I will fulfill the prophecies and destroy Sigmund even if it's with my last breath. Will you help me?' Those were thy words. They and thy solid faith in the Creator-Father, stirred my heart and lent me strength. I will return this favor. Thou wilt not face the evil spawned by the living darkness alone. I will return with thee. I and any Kindred who chose to accompany me."

29

The second morning after Rayne had been taken, Cailyn knelt at the mossy edge of a swift-moving, chuckling stream, cupping chilly water to her burning face. She had promised Seth success, but the truth was, she had lost any sense of Rayne within hours of leaving the altar stone. Unwilling to admit defeat, she followed the slight signs Arnulf had pointed out. A snapped twig here, hoof prints in the mud near one of the many streams they crossed.

"Two horses." The man's deep bass had rumbled. "Pretty smart. Not smart enough. Left enough of a trail someone with tracking skills could follow. North. They've gone north."

"The Rockhall Province Road would take them back into Inverness. They're probably going to try and skip off Nemora." Cailyn mused.

After pursuing the tracks into the next day, the signs petered out. Hours were lost trying to pick up any trace of the vanished trail and Seth was livid. With nothing to follow, they set up camp for the night. Now, as the sun rose on another morning, the truth was clear. The trail had been a diversion.

"Stupid woman!" Seth stormed, his face a curious shade

of reddish purple as a pulsing vein appeared next to the strands of gray hair at his left temple. "How could I have been so foolish as to trust someone as weak as you?"

Though Arnulf patiently received his share of Seth's anger as he proceeded to pack up their supplies and saddle their horses, the brunt of Seth's fury was poured out on Cailyn.

Though she had expected Seth's rage, his cruel words cut deep, reducing her to a trembling weakling. Tears threatened and with her face growing hot, she ran.

Memories of her inability to compete with Rowena as a child surfaced and she plopped down on the damp moss. Frustration burned like a wildfire in her veins.

"Stupid. Stupid. Stupid," she hissed into the dense, misty morning air while tearing up fronds of the blue-green ferns growing out of the moss and flinging them into the water. "Of course he'd head south. To Neth. To the Kindred. Stupid ancients. They helped him before. I should have remembered that."

"So ... my dear ... your hypothesis that the Binder's rescuers would circle back to Inverness and attempt to leave Nemora was mistaken. It took you this long to realize he would have sought help in Neth? Foolish woman!" Seth's voice sliced through the air as sharply as Arnulf's knife sliced through skin.

Cailyn gathered her wits. *By the seven, he must have followed me. Buck up Cailyn. You're better than this. Yes, I am ... I'll show him. I'm not weak. My strength summoned the High Guardian. Seth needs to be reminded. I will not be weak again.* Laying hold of the willpower her desire for vengeance had birthed in her, and fixing a haughty look on her features, she turned toward Seth. Without a word, she reached out and waited for him to help her up. Several seconds passed but then, with a growl, he stepped forward and took her hand, assisting her to rise. She strode toward their campfire, Seth's presence behind her like a living wall of seething emotion.

You can do this Cailyn—No—Lady Mother. Face him and prove how strong you really are. Lowering gracefully onto a log set by the ashes of their fire, Cailyn patted the seat next to her and looked up to meet Seth's smoldering eyes.

She swallowed as he lowered his bulk down next to her. "You are right to be angry with me, Seth. I lied to you. But I did honestly believe I was strong enough to follow Rayne's trace despite the Ferris Weed. I was wrong. When Arnulf picked up those hoof prints, I was relieved. I believed that, in time, the Ferris Weed would wear off and I would again sense the Binder's presence. I was wrong. But, Seth, remember. I am Duchess of Nemora. And it was I who pulled together the heavy magic needed to call forth the High Guardian of the Scrolls in the first place. I may have misjudged this time, but I will not fail you again. We need to work together; put this mis-adventure behind us and focus on what we need to do now to correct the situation. Your anger will not help."

Seth turned toward Cailyn, his eyes wide, eyebrows crawl-ing up his forehead. "By the seven, you're right." He paused, a calculating look filtering into his eyes. "Yes. Yes. Your words are wise, Lady Mother. Though you have disappointed me, and your lie has cost us much. This is something we can remedy. As you say, now is the time to hasten our search for the Binder, not sit here bickering amongst ourselves."

He nodded as a faraway look came into his eyes. "Yes. We might yet salvage this attempt to retrieve our sacred scrolls. If … If … Come. There is no time to waste. Arnulf. Quick man, we must leave now and head due south. We must hurry. And if the High Guardian is willing, we may perchance meet up with First Associate Shepherd Creedoff and his soldiers along the way."

Moments later, as Arnulf was giving Cailyn a leg up, voices and the jingle of tack reached their ears.

"Prime Shepherd Hamlin, is that you?" Vartan's voice called out. Soon they were surrounded by riders dressed in the tunics and trousers of the USO militia. "They went north? Headed back to Inverness?" Vartan's questions elicited a growl from Seth.

Without answering Vartan, Seth waved for Arnulf to mount. Turning his horse's head south, Seth kicked the animal in motion, following the stream.

Cailyn clothed herself in her icy veredium cloak of unfeeling and followed. Two hours later, Cailyn now guiding, they moved onto the first of several small paths that would eventually lead to the main trail that skirted Neth on its way to Annesley. They stopped in a few small villages for food and to rest the horses along the way but continued to push at a ground-covering pace whenever the trail permitted.

Five days later, they left the trail, headed down into a wooded valley, and pulled up at the edge of a heavy stand of huge old-growth hardwoods bathed in a dense, blue-tinged fog. Neth Forest.

Cailyn's eyes scanned the woods, attempting to penetrate the mist. "We must be careful in Neth, ride the horses only when the path is clear and then only at a walk; anything more, the trees will notice and alert the Kindred."

At the mention of Kindred, a murmur of voices and shifting mounts greeted Cailyn's ears.

"Kindred?" Seth asked, moving his horse next to Cailyn's. "You mentioned them before. Until now I thought they were just a legend; the stuff of fairy tales, stories told to children to make them behave."

Cailyn huffed out a breath. "No. They are quite real. Ancients who've been here longer than humans. I've lived on Nemora my whole life and never seen one, but the reports from this area suggest they are very real, prefer to be left alone, and tend to scare off anyone stupid enough to wander into their forest. And there are the stories of those who have entered here never to be seen again. However, when the Binder was trapped in the old man body and near death, they welcomed him and helped him, even allowed him to retrieve the Nemorian scroll from the Heart of Neth. He has a *special* relationship with them."

"Can you sense him yet, Lady Mother?" Seth's tone of respect eased Cailyn's nerves. Seeing the deep blue-gray fog had sent a shiver of doubt through her. Seth's deep, matter of fact voice soothed her, reminding her of who she was and what had brought her here. Seth understood her—her need for renown and vengeance. Despite his hurtful words days before, he knew her strength and respected it. Never before had she been shown the kind of respect she now received from Seth and the believers of the United Scrolls of Ochen

"Allow me a moment, Prime Shepherd."

Cailyn closed her eyes, opening her mind to the surrounding energy. The power here was richer than elsewhere. She'd forgotten how intense it was at the edge of Neth; it had been years since her last visit to this area. She recalled Rayne's report that the Source, located in the Heart of Neth, was the fount of magic energy for all Ochen, spreading from Neth to all seven worlds. Here the power was light-filled, alive, and pure; so very different from the smothering dark energies she had been manipulating lately. A pang of regret blossomed in her chest. She squelched the rising guilt and hardened her heart, then began sifting the energy, pulling it to her. The intense potency almost overwhelmed her. When she was ready, she projected a sense tendril into the dense, mist drenched forest before her. *How easy it is with this amount of power available.*

She pulled in a sharp breath. Something else, something stronger and higher inhabited the light. *Vengeance belongs to me.* The words were planted in her spirit, the thought clear as a bell though actual words weren't spoken. Cailyn puffed out the air she had been holding.

"No." The word hissed between her teeth.

"Lady Mother?" Seth's anxious eyes met Cailyn's.

She shook her head. "Nothing. It's nothing." Closing her eyes again, she picked up the tendril and followed it. Due south. Into the heart of Neth.

There. Yes. It's him. Rayne's distinctive savor was unmistakable, strong and radiant, so like his mother's. "I have him."

"Arnulf, you will come with the Lady Mother and me. Pick twenty men to accompany us." Seth's gaze shifted from Arnulf to Vartan. "Vartan, take the remaining troops and move to the river. If he's got any brains, the Binder will change direction and head back to the portals in Inverness. If he does, we'll trap him between us." His lips turned down in a sour expression as he scanned the ranks of trees before them. "Keep alert. This forest has an unsavory feel to it. It reeks of

One worship. If we do not join up with you within a week, set fire to these loathsome trees."

Cailyn's eyes bulged. "What? No! You can't do that. The Source is in there; all the Kindred. We'll be in there." She swallowed. "You can't burn Neth. It's sacred."

"Can't?" Seth sneered. "I can and I will. These trees are not sacred." He waved a hand at the wall of trunks. "The Kindred are helping our enemy. No. The scrolls alone are sacred."

He dismounted and paced to stand at Cailyn's side. Looking up at her, his eyes narrowed, he hissed in a low voice that only Cailyn could hear. "Or have you forgotten what will happen to us—not just me, us—if we fail to complete the sacrifices?" He shuddered. "No. I will not fail. If I must reduce all Nemora to ashes to accomplish the High Guardian's bidding, that I will do. Unless you prefer to become a slave of the High Guardian for all eternity, I suggest you put your skills to good use and track down our final sacrifice. Now!"

Cailyn startled as he shouted his final word. She blinked several times in succession while gathering her wits. *Slave of the High Guardian? But ... but ... O Lord. I have no choice.* Words spoken by the dark figure nearly two months ago surfaced in her mind, the memory sharp and crisp. *To fail once you have begun, is to lose your soul to me for all eternity. Do you accept this bargain?*

Straightening her spine, she met Seth's angry gaze. "Of course, Prime Shepherd Hamlin. I too am most eager to serve the High Guardian without fail."

30

Rayne followed Giles's footsteps along the faint path, his eyes flicking over massive tree trunks as they appeared like ghosts emerging from the hazy forest before receding back into the damp, blue-tinged mist. His cousin's back, stiff and accusing, drew Rayne's eyes like a magnet. Giles hadn't spoken to him since the morning he announced his intent to return to Inverness and speak the One's words to the scroll worshipers. Rayne released an internal sigh. *It's not like I'm looking forward to doing this. Why can't he understand?* The groan that rose in him almost escaped into the fungi-scented air, but he clamped his lips shut, holding it in as he called to mind his meeting with the One by the side of the lake two nights ago.

You are my chosen. The One's voice had thrummed through Rayne, igniting his light in response, its radiance reflecting in myriad sparks across the lake.

"But haven't I done enough already?" Rayne whispered back. "Haven't I suffered enough? They're sacrificing innocent people just to bring Sigmund back. Using my blood to call to him, to break your word of banishment." Rayne paused, listened. The varied sounds of nighttime creatures floated on the slight breeze, filling the quiet. Nothing more.

"What if they take me again? Use me to finish the final two sacrifices? Won't all I've done before be meaningless if Sigmund and the Demon Master return?"

Do you no longer trust the prophecies? Do you no longer trust me?

Rayne pushed up from his knees, his face set in a grimace, hands fisted. "I don't know what to think. I mean, I know you were with me in that pit, but for all those weeks it seemed as if I was alone. And those sacrifices…" He shook his head, then swiped errant strands of untrimmed hair out of his eyes. "I've spoken to scroll worshipers before." His fingers traced the scar on his cheek as he began pacing along the edge of the lake. "Got this trying to reach them. They won't listen."

I have prepared many hearts among them.

Rayne stopped pacing; his churning thoughts stilled.

Will you go for me my beloved Light Bringer? Speak my words into hearts yearning to be freed from the bondage in which they now live? Did I not choose you, strengthen you, for this very purpose?

The spark the One had placed within Rayne's spirit so many years before flashed—warm and supporting, filling him with peace—just as it had in the past when Sigmund tried to break him. And Rayne knew he would yet again answer *yes* to the One's calling. "You have prepared them?"

My words, spoken through you, will call many out of the darkness into the light. Do you trust me?

A sad half-smile tweaked one corner of Rayne's lips. "How many times have you needed to ask me this?" He closed his eyes. "Too many. I know, too many." He glanced down at his softly glowing hands and nodded. "I trust you, my Lord. Please help me to always trust you. I will go." The warmth within him grew as the spark glowed bright.

The smile hovered at Rayne's lips as he relived the conversation. *But now, how do I make Giles understand?* Catching his foot on a tree root, Rayne stumbled. *Not good. I'd better focus on this path before I break my neck. I'll talk to Giles when we take a break.*

Rayne didn't get a chance to talk to Giles until they stopped for the night. He caught his cousin's eye and inclined his head toward the sounds of a chuckling stream in the darkness beyond the flickering light of the campfire. With a nod, Giles rose and preceded him into the deeper shadows under a cluster of Weeping Willows at the water's edge. Rayne followed, his eyes smarting as the breeze shifted and a plume of smoke wafted in his direction.

Once again Rayne stared at his cousin's board-stiff back while Giles stood on a moss-covered shelf jutting out into the water. Judging by the tilt of his head, Rayne knew Giles was watching a whirlpool caught on the upstream side of the spongy bank on which he stood.

"Are you going to talk to me or avoid me for the rest of your life?" Rayne said. With a huff, he jumped onto the muddy peninsula and knocked his shoulder into Giles's side.

Arms wind milling, Giles lost his footing and landed in the ankle-deep water. He stood still for a moment, the water swirling around his feet, before raising angry eyes to Rayne. "You're an idiot, you know that?" A growl escaped his lips and he grabbed Rayne's arm, dragging him off the muddy bank and into the swirling stream.

A smile worked its way across Rayne's face as a memory bloomed in his mind. He looked up, meeting Giles's gaze. "Remember Ferry Harbor?"

Anger and confusion bathed Giles's face, then a light of comprehension brightened his eyes. He nodded. Shifting his feet, he climbed onto the bank before turning back and reaching to help Rayne out of the stream. Moving to solid ground, he sat with his back to one of the huge willows and yanked his boots off.

"I'm irredeemable. Do you remember? That's what you told me that morning. Is it still true? Or can I hope that your rescuing me means something more?" Rayne kept his voice even as he sat on the opposite side of the willow from Giles, not wanting to push his cousin into saying something he would regret.

At first, he got no response, but then Giles mumbled, "You're still an idiot."

"You're probably right. But I *still* want to know ... why did you rescue me? You disappeared the day Sigmund was bound; you could have stayed away, and yet you didn't. Now you'll have to face trial for your part in Sigmund's plans. So I ask again, why did you rescue me?"

Giles snorted. "Why do you think? Or, let me put it this way; why are you putting yourself in danger by returning to Inverness to speak to the very people who just tried to call Sigmund back using your life as bait?

"I mean you *were* drugged out on Ferris Weed, but even like that you couldn't miss the heavy magic they were churning up with all those sacrifices and blood. Oh, yes! Your blood! And now you're determined to return and give them another chance? Why? I'll tell you why I rescued you; I rescued you because I'm an idiot too, thinking you might have finally developed an ounce of self-preservation in the last three years. I should have just disappeared with Marius when he left. He's the only one of us with any sense."

"So you have changed." Rayne pushed up onto his bare feet and walked to the other side of the wide trunk as he spoke.

Giles huffed, his mouth opening and closing a few times as if he wanted to rebut Rayne's statement. Pinching the bridge of his nose with his thumbs, his fingers clasped in front of his forehead, Giles responded in a breathy whisper. "Yes."

Elation flooded through Rayne. "I knew it. I just knew the One was working on you all that time we were together. You fought it, but he had you in his sights, and he never loses."

"You weren't so certain of that on Binding Day, were you? When Marius and I disappeared. Like you said, I'll have to face trial for my actions."

Rayne allowed a grin to surface. "True. But now we can offer your actions in rescuing me from the scroll worshipers' sacrifices as part of your defense. You've changed. It'll work out, you'll see. You just need to trust the One."

Rayne reached out to pull Giles to his feet as Neal, one of the Kindred warriors, ghosted into view. "Thou must come now." His soft words wafted through the dark shadows. "Fallon is calling for thee. Scouts have arrived reporting newcomers in the area."

Rayne grabbed his shoes and sprinted to the camp with Giles following.

"Two groups," a scout Rayne didn't recognize was saying. "One from the newcomer's road and another, closer to thee. Thou will meet them by sunrise if thy path is straight ahead."

"In Neth, thou says?" Fallon's face was hard. "How? How were our traps not effective against the newcomers?"

The Kindred scout shook his head. "It's the animal. A dog … It be leading them aright. Down past our deterrents, no mistake."

"A dog?" Rayne pressed forward to face the Kindred. "What does it look like?"

"Dark, like night. But there be a streak of white, like a bolt of lightning between the eyes."

Joy flooded through Rayne. "Could it be …" he mumbled, shaking his head. He raised his gaze to meet Fallon's. "It must be Boone. She could track me anywhere."

"Dost thou know these newcomers then?" Fallon asked, his expression growing dark.

"If the dog is Boone, then those with her are friends."

"And this other group? Hast thou invited even more newcomers into Neth?"

Rayne shook his head. "I can't be sure, but the scroll worshipers were hunting us. So, I am probably, once again, the reason newcomers are traveling into Neth."

Giles moved next to Rayne. "We were followed from Inverness. I still can't believe they didn't catch us on the way here; Marius covered our tracks and tried to mislead them, but we couldn't travel very fast with Rayne in his condition. If the closer group with the dog is friendly, I suspect the second is the bunch of scroll worshipers who've been tracking us. What I don't understand, though, is how anyone was able to get between us and the scroll worshipers."

"However that may be, we must decide if we will intercept these newcomers, or avoid them." Fallon's dark eyes met Rayne's amethyst ones. "What is thy wish, Light Bringer?"

Rayne considered for a moment, lifting a quick prayer to the One before speaking aloud. "I will not put the Kindred at risk. We'll keep on this track, continue toward the people with the dog. If they're friends, we'll greet them; if they are enemies, we'll confront them. Once we've dealt with that band, we'll check out the other. I'll not leave Neth until I'm certain neither of these parties pose a threat to the Kindred."

31

Reality crashed into Lexi's thoughts, flinging them from her mind, as Boone yanked the lead from Andrew's hand for the third time since entering Neth. Thorvin flung the reins of the horse he was leading in Lexi's direction and huffed out a grunt. He sprinted after the dog whose nose vibrated as she snorted and sniffed the faint breeze stirring the moisture-laden air. Avoiding Thorvin's attempt to grab her, Boone circled the man twice before Mayda darted in and seized the dog's trailing leash.

Andrew rose and endeavored to wipe the newest layer of mud from the knees of his trousers before slinking to Mayda and snatching the leash. Lexi stifled a giggle at his expression. A combination of embarrassment and frustration evident in the reddish tint worming its way up his clenched jaw.

"One more time … this happens one more time … I'm taking that lead from you and holding onto that irritating mutt myself." Thorvin's words hissed through clenched teeth as he reached to take the reins of his horse from Lexi's outstretched hand. "If we lose her, we'll be looking for a needle in a haystack. Neth is a big place and Rayne could be anywhere in here."

"I know. I know," Andrew mumbled. "But we tried. Every time you took her leash, she just sat and watched you. Wouldn't even move. That didn't help."

"Well at least she can't pull the stupid thing out of my hand. Maybe we need to try again."

"Here, girl." Andrew gave a light tug on the leash, and Boone trotted to him and plopped down at his side.

Lexi couldn't be certain, but it seemed as if the dog was grinning at the boy as she panted, her eyes locked on Andrew. "Okay you two. We didn't lose Boone and I think we all need a break. What do you say, Thorvin? It must be close to noon. Though with this mist and the heavy tree cover, I can't be sure. I just know I'm hungry. What do we have left?"

Thorvin's lips flattened and he shook his head. "Berries and some dried fish. That's it."

"We've got plenty of mushrooms," Mayda held up a lumpy bag. "They're all around."

Thorvin growled. "I *despise* mushrooms."

"We know," Lexi, Mayda, and Andrew all said together.

Thorvin sniffed the air, his nostrils flaring. "Boone's been following this stream since we entered Neth. If we're still tracking along it when we stop for the night, Andrew, you and Mayda fish. Catch as many as you can. We'll eat some fresh and smoke the rest overnight." He snorted then muttered, "Boone can't eat mushrooms."

The mist continued through the day, turning at times to a soft rain. Later, near evening, the cloud cover broke and blue-tinged light filtered through the canopy of purple leaves and gray-green needles. Boone continued to follow the stream, never wavering, her course pressing south. Thorvin tried several times to hold her leash and give Andrew a break, but each time, she dropped onto her belly and stared up at the large man.

When the stream widened and the bank flattened into a moss-covered glade, Thorvin called an early halt. Within minutes, Mayda and Andrew retrieved their net and set out to catch supper.

Thorvin tied Boone's lead to a tree. She lay facing south,

alert, just like every other time they stopped. Lexi pulled an empty sack from her pack and wandered off to hunt mushrooms. Though the large warrior hated the taste of mushrooms, his knowledge about which Nemorian mushrooms were edible had proven invaluable.

Lexi returned with a bulging bag soon after heading out and sat next to Thorvin. She leaned forward, placed the mushrooms on the ground, then clicked her tongue, making sweet sounds and rubbing Boone's ears. "Who's a good dog? Boonie's a good dog. Yes, she is."

Boone's tail thumped the mossy earth and when Lexi shifted her hands to rub a certain spot behind Boone's front leg, she triggered a response. Boone's hind leg on that side jumped as she tried to scratch at nothing. Lexi chuckled and stopped. "Sorry, Boonie. I just couldn't resist." Scanning out over the stream she watched for a bit as Andrew and Mayda scooped up another fish. It looked as if they already had several set out on large blue leaves, away from the water.

Shifting her gaze to Thorvin she broached a subject that had been on her mind for the last few days. "For someone who loathes mushrooms you seem to know a lot about them. Have you always had this aversion? According to my father, all Nemorians love fungi. Like it's a planetary directive or something. *All good Nemorians must love mushrooms.*"

Thorvin grunted. Lexi waited. Just when she decided he wasn't going to say anything, Thorvin said, "You can blame the queen. It's her fault so you'll have to get the story from her."

Lexi's interest aroused; she pursued the matter. "What? She didn't do something like feed you bad mushrooms when you were kids, did she?"

Catching Thorvin's dark expression, Lexi rounded her mouth into an 'O'. "Oh my! She did. Was it on purpose?"

If possible, Thorvin's face turned an even deeper red. "I told you. You have to ask her."

Lexi knew Rowena had a bit of a wild side to her, especially when she was younger. Growing up together here on Nemora, she and Thorvin must have shared some amazing adventures. This sounded like too juicy a story to pass up—and

Lexi needed a distraction to get her mind off Rayne, and the fact that she was stuck traveling with a scroll worshiper. Ignoring Thorvin's storm-cloud demeanor, she pressed. "I would ask her, but she's not here. You are. You know I won't let this rest until I hear the whole story. So, spill, Thorvin. Out with it. What happened?"

"What happened when?" Andrew's voice startled Lexi as he dumped a load of fish wrapped in several large leaves on the ground, lowered himself to sit cross-legged next to the pile, and stared at Thorvin. Ghosting his footsteps, Mayda copied his actions, taking a place next to Andrew.

Thorvin pushed up onto his feet. "Nothing happened. I'll get kindling so we can smoke those fish. Andrew, you and Mayda, clean them. Lexi ... well ... you help. This discussion is over." He stomped across the clearing; his shoulders hunched.

Andrew's gaze met Lexi's. "What was that about?"

Lexi crooked a half-grin. "I'm not sure, but I think Queen Rowena might have fed our man Thorvin a bad mushroom when they were younger."

Andrew's eyes grew large, then, a thoughtful expression setting his brow in wrinkles, he nodded. "Yep. I can see that. I've heard some of the stories. She and Cailyn were noted for doing crazy things when they were younger. And Her Majesty was always the instigator."

"Cailyn?" Mayda said, her eyes squinted in curiosity. "You mean the duchess?"

"Yeah." Andrew's voice went icy. "The duchess. Rayne's aunt. The *Lady Mother.* I don't understand how she could do what she's doing. Sacrificing her own nephew to that *thing!* Especially since she and the queen were always so close. It doesn't make any sense."

"Maybe it does." Lexi paused listening as the faint rustlings of forest creatures settling for the night invaded the silence.

"Well?" Andrew pressed.

"Well ... she blamed Rayne for killing Brayden even though he tried to save him. She tried to hide it, but it was obvious every time they were together. I'd catch her staring daggers at Rayne. I tried to talk to Rowena and Rayne about it, but they couldn't accept it. Then when Miles ... killed himself. I think it was all too much for her. After that she stopped coming to Westvale and turned hermit in Inverness. Now I know why. She was teaming up with that Seth person, plotting against the Church of the One and Rayne. Plotting to invite the darkness back into Ochen.

"Argh! How could she? I understand she was hurting, but to do what she's doing. There's no excuse. I hate her almost as much as I hate scroll worshipers ... wait. She's a scroll worshiper too. Just another reason to hate her even more."

Mayda's chin dropped to her chest and her hands stopped working. "I guess you hate me too."

Her words were so soft Lexi almost missed them. The rage Lexi kept submerged bubbled to the surface. Ever since the scroll worshipers on Arisima had sprung a trap and almost killed Rayne more than a year ago, she vowed to hate all scroll worshipers. Rayne warned her of the damage nurturing bitterness could cause her spirit, but despite all his arguments, she refused to forgive.

They don't deserve your forgiveness. She had thrown her words of loathing at Rayne more than once over the last year.

Fixing cold eyes on Mayda, Lexi said, "Yes. I hate you! We may have to travel together for now, but I won't forget what you are, what you've been part of. You were there, participating in those sacrifices. You're no better than the rest of them."

Mayda's fear was palpable in the light of Lexi's animosity, her eyes wide and face ashen in the diminishing light. *Good! Feel fear like I've felt fear! When Rayne was scarred by scroll worshipers. Poisoned by scroll worshipers.* Lexi narrowed her eyes at the younger girl, staring, sending shards of loathing at her as her hands cupped the grips of her twin daggers. Until Andrew's voice pierced her outer armor.

"Lexi. Lexi. Stop it. Mayda's our friend. She's not like them. She's helping us. Lexi!" Then Andrew echoed Rayne's words. "You need to forgive, Lexi."

Lexi stuffed down the overwhelming need to scream.

Instead, she hissed through clenched teeth, "No. No I don't *need* to forgive. Rayne does enough of that for the both of us."

After throwing a last angry glare in Mayda's direction, Lexi stormed off into the gloaming. She would not sit and pretend she could forgive the scroll worshiper no matter how helpful the girl had been or how many promises she made. Someone needed to protect Rayne. She knew he wouldn't do it for himself despite how he'd been hurt. He'd preach forgiveness like he always did. That left his defense to Lexi and she wasn't going to allow anyone or anything to stand in her way. She *would not* release her hatred. She couldn't give it up, not when it burned within her, strengthening her resolve.

Night had fallen and the cloud cover returned to blanket the sky by the time Lexi returned. Thorvin opened his mouth to speak, but after one stern look from Lexi in the flickering light, he clamped it shut. Without a word, she pulled a blanket from her pack, wrapped it around her, moved away from the others, and settled at the base of a cypress. It was going to be a damp, chilly night but she denied her need to move closer to the fire.

As morning approached, the mist-laden air grew brighter and forms began to take shape. Still Lexi clung to her self-righteous anger. Though the voice of the One whispered within her spirit through the night, telling her to let it go, she refused, locking out the voice. Instead she fed on Mayda's words describing the sacrifices and what had been done to Rayne. Allowed them to stir the boiling pot of abhorrence.

It isn't fair. Why do we always have to be the ones to forgive? Why does Rayne? If he won't stand up for himself, and you won't defend him, I'll do it myself. Those barbaric scroll worshipers need to be taught a lesson. I just hope King Theodor has come and set an army on them by now. That would serve them right.

She avoided talking to anyone as they grabbed a quick breakfast and broke camp. Boone tugged Andrew along, scrambling at the mud and ferns at her feet with unrelenting doggie energy. Lexi followed, leading her horse, with Mayda behind her, and Thorvin bringing up the rear, leading his horse and Andrew's.

Morning passed. No one spoke. The soft thuds of horses' hooves, the rushing of the churning stream and occasional dripping from moisture-heavy leaves, combined with the periodic scrambling noises of small animals and a non-stop symphony of bird songs masked the absence of conversation as the four continued their trek south.

Exhausted after her sleepless night, Lexi placed one foot in front of the other, lulled by the soft forest sounds. When Boone howled, her head shot up and her mouth dropped open at the shock. Then Boone was barking and dragging Andrew through a patch of ferns taller than the dog. It looked as if Andrew was being propelled forward by the wildly waving ferns themselves.

⁂

Rayne ran his fingers over the coarse bark of an immense green-needled cypress tree, his eyes riveted on Neal as the Kindred champion worked his way up the side of a large outcropping of rock rising at the edge of a rushing spring. Small rivulets of water splashed down the stream side of the slick, moss-covered rocks. Neal's form vanished then reappeared as he shifted into a position overlooking the foaming water, scanning upstream.

Giles and the other Kindred waited downstream a short distance while Neal reconnoitered. Rayne dogged the warrior's steps, refusing to wait. According to the scout's report, the newcomers with the dog were following this stream south. They had to be close.

Rayne lowered his head to his chest and shook his arms out, releasing a portion of the tension that had built in his neck and shoulders. He grabbed the hilt of the sword Neal had given him before leaving the Heart.

They've got to be close. He nearly jumped out of his skin as the baying of a dog drove all thoughts but one from his mind. *Boone?* A tentative smile worked its way onto his lips. Sharp barking erupted, volume increasing by the second. *I know that bark. Boone!* Rayne stepped away from the cypress and whistled low and long. A black blur sped through the trees toward Rayne, staggering him as Boone crashed into him, whining. She turned circles around him then jumped up, planting her front paws on his chest, covering his face in slobbery doggie kisses. Rayne knelt, pleasure at Boone's greeting igniting deeper emotions.

Rayne. Boone must sense Rayne. And he's close. Energy surged through Lexi. She began running after Boone. Coming around the back side of a jumble of rocks that rose out of the stream they had followed since entering Neth, she stumbled to a halt.

Rayne knelt before her, his hands wrapped in Boone's fur, the dog whining and trying to jump on Rayne's head. He looked like something out of a dream in the swirling mist. Releasing a sob of joy, she sprinted toward him. He rose with arms spread to pull her to him. She gazed up into his amazing amethyst eyes as his lips lowered to hers. All else was forgotten.

Rayne's eyes rose, tugging him to his feet. Joy flooded his spirit. Lexi, Thorvin, Andrew, and a girl he didn't recognize appeared through the light mist, moving toward him around the base of the rocky outcropping.

A squeal of delight pierced the air as Lexi froze for a moment, then sprinted toward him, her arms spread wide. Rayne's eyes fixed on hers. Then she was in his arms, warm and so very real, and her sweet savor surrounded him. He cupped her cheek and lowered his lips to hers tasting the salty wetness of tears there.

32

Rowena's prayer ended. For the past two days she had fasted and spent hours in prayer. Now the time had arrived, and prickles of doubt shredded her confidence. "It's in your hands, holy One. I rest in the truth that it is you, not me, in control. And you never fail."

The One's comforting warmth seeped through her. *I have claimed many here for my own. Calm your fears my daughter. Watch and see what I will do. My Light Bringer will speak, and I will ignite hearts prepared. Trust.*

Rowena rested in the peace that came with trusting the One. She opened her eyes and met Mite's gaze across the pitted table in the cottage behind Castle Inverness. He nodded. "Now? We go now?"

"Yes, Mite. Are you ready?"

The slight ancient jumped from his seat and bounced from foot to foot. "Ready. Ready. The time is now. The Creator-Father promised. We go. We go."

Rowena smiled at Mite's antics, allowing the peace to take deeper hold. *Trust. It's such a simple word. And yet ... it holds a world of meaning. I have learned much about trust from my son.* She permitted a chuckle to emerge. *And from Mite.*

Gwyn pushed his square bulk up onto his feet and met Rowena's gaze. She swallowed, yet again weighing the ex-scroll worshiper's profession of belief in the One. "Don't make me regret trusting you."

Gwyn nodded, but said nothing.

All five donned USO cloaks—Mite a child-sized one—that Noah and Sashi had lifted from various clotheslines throughout the camp. Noah and Sashi moved in behind Rowena, Mite, and Gwyn as they left the cottage. The group shunned the main thoroughfares, slipping down smaller lanes and alleys until they stood in the shadows at the corner of the Blue Moon Tavern, staring out at the line of guards blocking the entrance to the portal station.

Rowena turned to face the others, catching each one's eyes, comforted by the determination she met there. "I want to go over the plan one last time before this starts. Mite, once you've drawn these guards into your illusion, we'll need to get into the portal station and set the illusion there.

"Noah. Sashi, When I give the signal, you'll open the portals for Sorial and Corylus. No matter what happens we must open those portals.

"Gwyn, remain here. *If* it looks like Mite's illusion is weakening, do what you can to draw the guards' attention away from the station, even if it's sounding an alarm that they are needed back at the camp."

She reached out and laid her hands on Noah's and Sashi's shoulders. "If for some reason the illusion is broken before we're ready, you two will need to keep the guards busy until Theodor and his men skip. Mite and I will do our best to help you, but we're not soldiers."

Rowena scanned the faces of her people once more. "Let's pray." A few moments of silent prayer passed, and Rowena opened her eyes. "Okay Mite. Let's do this."

Rowena let her eyes slide shut again and began summoning the magic energies of Nemora to her, balancing them, weaving them, and feeding them to Mite. Within seconds, she felt his illusion blanket the square in front of the portal station. It was as she had suspected. With the level of energy available, and the guards bored with their duty, they were all staring, glassy eyed, less than a minute later, immersed in Mite's illusion.

Blinking in the blue-tinged sunlight, Rowena led Mite, Noah, and Sashi through the line of oblivious guards and up the three steps into the cathedral-like building. Following the plan, the four grouped together imitating a family and moved to sit on one of the benches closest to the entryway. Rowena's breath came out in a sigh when no one took notice of their arrival. Not wasting a moment, she closed her eyes and again began pulling in energy and threading it to Mite. She was amazed by Mite's skill and power as he received all she sent him and crafted the illusion.

"Done," Mite whispered. "All done."

"Now." Rowena's voice sounded loud in her ears as she gave the signal to open the portals.

Noah took off toward the Corylus portals while Sashi angled toward the Sorial lines. In less than a minute, Noah had already jumped the counter, opened the individual portal, and was heading to the massive freight portal. Then the unexpected happened. One of the guards sneezed several times, shook his head, and broke free of the illusion. His eyes blinking and a look of confusion on his face, he stumbled to the man next to him and shook him. "Intruders. There are intruders in the station."

Within seconds of his yell, several more soldiers began shaking their heads and looking around, dazed, but surfacing from the illusion into full awareness far too quickly.

Sashi stopped—like a frozen statue she stood immobile as her panicked eyes focused on Noah.

"Don't stop." Rowena shouted, trying to understand how Mite's illusion could have lost effectiveness after the amount of energy she had funneled into it.

Sashi turned and sprinted the rest of the way to the Sorial portals. Sliding past the railing, she opened the personal portal. Two guards were on her before she could get near the freight portal and she turned with a snarl to face the threat.

Noah, pressed by several angry guards, backed into a wall. Rowena needed to do something to help them. Neither her magic nor Mite's was suited to warfare, but she knew the human body well from working as a healer. She just needed to get closer. She glanced again at Sashi, who seemed to be holding her own against the two guards harrying her, but Noah couldn't hold out much longer against the greater numbers.

Just as she determined to move, soft singing broke through her awareness. Mite. He was attempting to shield Noah and Sashi with a song of protection. *Better idea, Mite. Much better.* For the third time that day, she pulled in magic energy and fed it to the child-like ancient. He continued singing, weaving protection around Noah and Sashi, baffling the guards whose swords seemed incapable of penetrating the invisible barriers surrounding the two.

The barriers wouldn't hold for long, but even as Rowena pulled in more energy, soldiers wearing Westvale Palace Guard uniforms began poring through the Corylus portal. Captain Fontaine appeared in the Sorial portal. His gaze flicked over the scene as he waved in a line of men and women dressed in Ochen army uniforms. He grabbed a couple as they passed and sent them to open the freight portals. Within minutes, soldiers filled the station, overwhelming the USO guards and herding them together as prisoners.

Rowena startled as arms clothed in army brown wrapped about her from behind. An angry retort formed on her lips but then her eyes went wide as she looked over her shoulder and gazed into Theodor's warm, chocolate eyes. "What ..."

Without a word, he spun her around and planted a kiss on her lips, drawing her closer to him.

"How?" Words were impossible and Rowena sighed before relaxing into another kiss.

He turned her again, pulling her back into his chest, wrapping her in a soothing embrace. "Watch," he whispered into the back of her neck.

She swallowed the lump in her throat as troops continued to pour into the Nemora Portal Station. Encircled in Theodor's arms her confusion dissolved when she caught sight of a man, looking very like Theodor, riding his war horse through the Corylus freight portal, a cavalry unit following in his wake.

"Is that supposed to be you?" she said, her fine fingers wrapping around his strong arms.

His chuckle rumbled through her back as he brushed his bristly beard against the top of her head.

"No. Stop that." She turned in his arms. "Explain yourself. Why is the king of Ochen parading around as a common soldier?"

"It was my idea, but Anton and I discussed it and Captain Ellis agreed. If the portals closed before many troops were able to skip, Anton was to take command of those who skipped, and negotiate in my name. I wanted the freedom of anonymity. As a common soldier, I could plead sympathy with the scroll worship cause and infiltrate their camp if need be. After conferring with Shaw and Anne we thought this would be a good back up."

A crooked grin tugged at the corner of his lips. "And I couldn't resist the opportunity to be part of your little rebellion." His expression turned serious. "Has your plan to destroy the weapons stores worked? Do you know what's happening outside?"

"As of our arrival here, there was no word that the fire had been started. As for outside ..." She shrugged. "We'll find out soon enough."

A shiver ran through Rowena as Theodor dropped his encircling arms, withdrawing their warmth. She reached out and took one of his hands, longing for the connection, then caught sight of Captain Anton Fontaine, Noah, and Sashi heading toward them.

Captain Fontaine smiled at Rowena and inclined his head. "I am gratified to see you are safe, Your Majesty." He saluted Theodor. "Sire, the enemy soldiers are secure, and Captain Ellis is overseeing the arrival of our remaining troops. Do you still plan to enter the city in disguise first, or shall we approach the camp with significant numbers for a show of strength? We had discussed both options."

The king's focus shifted to Rowena. "You know the situation here. What would you recommend?"

"Mite?" Confusion and a smidge of irritation filtered

through Rowena as she scanned the station for Mite. "He was just here. Where could he have gotten to?" She sucked in a breath and released it with a huff, returning her attention to Theodor and Anton. "I can't be certain but judging by how quickly the scroll worshipers in here were able to repel Mite's illusion, I suspect it has already ceased to have any effect on the guards surrounding the station. The fact that they haven't responded to the turmoil in here would seem to indicate they've been … distracted. Perhaps by a summons back to camp to deal with a fire. We can only hope. But … rather than take a chance and lose the element of surprise, I suggest that you allow Noah, Sashi, and me to investigate then report back to you."

"I'll come with you," Theodor said.

"Not like that, my dear."

Theodor's eyes dropped to examine his uniform and he nodded. "Good point."

Without another word, Noah sprinted to where the scroll worshipers were grouped against the wall, seized a cloak, and delivered it to the king with a bow. "I think this should help, Your Majesty."

33

న

A few minutes later, as the last of the soldiers filtered in through the portals, Theodor, Rowena, Noah, and Sashi slipped out the front doors of the station into a quiet and empty square.

Deep blue-gray clouds churned overhead, and a distant rumble of thunder held the promise of rain. Rowena hoped the rain would hold off long enough for Benning, Bram, and their people to complete their work of destruction. As she lifted a prayer for their success, Mite scurried toward her. Following the diminutive ancient, Gwyn's bulk plowed forward, looking even more weighty in contrast to Mite's slight form.

"Must go now. Must go quick, quick. Now. Now. Now," Mite called as he sprinted across the square.

"He's right." Gwyn huffed out heavy breaths as he drew closer. "A man came from the camp shouting, 'fire! Our weapons are burning. Tents too. You must come now.' The guards shook their heads and woke from the spell. They ran off leaving no one behind."

Gwyn inclined his head to Rowena, a grin lifting one side of his mouth. "If we go now, we can, perhaps, use this to our advantage just as you hoped. But we must act quickly. Catch them off guard and panicking. Under those circumstances, an appropriate show of force may turn the tide in our favor." He paused and shuffled his feet. "We should at least try to end this without bloodshed. The One knows they aren't warriors for the most part. Just disillusioned families, farmers, and trades-people."

He caught Rowena's eyes with his own pleading orbs. "I know you would save all if you could. Perhaps this is your chance. Please!"

Theodor moved to stand between Gwyn and Rowena. "And you are?" His words came out cold and clipped.

Rowena placed a hand on Theodor's right arm, knowing he itched to draw the sword hidden under his cloak, and nodded toward the ex-scroll worshiper. "Theodor. This is Gwyn. He was one of the leaders of the United Scrolls of Ochen but now claims faith in the One. Gwyn, this is His Majesty, King Theodor."

"Is this one of the enemies who have been using my son as part of their weekly ritual of human sacrifices?" Theodor's eyes went flat as he ground the words out between his teeth.

Gwyn's gaze dropped to the paving beneath his feet and he began to lower his hefty frame to his knees.

"Gwyn, stop! This is not the time." Rowena's words came out sharper than she wanted, but they needed to stay focused. Taking Theodor's arm, she pulled him around until he faced her. She understood his anger, had felt it herself not long ago. But Gwyn wasn't the enemy they needed to battle now. Willing her husband to understand, she locked eyes with him. "For now, trust him. Trust me. I will explain things later. But for now, Gwyn is right. We can't waste this opportunity."

Theodor's inner struggle worked its way out on his face. Several seconds later, he released a growl and shook his head, then nodded. "Okay, Ro, this is your call. I trust you." His gaze shifted back to Gwyn as he gently propelled Rowena from between them. "But you and I will have words when this is over."

Another growl emanated from Theodor's throat. He

glanced down to Rowena then scanned the square. "I hope Captains Ellis and Fontaine are ready. We're going to confront a bunch of scroll worshipers and we're doing it now."

"Plan B." Theodor's resonant voice fanned-out ahead of him as he paraded back across the cavernous, crowded, portal station, drawing not only his two captain's gazes, but the alert attention of the soldiers.

Rowena jogged to keep up with her long-legged husband. Relief eased the taut muscles between her shoulders when she realized that those who had skipped were already formed up in the tight space, organized into structured, well-defined units. The cavalry troops, though small in numbers, were the best trained mounted troops Ochen had to offer. The echo of horses' hooves striking the stone paving on the floor rang from the dark, vaulted ceiling above, sharp and distinct against the susurration of troops preparing for battle. One company's uniforms caught Rowena's eye; as part of Captain Ellis's elite cavalry from Arisima they wore the distinct beige robes and maroon turbans of the desert world.

Rowena shifted her gaze as Theodor stepped up to the tight band of officers surrounding Captain Ellis and Captain Fontaine, and said, "Their weapons are burning as we speak. The camp is in chaos. Let's try to end this right now. Stick to the strategy we set in place when we discussed this with Shaw. You still comfortable using the troop placement we set out on his map?"

"Yes, Your Majesty." Anton saluted.

Theodor turned to Captain Ellis. "Captain, as we arranged, Captain Fontaine will take charge of the foot soldiers while you lead the cavalry. We will be counting on your ability to shift positions quickly and create even more chaos in the process. Are you ready?"

"Yes, Your Majesty."

"Then let's do this!"

"Wait. Oh, wait, wait, wait." Mite's high-pitched voice rose in a wail. "Must pray. Must pray first."

"I will pray." Gwyn's voice rumbled.

Her eyes wide, Rowena turned toward the ex-scroll worshiper, a denial forming on her lips. But Mite spoke up again. "Yes. Yes. Yes. Scroll man not scroll man any longer. Chosen. He is chosen. Must pray. Must pray now."

As if a stone had been thrown into the pond of the portal station, rings of silence moved outward from the center. A heavy, pregnant silence. Gwyn's face took on a peculiar pallor and he stood as if frozen, except for his eyes which blinked several times in rapid succession. Rowena expected him to turn tail and run in fear, but as she watched, a change came over the man. Peace erased the fear and his eyelids dropped over calm eyes. When he spoke, the sound of his voice carried into every corner, behind each column, and reached the ears of all the men and women gathered there with a force Rowena had only experienced when listening to Rayne speak the Words of the One.

"Precious Lord, I come before you as a sinner. Unworthy. I have followed a demonic teacher and have sought the harm of your people and your Light Bringer. And yet ... you now fill me with a peace I cannot comprehend. You have called me to pray for these soldiers as they venture forth to face those I once called friends and fellow believers. I do not ask for these soldiers of Ochen to stay their hand, but I do ask that they may show mercy and compassion when possible. Protect them and guide them. Help those who worship the scrolls to see the error of their ways, throw down their weapons, and surrender to the authority of the king and queen. And may they seek your truth. Extend to King Theodor, Queen Rowena, and their military leaders wisdom beyond human understanding and give them strength. Thank you."

The final words of Gwyn's prayer echoed across the room and Rowena opened her eyes, pulled in a deep breath, released it in a slow exhale, and reveled in the incredible peace of the One that permeated the station. Though she hated the idea of strife between her people, she now understood; a clash was inevitable. She needed to trust that even in these times of turmoil and confusion, the One was in control. She and Theodor must be strong for all their people.

She glanced down at the USO robe and shook her head. "This won't do. Theodor!"

Her husband turned to her, reaching out. "Ro, are you alright?"

"Fine. We need to change before we go to the camp. We... need to show who we are. Project our authority."

He nodded. "I agree. But we need to make this quick."

Within minutes, they were waiting for Noah and Sashi to skip back in from Corylus. When they arrived with several pages in their wake, Sashi handed Rowena a long shirt made of silver chain mail. "I've brought these as well, but you'll need a place to change." She waved behind her. Three page boys stepped forward, one holding, a charcoal-gray, feminine-cut gambeson, and a charcoal-gray, leather split skirt; another clutching fine, silver-embossed, black leather boots. The third held out Rowena's rapier.

"Let's move behind that pillar. It will have to do." Rowena lead the others to a shadow-drenched corner behind a far pillar. The soldiers standing there all turned their backs, giving the queen a degree of privacy. She stripped down to her small clothes. Sashi held out first the gambeson, then the skirt, before helping Rowena slip on the chain mail, taking care to not catch strands of hair in the links. Moving to the nearest bench, Rowena sat as the page with the boots assisted her in pulling them on. Finally, the page with the rapier, buckled on the scabbard over the chain shirt.

By the time Rowena lifted her eyes, Theodor was wearing a set of light armor and buckling the scabbard for the King's Sword. He looked up and, when she caught his gaze, she nodded her admiration. *Perfect. A fine show of royal authority. Now we just need to hope this brings about a quick resolution to this upheaval.*

As Rowena walked back to Theodor, Captain Ellis approached, leading her favorite horse, a silver dapple, with white feathering on his hooves, named Mosley. She gave Mosley's velvet nose a fond rub, then smiled at Theodor.

"Are you ready?" He dipped his head, approval shining in his eyes.

"As ready as I'm going to be." *At least on such short notice. O One, please help us!* "Yes. Let's do this."

"Your Majesty." Gwyn stepped before King Theodor and

spread his arms in a pleading gesture. "Your Majesty, please … let me come with you. Maybe I can talk to the people, explain… things. They know me. At least they used to. They respected me."

Theodor crossed his arms and studied the man for a moment, then nodded. "Perhaps you will be of help." He flicked his gaze to Rowena. "Ro, what do you think?"

Before Rowena could answer, Mite slipped in next to Gwyn. "Yes. Yes. Yes. Gwyn must come. Must."

Rowena's brows climbed her forehead. "Well, I guess you have your answer."

They led their horses out, followed by Captain Ellis's cavalry as the portals were again activated and more soldiers began arriving.

Theodor and Rowena rode at the head of what soon became a long procession. Mite and Gwyn shared a mount directly behind the king and queen, with Captain Ellis behind them. To the north west, a thick column of ominous grey smoke blotted the sky. As they traveled down the main thoroughfare, losing sight of the smoke, the sun peeked out from behind the dispersing thunderheads, drawing steam from the paving and glinting on Theodor's armor and Rowena's mail. Soon word of their arrival preceded them, and the inhabitants of Inverness began to line the route, cheering.

"It's King Theodor and Queen Rowena. They've come to help us."

"Thank you!" several voices called. Others followed. Soon, many voices were raised.

"The One bless the king and queen."

The crowd thickened and as the procession passed Castle Inverness, servants came rushing out, lifting their voices in praises and blessings as well. After leaving the castle behind, the dwellings thinned and the pavement narrowed until, a bit farther on, they were riding on a packed-dirt road. Five miles ahead, in a sheltered valley Rowena remembered hunting in with Cailyn when they were younger, sat the USO camp.

Another mile and Theodor signaled Captain Ellis and a man Rowena didn't recognize, also wearing Arisimanian beige and maroon. With their horse soldiers riding in formation behind, they headed off in opposite directions to take up predetermined positions in the surrounding foothills. Rowena shivered to think of the damage armed riders could inflict on untrained civilians when charging down the sides of those hills. Though the scroll worshipers outnumbered the king's troops ten to one, and many of the USO soldiers had been training for months, they would be no match for the seasoned warriors now preparing to confront them.

A lump formed in her throat as she watched Noah and Sashi ride off with Captain Ellis's troops. *Blessed One, please keep those two safe.* Glancing back past Gwyn and Mite, she scanned the next company of cavalry moving in. The lump enlarged and the backs of her eyes burned. *How many young people are risking their lives because Sigmund initiated this false religion, my Lord? How many of our people will die? On both sides? Please bring this whole, absurd conflict to a quick end. Help those who have been deceived to see your truth ... and please be with Rayne, wherever he is.*

The heavy growth of pines they rode through thinned as they climbed a short hill, giving way to intermittent stands of oaks. A stiff breeze tossed branches and the thick column of rising smoke they had spied on the way from Inverness now hugged the ground and filled the air around them with a shifting, choking haze. They crested the rise and as the wind kicked up again, Rowena caught her first sight of the scroll worshiper camp. Though her friends had warned her of its size, she hadn't expected it to fill the entire valley.

Theodor shifted into position beside her, his face grim. His eyes scanned the hundreds of tents that appeared then disappeared like imaginary phantoms as the smoke swirled and shifted. "This is unbelievable. How did they ever manage to bring so many together without us knowing?"

"Cailyn." Rowena squeezed her eyes shut against her tears and the stinging smoke. She shook her head, then opened her eyes again, trying to take in the immensity of what lay before her. "Oh, Theodor. Cailyn was working with that *Prime Shepherd* Hamlin. How could she do this?"

"Cailyn was involved with this?"

Rowena groaned. "I'll tell you all about it later when we have time. But, yes, Cailyn was—is—involved." Rowena leaned toward Theodor, searching his features. "She was behind Rayne's kidnapping. It will take time to tell all I know, but for now ... let's go make an impression on some scroll worshipers."

34

Tears pricked Rayne's eyes, but he blinked them back. Lexi's warmth within the circle of his arms beckoned his spirit to release the burden pressing down on him and rejoice in this moment. She was home, she was life, she was his heart. And her heart was beating a welcome rhythm of its own through her chest into his. *Thank you, my Lord. For this moment. For Lexi.*

"I was so worried. When we heard about the sacrifices, I feared I had lost you." Lexi raised her golden eyes to Rayne's face then followed with her hands. She cupped his cheeks and wiped the couple rebellious tears that had found their way past his lashes to her fingertips. He mirrored her actions, wiping the salty wetness from her face.

"But you're here." She lowered her hands to grasp his arms and pushed him away to run her gaze from his face to his feet then back again. "You're whole and you're here." Her voice broke and she hugged him close again as she sobbed into his chest, leaving damp spots on his robe.

After a couple minutes, Lexi's crying subsided into sniffles and hiccups. Rayne shifted her to a position where he could wrap his left arm around her shoulders, then reached out to

Thorvin. "Come to rescue me again?" Rayne asked with a wry grin.

Thorvin stepped in to grasp Rayne's hand but as his eyes shifted past the prince, he stopped midstride, hand still out-stretched but now stiff. A low growl rumbled from his throat and a muscle jumped in his clenched jaw. "You! You filthy betrayer!"

Rayne glanced back over his shoulder and Thorvin reached for his sword.

"What ..." Lexi mumbled as she too shifted to see what had upset Thorvin. "Oh!"

As the one syllable puffed from Lexi's mouth, Rayne caught sight of Giles standing about twenty paces behind him. Slipping his arm from Lexi's shoulders, he moved to block Thorvin's advance before his old trainer did something he would regret. But before Rayne could get between the two, Neal was there, his staff at ready. "Do not act in violence within Neth, newcomer." His eyes bore into Thorvin with an intensity that stopped the large man in his tracks. Tilting his head, Neal added, "And, to react before hearing the whole story would bring dishonor on us all."

Though Thorvin had been brought to a halt by Neal, Lexi still marched toward Giles, her twin swords hissing as she pulled them from the crossed scabbards on her back. "You traitor! We trusted you. Rayne trusted you."

"Stop, Lexi!" Rayne's words seemed to fall on deaf ears as Lexi's advance continued unabated. "Lexi! Please, listen to me. He saved me from the sacrifices! Stop!"

Lexi slowed, then stopped and turned to face Rayne who came up behind her. Her arms drooped to her sides, her swords dangling. Anger flowed from her as she stared at Rayne, her brows pulled together, and her mouth flattened into a stern line. "What? What are you saying, Rayne?"

Rayne took hold of Lexi's arms and willed her to focus on him. Sorrow choked him as Lexi's muscles stiffened under his fingers. Cold fury streamed from her eyes, signify-ing the all too familiar storm that raged within her. It first appeared when he was poisoned while confronting Vagrants of the Scroll on Arisima a year ago, and, in the time since, he had seen it take hold of her spirit, erupting in moments of rage. His heart broke for Lexi as he watched the anger fade from her eyes leaving a conflicted confusion behind as she dropped her swords.

"Rayne?" Her eyes rounded. "I ... I ... He helped you? But what about before?" She drew in a shaky breath and with a moan, wrapped her arms around him. "I was so afraid for you." Her face nuzzled into Rayne's robe once again and another moan escaped her lips.

"It's okay, heart of my heart. It's okay," he murmured into the top of her head.

Thorvin's rough voice pulled Rayne's attention from Lexi. "Well, Your Highness, are you planning to explain what happened in the near future or leave us wondering why you are defending this worthless snake?"

Rayne met Thorvin's gaze.

"Light Bringer?" Fallon's words broke the connection and Rayne looked over his shoulder.

"Other newcomers approach," Fallon said. "They have entered Neth and are close. If thou wouldst evade them, we must make all haste now while it is still possible to do so."

The Kindred leader inclined his head toward Rayne. "But if thou wishes to converse with thy friends before we continue, Neal and I will attempt to distract those who have entered here with violence in their hearts."

"No." Rayne shook his head. "I'll not risk any Kindred." He shifted his eyes back to Thorvin. "We'll talk later. Now we need to move."

Tenderness infused his spirit as he set Lexi back. "You understand? We can talk later, Lexi." Shifting his eyes from Lexi to Thorvin and back, he continued. "I promise I'll explain everything ... later."

Lexi nodded and stooped to pick up her swords. Rayne's gaze drifted from her to Andrew. Donning a half-smile, he winked at the page then raised his eyebrows in question as he noticed the girl chewing her lower lip, half-hidden behind Andrew. "I think it will take some time to sort things out."

He slapped his thigh and whistled for Boone who yipped then took her place at his left heel, ready for his commands.

Neal headed out, followed by Ean, Rayne and his friends, while Fallon trailed behind. As the day progressed, Neal kept a stiff pace. When the forest thinned, the newcomers mounted and rode while the Kindred ran in their swift fashion, shifting through the thick forest like living shadows.

Morning drifted into afternoon and by the time Fallon called for a break they were once again walking, leading their horses along a narrow path following one of the numerous streams that flowed through Neth. The blue tinged light of the sun angled weakly through the dense canopy above as late afternoon shadows deepened beneath the forest giants.

Though the One had done a wonderful work in healing Rayne, his body struggled to keep pace with the others. Relief flooded through him when Fallon's words penetrated his numbed state. He stumbled to a halt and turning, handed his reins to Thorvin without protest when the man reached out, saying, "I've got this for you, Your Highness."

As Rayne's hand dropped limply to his side, Boone was there, pushing against his palm, seeking his attention. "Who's my good girl?" he asked, his voice soft and spent.

"She really is a good girl." Lexi stepped in front of the dog and squatting down reached over to scratch behind her ears. She led us to you, you know. I think she would follow you anywhere." Her eyes searched out Rayne's and warmth spread through him at seeing her regard. The desire to wrap his arms around Lexi shot through him, but weakness kept him from acting on the impulse. Instead he just stood over her, staring, with a loopy half-grin plastered on his face.

"Thou must be exhausted," Ean huffed as he joined the two. "Come, I've spread a blanket near the stream. I will help thee."

Succumbing to his undeniable exhaustion, Rayne allowed Ean and Lexi to help him to the blanket where he dropped like a sack of potatoes to the ground. Lexi lowered herself to a place next to him.

Ean nodded, a satisfied expression on his face. "Thou

must stay put while I prepare something to help thee regain thy strength." A grin split Ean's wide face and his cheeks turned a deep pink. "Thou and thy lady friend look good there together. Don't bother thyself with anything, just rest."

"He's sweet," Lexi murmured as Ean bustled over to Fallon. Fallon's brow lowered and he shook his head at Ean's words.

"I don't think we're going to stay here long enough for him to do anything," Rayne said. "Fallon doesn't look happy." While Ean and Fallon continued to talk, Rayne sought out Andrew and the mysterious girl who was with him. The two were helping Thorvin water the horses farther downstream from where Rayne sat. "Who is she?" he asked Lexi, flicking his eyes in the girl's direction.

Lexi glanced over and huffed. "Oh! Her! She's just some dirty scroll worshiper Andrew picked up. I don't know why she even came with us. She belongs with her people, not here. I mean, for all we know, she could be a spy working for them, just waiting for the chance to turn you over again. I don't trust her."

"So …" Rayne's thoughts jumbled over and around each other. "She's a scroll worshiper, but she came with you to help me? Does Andrew trust her?"

"I suppose so. At least he seems to. But her father's some big leader in the USO." Lexi shook her head, the ends of her pinned-up hair flinging around like a faint halo. "But I don't want to talk about her; I want to know what happened to you. Your mother and I kept sensing your terror and darkness. We all feared the worst. But you're here now. Are you really okay? Please, tell me. What did they do to you?"

Rayne released a deep sigh and ran his hands through the thick, black fur at Boone's neck, finding comfort in the familiar motion. He couldn't tell Lexi the truth of what had been done to him; she carried far too much hatred of any who worshiped the scrolls already. And when he confessed his plan to speak the One's words to the people who had just tried to use him to bring Sigmund back from where he had been bound, she'd never understand. Instead, she would do all she could to try to stop him. He couldn't tell Thorvin either; the man would agree with Lexi and tell Rayne he was crazy.

Avoiding the question, Rayne waved Andrew and his friend over. When he got to Rayne, Andrew leaned in and gave him a gentle hug then stepped back, his eyes squinted with worry. "I'm so sorry we didn't rescue you. Everyone tried to get to Nemora sooner, but we couldn't. I knew Boone could find you. Your father said I couldn't come, but I had to ... so I followed."

"It's okay, Andrew," Rayne said. "You did what you needed to do. I'm glad you're here and that you brought Boone. Would you introduce me to your friend?"

"Oh ... yes!" Andrew shifted from foot to foot then stepped aside, waving for Mayda to approach Rayne. "Your Highness, this is Mayda Creedoff. Mayda, this is His Highness, Prince Rayne of Ochen."

Mayda took a hesitant step forward and dropped into an awkward bow. She opened her mouth but closed it several times before whispering, "I ... I ... I'm glad you're okay. I'm sorry for what we did. I ... I'm so sorry. I didn't know about you or what really happened until Andrew explained things to me. If you are mad and want me to leave, I understand ... I mean if you don't want me near you ... I'll find my way back on my own."

"Of course." Lexi's voice dripped sarcasm. "Now that you know where Rayne is, you offer to leave like you're doing us a favor. You'll probably go to your father and point him straight to us. Just like the bloodthirsty traitor you really are."

"That would not be necessary, if that is indeed the young lady's plan." Fallon's soft voice broke into the conversation before Rayne could object. Fallon turned his gaze to Rayne. "It seems those who have been tracking thee have turned to intercept us. We must make haste if we are to avoid them."

"How?" Thorvin's attention riveted on Mayda. "How did you do it? You must have signaled them somehow."

Mayda took a step back as the big man towered over her, his hands clenched in fists. "No," Mayda puffed out the word, shaking her head. "I wouldn't do that. I couldn't. Please, you have to believe me."

"I believe you." Rayne pushed up onto his feet, reached out and grabbed Thorvin's arm, pulling until his old mentor turned to face him. "Thorvin. I believe her. The truth is they wouldn't need her help to track me. Aunt Cailyn is with them. She's probably using a searching tendril to find me. She's one of their leaders. We need to listen to Fallon. The closer Aunt Cailyn is, the easier it will be for her to sense me. You know this." He blocked the pain of his aunt's betrayal as he focused on the more important goal of returning to Inverness. "We can't be fighting among ourselves when our enemies are close. Please, let's get moving."

Thorvin stared at Rayne for a moment, his jaw hanging, then shook his head. "No. That makes no sense. I know Cai; she wouldn't do that. Why would she be involved in any of this? She wouldn't do it."

"For vengeance." Rayne's eyes shifted to scan the woods to his right. "She wants me to suffer because she blames me for Braydon's death and Miles's suicide."

Rayne's gaze returned to meet his friend's. Rubbing his chin, Thorvin's eyes went wide as he nodded once, slowly. "Yes. Rowena was concerned something happened to her sister."

Rayne turned to Fallon. "Are your scouts still tracking the other group?"

Fallon nodded.

"Good. Let's try changing direction and see if they follow. If they do, we'll need to find a way to lose them. If we head due east from here instead of north, Fallon, will we still be able to get out of Neth soon?"

"Yes. We are not far from the Neth River here. We can travel east then follow the river north."

With a sharp nod, Rayne said, "Then that's what we're going to do."

35

ℵ

Near noontime two days later, Rayne stood on a rocky rise overlooking the banks of the Neth River. Fallon was talking to Neal and the scout, who had returned a few minutes ago, appearing like phantoms from a thick stand of old pine trees. Thorvin watered the horses while Ean told Andrew and Mayda a story. Giles stood off by himself upstream from Rayne's position. A light breeze ruffled Rayne's ragged hair and brought the heavy scent of pine to his nostrils as he watched sunlight turn the water into sparkling sapphires on the churning river.

"Was I seeing things, or did Neal disappear and reappear?" Lexi touched Rayne's arm and waved toward where the three were talking in their native tongue.

Rayne chuckled. "No. It's not your eyes playing tricks. The Kindred aren't solid in the same way we are; they're more spirit than flesh. Ancients with the ability to manipulate the magic of Nemora, they can do anything we can, just not in the same ways.

"Although you shouldn't mention the disappearing to Fallon or any of the others. They can be touchy about it."

Fallon waved Rayne and Thorvin over. "I'll be right back." Rayne wrapped his fingers around Lexi's hand that had hovered over his upper arm, giving it a slight squeeze.

Lexi's eyebrows rose. "Oh no; you're not getting away from me that easily." With an expression that brooked no disobedience, she motioned him forward and followed on his heels.

"Neal and Gavin have succeeded in distracting those who are tracking thee. At the present time, they are moving southeast. If it meets thy approval, Light Bringer, I propose we follow the river upstream to one of our established campsites at Neth's borders. We can take our ease there for the night before leaving the protection of the forest. Neal will rejoin us while Gavin continues to monitor the movements of those who have entered here uninvited. Dost thou agree?"

Rayne nodded; his brows drawn together in thought. "That is good news. And I appreciate your offer to spend the night resting. But … I … fear stopping for the night. We can't lose the time." He paused, his eyes flicking toward the river again. "We'll stop, but only for a few hours, then press on to Inverness."

Ean walked up at that moment, a look of concern crossing his face. "Thou cannot mean to push thyself so much. If thou dost not allow time for rest, thou wilt once again fall to thy sickness."

Rayne groaned under his breath as everyone else drew near. They would all argue for him to pace himself, but the One's internal prompting demanded he keep moving. With no choice left him, Rayne drew himself up to his full height and spoke in the commanding voice he heard his father use when demanding obedience. Though he put on an outward show, speaking to his friends in such strong language churned his stomach. "Am I not the crown prince of Ochen? Am I not the One's chosen Light Bringer? I believe I own both those titles. And, as such, my word must be obeyed. We leave now for the border of Neth. We will camp there for a few hours, then we *will* head north to Inverness."

Seeing the protest forming on Lexi's and Thorvin's faces,

Rayne raised his hand, silencing them. "No. This is not up for discussion. We move now."

Several hours after leaving the cover of Neth Forest, Rayne pushed both the horses and the Kindred. Ean had turned back with Gavin at the Neth border while Neal and Fallon continued to travel with the party, committed to following Rayne to Inverness. Now, with night falling they stumbled upon a thick grove of Ash and River Birch trees in a hollow flanking one of the myriad streams that populated Neth, Thorvin insisted they set up a camp and rest for the next few hours.

Lexi hovered behind Thorvin as the big man ignored Rayne's objections, reached up and grabbed Rayne's left arm and, with little effort, dragged the prince from his horse. When Thorvin pulled the arm over his shoulders, Lexi slipped in under Rayne's other arm and helped him hobble on unsteady legs until Thorvin lowered him to sit on a fallen tree trunk.

"Now stay put," the big man growled. "And listen this time." He huffed and softened his voice. "You can't keep pushing yourself. Let us take care of setting camp. You need to rest."

"He is correct." Fallon gazed down at Rayne, his eyes large and filled with sorrow. "Thou hast pushed past thy limit and must listen to his good advice. I will make thee some of Ean's healing tea once a fire has been started."

Rayne squelched the protest blooming out of the frustration that bubbled within and, clamping his lips tight, nodded. Since waking in the Heart of Neth, he had struggled with bouts of chronic exhaustion. And though he felt the pressure of time speeding by, it would do no good if he broke his neck in a fall from his horse. He shifted to the ground, leaned his back against the fallen tree, and closed his eyes.

"Is there anything I can do for you?" Lexi's voice penetrated the haze already dragging Rayne into sleep.

"No," he murmured. "I'm going to try and get some sleep."

He had only rested for a couple minutes when Boone's wet nose nudged under his hand drawing him back from the edge of oblivion. He lifted his arm slightly and the dog wormed her way forward to lie next to Rayne.

Hours later, when Rayne awoke, the fire sputtered, now nothing more than low embers. Overhead Rem's silver light reflected off a bank of clouds to the north while Ledia's blue hues skimmed knife-like over the tops of the trees now hiding her bulk.

"Good morning, Light Bringer." Fallon's voice was soft but clear. "Thy friends sleep. Neal and thy cousin Giles are watching. The sun will break soon. Dost thou feel rested?"

Rayne thought about the question. Blinking several times, he sucked in deep breaths of air and he ran his hand over Boone's fur, enjoying her presence next to him. "Better than I was. But ..." Rayne tried to pierce the darkness in the direction of Fallon's voice, but he couldn't make out the Kindred and he sighed. "I know the One is with me. He has proven that time and again. And yet ... I fear the coming moment when I must stand before the scroll worshipers and speak of the One's love. I've faced others who denied the existence of the One, but never so many who were intent on denying the One."

"Before we left the Heart, thou told me the Creator-Father called thee to this task and that he has prepared hearts. Thou must cling to that truth. Hast thou lost faith in the Creator-Father's promises?"

"No!" The word came out with a force that surprised Rayne and he scanned the sleeping forms around him. When no one stirred, he continued in a lower voice. "No. I don't doubt him. I doubt me."

Rayne's hand slipped from Boone's back as she rose and padded toward the stream.

"In the past, when I declared his words, his presence was strong within me. I spoke out of a center of peace and strangers were touched. But ... now ..." He shook his head, flinging strands of unruly hair about. "Fallon, I can't find my center of peace. It's like that part of me got locked away while I waited in the dark for those sacrifices, seeking to lose myself in Ferris

Weed. I'm not who I was. I can't even reach through to the heart of the one I love. Somehow, no matter what I say, I can't convince Lexi to release her hatred of scroll worshipers. If I can't get through to her, how am I going to influence people who are filled with so much hatred they not only slaughtered innocents on their altar, they sought to use my blood and eventually my life to bring Sigmund and his kind back." Rayne twisted a twig in his hands, his powerlessness to reach Lexi sliced through him like a knife. "The One expects so much of me ... so do you ... my parents ... so many others ... but what if I've changed? What if I can't do it anymore ... what if I ... fail?"

Fallon walked over to the fire and threw on some kindling. It ignited and he added two small logs, his face ruddy in the growing flames. "Thou hast talked with Andrew's young friend, Mayda. She had been one of those whose hearts you would touch with your words. Has not her heart been softened? Has it not been prepared so that when Andrew arrived, she was ready to help him even though it meant leaving her father? Take heart, young Light Bringer. If the Creator-Father promises a thing, is it not certain that thing will come to pass? I believe this is so."

Rayne stared at the flames without speaking as they crackled and licked around the wood. Though he appreciated the Kindred's words, doubt remained. *I worry for Lexi, but I wonder? Can I forgive yet again? Am I so different from Lexi? ... Can I face those who sought to use me to bring back the darkness? Not allow bitterness to cloud my judgment? Will I speak the One's words as he has asked, or will I, like Lexi, give in to a desire for vengeance?*

The need to move drove Rayne to push up onto his feet and walk on stiff legs to the edge of the stream where he found Boone, sitting, staring into the woods on the opposite bank.

The stream's gurgling surrounded Rayne, loud, insistent, stirring within him the droning voices from his past that he hadn't been able to escape during his dark imprisonment. Without warning, a surge of pain followed, and he bit back the need to cry out at the sudden onslaught. Quiet, unbidden, as he focused to overcome the agony, a subtle whisper bubbled to the surface of his troubled mind ... *Seek out Ferris Weed. Seek out the sweet. It will take the pain away ... help you. You need it. Release ... your pathetic desire to help others. You're too weak. Leave here now. You can make the Camp of the Forgotten in three days on horseback. Why suffer needlessly?*

It would be so easy, so simple. He could leave now and not be missed until morning. A waft of cold air sent a shiver through him, raising pimpled flesh on his arms. Boone's whine cut through his thoughts and the One's words spoken days before soothed his spirit like a warm balm. *Though the sweet calls to you, cling to my voice and I will strengthen you.*

Rayne shook off the siren call of the Ferris Weed. Stepping with care to the edge of the stream, he hunkered down, bent over, and splashed icy cold water onto his face, running his hands through his hair and over the back of his neck. "Thank you, my Lord." The soft words seemed to echo around him. Thorvin's voice broke the spell.

"Rayne? Rayne? Where are you? Is Andrew with you?"

36

Tracking Rayne had been easy. The abundance of available energy in Neth fueled Cailyn, allowing her to extend her quest farther than she had ever done before. Her confidence soared as they traveled mile after mile, the distance between Rayne and Cailyn shrinking as the hours passed. Her searching tendrils locked onto his unique life force with such a potent bond she felt as if they were physically linked. Until, three days later when thick growths of understory bushes or steep channels cut by racing streams blocked every path forward. After turning south, then working their way east, they began to, once again, diminish the gap between them and Rayne.

Cailyn lead, focused on tracking Rayne, with Seth at her back. Arnulf followed the two, the soldiers spaced out behind him, leading the horses through dense stands of pine and fir. The air was thick, heavy with the scent of dried, crushed pine needles. The chuckling of one of the many streams had become a dull droning and the small scratching sounds of animals and myriad bird songs lulled the group. They marched forward in a mid-afternoon daze until a strange, high-pitched whine vibrated the trees around them.

"What's that?" Seth's voice rose above the noise as his hand grasped Cailyn's shoulder and he turned her to face him. She opened her mouth to respond when, with panicked neighing, several horses reared and struck at those leading them. The other mounts joined in and within less than a minute, most of the animals had broken free and were galloping back the way they had come. The sound, now louder—closer—filled the air, driving soldiers to their knees, hands shielding their ears.

The noise faded, replaced by wild laughter that bounced off the surrounding trees as if it came from every direction. "Silly stupid newcomers. Thou hast chosen poorly in entering here. Leave Neth before thou loses more than a few flea laden nags." Again, the laughter reverberated for another moment, then silence pounded against Cailyn's eardrums. Not even a bird song or the rustling of a small animal broke the eerie hush.

"Don't just stand there you fools, get the horses." Seth waved toward the retreating animals before turning to Cailyn. "By the seven, what was that?"

His voice broke the spell that froze Cailyn. Shaking off her shock, she closed her eyes and whispered, "I don't know. I've never experienced anything like it before."

Tales she had heard as a child flitted through her mind and her eyes popped open. "No. Wait. I do know what ... or rather who ... that was." She rounded on Seth. "I warned you, didn't I? The Kindred don't take kindly to newcomers invading Neth. We need to leave here. Now. This is just the beginning. A warning."

Seth's jaw dropped for a second until he snapped it shut, sparks flying from his eyes. "And what do you propose we do? Give up the search? Just let the Binder go?" He ground his teeth and broke eye-contact with Cailyn to stare out past her shoulder. "No." His gaze flicked back to her. "You know as well as I do, we can't let that happen."

Cailyn clasped her hands together to mask their trembling as stories of the Kindred's wrath toward trespassers stirred the old fears of childhood. Of travelers who ventured into Neth never to be seen again.

Cailyn swallowed the rock-like lump that formed at the

back of her throat. "Seth, you don't understand. Whatever the High Guardian may or may not do, will become a moot point if we don't survive Neth."

Anger distorted Seth's handsome features and Cailyn noted the fear in his expression as he turned from her to confer with Arnulf. *This isn't the first time I've seen Seth's fear. But if the High Guardian's return with the scrolls is our ultimate goal—if he's good—why would Seth fear serving him?* Cailyn suppressed another shudder. *But Seth ... No! Seth knows what he's doing. I will not disappoint him. If ... If ... no ... I can't turn from my path now. I will not allow Brayden's and Miles's deaths to be meaningless.* Glancing over her shoulder at Seth and Arnulf, Cailyn bit her lip. *And yet, is bringing the mysterious High Guardian back really going to help the people of Nemora? What do I do?*

The quiet voice whispered into her spirit. *Trust me and forgive. Release your ill-advised need for Seth's praise. Seek me instead. I will lead you on paths of peace.*

Cailyn stared ahead, unseeing, as she chewed her lower lip.

Until she met Seth, she'd struggled with depression and the deeply buried fear that she was nothing more than a disappointment to her parents. She tried hard to follow Rowena's example, be the perfect daughter. But she couldn't compete. Her childhood hero worship turned to envy which birthed hatred; though she hid it well as she pretended to be Rowena's best friend as well as sister. Perhaps her hatred had fueled her son's. *No, I can't think about that now.* She shook her head, throwing off the flooding guilt that threatened to drown her.

"Lady Mother." Seth's call pulled Cailyn's attention back to the present. "We have decided to cut straight north and leave this cursed forest. Our enemies appear to be heading toward Inverness, probably seeking to escape Nemora through the portals. We will rejoin our fellow believers who have been tracking along the outskirts of Neth and intercept the Binder between Neth and Inverness. Can you continue to track his presence if we do this?"

Cailyn swallowed as she walled off the guilt that battered against her resolve and nodded. "As long as he doesn't get too far away, I can."

"Good. Once the men have retrieved the horses, we will proceed." Seth's icy expression softened. "You have done well, my lady." A gentle smile lifted the corners of his mouth. "I know this is hard, but it will be worth it in the end."

"And what will that end be, Seth?" Cailyn pulled in a deep breath and met Seth's gaze. "I've seen the fear in your eyes whenever you mention failing to fulfill our pact with the High Guardian. If he is so terrible, how can you trust him to bring back the scrolls? And if he does, will they truly bring us power and peace?

"I was raised to believe in the One; to trust that he seeks good for his people. Can you honestly tell me we can expect the same from the High Guardian?"

A fleeting instant of irritation surfaced before compassion spread across Seth's features. "You question. That is good, my lady. But you must let go of the false teachings of your past and embrace the truth that peace can only be achieved through power—and our greatest source of power resides within the promised scrolls. And only the High Guardian can bring them back to us.

"His return guarantees a restoration of Ochen's power and glory. Of course I fear him; just as I would fear any being possessing that level of power. Even One worshipers are said to *fear* the One. You fear this forest. Why? Because it has power you can't understand. I respect the High Guardian for the same reason. I would be foolish not to. Can you not see this?" He paused and Cailyn's gaze shifted to the deep shadows surrounding them. An errant breeze filtered through, blowing strands of hair across her face and swaying branches. Patches of light and dark played a swift game of hide and seek, as if the shadows were alive.

A faint chuckle drew Cailyn's blinking focus back to the charismatic man before her. The soft sound morphed into a gentle laugh as he shook his head. He puffed a breath out his nose. "Even you, my dear, sweet lady. Your power, your ability to manipulate the heavy, magical air of Nemora. I respect—yes, and even fear—you. Do you understand now?"

Plunging into the depths of his matchless eyes, remembering

how he had given her strength and encouragement since Miles's suicide, Cailyn nodded. "Yes, Seth. I begin to see."

He stepped in closer and set his firm hands on Cailyn's shoulders as a soothing smile quirked the corners of his mouth. "You are amazing, my lady. Our cause would have died an ignoble death a year ago if not for your support." His voice dropped, barely heard above the murmuring pine needles and buzz of insects. "I ... I ... think ... I love you." His lips lowered to meet Cailyn's, so soft, so persuasive. Without thinking, Cailyn lost herself for a few seconds before pulling away.

"Seth. No. We can't."

"I know." Understanding creased the skin around eyes that spoke of an insatiable hunger. "I will wait. But be forewarned my lovely mage, once we've achieved our goals, I will not be put off any longer. Come. Let us succeed quickly."

Cailyn shook off the effects of Seth's proximity and pulled in several breaths, her gaze locked on Seth's muscular form as he strode toward Arnulf. *He loves me? When did that happen? Our goals ... always it had been about our mutual goals. But now ... can it be? Do I love him? We've shared so much. I'll have to think about this.*

Her horse plodded forward through the thinning trees as they approached the edge of Neth Forest and Cailyn replayed the scene of Seth's pronouncement of love from two evenings before in her mind, dissecting it, scrutinizing it. Though she wanted to believe his words, she couldn't accept that someone as alluring as he could fall in love with her. And yet, every time she glanced in his direction, she met his eyes and he winked.

They made camp in a shallow depression where a stream meandered through a grove of willow trees before disappearing in the deeper shadows of the forest proper, now fading in the twilight.

A shiver of delight traced its way up Cailyn's spine as Seth stepped behind her, shifted her braid, and placed a feather-soft kiss on the base of her neck before striding toward Arnulf who stood like some mythic statue, scanning.

"Anything?" Seth's voice drifted to Cailyn.

"It seems quiet. I can't shake the feeling we're still being watched."

"We've left their cursed trees so we should be safe. Tomorrow morning you'll need to send men in both directions. Our fellow believers should not be far. And … with the High Guardian's favor, they'll join us before we catch up to the Binder and his friends"

Arnulf shifted and lowered his voice. Cailyn closed her eyes to focus on the conversation. "…still tracking him?"

"Yes, she believes he's still east of us. Probably on one of the Kindred's trails, maybe even out of the forest by now. We'll catch him tomorrow or the next day for sure."

"And she's past all that doubting? You've convinced …" Arnulf draped an arm on Seth's shoulders and shifted away from the camp. They continued speaking, but Cailyn could hear no more.

Exhaustion left Cailyn with little appetite and after a light meal of rabbit stew, she sought out her tent. Within minutes of settling in her bedroll, her eyelids drooped, and she drifted off into fitful sleep. Predawn dark enveloped her when raised voices tugged Cailyn out of a disturbing dream. She blinked, attempting to dislodge the grit of sleep from her eyes and the dream from her mind as she pulled on her boots. Still groggy, she slipped out the tent flap. The group of believers who split off before she and Seth entered Neth had arrived during the night. They stood around the now blazing fire, focused on several forms, backlit by the blaze. The scent of brewing coffee laced the smoky air.

Cailyn's eyes followed everyone's line of sight and locked onto five people. Recognition drove off the vestiges of sleep as she murmured, "Andrew? What are you doing here?"

Associate Shepherd Creedoff and his daughter Mayda were arguing loudly, her arms swinging in wild arcs to emphasize her words. Next to them, Andrew, Rayne's page, struggled in Arnulf's grip.

Seth's shout drowned out the argument. "Vartan, explain yourself. What is going on here and who is this boy?"

37

Silence followed Seth's shout, but only for a moment as all eyes locked on him. Mayda, her lips thinned in anger, snorted and resumed her argument. "Please father, you have to listen to me. You remember Andrew, don't you? My friend from camp? I came looking for you and Andrew wouldn't let me come alone. You can't punish him for that. Please! Tell Arnulf to let him go."

Cailyn pulled her cloak closer as the chilly nighttime air set gooseflesh to rising on her arms, then followed Seth as he approached Associate Shepherd Creedoff.

Seth huffed out an annoyed breath and signaled Arnulf. "Arnulf, let the boy go ... for now." His gaze landed on Andrew for a few seconds, his eyes narrowed in suspicion, before his stormy gaze shifted to Vartan and Mayda. "Vartan, care to explain to me why your daughter is here. And, more to the point, how she even found us? And by the seven, who is this boy? I need explanations and I want them now!"

Cailyn slipped past Seth and moved closer to Andrew. The boy slumped next to Arnulf, his chin to his chest, eyes focused on the ground as he kicked a patch of moss at his feet.

"Andrew." Cailyn spoke in a hushed whisper. Her eyes shifted to Seth whose back was turned as he questioned Vartan and Mayda. "Andrew." She raised her voice to a louder whisper once Arnulf released the boy and walked over to Seth. She met Andrew's burgeoning anger head on, his disgust obvious in the slope of his lips as she asked, "Nemora's moons, what are you doing here?"

Andrew's chin came up and his eyes flashed. "I could ask you the same thing, my *lady*. How could you be part of this?"

"Shhh." Cailyn waved Andrew to silence. "Seth can't know who you are, or you'll be in great danger."

"And just who is he?" Cailyn gasped. She hadn't heard Seth's approach and now he spoke at her shoulder. "Obviously you know the young man. I think introductions are in order."

Beyond Seth, Mayda's eyes grew wide. She started forward but her father grabbed her arm. "Stay out of this daughter."

Cailyn's circling thoughts landed on one fact; she couldn't let Seth know who Andrew was. Regardless of what Rayne had done, she would not allow Seth to sacrifice the page who had shown her kindness in the past. And, if he learned the truth, that is exactly what he would do—use Andrew to lure Rayne to him then sacrifice both.

Shifting her fingers along the edges of her mantle with a show of calm despite the chaos churning within, she smiled at Seth. "Yes, I do know this young man. He is a family friend. I've known him since he was a wee baby. His name is Andrew." Cailyn waved a hand toward Seth. "Andrew, have you met Prime Shepherd Hamlin?" She met Andrew's eyes, willing him to understand as a slight shake of her head sent her braid shifting across her back.

Andrew stiffened, then understanding blossomed. One subtle nod of his head birthed relief in Cailyn. He understood; he would play along.

"No, Your Grace, I haven't had the honor."

Donning the mask of her office, Cailyn allowed a slight smile to surface. "Well, then I shall introduce you. Seth, please meet Andrew Weiland originally of Corylus and more recently of Nemora; Andrew, this is Seth Hamlin, Prime Shepherd of the United Scrolls of Ochen and a close friend."

Andrew inclined his head. "It is a pleasure to meet you. My friend Mayda has told me much about you."

Seth's eyes narrowed. "And how did you come to meet Mayda? I didn't think she had any friends who didn't believe in the scrolls."

"Oh, he's a believer all right. Aren't you boy?" Vartan's over-loud voice broke Seth's stare. "Met him when we skipped. He's been with Mayda and me ever since. Right nice young man, he is." Vartan paused, his brows drawing together. "Wait. You had a dog with you, didn't you? What happened to your dog?"

Andrew's mouth opened but nothing came out.

"We left her back at the camp when we came looking for you." Mayda scooted around her father to stand next to Andrew. "Some friends are taking care of her. We didn't think bringing her along was a good idea. Right, Andrew?"

Andrew nodded, then mumbled, "Yeah. That's right. We left her with friends."

"Seth." Arnulf's eyes locked onto Andrew before shifting to Seth. "We need to talk."

Seth focused on the big man; his eyes questioning. "Of course.

"Lady Mother, please excuse me a moment." Seth smiled at Cailyn and patted her hand before walking off a short distance with Arnulf.

Her attention fixed on Seth and Arnulf, Cailyn stepped in front of Andrew. Conflicting emotions churned her stomach and head. *Only one reason he could be here now. He's been with Rayne. How? How is that even possible?* She ground the tips of her fingers into her forehead, then met the boy's gaze. "Andrew, you can't be here. Find some excuse and you and Mayda leave now. Go back to Inverness. If Seth finds out who you are, he will not hesitate to use you as a sacrifice. You are not safe." Her gaze drifted back to Seth and Arnulf. *Arnulf knows!* A distressed sound slipped past her lips. "Why? Why did you even come here?"

"For my pop." Mayda's voice cracked. "He doesn't understand. I have to help him, convince him what you are all doing is wrong. Don't you see that? Sacrificing people to call the High Guardian is just … evil. Andrew…" She reached over and grabbed Andrew's hand, wrapping her fingers around his. "Andrew wouldn't let me come alone. If anything happens to him, it's my fault. I thought if I could convince Pop to leave Prime Shepherd Hamlin and return home … things could go back to the way they were. I wish we'd never come to Nemora."

She swallowed hard, blinking back tears that clung to her lashes. "It wasn't supposed to be like this. So stupid! Stupid Arnulf had to see us. Oh, Andrew, I'm so sorry."

"What are you talking about?" Vartan said, confusion drawing his brows together. "You came here for me? To tell me I don't understand. I thought you believed in the High Guardian. You never told me you had questions."

Mayda groaned. "I didn't. At least not until we began those horrible sacrifices." She shuddered. "All those people; all that blood. Then I met Andrew … met the Binder—Prince Rayne." She shook her head. "He's not what we were told. The One isn't what we were told. Oh, Pop. We were wrong."

"Really?" Seth lingered over the word, drawing it out.

Cailyn jumped at the sound of his voice next to her ear. Arnulf stood to Seth's left, a self-satisfied smile curling his lips.

"It looks as if we have some One worshipers in our midst, Arnulf. Do you agree with your daughter, Vartan? Have you given up our dream to reclaim our scrolls of power and fallen for the lies of a false god?"

Vartan stepped back, shaking his head. "No. No … I don't know." He paused, his eyes glazing, then he lifted his hands in supplication. "Seth, she's my daughter."

"Yes. Your daughter. A member of the USO's next generation. It seems to me that the Binder—and his little servant here—are attempting to corrupt our youth. Arnulf, you know what must be done."

Cailyn stifled a scream as Arnulf and four other soldiers jumped forward, grabbed Andrew and Mayda, bound them, and pushed them to their knees next to the smoldering remains of the fire.

She wanted to run back into her tent, ignore what was happening, but instead her feet moved as if of their own accord, propelling her to stand in front of Seth. Trembling and biting back her fear, she confronted him. "What are you going to do with them?"

Seth's smile sent waves of fear through Cailyn. "Why, nothing. At least nothing yet. Let's see how much the Binder is willing to sacrifice to get back his little friend, shall we? You, of all people, should be delighted at this turn of events."

Delighted? I should be... Oh, Lord, how did I get to this place?

38

Anger glinted in Theodor's eyes at Rowena's statement, but at that moment, word came to them that everyone was in position. The time had arrived for them to display force and confidence in their bid to end this battle before it even began. "We'll discuss this later, Ro. You, me, and that *ex*-scroll worshiper."

Theodor nodded to his flag bearer who carried the white flag of truce, now furled, then signaled his trumpeter. Offering a smart salute, the young man raised the horn to his lips and blew the notes that signaled the soldiers of Ochen to reveal themselves. Others followed his call, their shrill notes penetrating the smoke and chaos until their voices blended, echoing across the valley.

At first, the scroll worshipers seemed unaware of the army surrounding them as they continued to struggle against the enveloping smoke that obscured the sloping hills and the fire that now engulfed several dozen tents and a large wooden structure. A moment later, first one, then several raised their eyes and pointed; shouts followed.

Rowena made out some of the words over the clamor as

tears brought on by the acrid smoke blurred her vision. "The king…" "The king…" "Army…"

One voice rang out above the chaos, deep and strong it barreled through the valley as if aided by magic. "To arms. To arms. Men and women of the USO. Now is our time. To arms!"

She couldn't see who was calling the milling mass to order below, but the response to his cry was evident as people began to scramble, some moving into ranks while others scrambled out of their way.

"Are you ready?" Theodor's voice drew Rowena's attention. He stood in his stirrups; his eyes locked on a point below. Somehow, despite the smoke and activity, Theodor must have spotted the man in charge of the scroll worshipers. Blinking, she wiped the tears from her cheeks and nodded.

"Unfurl the flag," Theodor ordered, then kneed his charger into a slow trot down the grassy incline, skirting the few trees still left standing along the way. The flag bearer moved to his left as Rowena shifted to flank him on the right. The jingle of tackle and muffled horses' hooves were soon drowned out by the overwhelming noise as they rode into the camp. Fear rounded the eyes of most of those they passed, though anger was evident in clenched fists and flattened mouths as well.

Rowena followed Theodor's example, keeping her eyes focused forward and her horse in motion. Smoke continued to swirl, revealing then concealing the scroll worshipers; men, women, and children, dressed in USO cloaks smudged and grimy from fighting the fires.

The crowd before them split until they faced several rows of armed individuals. A well-built, middle-aged man with salt and pepper hair and a scarred face, holding a sword as if he knew how to use it stood before the group.

Theodor pulled to a stop and Rowena let her eyelids lower, preparing to fortify his voice with heavy energy so all would hear his words.

The king sat, statue-like and regal. His presence exerted the hoped-for influence. As the people around him grew quiet, the sounds of flames crackling, and wind hissing filled the void.

"I am Theodor, heir to Nathan, and King of all Ochen." He paused, his eyes roaming over the crowd. "Your presence here as off-worlders on Nemora, taking control of the skipping lines from Corylus and Sorial, and your efforts to raise an army all signify treason. To excuse your rebellion would be to betray Ochen. Look to the hills circling this valley. Take note. You are surrounded by the well-trained troops of the confederation who stand ready to defend our worlds against insurrection.

"I do not wish for war; I don't think you do either. Before this upheaval blows up into the conflict we all desire to avoid, I would speak with your leaders to see if a compromise might be reached."

Though he didn't raise his voice, it cut through the valley like a carillon call. Rowena glanced over her shoulder to see Mite with closed eyes, muttering. He was aiding her magic, increasing the force of Theodor's voice. *Well done, Mite. Thank you.*

The man with the military bearing, who seemed to be in charge, took a step forward. Planting his feet shoulder width apart, he spat on the ground. "I am Captain Theada. I command the USO Militia. And I speak for Prime Shepherd Hamlin. We don't own you as our king. You serve a false god. We will not bow to you."

"I see," Theodor said in an even tone, though Rowena read the suppressed anger in his voice and his horse shifted beneath him, tense, pawing the ground. "You may not claim me, but I claim you. As you are my people, citizens of Ochen, I seek to avoid bloodshed this day. Do not misjudge me here, though. If you will not throw down your arms and surrender, I will set my army on you and your people. I will not—cannot—allow you to question my authority as King of Ochen."

A scream. Shouts. An arrow whistled by Theodor's head, piercing the flag of truce. Rowena redirected the power within her and set a barrier of protection around Theodor, herself, and those closest to her. Strength flowed into her from Mite, and she expanded the circumference of protection while wishing she could do more.

Other shouts followed. Chaos erupted. Panic ensued, as portions of the Ochen troops rushed down into the valley. Scroll worshipers ran in every direction, some skirmishing with the regular soldiers while others attempted to fight the fires now raging out of control. Captain Theada yelled, "Get the king!" He and his followers rushed toward Theodor.

Along the edge of Rowena's energy shield, Ochen soldiers rushed to defend Theodor as Captain Theada and his supporters slammed into them.

"Enough!" Theodor ground out between clenched teeth. "Ro, I need to be heard!"

Rowena once again redirected the energy she was holding to reweave the spell that empowered Theodor's speech.

As skirmishes took place across the valley, Theodor's words rang across the glen, reaching those who struggled to escape the tumult as well as those who fought. "Come to your senses, my fellow citizens of Ochen and cease this senseless rebellion now. Today I extend grace to you. I make no promise for tomorrow."

Theodor signaled Rowena to cut her support, then turned to his trumpeter and said, "Sound stand down."

Within seconds, the sound of multiple horns echoed across the hills. Rowena held her horse in check as Theodor turned his horse in a circle, stopping when his eyes caught on something. Captain Theada. Understanding his goal, Rowena followed, reforming her protective shield around Theodor, Gwyn and Mite who remained close at her side, the flag bearer, and herself, as Theodor spurred his horse, pulling up in front of the belligerent captain.

The King's Sword hissed as Theodor pulled it from his scabbard. He pointed it at the man, holding him at bay. "You would be wise to take my advice. Gather your people and determine your course. I will return tomorrow. Empty threats and angry shouting will not help you or your people. Be ready to sit down and discuss this as fellow citizens of Ochen when I return."

His face stern, he turned and pressed into a canter up the hill. Rowena took note of the few fights still going on nearby as she followed. Scanning she realized most of the scroll worshipers had resumed fighting the fires while all around her, Ochen soldiers scrambled to return to their positions on the hills.

She was nearing the top when a familiar voice shouted her name. She turned to see Benning and Oliver, faces and clothing sooty. Bram and his people trudged behind the two soldiers also looking bedraggled and exhausted. She turned her horse back and lowering her shield, pulled to a stop even as Theodor continued. Gwyn and Mite remained at her side.

Bram squinted his one eye and huffed out a breath. "Well, Yer' Majesty, it didn't do all we was hopin' it would but you'll be happy to know I ain't killed no one." He coughed, triggering a round of coughing among the group.

"Well done, Bram. Thank you and your friends. What will you do now? Do you have family here?"

"To tell you the truth, I kinda like helpin' Benning. He and Oliver are okay … for soldiers. We was wonderin' if we could … tag along with them a while longer?"

Rowena shifted her gaze to Benning. "What do you think?"

"Ollie and I appreciated Bram's help. He…"

Rowena's breath hitched as the ground rushed up to meet her. A sharp pain pierced her right side and a weight fell on her back. She tried to pull air into her lungs. Pressed into the ground, it was impossible. Panic flooded, followed by relief as the weight lifted off her back. Turning over, she groaned at the pain in her side as she dragged in deep breaths.

Above her, Benning and Oliver wrestled with a large man in a USO cloak, wielding a dagger. Coming up behind the man, Bram ran a short sword through the scroll worshiper. Bram shook his head and looked down at Rowena. "I tried, Yer' Majesty. I tried. But he shouldn't a jumped you like that, no he shouldn't."

Rowena's hand found a spot of liquid warmth spreading across her right side. She raised her eyes to Bram and as shock widened his one eye, darkness claimed her.

39

Light streamed through a familiar window as Rowena opened her eyes and turned her head. *How?* The last thing she remembered was being knocked off Mosley. *That man ... he stabbed me.* Slipping her hand beneath the blanket that covered her, Rowena found a layer of stiff bandages wrapped around her waist. The memory of what happened after her fall blossomed in her mind and she groaned. *'He shouldn't have jumped you like that.'*

"Oh, Bram."

"Thank the One, you're awake." Theodor's voice preceded him into the bedroom of the Royal Suite in Castle Inverness. A couple long strides brought him to Rowena's side; he leaned over and a soft kiss fluttered at Rowena's cheek.

"I was so worried. I wanted to be here when you awoke." He looked down at his hands then reached for Rowena's left hand, taking it up gently in his right, running the fingers of his left hand over hers. "A delegation from the scroll worshipers showed up at the castle two hours ago. I couldn't miss this opportunity to talk to the group who came in response to my daily visits to their camp."

"Mite stayed. Yes, yes, yes. To keep Light Bringer's mother company when she woke up. Yes, yes."

Rowena's eyes were drawn to the ancient who sat on a burgundy leather loveseat, his legs dangling inches above the ground. She rubbed at the tight bandage that covered her throbbing side.

"What happened?" she asked as Theodor took a seat at the far end of the bed.

Theodor redistributed his weight on the bed; his gaze drifted to the window and he ran a hand through his disheveled hair. "I am so sorry. I was stupid. Leaving your side when our enemies were so close was a foolish mistake. At least you weren't alone." He huffed, sorrowful eyes meeting Rowena's. "Some crazed scroll worshiper tried to kill you. But you're all right now."

Rowena slid her eyelids shut as she groaned. "Yes. I remember. Bram killed the man."

"And if he hadn't, I would have." Theodor's face reflected an unsettled anger within him. "To attack you like that was cowardly. You could have been killed."

"It's not your fault. I shouldn't have disbursed my shield and I should have been paying attention, not gotten distracted when I saw Benning." Rowena's brows drew together. "Wait. You said *daily visits* to the camp. How long have I been here?"

"Three days, Your Majesty." The familiar voice pulled Rowena's focus to the door. Anne walked in carrying a tray with several mugs. "I heard you were awake, so I brought some tea."

Anne set the tray on the sideboard while Theodor helped Rowena into a sitting position, fluffing several pillows behind her back. Anne handed cups to Theodor, Mite, and Rowena as a spicy aroma permeated the air above the steaming mugs. Taking one for herself, Anne left two on the tray and moved to sit next to Mite.

Rowena swallowed a sip of tea then returned to her question. "If I've been here three days, someone please tell me what all has happened." She shifted her gaze from Anne to Theodor.

"Yes. Daily visits to the camp." Theodor pushed up and

walked to the open window. He pulled in a deep breath, released it with a hiss through his teeth, then turned back to Rowena. "It's been a rather full three days." He raised his eyebrows and flattened his mouth. "Let me start at the beginning.

"After your injury I left things at the camp in Captain Ellis's capable hands. It wasn't an easy task. That USO captain, Theada, escaped with at least a couple hundred of his militia. They have been randomly attacking our troops and raiding outlying farms ever since, especially at night, creating havoc and leaving a trail of bodies.

Captain Ellis formed a special cavalry unit to pursue them." He paused, his brow wrinkling. "The majority of the scroll worshipers appear unwilling to push things to that level of violence. They are angry and sullen but remain close to their tents, making no threatening moves. Or at least they have remained close to their tents ever since the fires were put out the evening of that first day. But there have been others who have snuck out of the camp and joined Captain Theada, increasing his ranks.

"I've gone to the camp the past two days; threatened punishment for rebellion, offered amnesty for those who are willing to renounce the USO, and asked to meet with those in charge. It seems everyone who has authority within the ranks of the USO, except Captain Theada, are with Prime Shepherd Hamlin and ... Cailyn ... pursuing Rayne."

His eyes shifted from Rowena to Mite, then to Gwyn who now stood in the doorway, Shaw behind him. "But you know that already." His eyes returned to Rowena's. "That's what you didn't want to tell me, isn't it?"

Rowena nodded. "Yes. It's not that I didn't want to tell you. The timing wasn't right. I knew you would need time to process the information. The One knows I did. I planned to tell you everything once we returned to Castle Inverness."

Theodor nodded as a small smile crooked one side of his mouth. "I know. While you were unconscious, Gwyn and Benning filled in the gaps for me.

Anne rose, handed Gwyn a mug, then gave one to Shaw. Shaw took the tea, planted a kiss on Anne's cheek, then sat on a high back chair near the fireplace where a low fire burned. Ann retrieved her own tea and perched on the arm of Shaw's chair. Gwyn moved to the window, staring out as Theodor had done moments before.

Theodor's attention settled on Gwyn. "Gwyn has also been speaking to small gatherings of scroll worshippers who know him and are willing to listen. He's had some success and those coming to hear him are spreading his words to others.

"What do you think, Gwyn? Did those who came to the castle earlier come because of what you said? And are they a true representation of the current feelings now spreading throughout the camp?"

Gwyn sighed and turned to face Theodor. "Yes, and no, to both questions. They have come because they are curious, but they will not give up their belief in the scrolls and the High Guardian easily. And yes, they were sent to represent the camp, but not the whole camp.

"Without Prime Shepherd Hamlin's guidance, the people are at a loss. They are confused and they are afraid you will seek retribution for what has been done to your son. They did listen when I spoke of the One and reading his Words without attempting to kill me for blasphemy; that would never have happened before. But once Seth returns, I can't promise what they'll do. He has … a way of …" Gwyn huffed out a breath. "He's a natural leader that people want to follow. His influence will be hard to combat. It wouldn't shock me if he called his followers to attack your soldiers unarmed and, despite their current confusion, they obeyed.

"But … with him away, and his influence waning." He shrugged his broad shoulders. "I suspect that's why the One called me to speak now. Perhaps I am fooling myself, but I think my words are impacting many." Gwyn turned back to the window, blinking against the tears pooling in his eyes. "I have never felt the presence of the One like I do now. When your son returns, I believe that scores of people who have been blinded by the High Guardian and Prime Shepherd Hamlin will have their eyes opened to the One's truth.

"Unless he returns as Seth's prisoner." He shook his head,

a slow steady motion. "Last Binding Day, there was no ritual sacrifice. The final offering needs to take place in two days; the offering that calls for seven victims and the Bin ..." Gwyn dropped his gaze to the floor before continuing. "His Highness's death." He raised his eyes to meet Theodor's. "If Seth returns with Prince Rayne as his prisoner, he will do everything in his power to offer the prince's life blood to the High Guardian. And I can't guarantee the people won't back him. If that happens, all we've accomplished here will be for naught.

"Blood for blood; blood for power; blood for vengeance." Gwyn's voice turned deep and menacing and his words vibrated the air. Dark shadows filled the corners of the room. Rowena shivered in response to the heavy energy and dark power. "It is a potent call," Gwyn continued. "One which followers of the High Guardian are trained to heed."

"But you can change that," Rowena said as she threw off the effects of Gwyn's chant. "You just said you have never felt the presence of the One as you do now. He will be your strength just as he has been my son's strength for so long. You have been called; and if you have been called, the One will be with you. Trust him."

40

Fear for Andrew and Mayda squirmed within Rayne, like some loathsome serpent seeking release. Though he followed Thorvin and Lexi without a word, pushing his horse into a canter whenever his old trainer pushed for speed, his spirit was focused on a buzzing in his head. It hovered, just at the edge of consciousness, irritating and alarming.

Lexi reined in and came alongside Rayne. "Are you okay?" She bit her lip. "Stupid question, right? Of course you're not okay. You're worried about Andrew. We all are. That traitorous little scroll worshiper is probably leading him into a trap. I don't know why we ever trusted her."

"I'm sure wherever they are, Mayda isn't betraying Andrew. Even though I just met her, I could see she likes Andrew. And he, her. No. Whatever reason Andrew had for leaving us, must have been a good one. I trust Andrew. We'll see the two of them when we get to Inverness."

"You are too trusting. And too kindhearted to admit all scroll worshipers are despicable. I mean, why else would they try to invite that demon Sigmund and his darkness back to Ochen? Even if you chose to forget what they've done to you,

I can't. And talking nice isn't going to convince a bunch of zealots to change their beliefs."

Rayne tried to ignore the headache forming at the base of his skull. Lexi's ongoing prejudice grated on him, causing the throbbing pain to increase. As the sun rose higher and the mysterious vibration in his skull amplified, it became a struggle to concentrate. Lexi had remained by his side through the morning. He was certain she was doing her best to help him relax as she told him stories about her father-daughter trip on Veres. Try as he would to listen, he couldn't focus. He needed peace to think past the noise in his head.

When they stopped for a drink at a stream, Rayne held back until Lexi rode out with Thorvin. *The two are probably comparing notes on how to keep me safe.* Rayne smiled.

Hemmed in by a growth of giant trees, they slowed to a walk. Rayne's horse continued to follow behind Thorvin's so Rayne took the opportunity to pray. *Creator-Father, I promised to always trust you. That, whenever you called or whatever you asked, I would never say no. And you've always been with me. Please be with Andrew and Mayda now. I don't know where they went but I have a bad feeling about this.*

He looked back over his shoulder, grimacing at the increased pain the movement caused. Giles had dismounted and was leading his horse as he talked with Fallon and Neal, the two constantly scanning their surroundings as they spoke. As if he knew Rayne was watching, Fallon looked up, his eyes locking onto Rayne's. He said something to Neal who sprinted off into the woods, flanking the group. Then Fallon jogged up to walk alongside Rayne's horse.

"Thou dost feel the energy," Fallon said. "I cannot understand it; it is a message for thee. But I feel the vibrations in the energy."

"I don't understand it either." Rayne dismounted, grabbed his horses' reins, and walked next to Fallon. "All I know is, the back of my head is throbbing, and I don't know how to get the buzzing to stop."

"Listen." Fallon nodded as Rayne shifted his eyes to glance sideways at the Kindred. "Thou must focus and listen. Until thou clears everything else from thy mind and accepts the message, it will continue to pulse but not get any clearer."

Rayne nodded. "Thorvin," he shouted. "Keep going. Fallon and I are going to stop for a few minutes. We'll catch up to you shortly."

Thorvin turned his horse to face Rayne and pulled it to a stop, his brows drawn together. "No. That's not a good idea. Especially with Andrew missing."

Lexi stared at Rayne as if he had just grown a second set of arms. "Thorvin's right. You shouldn't be alone."

"We'll be fine. Fallon will be with me and he knows the area. And Neal is close by scouting. Don't worry. I have the sword Neal gave me, so I'm armed. We won't be long."

The two continued to stare and Rayne shook his head. "Why must you always question me? Fallon and I just need to talk alone for a few minutes, with no distractions. Trust me."

Thorvin's sigh of long suffering bounced off the trees but he huffed his agreement.

"You too, Giles." Rayne waved his cousin ahead.

Giles gave Rayne a hard look. "Remember. Don't do anything stupid. I will not come to your rescue again."

Rayne chuckled then ground his teeth at the pain. "No problem."

He watched the others disappear beyond a bend in the trail, then turned to Fallon. "How do I get this out of my head?"

Fallon tilted his head and studied Rayne for a moment. "The meaning of this message is not unknown to thee. That is why thou hast sent thy friends away."

Rayne looked away, unable to meet Fallon's eyes. Flicking his focus back to the Kindred, Rayne nodded. "Yes. I suspect it has something to do with Andrew and Mayda's disappearance."

"Thy friends would not understand what thou might need to do."

Again, Rayne nodded.

Fallon stood for a moment, indecision creasing his brow, then scanned the surrounding woods and pointed out the large trunk of a downed oak. "Sit, young Light Bringer." Rayne settled on the rough bark, planting his feet on the leaf-mulch covered ground, stirring up the scent of rotting things.

"Now, close thy eyes and relax. Relax and think of the vibrations as a song. Someone is singing to thee over a great distance. Listen but not with thy ears, with thy mind."

As Rayne calmed and allowed his thoughts to roam freely, words came to him. He stiffened when he realized who was speaking through the tendril—*Aunt Cailyn*—but he lost the thread of words, so he shook out his hands, took several deep breaths and settled again.

"... will not be harmed as long as you come alone."

Silence. Stillness. Then the message began again. "Rayne. We have Andrew. We will release him if you follow this tendril back to me. Prime Shepherd Hamlin doesn't want to hurt him, but he will sacrifice him if he must. Andrew will not be harmed as long as you come alone."

The words sank in like a boulder pressing on Rayne's chest. The buzzing stopped and the throbbing headache eased. Rayne sat still and silent for several minutes before awareness of a thin, smoky line leading off to the north west stirred feelings of revulsion within him; it was Cailyn's tendril. He had seen his mother's in training and Cailyn's was similar, but where Rowena's threads tended to a light smoky gray, Cailyn's was charcoal with snakes of black slithering through it. Heavy magic weighed on Rayne.

Fallon's voice broke Rayne's focus. "What wilt thou do?"

"You heard?"

Fallon nodded.

"I need to pray. Alone."

"Is it to pray that thou wouldst ask me to leave, or to follow the thread now fastened to thee?"

"Fastened?"

"Once the message was heard, the cord attached to thy spirit." Fallon cocked his head to the side. "But this is not news to thee. Thou hast practiced the same with thy mother. Is this not right?"

Irritation at Fallon's words drew Rayne to his feet. "Not with the message part, but yes. How did you know?"

Fallon merely shrugged. An awkward silence followed.

"I need to pray. And I need to do it alone. Perhaps you should return to Neth now. Find Neal and go."

Fallon shook his head, a disappointed look on his face. "Yes, prayer is needful. But no. I will not return to Wife Neci until I have done what I have committed to do. But I will send Neal back. And," Fallon gave Rayne a knowing look. "I will not lie to thy friends. This is a trap. Thou knowest it. And thou wouldst not have them follow thee. I understand. But I fear thou will come to harm if thou follows that darkness-infused line alone."

"Please."

"As thou hast said, prayer is indeed called for. If thou dost decide to go *after* speaking with the Creator-Father, I will not stop thee. I will continue on to Inverness with thy friends and will not tell them where thou hast gone. I will keep thy secret. But thou must promise to pray before deciding."

"Thank you." Rayne ground his knuckles into the sockets of his eyes. Rising, he walked over to Fallon, then held out his hand to shake Fallon's. "I can't let them sacrifice Andrew."

Fallon grabbed Rayne's hand and pulled him in, wrapping his arms around Rayne. "This I know. May the Creator-Father be with thee and guide thy steps, young Light Bringer. I have faith I will see thee again in Inverness."

"Fallon?"

"Yes?"

"When you get to Inverness, please tell everyone I'm sorry." He paused, pulled in and released several quick breaths in succession as he ran a hand through his hair. "Tell my parents I love them ... and whatever they see, whatever happens, they need to trust that the One is with me and I'm obeying his will. They need to make certain no one interferes with the scroll worshiper's ritual of sacrifice no matter what. They must trust me. This is really important.

"And Lexi. Tell her I love her and that if she loves me, she needs to trust me."

Fallon nodded.

Rayne bent down and ran his hands behind both Boone's

ears. "Go to Lexi. Protect her. Stay with her. No seek Rayne. No. Go. Now!"

Boone whined and her tail gave an aborted wag but then she bounded off in the direction the others had headed.

41

Rayne watched as Fallon disappeared into the shadows of the trees. A faint roll of distant thunder presaged a coming storm. He focused on the thin, thread that connected him with his aunt and followed it until he came to a stream where he found a sheltered spot and sat. Winds from the coming storm blustered through the willows lining the stream. Unseen clouds above devoured the remaining sunlight and lightning flashed.

Rayne knelt in a patch of ferns, drew the hood of his cloak over his head, closed his eyes, and reached out to the One. *Blessed One, you have called me to return to the place where I was being sacrificed one slice at a time, my blood blending with the very lifeblood of others. Where those who worship darkness are working to summon the demons you have bound. Blinded by Sigmund's false promises, they seek the demon's return to Ochen.*

I vowed to never deny you anything you ask; and yet, this ... this willing return to evil seems like pure foolishness to me. And if I misunderstood what you said back in the Heart of Neth, my actions could bring disaster to all. It is not you I mistrust; it is myself. Please help me to understand. I will do this if it is your will, but I must be certain.

Please help me. Do I continue to follow Aunt Cailyn's tendril, or do I seek to catch up to my friends?

Droplets of rain threaded through the overhanging branches, dripping onto Rayne's already tear-dampened cheeks, soaking the knees of his trousers. Time passed as did the storm and still Rayne knelt.

O blessed One, I am desperate and lost.

A warm breeze surrounded Rayne. The lights within him responded, turning his body into a glowing lantern. *My beloved child. I have asked much of you and you have pleased me though it has been costly. Go to Cailyn. She is drowning in self-perpetuated lies. Speak to her of my forgiveness.*

Do not fear the darkness; I am with you. Reveal yourself to the prime shepherd. Because he is proud, he will accept my challenge. Know that I will protect you and strengthen you. When you have destroyed the seat of evil, you will speak to my people who have been prepared and they will be changed. Be strong; be courageous. I am with you.

Rayne rested in the comforting warmth. Though his battered spirit quailed at the thought of placing himself in Prime Shepherd Hamlin's hands and facing the bloody stone, he drew strength from the One's words. He would do what he had been called to do and trust. Oh, but even after all this time and all that had happened, the trusting came hard.

Lexi's words from earlier in the day ghosted through his mind. If things had gone as planned, he and Lexi would be on Amathea now, enjoying their honeymoon at Cashel Monastery on Shiloh Island. His mind churning, he ran a finger down his scarred cheek as he pondered her words and why the One had not allowed them the peace they desired. Would Lexi still be content to marry him after he again spoke of the One's forgiveness to the scroll worshipers she detested? Her hatred had grown since his disappearance. Could she be saved from the root of bitterness to which she now clung? Were the words Rayne had been called to speak as important for Lexi's spirit as they would be for the people deceived by Sigmund's lies?

Blessed One. Have mercy on Lexi. Free her; help her to release her hatred.

I pray for my family and friends. Help them to forgive as you are helping me to forgive. Without your strong presence, my faith would dry up like water in the desert.

Awareness of the cord that now bound him to Cailyn surfaced as it tugged at his spirit. "I'm coming Aunt Cailyn. I just hope you're as ready as the One seems to think."

N

Rayne pulled in a deep breath as he scanned the camp of USO followers the morning after he had left Fallon and his friends. Cailyn sat with Mayda and her father at a cook fire where a pot of something simmered.

Andrew's face was a mask of disgust as he tugged at a rope that tethered him to a tree; the large master of sacrifices sat near, watching him, sharpening his deadly knife. Rayne rubbed the remnants of scabs along the right side of his neck, remembering the feel of that blade as it sliced his skin.

He caught sight of Prime Shepherd Hamlin's distinctive, silver hair. He sat on a felled log, across from Cailyn, holding a mug with both hands. He leaned forward and said something Rayne couldn't hear.

Looking over his shoulder, Rayne caught a glimpse of Marius. The man had shadowed him since he split off from the others and Rayne wasn't sure of his intentions. He seemed unable to make a choice and switched sides as easily as a dragonfly could dart back and forth over a pond. Rayne didn't know if Marius had followed them from Neth, but it seemed right that Marius would be with him now, just as he had accompanied Rayne from Arisima to Corylus on his way to confront Sigmund and the Demon Master.

Lord, you know his heart. Please keep him from trouble and help him to finally commit to you.

Moving with quiet grace, Rayne snuck closer to the camp. Only a few trees now separated him from his enemies. Nearness to Cailyn triggered the throbbing in his skull. Squinting against the pain, Rayne hesitated. Once he walked into that camp, his freedom would, yet again, be lost. Prime Shepherd Hamlin viewed him as nothing more than an enemy, a pawn to be used, just like Sigmund had.

Rayne glanced back toward Marius again. He was gone. *Figures. The man has no real identity, just like some lost phantom.*

Lifting another prayer to the One, Rayne squared his shoulders and slipped past a towering evergreen to stand exposed but unannounced, at Hamlin's back.

Within seconds, the camp teemed with activity. Arnulf's eyes widened when he saw Rayne. Leaping to his feet, he sprinted forward, swinging his knife. "Seth. Behind you. The Binder."

Rayne unsheathed Neal's sword comforted by the familiar grasp of the blade. He held it loosely, tip pointed toward Arnulf's heaving chest, pulling the man to a stop before him. Arnulf's nostrils flared as he wove his knife through the air, seeking an opening, ready to attack.

Adrenaline surged and Rayne clamped it down, maintaining control even though all his instincts screamed *protect, defend.*

"Well, well, well." Seth's drawn out words drew Rayne's attention. "The Lady Mother told me you would come for this child, but I had my doubts." Seth moved to Arnulf's side. "Put that thing away, Arnulf. The Binder is an honorable man. He has come of his own free will. If he wanted to kill us, he would have done so from the cover of the forest. No, he means to accept my terms of surrender."

"Not exactly." Rayne kept his voice soft and even, a difficult task under the circumstances.

Seth stared, his eyebrows riding up his forehead in question.

"I have come with a message from the One." Rayne watched a kaleidoscope of emotions play across Cailyn's features as he spoke.

For a moment, Seth's mouth formed a circle then he laughed outright. "*The One?* Don't make me laugh. If he truly existed—which of course we know is ridiculous—he would have rescued you from our dark hole before Arnulf here ever sliced you on the altar stone. No. Your attempt to ensnare us with empty words is pathetic."

"My words are not empty and, to be honest, after what you've done to me, my sword thirsts for scroll worshiper blood.

Do not be deceived. The only reason you are still standing is because the One has forgiven me and bade me do the same for my enemies. I bring you his message."

"Oh, I see." Seth turned, his arms spread, palms up, and addressed Cailyn. "What say you, Lady Mother? Shall we listen to this *message*?"

"Seth." Cailyn's eyes were large and filled with fear. "Don't mock the One. He ..."

"Oh, come now, Cai. Don't tell me you are now cringing before this misguided *Light Bringer* and his false god." His focus shifted from Cailyn to Rayne and back again, a sly grin forming on his lips. "I see what's happened. You've lost your nerve." He shook his head. "I knew it. I could see it coming. Your sympathy for this enemy whom you claimed to hate will be your undoing. Think what you are saying before you join my old friend Gwyn and become a liability, fodder for sacrifice.

"Arnulf, watch her. I will deal with her after I take care of our guest."

Awareness of Andrew struggling flickered at the edge of Rayne's attention as Seth turned back. "Now, my young friend, where were we? Oh yes, you had a message?"

"The One has sent me to warn you. If you do not turn from the path you are on, his wrath will descend on you and your followers. I bring you his challenge. If you swear to abide by the constraints he sets for this test, I will abide by them as well.

"These are the words of the One: I alone am God; there is no other. You worship a false god to your destruction. Put him to the test. Bid him appear. Call to him in any way you wish other than the use of human sacrifice which I abhor and forbid; let him display his glory for all to see and prove your authority. If he is as you claim, the true power on Ochen, he will appear without the need of sacrifices.

"When you call and he does not appear, you will make way for my Light Bringer. I have charged him to surrender and accompany you to the site of evil without resistance. My Chosen will call the High Guardian of the Scrolls. Not by knife, nor by sacrifice, but by my power the guardian shall appear. By this will truth be revealed. I have prepared hearts; the time comes when they will listen to my Light Bringer and embrace my Words."

Seth folded his arms across his chest and snorted. "You think I will fail, and you will succeed? Don't make me laugh. I will summon the High Guardian and he will thank me for bringing you to him."

He snickered. "You're insane." He paused and narrowed his eyes. "Why would I even agree to this farce of a challenge? My soldiers surround you; they could take you even now. Do you think you could defeat them all? You are alone."

Rayne shook his head, resting in the calm center of warmth at his core. "No. I am not alone; the One is with me always. And yet, if you did attempt to take me without my consent, you would become a sacrifice to your own pride. I am armed and quite dangerous. And you would be the first to feel my blade."

Seth took a step back, understanding blossomed in his eyes. He inclined his head. "Well played, Binder. I see you are most serious."

Rayne raised the tip of his sword. "Indeed."

Seth made as if to laugh yet again but swallowed his mirth instead. "I have been warned not to underestimate you. What must I do to gain your compliance?"

"Swear on the seven scrolls of power and their High Guardian."

Seth's face turned a curious shade of red. "Blasphemy! You ask me to swear an oath I cannot make. You make a mockery of my beliefs."

"Perhaps. But it is the only oath I will trust. Swear the oath or I will grant my sword its wish to taste the blood of one who sentenced so many to death on his altar." Rayne focused a stern look on the man then shouted, "Now!"

Seth startled. Anger suffused his features, contorting his face. "I swear on the holy scrolls of power themselves and on their mighty High Guardian that I consent to this challenge as presented. You will remain unharmed until I succeed in summoning the High Guardian—and I will succeed. And when he appears at my bidding, this challenge will end. Then you will lie unprotected on the stone of sacrifice and the High Guardian himself will shed your blood. Together we will see where true power resides." Seth's cold eyes fixed on Rayne. "This is ridiculous! But now that I have sworn according to your request, will you keep your word and lower your sword?"

Andrew's cry blended with Mayda's, echoing off the encircling pines, "No!"

Rayne kept eye contact with Prime Shephard Hamlin as he stooped and laid his sword on the ground between them. He closed his eyes and lifted a quick prayer as USO soldiers dragged him away from the prime shepherd, bound his hands behind his back, pushed him to the ground next to Andrew, and tethered him to the same tree.

42

W hy did you come?" Andrew whispered, his focus locked on Seth and Arnulf as the two conversed in quiet tones. Cailyn stood with the men, her face a stone mask.

Rayne leaned his head back against the rugged bark of the tree behind him and sighed. "Why did you leave?"

Something that sounded like a mix of anger and misery leaked from Andrew. "We weren't supposed to be caught, Mayda and me. She just wanted to talk to her father, help him see how what they are doing is a mistake. But it all went wrong. I'm sorry; I'm so sorry. This is all my fault. You're going to be sacrificed and that darkness is coming back. And it's all my fault."

"No. This is not your fault. This ... my surrender ... needed to happen. Your actions may have changed how it came about, but you heard what I told the prime shepherd, this was inevitable."

"But why? Why would the One want you to die? You're his Light Bringer. He banished Sigmund, why would he want him back now? I don't understand."

Exhaustion sucked Rayne's energy, even his bones ached.

He wanted nothing more than to close his eyes and lose himself in the oblivion sleep would bring, but he couldn't leave Andrew to deal with his guilt alone.

"Andrew?"

Sniffle. "Yes?"

"You trust the One, right?"

Another sniffle. "Y-y-yes."

"You trust me, right?"

"Y-y-yes."

"Then trust us now. I don't understand the One's plan; but I am certain everything will work out. He told me I would survive to speak to the scroll worshipers for him. I believe he will make that happen. I trust him. He's never abandoned me in the past. You need to trust as well. Okay, Andrew? No matter what happens, keep trusting."

"I will."

The camp settled into a routine of breakfast. Prime Shepherd Hamlin kept Cailyn at his side. He spoke to her at length and from time to time she nodded agreement. Rayne wondered what they were saying. If he understood the One's words from earlier, Cailyn was harboring doubts about her relationship with the prime shepherd, the USO, and the sacrifices. She seemed tense and Rayne remembered how much she shrank from confrontation. *Please, Creator-Father, give her the strength she needs to break away from the chains of darkness that have led her to desire vengeance and power.*

Once everyone finished eating, they broke camp. Arnulf rose from his seat near the fire and strode over to Rayne and Andrew. Rayne looked up at the Master of Sacrifices as the man towered over him, twirling his knife, a hungry expression on his face.

"Prime Shepherd Hamlin says we can't harm you so you can be a perfect sacrifice once he summons the High Guardian. But if you try anything, I won't hesitate to spill some of that special blood of yours. Just so long as you have enough left to soak the altar tomorrow night.

"In his mercy, he has decided to allow your little friend his freedom as he promised. If I had my way, the two of you would be dragged behind my horse. But it is not my decision."

The man waved his knife in Rayne's face. Grunting, he bent over and severed the rope tethering Rayne to the tree. He stepped in front of Andrew and cut his rope as well, then the bindings around Andrew's wrists. "Get up."

Rayne stumbled his way across the remnants of camp and Andrew followed. They stopped at the line of horses and waited for Arnulf's direction. Most of the USO soldiers ignored the two, but a few cursed at them and one spit on Rayne.

Arnulf laughed. "Where's your precious One now, Binder? I don't see him wiping the spittle off your face. Looks like you'll just have to live with it." He paused. "At least until tomorrow night. Then it won't matter anymore." The soldiers all laughed.

"Enough," Seth said as he approached, Cailyn on his arm, Mayda and her father on their heels. "We don't have time for games.

"You." He waved at Andrew. "You will ride with Associate Shepherd Creedoff. But make no mistake boy, if you give us any trouble, you'll be reduced to bound prisoner again."

His eyes sparking, he shifted his focus to Arnulf. "Get the Binder on a horse. We need to move if we're going to make the sacrificial stone by midnight tomorrow."

Leaving the clearing, they walked the horses until the trees gave way to a field. Setting a course northwest, they soon crossed the Verness River at a point where it flowed wide and shallow. As the last of the sun's light disappeared, they picked up the road that ran from Annesley to Inverness. Turning right onto the road, they traveled another mile before setting camp in a meadow along the side of the road.

Hunger and exhaustion plagued Rayne, but even more, thirst. Though they had stopped to water the horses at the river and the few streams they crossed along the way, and the soldiers had drunk their fill, no one had offered any to Rayne. And when Mayda and Andrew tried, Arnulf stopped them.

Bickering erupted among the soldiers after the long ride. Within minutes, however, a line was set for the horses. Arnulf helped Rayne dismount. The soldier who had spit on Rayne retrieved his horse and Arnulf waved him to the trunk of a massive White Oak where he tethered him once again. Within minutes, Andrew and Mayda crouched behind the tree.

Rayne sought to pull moisture to his mouth before he attempted to speak. "Andrew? How are you holding up?"

"Okay, I guess. You must be thirsty."

"Yeah, I am." Rayne scanned the soldiers hoping to see Cailyn. His muscles tightened when Mayda stepped from behind the tree holding a water skin close to her leg. Her eyes met Rayne's. She shook her head and mouthed, *shhh*.

Mayda glanced behind her then moved in front of Rayne. She set the bag at his lips and Rayne almost moaned as cool, fresh moisture coated his dry throat.

Rayne finished and Mayda stepped back. She huffed and Rayne looked up over her shoulder. Prime Shepherd Hamlin stood there. "What are you doing here, Mayda? You should be with your father. Go."

The prime shepherd's cold eyes set Rayne's stomach to churning. Avoiding the man's glare, Rayne focused on the soldiers who were now settling in. A few minutes later, he relented and sought the prime shepherd's gaze. Rayne waited for the man to speak, but when he continued to stare without speaking, Rayne said, "Yes?"

"I'm not a bad man." Seth squatted to meet Rayne eye to eye. "I know you think I am. But all I do, I do for Ochen."

"I know you believe that. But your actions don't line up with your words."

"You don't understand. I've fought for the Scrolls of Power for the last ten years; first on Glacieria then on Arisima and Corylus. I have seen how the Church of the One grinds down those who don't believe as they do. And I've seen the power of the High Guardian displayed. That was before you destroyed our precious scrolls and took their power for yourself. You claim the One is the true force behind everything, but I know you lie. The One is a myth perpetuated by your family to solidify your reign. You lead the people astray, telling them to read the scrolls. They were never meant to be read, only to be venerated. Now you have taken the power for yourself and unless I stop you and your misguided One followers, we will all be forced to grovel at your feet."

Seth shook his head. "Even now. Do you think I don't see that unholy radiance about you? It's the power you stole from the scrolls and keep to yourself. I know what you can do, I've seen you shine so bright, tricking your pathetic followers. But you won't hold on to what you've stolen much longer. Once you've been exposed to the true might of the High Guardian and the light has been restored to the scrolls of power, they will, once again, return power and glory to the worlds of Ochen."

Rayne sat with his mouth hanging open, unable to grasp the depth of the deceit Sigmund had fostered in this man. It was a series of lies built on lies. Rayne shook his head. "You're wrong, Prime Shepherd." Rayne pulled in a deep breath and released it with a groan as he sought to find an argument that would reach past the man's unquestioning belief. He wished his hands were free so he could massage his face "You call yourself a shepherd and yet you slaughter the very people you claim to care about on an ancient altar that has been a symbol of evil for centuries. How can that help the people of Ochen?"

Hamlin rose, pulled his shoulders back and looked down at Rayne. "How can that help the people of Ochen, you ask? By rescuing them from the grasp of your malignant and deceitful family. I sacrifice the few to save the many, something you cannot possibly understand.

"I gave you a chance to repent, *Chosen of the One*." Seth grimaced, his teeth bared. "Your words are words of deception. I will listen no longer. Pray to your false god while you can. Soon now, you will be past praying."

The man stalked away, his frame jerking with repressed anger as he waved Arnulf to himself. He looked over his shoulder, his eyes boring into Rayne like daggers, before turning back to Arnulf. "Guard him. Do not allow him to speak. In fact, gag the Binder. I now understand why the High Guardian commanded he be kept in darkness and silence. Gag him and bind his eyes as well. Then throw a hood over his head. I cannot allow any of our people to hear his blasphemous speech. If only we had some Ferris Weed; I'd pour it down his lying throat."

His eyes drifted to where Cailyn sat with Andrew, Mayda, and her father. "Have one of the men keep a close watch on them as well. I fear they have all become corrupted by associating with the Binder."

43

Lexi struggled to hold back the fury that steamed in her, as if she was a tea kettle whistling with no one to turn off the heat that built within her. *How could he do this to me? Stupid, stupid, stubborn man.* Part of her wanted to cry at the pain of losing Rayne while another part wanted to thrash him for his actions. It was an affront to her. *What did I do to deserve this?*

The soft voice within that had been plaguing her since Rayne's departure impressed into her spirit the words she refused to acknowledge. *Consider my daughter, he is not leaving you; he is obeying my will. When you are ready you will understand why I call for forgiveness.*

Lexi drew her mouth into a flat line and ignored the voice. Rayne had spoken to her need to forgive more times than she cared to remember these past few years. She mumbled under her breath. "When I'm ready. Yeah, right! You can just wait for that."

Her spirit quailed at her rebellious words and part of her wished she could take them back. But they were gone and could not be recalled. Besides she was too angry and afraid to begin to consider releasing her need for vengeance to the One.

It was hers and she clung to it. Eventually she would need to confront the distinction between righteous anger and just plain self-absorbed fury. But not yet, not now with Rayne probably in the hands of dirty scroll worshipers.

She looked sideways at Thorvin. He hadn't said much since Rayne's disappearance, but she could tell he was furious with Fallon for letting Rayne go. It didn't matter that Fallon couldn't stop Rayne if he had made up his mind; Rayne was in danger because Lexi and Thorvin couldn't stop him.

She and Thorvin knew Rayne was gone even before Fallon confessed letting him go. Lexi's heart had taken residence in her throat when Boone trotted out of the trees without Rayne. He took up position at her side and remained there. Only Rayne's command to guard her would convince the loyal dog to leave his side.

Giles had been more vocal in his protest, turning his horse back and wasting hours trying to track Rayne. He even attempted to get Boone to leave Lexi and search for her master. But each time, Boone circled back to Lexi.

When Giles finally gave up, he refused to talk to anyone, ignored Fallon, and rode in silence behind the others. Fallon took it all with a stoic acceptance and just continued to walk alongside Thorvin's horse as if nothing had happened.

They planned to skirt the main city of Inverness, intent on sneaking back into the USO camp without drawing attention to themselves, but as they got to the outskirts of the city, they noticed things had changed. More people were traveling to and from the city and soldiers wearing Ochen Army uniforms were everywhere.

"What do you think, Thorvin?" Lexi asked as they passed another group of soldiers. "If the troops are here, King Theodor must have arrived. The portals must be open."

Thorvin pulled to a stop. Lexi couldn't miss the look of dread on the man's face. "What?" she asked. "If the king is here that means things are going to be okay, right?"

Giles pulled up next to the two. "Yes. But that won't help us when we face King Theodor and Queen Rowena and tell them Rayne took off by himself to go after Andrew. And—by the way—speak the One's words to the USO. Yes. That should go over well."

"Oh." Lexi let the word hang for a moment. "I see what you're saying. We will be the messengers who bring the bad news."

Thorvin grunted. "Not you. Me. I'm supposed to protect Rayne. I'm the one they are going to hang for losing him. A-gain!"

Fallon had hung back, but now he stepped next to Thorvin and took hold of his horse's bridle, stroking the animal's nose in a calming manner. "Thou had no choice. The Creator-Father called, and his Light Bringer answered. It is as it should be. Thou could not have stopped it any more than thou could stop the sun from rising or the wind from blowing. The king and queen must accept this as must we all. We need to trust the One, just as the Light Bringer trusts."

"You make it sound so easy," Lexi said, anger drawing her eyebrows down and casting a sour look to her mouth. "Maybe it is for you, but ... but ... argh! I can't believe Rayne left us like that. I would have stopped him if I knew what he was planning." Her eyes shifted to Thorvin and Giles as she blinked back tears. "By the seven, we all would have stopped him."

"And that is why he left the way he did. Thou would have tried to stop him and yet he needed to go." Fallon shook his head, his translucent form shifting out of sight for a moment. "Do not mistake my trust for lack of concern. I too worry for our friend. Yet, I continue to pray and trust the Creator-Father."

The four remained silent for a few minutes until Thorvin said, "Standing here isn't going to solve anything. If the army is here, there's no chance we can sneak into the USO camp. Besides, it makes no sense to go there now. The king and queen are probably at the castle. Come on."

Lexi peeked in the door of the suite where Rowena was resting and found the queen sitting up in bed, several pillows behind her, talking to Anne and Shaw. Lexi released a squeal of delight and charged into the room, Boone trotting in behind her. She hugged Anne and Shaw before recalling herself and bowing to the queen.

"None of that now, my daughter," Rowena said, a bright smile lighting her face. "Come, sit beside me. Tell me all about your adventures. Did you find Rayne? He's here, isn't he? Of course he is. If Boone is here, he must be as well."

Lexi attempted a rather stilted smile as she moved toward the bed, but her focus shifted back to the doorway. She hoped Thorvin and the others would walk through before she needed to answer any of Rowena's questions.

She nearly jumped when Theodor appeared in the doorway, looking back over his shoulder and shouting, "What do you mean you lost him when he went after Andrew? What does his page have to do with anything?"

No one spoke as Theodor stalked to the bed and stood, glowering, at Rowena's side. Thorvin and Giles followed, appearing cowed by Theodor's outburst. Fallon walked in behind the others, bringing with him an aura of calm that spread like a cool mist on a hot day throughout the room.

Lexi rounded her shoulders and slunk back against the wall near Anne. Boone joined them, plopping down with a groan between the two.

"Well?" Theodor's voice echoed around the room. He shook his head and looked at Fallon. "Who might you be and why are you here now?"

Fallon inclined his head to Theodor then to Rowena. "My name is Fallon. I am an elder of the Neth Kindred and a friend of the Light Bringer."

As Fallon spoke, Theodor's angry stance relaxed. "You know my son?"

"Fallon. I know that name," Rowena said. "You're one of the Kindred who befriended Rayne when he was trapped in that old body. He has spoken of you often. Why are you here now? I thought the Kindred never left Neth."

"I decided to come away from Neth after the Light Bringer came to us in need of healing a second time. That he was not received with honor ... troubled ... me. I left my people to see how such a thing could happen. It has indeed been many centuries since any Kindred left Neth. I offered to help Prince Rayne in any way I could in his appointed task to bring the Words of the One to those thou hast named scroll worshipers."

The room got silent for a few seconds, Theodor and Rowena processing Fallon's words. Theodor spoke first, his voice tight. "What appointed task? Appointed to speak to the scroll worshipers? Fallon, tell me. Where is my son?"

Thorvin's gravel-filled voice sounded loud in the room. "He's got some notion that the One has done something to make these scroll worshipers ready to hear him."

"But that doesn't explain why he left us," Lexi said, her voice barely a whisper as she struggled to control the trembling now invading her body. She knew. Ever since Andrew disappeared. If Rayne went after Andrew, and the boy had been captured by the scroll worshipers who had followed them in Neth, then Rayne walked right into a trap. The "no" exploded from her mouth before she could stop it.

Rowena pushed up from her pillows, her focus locked on Lexi. "What?"

Tears came, flooding Lexi's eyes, burning and relentless as she sought an answer to Rowena's question. A sob fought its way between her lips and Anne was by her side. "It's okay, Lexi, come sit down. Take a deep breath. There. That's better."

Lexi sat on the brocade loveseat where Anne had been sitting when she walked in, next to Shaw who put his arm around her shoulders. Anger battled with fear within her. Again, the question surfaced from the chaos in her mind, "how could he do that to me?" The realization she had spoken aloud flooded Lexi with shame. Rayne's actions impacted everyone in this room, not just her. She lowered her eyes to her hands and watched them twitch.

"He did not do this to thee." Fallon's soft voice drew Lexi. He nodded when she turned to him, a slight smile crooking the sides of his lips. "His parting words to thee were, 'tell Lexi I love her and that if she loves me, she needs to trust me.'"

Fallon's gaze shifted around the room. "Those were his words to all of thee. To trust him and to trust the One, the Creator-Father. That he is in control of all that happens. No matter what happens." He took a step to stand before Rowena. "Thou wouldst save thy son." His focus shifted to Theodor. "I understand this. I too would save the young Light Bringer from this task if I could. But ... this is what he has been called to do. To challenge those who would use him for evil ends and by doing so, defeat them."

Fallon's eyes, filled with compassion, turned back to Lexi. "We must not interfere. The Creator-Father will work through that which he has put in motion."

He searched the eyes of those around him again. "The Light Bringer's greatest fear was that we who love him would try to stop what must happen. That we would not trust him or the Creator-Father enough. I pray we will not stumble. His task is to trust and obey; ours is to do the same. We are called to the hardest thing. That is, to do nothing."

"Not nothing," Shaw said, his voice stronger than Lexi would have thought possible. "No. Not nothing. We will pray."

44

Rayne's bound eyes itched. A rough bag reeking of mildew covered his head and the weight of dark, heavy magic pressed down on his spirit. He was back in the hollow near Castle Inverness. Uncertain how much time had passed since they had arrived at the hollow, Rayne prayed. Soon he would be standing next to the altar in front of a mass of scroll worshipers seeking his death. He refused to think about that. He sought the warmth of the One which sustained him.

I am here, Lord. In the place you have called me to. I fear Prime Shepherd Hamlin will betray me and have Arnulf slit my throat rather than try to summon Sigmund as he vowed. I have no way of knowing what will happen. This trial presses on me. In some ways it was easier when I didn't know as much as I do now. It was simple to just trust. Now, the trusting comes at a price.

I know. I know. Change my focus from myself and my fear to you. I pray you will keep those I love safe. Lexi, Mother. Father. My friends. Anne and Shaw. Keep them from interfering in your plan and give them peace no matter what happens. Especially Lexi. She is full of anger and if this goes wrong, she will cling to that hatred like an anchor. Save her from that. Help her to embrace your love and forgiveness not only for herself, but also for those who have been deceived.

Releasing his friends and family to the One, Rayne continued to lift praises. He lost track of time and place as he retreated into the depths of his spirit, seeking the Spirit of the One, the flame that had sustained him for so long.

Sleep found him as he prayed and when Arnulf's rough hands pulled him to stand, he stumbled as he scrubbed the fog of slumber from his mind. Arnulf pulled the bag off Rayne's head, undid the cloth from around his eyes, and cut the ropes from his wrists. Rayne shook out his hands, grimacing at the pins and needles brought on by returning blood flow. He blinked in the blue glow of Ledia's full light. Rem, nothing more than a sliver, hung over the treetops edging the hollow. His eyes teared and he squinted at the ground as Arnulf propelled him toward a group standing near the altar. Hamlin's voice, strident and filled with venom, battered Rayne.

"This can't be happening. After all I've done, all I've given up, to get to this point, I'm not going to lose now."

A man Rayne remembered seeing at earlier sacrifices bowed to the prime shepherd. "I'm sorry Seth. We've done the best we could. But when the king and queen showed up with a whole army, our people acted like the cowards they are and refused to fight. My men and I, and those who joined us in the days that followed, we're here for you. We proved our loyalty. Can't you do the ritual with us? Forget the others?"

"No, Captain Theada. They are ... too few." Hamlin's fists curled, and he ground his teeth. A deep line formed between his brows. "Just give me ... let me think."

Several minutes later, he raised his eyes to Cailyn. "Yes. I have it. You, Lady Mother, you can summon the faithful. We must have witnesses." His eyes skirted the area, landing on Arnulf. "How long until the time of sacrifice?"

Arnulf shifted the front of his USO robe and pulled a timepiece from an inside pocket. "A little less than two hours, Prime Shepherd."

"Good. Good." Hamlin nodded. "Yes." He grabbed Cailyn's arm and pulled her away from the others, too far for Rayne to hear what was said. Cailyn's face went red, then all the blood drained from it, turning her a sickly shade of pale in the blue light. She chewed her bottom lip and blinked repeatedly as if to hold back tears, but nodded consent.

The heavy energy in the air thickened as Cailyn closed her eyes and began to weave hundreds of tendrils. As they developed, Rayne shivered at the malevolent texture of the mounting energy. Time passed and still Cailyn wove, pulling an incredible amount of power into her small frame. Her release speared through Rayne. Cailyn had done the unthinkable, blanketing the entire area around Inverness with a call that summoned all who heard to the stone of sacrifice.

"Well?" Impatience laced the Hamlin's voice as he towered over Cailyn. "Have you done it?"

Cailyn gasped and nodded. Her body slipped to the ground and she lost consciousness. Prime Shepherd Hamlin waved several soldiers over. "Take care of her."

Hamlin's eyes glinted in the moonlight as he squared his shoulders and addressed the group surrounding him.

"Don't you see?" he said, after explaining Rayne's challenge. "This will gain us everything we have ever wanted. Once the royals and their army witness the power of our scrolls and our High Guardian, they will bow to them. That is why I had the Lady Mother call out to everyone. We will demonstrate beyond any doubt that the Church of the One is nothing more than a sham bolstered by the Kierkengaard family. The spectacular death of the Binder will be something our children's children will read about. It will be splendid in its finality.

"This was meant to be. Why else would the Binder deliver himself to us like a lamb to slaughter?" Hamlin threw his arms wide and turned in a circle. "Breathe it in my friends, my fellow believers. The air is ripe with energy. This is a night that will be written about in the histories of Ochen. And we few will be remembered down through the ages as the loyal servants of the High Guardian who brought this to pass. Can't you feel it?"

Unable to stand silent any longer, Rayne spoke in a soft voice. "What you feel is heavy energy, like the atmosphere before a storm. You can still repent and turn from this foolish endeavor."

Arnulf growled, pulled his sacrificial knife and lunged at

Rayne. Rayne back peddled, lost his balance, and landed on his back. Arnulf stood over him, then dropped to a knee, grinding an elbow into Rayne's chest.

"No. Arnulf stop. Stop!" Hamlin's voice shredded the night as Arnulf's blade sliced downward toward Rayne's neck. But the man ceased his downward plunge, grunted, then stood to his feet. "Keep your filthy mouth shut, One worshiper."

The big man turned to Hamlin, his shoulders hunched, his hands fisted. "I understand. You have promised no harm shall come to him until the High Guardian arrives. Only for you and for our High Guardian of the Scrolls would I pull back a strike. When the time comes, may the High Guardian enjoy this offering."

He stalked off to stand near the man in charge of the soldiers, muttering under his breath.

Two of the soldiers who had approached Arnulf grabbed Rayne's arms and pulled him before Hamlin. "It is almost time. You will now see how wrong you have been to place your trust in a myth. You tell me it's not too late to repent; I offer you the same. Repent of your misplaced belief and bow to the High Guardian of the Scrolls when he appears. Perhaps he will have mercy on you and make your death quick."

The prime shepherd led the way as the group marched to the stone. A few minutes later, Cailyn joined them, the hood of her USO robe pulled forward, hiding her features. She shivered from time to time as if plagued with some disease. USO soldiers spread out, lighting the numerous torches that had been planted throughout the dell.

People began filing into the hollow, slowly at first but soon in great numbers. At first, most wore USO cloaks but as time passed Rayne picked out groups of Ochen soldiers, some walking, some riding.

He caught sight of Stevie, Noah, and Sashi riding with Captain Ellis and soldiers in Arisimanian clothing.

His knees almost gave way when he saw his mother and father. With them were Lexi, Anne, Shaw, and Thorvin. Fallon stood at Thorvin's side, fading in and out. Even Mite was there, walking alongside a stout man Rayne recognized as one of the leaders of the USO. Curiosity piqued, he wondered how the man had ended up with his friends but let the thought go when Prime Shepherd Hamlin stepped up to the stone and raised his hands for silence. Cailyn accompanied Hamlin, already pulling in energy to magnify his voice so all could hear.

"People of Ochen. I, Prime Shepherd Hamlin call you to witness as true power manifests itself.

"A challenge has been issued and I, as leader of the United Scrolls of Ochen, have taken up the gauntlet. In the past our High Guardian has required the sacrifice of humans for him to come to us. Those who do not accept the truth believe this is because our high guardian is weak."

Hamlin paused, his eyes scanned the throng, waiting. The crowd stilled. His voice rang out. "He is not weak! His power knows no bounds! The sacrifices were a necessary duty to remind us of his supremacy, and our need to worship and honor him.

"Now we will summon him by *our* calling and *our* blood, and he will honor us as his worshipers."

He waved for the soldiers who flanked Rayne and they brought him to Hamlin. "My fellow believers, before me stands the Binder."

Shouting and obscenities sounded from around the glen. The prime shepherd motioned for silence.

"He came to me and offered a challenge from his false One. How could I refuse when by accepting his terms, our High Guardian of the Scrolls can demonstrate his supremacy to all who will bear witness to his appearing. I promised the Binder a chance to speak. I give him his moment now."

Rayne met the prime shepherd's triumphant look then turned to face outward, scanning the myriad faces, eyes glued to him. He cleared his throat and looked toward Cailyn. She nodded.

"I want to—no need to—ask that no one disrupt this challenge. It has been put in place by the One himself." Boos arose from the scroll worshipers. Several threw stones and Rayne ducked. Soldiers standing near those flinging the stones reacted and within minutes several fights broke out.

"Stop! All of you, stop. Let him speak!" Cailyn's voice startled Rayne as she spoke through the amplification she had set, disrupting the fighting as those involved turned to her.

"You know me, fellow worshipers of the scrolls of power. I am your Lady Mother.

"You know me, soldiers of Ochen, I am Duchess of Nemora.

"Please, I beg you, refrain from such demeaning behavior. Prime Shepherd Hamlin has assented to this challenge sent from the One and delivered by His Royal Highness, Prince Rayne. Now, honor them with your attention and silence."

She turned to face Rayne again, sorrow weighing on her features. "I am sorry."

Rayne took a deep breath and continued. "The challenge has been issued and accepted. I am at peace with it. Let no one interfere."

Rayne turned to face the alter stone; he hardened himself against the painful memories of what he had suffered here, and his all-too-human dread of what would now take place. Rayne took one final glance over his shoulder at Lexi and his parents, then nodded to Prime Shepherd Hamlin.

45

The air pulsed with power and Lexi fought the urge to run to Rayne as he closed his eyes and went deathly still.

A disturbance in a stand of pines near the stone snared her attention. A man half-hidden by shadows stood with a bow drawn. His arrow, nocked and ready to release, pointed toward Prime Shepherd Hamlin. Shouts rang out, but she couldn't make out what was being said. Panic took hold of those near the prime shepherd and they began to scatter.

Without thinking, Lexi bounded down the hillside. Footsteps thudded behind her, but she didn't stop to look back. As though guided by an outside force, she skirted knots of scroll worshipers and soldiers alike without slowing her pace.

The bowman's shout rang out. "Death to all who worship the scrolls." Lexi gasped as time slowed. The arrow left the bow.

Tracing forward along its trajectory, Lexi's eyes landed on Mayda standing next to a man who must be her father. No ... not standing ... shifting, moving in front of him as he shielded Prime Shepherd Hamlin.

Time resumed its normal pace. It happened so fast Lexi's

brain scrambled to process what transpired as she skidded to a stop and a scream of denial forced its way past her lips. Four slow, numb steps brought her to the level ground near the stone, where she came to a standstill.

Andrew sat before her, tears streaming down his face as he cradled Mayda's head in his lap. "Help her! Please, someone help her."

Rowena slipped past Lexi. "Andrew. I'm here. Let me see." The queen dropped to her knees next to Andrew and examined the wound.

Anguish wormed through Lexi and she couldn't breathe when Rowena looked up to Andrew's expectant face and shook her head. "I'm sorry," she said. "The arrow pierced her heart. I cannot pull it. You have very little time."

Lexi's own hateful words spoken to Mayda circled in her mind, like vultures seeking to feed. *No! This isn't what I wanted. Not Mayda!*

Andrew's attention dropped to the girl in his arms as the man Mayda had saved wailed a tormented cry and collapsed to the ground. "My Mayda. My beautiful little girl. Why? Why?"

"Andrew?" Mayda's soft voice drew Lexi's eyes from the man who now sobbed into his hands.

Mayda blinked and her eyes wandered before they focused on Andrew. "You were right. The One is real. He … he's here right now." A weak smile turned up the corners of Mayda's lips and Lexi's heart pounded at the peace she saw in Mayda's eyes.

"He's so bright and so beautiful." Mayda stared at a spot behind Rayne. "He's smiling… He's calling … scroll … worshipers to him.

Mayda's expression clouded. "Andrew, you must forgive … forgive the man … who shot … me. We all … need … need to … forgive. Thank you for being my friend…"

Lexi's throat seized and tears flowed, mirroring Andrew's as he rocked back and forth. His cries cut at Lexi's heart. Regret for the way she had treated Mayda threatened to choke her.

Several men wrestled the archer to stand in front of King Theodor who now stood with his arms wrapped around Rowena.

"I only wanted to protect the prince," the man said, his voice cracking. His gaze shifted to Rayne, who now stood between the prime shepherd and the archer. "I owed you that. I didn't mean ... to hurt the girl. I was aiming for the prime shepherd. Not the girl."

"Marius? What have you done?" Giles's words drew Lexi's attention. *When did he get here?*

"Giles ... Giles. You must understand. I wanted to kill the prime shepherd. He deserved death for what he did to Rayne." His focus shifted back to Rayne who shook his head as tears glinted in the lantern light. "How he hurt you. I owed you that. You know, after Arisima. I wanted to stop what's happening." Marius went limp, like a puppet whose strings had been cut and his gaze dropped to the ground at his feet. He shook his head. "I ... didn't mean..."

"You didn't mean to hurt the girl and yet you did." Giles's voice took on a menacing tone. "You've heard Rayne speak. Didn't you understand? Vengeance is the last thing he wanted."

Lexi's heart burned with remorse. Gazing down on Andrew and Mayda, the words she had refused to say earlier came. *Please forgive me for not understanding until now. Help me to forgive as you forgive.*

Theodor released a growl. Lexi trembled at the sound of fury lacing through the king's voice as he commanded. "Bind that archer. We'll deal with him later."

Too much ... it's all too much. Lexi needed Rayne now, at this moment of understanding; his strength, his wisdom, his warmth. She turned to him and her heart sank. His eyes closed, he stood as if some alien statue, his mouth pulled downward in an unforgiving line. He blinked and turned back to Hamlin, his face a mask of stone even as tears streamed down his cheeks. "It is time." He shook his head. "No more innocent blood. Summon your High Guardian, if you are able."

A slight moan rose from Andrew, who still rocked the empty shell of Mayda's body. Lexi dropped to her knees next to him and wrapped an arm around his shoulders. A droning, like the hum of insects, filled her ears. Lexi shook her head. *What's that? Am I hearing things?* The sound grew louder, and she understood. People were chanting. Prime Shepherd Hamlin led them. His voice loud, insistent, as he waved his arms encouraging more scroll worshipers to follow.

"Blood for blood; blood for power; blood for vengeance." The words sent a shiver of foreboding through Lexi. More scroll worshipers picked up the chant and it echoed through the vale.

Lexi's gaze fell upon Rayne again. Only a few steps separated them. She wanted to run to his side, take his hand, and pull him to her. Tell him how sorry she was, how wrong she had been. But he stood rigid, his attention fixed on Hamlin. She wouldn't distract him, wouldn't disappoint him again; she'd let this play out according to the One's plan.

The scroll worshipers' chanting magnified when a large man wielding a veredium knife leaped to stand upon the blood-stained altar. He lifted his black blade and began slicing his arms and legs. "Blood for blood; blood for power; blood for vengeance."

His eyes wild, the man flung his arms wide. "My brothers and sisters, I am Arnulf, Master of the Sacrifice. Join me. We will make these unbelievers bear witness when we summon the High Guardian of the Scrolls. We do not need sacrifices. We will prove his supremacy without them. If we must shed our own blood to summon him, we will do it gladly. He will come for us. He will answer our call. Prove to these unbelievers that our High Guardian is the true god of Ochen."

Prime Shepherd Hamlin, his cloak flying behind him like a pair of unholy wings joined Arnulf. Others followed his example. They ran to the stone, knives flashing as they cut themselves, the chant growing frenzied, desperate.

Prime Shepherd Hamlin scaled the rock to stand next to Arnulf. "By the power of the scrolls we summon you our High Guardian. By the shed blood of your people, come to us now. Show your true power." He dropped to his knees and lifted his arms toward the sky, beseeching.

The clamor rose to intolerable levels and Lexi covered her ears. She wanted to close her eyes when blood began running off the altar and crazed scroll worshipers began dropping from blood loss. *Oh please, please, make it stop!*

But it didn't stop. For more than an hour, the turbulent activity continued, unabated.

"Do you need some help?" Rayne's mocking voice broke through Lexi's panic, drawing her widened eyes to his form as he strode forward and stopped in front of the prime shepherd. His head tilted back as he scanned the clear, nighttime sky, and he shrugged. "I don't even see a wisp of dark energy. Could you be doing something wrong? Is it possible the High Guardian can't hear you? Come on, put some effort into it. Try harder."

Spittle flying, Hamlin jumped from the altar. Lexi screamed, thinking he meant to attack Rayne. But the man raced past Rayne and grabbed Cailyn, dragging her back to the altar. "Use your magic," he screamed. "Call the heavy magic, the energy of Nemora. Do. It. Now."

Cailyn shook her head. Lexi strained to hear her reply. "I can't. It's gone. There is no energy. It's gone." She dropped to her knees a few feet from the blood-drenched rock and covered her face with her hands, her shoulders shaking as she sobbed.

Once again, Rayne approached the prime shepherd. Lexi's breath caught in her throat. She tried to shout, *what are you thinking? Don't taunt the man; he's not rational.* But the words froze on her tongue.

Still Rayne pressed. "Perhaps the High Guardian has gone deaf. Call out louder."

Arnulf roared. "By the Guardian of the Scrolls, I will end this." With blood flowing from multiple wounds and his cloak soaked and torn, the man lifted his knife high.

Trembling overtook Lexi as fear for Rayne speared through her, but the man turned the knife on himself, plunging it to the hilt into his own body. "A worthy sacrifice," he shouted, then collapsed onto the rock.

46

A weighty silence descended on the people. With Arnulf's death, the fire that had fueled the scroll worshipers' frenzy dissipated. They looked to the sky, but the dome of sparkling stars remained clear. No roiling darkness of heavy magic churned above.

The prime shepherd groveled on the ground before Rayne. Gibberish poured from his mouth. He lifted his eyes to meet Rayne's. "You! What have you done?"

Rayne shook his head. "I've done nothing. You have earned the One's righteous anger. Now. Watch and see the power of the One."

Rayne raised his face to the sky and Ledia's blue moonlight shone clear upon it, illuminating him. The spirit of the One flared at Rayne's core. *I am ready, my Lord. Use me as you will.*

Now. It is time. Call forth the demon, my Light Bringer.

Rayne lifted his arms and pulled in a deep breath. "Sigmund! By the power of the One I summon you!"

A thunderous ripping above drew everyone's attention to the sky. The heavens split and from the fissure stepped the most beautiful creature Rayne had ever seen. He spread white wings that sparkled blue and silver as he hovered in the air.

The being descended to the ground, pulled his wings in close to his back, and stood in front of Prime Shepherd Hamlin. The prime shepherd looked up from the ground, his eyes bulging and his mouth gaping. The winged man shook his head.

"Arise, my Prime Shepherd! Arise! Though you failed to offer the required sacrifices, the lapse will be forgotten before this night is over for you have delivered my enemy into my hands."

Prime Shepherd Hamlin pushed upright and ran shaking hands down the front of his dirty robe. "We welcome you, High Guardian of the Scrolls."

This is Sigmund's real form? Shock set Rayne back a step.

A smile lit the High Guardian's face, deep dimples setting off the perfect lines of his nose and chin. The pull of his presence drew Rayne like veredium shavings to a lodestone and he sought to reconcile the majestic creature before him with what he knew about Sigmund.

Penetrating, silver eyes lifted to meet his and the creature's smile deepened. He unfurled his wings then wrapped them around his body.

His gaze shifted to Rayne's right.

"Ah." He approached Theodor and Rowena. "The royal couple. It is indeed an unexpected pleasure to have you both here."

Theodor drew his sword and stepped between Rowena and the High Guardian, but the winged man turned to Hamlin. "I assume they will not be allowed to interfere?"

Captain Theada and several of his men rushed to surround the king. "I see. You have come to witness my triumph. How delicious."

Unfurling his wings yet again and stretching them out to their full spread, the beautiful creature turned in a slow circle and shouted, "Blood for blood; blood for power; blood for vengeance."

No other voice joined his. The High Guardian scanned the glen.

"You have disappointed me tonight. Where are my

chanters? Where are my seven sacrifices? Where is the blood you promised?"

"But ... but," Prime Shepherd Hamlin stuttered. "The Binder. We called and you didn't come. He called and you came. We ... he is behind you."

The High Guardian's eyes narrowed as he turned to face Rayne. "Impossible."

He walked around Rayne, examining him. The glow that always accompanied Rayne intensified; ribbons of light wound around him. Red, blue, and gold intermingled with a clear light that burned so brightly Rayne squinted. The lights combined into a sphere, enveloping him in a protective shield.

The winged creature Rayne now recognized as Sigmund reached out to touch the light but roared when it sparked.

Angered eyes lifted to the sky. "You think light tricks will defeat me? I will destroy your servant and take these worlds for my master."

Mottled gray spots appeared on his wings and he hissed. "They called me back; your creation. Of their own free will; they called out to me. You couldn't stop them. You set the rules and boundaries and now you must abide by them."

His gaze dropped to the silent crowd filling the glen. "What do you offer them? Truth? Forgiveness? Reconciliation? They don't want those things. They spit in your face and welcomed me back. Look at them! They love the darkness because the light you offer reveals their corruption.

"Now I will take your Light Bringer. I will bleed him and enjoy every second of it. They called me; you released me. Now I will celebrate my victory and you cannot interfere! This was your challenge."

The High Guardian circled the rough, blood-stained altar, his eyes fixed on Rayne. He moved in closer. Strange words spewed from his mouth, stirring old memories within Rayne.

A sword appeared in the High Guardian's hands. Formed from worked veredium, it glinted red in the light of the torches.

He swung the weapon as if to test its balance, a hungry look on his face as he stepped forward.

"You will not touch him." Thorvin, a glowing sword in

hand, stepped between the High Guardian and Rayne. The man's shoulders bunched, and a vein throbbed on his forehead as he planted his feet and held his sword at center. Thorvin's eyes locked onto the winged being whose magnificent stature and bearing made him look like a petulant child. "I swore an oath to protect my prince. I will not break that oath. You'll have to go through me to get to him."

The High Guardian's mouth widened into a grin exposing perfect, white teeth. "What is it that makes you humans unable to understand simple instructions? Though it would please me to put you in your place, trainer, I do believe the rules of this engagement forbade any interference. This challenge is out of your league."

The High Guardian's attention focused on Captain Theada.

Without a word, the captain waved more USO militia forward. Thorvin roared as he was overcome by the many soldiers and dragged away to stand next to Theodor, surrounded by USO soldiers.

"You can't fool me Sigmund, you piece of slime! Face me like a man," Thorvin yelled.

The High Guardian laughed. "Oh, that's precious. *Face you like a man?* I'm no man. I am beyond your puny comprehension. Be silent and watch as I demonstrate my power."

He lifted his sword and spread his wings. "I am the High Guardian of the seven Scrolls of Power!" His voice permeated the valley, piercing the air, splitting the night. "I have come to destroy the Light Bringer and wipe the lies of the One from Ochen! Lift your voices, my people. Sound the chant and worship our master as we take this, your final offering."

He lifted his eyes to the crack in the sky. "Now is the time!" He flung his arms wide. "Fill me with your power Master and I will destroy the servant of our foe. The human who sought to bring our plans to ruin."

Green, sickly lightning flashed, and the stench of decay filled the air as a mass of darkness lowered to hover directly above Rayne. It bulged downward.

Rayne lifted his hands. "O holy One, protect your servant."

The churning darkness dissolved into tiny bits of mist. A wind rose and the mist scattered.

The High Guardian stormed to the Prime Shepherd. "Seven sacrifices, you blundering idiot." He swung the blade in quick arcs. Within seconds, seven heads rolled on the ground at the prime shepherd's feet. "Next time, it will be your head I take."

Dropping the sword, he turned both hands palms up and cupped small flickers of dark fire. He spun and stalked back to Rayne, the small blazes growing into glowing balls of dense, oily flames. Rayne faced the furious demon, full faith in the One birthing confidence within him.

Heat from the searing balls drove those closest to the High Guardian back. Soon the entire space around the altar cleared leaving Rayne and Sigmund alone next to the altar.

The wings which had appeared pure and shining now hung in tatters. The face that earlier seemed beautiful was now charred and sagging. His compelling presence, now shrunk to the form of a spiteful, spindly travesty of the angel of light he had appeared to be.

A smile bared the demon's teeth. "So, little Light Bringer, we face each other again. This time I will not fail."

Rayne shook his head. "But you already have."

With an oath, Sigmund began to fling globules of dark fire at Rayne.

47

Once before Rayne had been held by the Son. Now, as a cocoon of light shielded him from Sigmund's fury, he again rested in the comforting presence. He wept as the call to leave pulled him back toward the physical world. His spirit clung to that perfect, holy being who made all things and offers forgiveness and acceptance to all who are willing to accept.

You must go back, my beloved Light Bringer.

"No. Why?"

You have not yet completed the tasks I have set for you.

"No. Please let me stay with you."

A deep, pleased chuckle vibrated the air. *Would you forsake your promise to me?*

The promise Rayne had made to always answer *yes* to the One whispered through him and he groaned.

Are you ready my child?

A vista opened below Rayne. Thousands of people filled a hollow lit by torches. It was night, but he saw everything as if the bright light of day filled the sky. His heart began to burn. Those he loved were below … and others … so many others whose spirits cried out to hear the One's Words. So much pain. So many deceived. The time had come for a reckoning.

Sigmund's corrupted true form stood next to ... *the sacrificial stone. That's my body. Like before. I'm here but my body is below.*

The voice hummed within Rayne. *Are you ready?*

"You will be with me?"

The warm presence vibrated with another chuckle. *Have I ever left you?*

The spirit of Rayne smiled. "Your love has always surrounded me. I'm ready. Yes."

The physical pressed down on Rayne and he blinked. Breathed in and out. He centered on the warm flicker of the One's spirit within him. He raised his eyes.

Rayne released his hold on the other place to fully return to Ochen—his world, his people, his calling.

When the barrage of dark fire ended, the demon leaned forward, hands on bony knees, his shredded, corrupted wings dragging on the ground, as he sucked in gulps of air.

The radiant ribbons of light surrounding Rayne had melded into an opaque shield. Rayne appeared as nothing more than an unmoving vague form within. Lexi squinted trying to make out his features.

"Move closer." Rowena's voice sounded hollow. The glen waited, silent, as if afraid to breathe.

Lexi nodded. Slow, even steps brought the two back to the level ground near the demon, still sputtering and gasping only inches from where Rayne stood encased in light. Sigmund's eyes locked onto Rowena.

"You! If I can't have him, I'll take you."

He sprang at them. Shoving Lexi to the ground, he wrapped long fingers around Rowena's throat, his eyes swirling with a mixture of white and black.

"Stop."

The word came soft as a breeze. Lexi turned. Rayne stood, unprotected, next to the unholy rock; his hands loose at his sides. "Leave her."

Sigmund released his hold on Rowena's neck and shoved her away. He licked his lips then grinned. "Finally."

With a calm assurance Lexi was certain she hadn't seen before, Rayne smiled at Sigmund, raised his hand and signaled, *come*.

ℜ

As the bands of light loosened around him, Rayne stepped toward Sigmund and Rowena.

Rayne smiled and again crooked his fingers for Sigmund to come. *That's right. Leave her. I am your challenge.*

"It's over." Rayne's shout rang like a clarion. "Do you not yet realize that you were called here by the power of the One, not by bloody sacrifices and chants. And by the power of the One you shall again be bound in outer darkness. That which you sought for others has now been delivered to you."

The demon started toward Rayne, scooping up his sword as he came, a smile revealing rotting teeth. He hadn't taken more than a few steps when he stopped short. A wild look came into his eyes and he tried to speak several times before he clamped his mouth shut. He backed a few steps away from Rayne, his eyes narrowing to thin slits. "You knew this would happen. You set me up."

Rayne shook his head. "You thought you could use these people. Worm your way back onto these worlds by deception. *You* know the One; *you* knew this would happen. Yet you continued to pursue a path leading to your own destruction."

Rayne raised his hands. "Worshipers of the scrolls. The time has come; the truth revealed. Power never resided in the physical scrolls. They were never anything more than wood and paper; their might a delusion. This deceiver now standing before you used you. Knowing the prophecy of the Binding would come to fruition as do all the One's promises, he paved a way to return after the Day of Binding."

Dropping his arms, Rayne turned to face Sigmund. "Now I will show you true power; the power of the One."

Rayne knelt and folded his hands in prayer. "Blessed One, Creator-Father, Redeemer and lover of souls, bestow on me the power you gave to your prophets on the old world. You have sent me to speak your words to those whose hearts you have prepared. Guide me now."

Rayne pressed onto his feet and comprehension flooded his spirit. He strode toward the USO soldiers surrounding Theodor and Thorvin, a path opening before him.

The men clustered together, placing themselves between the two they guarded and Rayne. Coming to a stop before the man who held the King's Sword, Rayne held his palm out and motioned for the soldier to hand it over. The man stared at Rayne, his eyes wide, his jaw hanging open. Though fear clouded his eyes, he pulled the sword in closer.

"I'll take that," Rayne said, reaching for the ancient weapon. The moment his hand touched the hilt; the blade blazed into the sword of light Rayne had wielded on the Day of Binding. Bands of red, blue, and gold luminescence circled a shaft of blinding white light, then compressed into the shape of a blade.

The USO soldier released the blade as if his fingers had been singed and Rayne wrapped his hand around the familiar hilt.

This is your battle, my Lord. I will not try to fight on my own again. What would you have me do?

Warmth filled Rayne. *Destroy this seat of evil so never again will it be used to summon creatures of darkness.*

His face set, Rayne returned to the ancient altar, stone of power and conduit for darkness.

His voice thundered over the valley. "Today you bear witness to the majesty of the One. Behold."

Rayne raised the sword over his head. He pulled in a breath, held it for a second, then, with a yell, sent the blade crashing down onto the blood-stained slab. A deep bell-like tone vibrated the air as blade met pitted surface and the altar trembled.

A high-pitched scream drew Rayne's attention back to Sigmund who began to wail. "No, no, no! You must not do this. Stop! Stop!"

As Rayne shifted his focus back to the evil mass, an explosive sound wave split the night and the altar shattered into tiny pebbles. Gusts of wind whirled above the pebbles, stirring them; they splintered and disintegrated into particles of dust.

Like strong currents within a squall, the wind howled, blowing harder. People stumbled and fought to remain upright as branches of surrounding trees swayed and bounced, some breaking with the force. Every particle of dust twirled up into the whirlwind, forming a brown funnel. Lightning cracked and thunder boomed.

The voice of the One pierced the night, "I am the One. There is no other. Never again will you set foot upon the worlds of Ochen, Sigmund."

The wind screamed. Sigmund stumbled and a blast of wind lifted him off his feet, pulling him up into the brown mass. With a final furious discharge, the dust scattered in every direction. Sigmund was no more.

An empty hole in the ground now marked the spot where the stone of sacrifice had stood.

Rayne raised his eyes to the sky. To the east, filtered rays of blue-tinged light announced the arrival of sunrise. Rayne turned his face into a shaft of light, allowing the warmth to calm the tremors that set in as the sword clashed with the altar. A new day was dawning for Ochen. The Source was gone. For the thousands of people Sigmund had deceived and manipulated, there was hope for new life and faith in the One.

48

Rayne dropped to his knees, spent, the Kings Sword clattering to the ground next to him. He lifted praises and thanks to the One as he stared at the cavity before him. He wanted to believe it was over. Needed to believe Sigmund was gone for good. He had thought so before ... before the full extent of Sigmund's influence over those who embraced his false religion became known.

The One's warmth filled Rayne and his words filtered through him. *Well done my faithful Light Bringer. You have served me like my prophets of old. You have been faithful.*

Rayne lifted his eyes. Though most of the scroll worshipers stood as if in a daze, and others gathered in small groups talking among themselves, offering no threat, Ochen Army soldiers were spreading out to oppose those still intent on fighting. The sun glinted off weapons. Screams sounded from various spots.

Captain Ellis and several soldiers confronted those who had surrounded Theodor and Thorvin. They surrendered without a fight. Rayne smiled to see his mother, one arm linked in Theodor's, the other holding her rapier as if ready to defend her husband.

Something thumped into Rayne from behind and a pair of arms wrapped around him. Twisting to look over his shoulder, he found a pair of gold-flecked amber eyes. Rayne pulled Lexi up with him as he stood, then turned in her arms. *Joy! Thank you, Lord for such joy!*

The world beyond them disappeared as Rayne's lips found Lexi's; soft, sweet, and so right. The kiss was cut short.

Urgency yanked Rayne from the all-too-brief moment of bliss back into the present as Prime Shepherd Hamlin's shrill shout rang out. "You! This is all your fault. I will not let you get away with this."

Rayne turned to face the man, shoving Lexi behind him.

Hamlin's face looked swollen. Mottled patches of red and black stood out on pale skin which had taken on a sickly green sheen of sweat. His lips drew back to expose perfect, white teeth as spittle drooled from the corner of his mouth.

Lifting a sword, he charged Rayne.

Rayne side stepped with ease, shifting Lexi with him. *Stupid! He's no swordsman. Crazy!* "Lexi, go to my mother. You'll be safe there."

He could sense her hesitation but shoved her away. The hurt look in her eyes morphed into understanding and she nodded.

Rayne returned his focus to Hamlin who reminded him of a provoked bull he'd seen once on Amathea. A quick shift of his eyes, and he breathed in relief to see Lexi sprint toward his mother. Thorvin passed her, running toward Rayne, a one-eyed man and several soldiers following.

The prime shepherd tossed the weapon he held and darted in to grab the King's Sword from where Rayne had dropped it. He bent and grasped the hilt of the ancient weapon. Rising he swung it in careless, wild arcs. He stopped and jiggled the sword, staring at it. "Come on. Glow for me!"

Rayne shook his head. "It's over, Prime Shepherd Hamlin. Your High Guardian has lost. Give me the sword."

A shift in the air at his back alerted Rayne to Thorvin's presence. "I'll handle this, Your Highness."

"No. I'll handle this." The feminine voice came from Rayne's right. *Aunt Cailyn?*

Cailyn strode up to the prime shepherd. "Like my nephew said, Seth, it's over. Now drop that sword."

"Lady Moth…"

'No!'

Cailyn's scream shook Rayne. So much anger and pain. *Was that what drove her to do what she did?*

"No, Seth. Don't you see? Look around you. The altar is gone, the High Guardian defeated." She cried out and dropped to her knees. "We were wrong, Seth. Think. Blood for blood? Wrong. We should have been binding up wounds, not making them worse.

"Blood for power? Wrong. Look at my nephew. Our bloody sacrifices couldn't pull up a fraction of the power he just demonstrated.

"Blood for vengeance?" She sobbed and raised her eyes to the sky before returning her focus to Hamlin. "Wrong," she breathed the word out, her voice breaking. "The worst wrong of all. The One warned me. 'Vengeance belongs to me,' he whispered into my spirit over and over.

"What now, Seth? The only thing left for us is to ask the very thing the One and Rayne have offered, forgiveness."

Cailyn's words had drawn attention. Those near enough to hear moved in closer to the level area where the ancient stone had sat. As they were drawn forward, those behind filtered into the gaps.

When Cailyn stopped speaking, Hamlin seemed to pull himself together. He wiped the spittle from his mouth with his sleeve, then pulled his back arrow straight.

"I will never concede defeat." He released a primal yell and, lifting the King's Sword overhead, charged at Rayne.

As Rayne stepped back, Thorvin slid into a defensive posture in front of him.

Prime Shepherd Hamlin, organizer and leader of the United Scrolls of Ochen, committed follower of the High Guardian of the Scrolls, plunged onto Thorvin's blade as if unaware of its existence. His eyes bulged as his gaze shifted from Rayne to the weapon now buried nearly to the hilt in his chest. He gasped his last breath and died on Thorvin's blade.

Cailyn's cries penetrated Rayne's consciousness, pulling his eyes from Hamlin to his aunt. She looked so frail, curled in on herself, kneeling on the ground. It would have been easy to hate her. Her need for vengeance had driven her to commit unspeakable acts. The old darkness within Rayne uncoiled itself, ready to feed lies into his spirit. *You have every right to hate her ... cling to that ... it is your right ...*

But her anguished sobs touched that part of Rayne where he had given the One complete control. He couldn't reach out to her now—his pain was too fresh—someone else would have to do that. But in time he would forgive her.

Love for Lexi and his mother drove the darkness back into its dormant coil as the two approached and knelt beside Cailyn. She would still need to face the consequences of her actions, but she would not have to face them alone.

Rayne didn't know how it happened, but Lexi had changed. Reaching out to Cailyn now was evidence of that change. The three women knelt together on the ground, talking for a few minutes. They bowed their heads in prayer, then Rowena waved a couple soldiers over. They helped Cailyn to stand and, supporting the still grieving duchess, walked her toward the castle.

Rayne suspected Cailyn and the other leaders of the cult would be taken to cells in Castle Inverness to await trial. The bigger question would be what to do with the thousands of people who had been deceived and come to Nemora looking for new lives and were now displaced.

Thorvin and several soldiers took Prime Shepherd Hamlin's body and laid it out in a shady spot with the others who lost their lives in the sporadic fighting that broke out during the confrontation.

So much death. So much pain. Rayne turned in a circle, taking in the milling uncertain crowd.

A line of gray clouds moved in, challenging Nemora's blue-tinged sunlight. A gentle breeze rustled branches and soft mist filled the air as beams of luminosity broke through in random spots. The misty morning reflected the mood Rayne sensed in those around him; mellow, hesitant. He too struggled with conflicting emotions; joy at having been used so power-fully by the One to combat Sigmund's plan, offset by sorrow for those whose lives had been destroyed by the demon's lies.

Rayne took comfort in the fact that the One's Words would now find fertile ground in the ex-scroll worshipers.

A smile surfaced on his face as Rowena and Lexi walked to him. Lexi held back, allowing Rowena to greet Rayne first. She approached Rayne and he held his arms out, she stepped into his embrace. He wrapped arms around his mother, her warm tears soaking through his tunic.

"I was so worried. Never, never do something so reckless again." Rowena's muffled voice rose from where she pressed into his chest.

Rayne's eyes met Lexi's as she stepped in behind his mother. "You had us all worried."

Rowena pressed back and withdrew her arms. "When you disappeared again, I thought I would die." A wavering smile fought against the tears that still trickled down the queen's cheeks. "But you're here now. Whole. Safe ... I hope."

Rayne allowed his smile to surface again. "As safe as possible. Thorvin even came to my rescue again."

"As well he should," Theodor said as he walked up. Thorvin, Mite, and the man Rayne had recognized earlier as a leader of the USO trailed the king.

Theodor pulled Rayne into a tight, back-thumping hug. He released Rayne and stepped back, looking him in the eye. "Are you alright, Son?"

Rayne nodded; afraid his voice would crack if he tried to speak. He was alright ... so very alright. Once again, unbounded peace flooded through him. Then Lexi was in his arms and he thought he would burst with the joy of it. She stepped to his side, pulling his arm over her shoulders. *So perfect.*

Rayne shifted his focus to the unknown stranger. "We haven't met, but I know you. You stood with Prime Shepherd Hamlin, overseeing the sacrifices."

Rowena spoke up. "Rayne, this is Gwyn Thomas. He tried to stop what was happening and almost became a sacrifice him-self. He's been talking to groups of scroll worshipers, telling them about the One's Words and encouraging them to read the scrolls. He did much to help prepare questioning scroll worshipers to hear you speak."

"Will you continue to work with those coming out of the USO then?" Rayne hoped the man might do so. His personal experience with the cult would help him reach out to others.

Gwyn glanced away, apparently unable to meet Rayne's gaze. "If you want me to. I'd understand if you'd rather I be tried with the others."

"Have you accepted the One and his Words?"

"With all my heart, Your Highness."

"Then I believe your penance is your calling. Go ... speak truth to those to whom you previously preached lies. If this is the One's will, you will be successful; if not, we will see where it leads."

"Thank you, Your Highness. I will try my best to serve him."

"That is all I ask."

Rayne scanned the group again, a furrow creasing his brow. "Where's Andrew?"

The silence that greeted Rayne's question dropped a rock into his stomach. No one would meet his gaze. "What? Where's Andrew?"

Thorvin's rough voice broke through the awkward silence. "Andrew's over there." Thorvin waved a hand in the direction where the bodies had been placed.

"No!" Instant tears burned the backs of Rayne's eyes. "Not Andrew. How?"

"Not Andrew." Rowena's quiet voice broke through Rayne's rising grief. He raised his eyes to hers. She shook her head. "Not Andrew. His friend, Mayda."

Marius's ill-fated attempt to kill the prime shepherd sent renewed grief through Rayne. Mayda was just a girl who deserved to live a long, happy life. And Marius hadn't meant to kill her. Sigmund's plans continued to birth evil.

"Andrew is sitting near her body." Theodor said. "He and her father refuse to leave her side. We didn't have the heart to arrest the man yet, but he's not going anywhere. The death of his daughter has broken him."

"I need to go to him." Rayne started toward the grove of trees.

"No, Son." Rowena's hand slipped over Rayne's arm. "Not yet. Andrew needs this time alone. Later. He'll need you later."

Rayne nodded. *Too much! Oh, holy Father, please be with Andrew ... and Mayda's father.*

49

In the days that followed, the weather turned, leaving behind the milder days of autumn. Heavy morning frosts layered the bushes and fields surrounding Castle Inverness, heralding the approach of winter.

The scroll worshipers continued to camp on the outskirts of Inverness. With few exceptions, they came together to listen whenever Gwyn spoke. Gwyn and Mite became inseparable, and it wasn't unusual to see the diminutive ancient and the hefty ex-scroll worshiper walking to or from the camp, deep in conversation.

Captain Theada and his followers continued to stage night-time attacks on both the Ochen Army soldiers patrolling the camp, and outlying farms. Thorvin led a hand-picked light cavalry unit formed specifically to run down the USO militia. After several close encounters, Captain Theada and his people disappeared. Concerned, the citizens of Inverness began to protest the camp remaining in the valley north of the city. They feared once the king and his party left, the rebels would return to cause havoc in Inverness.

Rayne announced that he would speak at the USO camp

on the second Binding Day after the One's challenge and defeat of the High Guardian.

Theodor issued a decree stating the day following Rayne's presentation, those who chose to remain on Nemora were to move south to the Camp of the Forgotten. There, they would be welcomed and have more room to spread out.

The king and queen held open court for many days after the confrontation, Rowena filling the role of Duchess of Nemora. Theodor listened to petitions from those wishing to return to their home worlds and granted permission for them to do so on the condition they signed pledges promising to never again participate in rebellion against the crown.

"You okay?" Rayne thumped Andrew on the back.

The page sniffled, wiped his nose on his sleeve, and turned to face Rayne. "I guess."

Boone circled the boy, pressing into him, the dog's tail waving like a flag. Andrew sniffed and scratched Boone behind the ears. "It's just so hard." His voice cracked and he turned to face the wall. "I'm sorry."

Rayne put a hand on Andrew's shoulder. "You have nothing to be sorry for. Losing Mayda hurt you deeply. Pain like that takes a while to work through."

"Sometimes I think I'm doing okay but then … it's like getting hit by a big wave. It sort of barrels over me and I start crying again."

"Look, if you have my clothes set for my talk, I'll get myself dressed. Why don't you take some time and visit your parents? You haven't seen them in months."

Andrew shook his head. "Thanks. But I promised Mayda's pop I would go with him to the Camp of the Forgotten; see him settled in. We're both missing Mayda. I like talking to him. He tells me stories about Mayda before I met her."

Andrew knelt to scratch behind Boone's ears again, but Rayne could tell he had something more on his mind. He remained quiet, giving Andrew time to work through what he wanted to say. A few minutes later, the page raised his eyes and said, "Rayne … do you think I'm too young to … you know… have loved Mayda? I mean, it's like the way you are with Lexi. How your face lights up and you get that funny feeling whenever you see her. That's the way I felt about Mayda. She was so special and … and do you think it's possible?"

"Sure Andrew. It's possible. I only knew Mayda for a short while, but she *was* special. I could see that.

"Is Mr. Creedoff leaving tomorrow with the rest of the camp?"

"Yeah." Andrew eyes went wide. "It's okay if I go, isn't it? I should have asked you sooner."

"Of course you can go, Andrew. I'll be back in Westvale by the time you get back, but I'll leave a pass for you at the Inverness Portal Station to skip to Corylus without charge. But—and I mean it—do not miss my wedding. I won't know what to do without you."

A hesitant smile quirked the sides of Andrew's mouth. "I wouldn't miss it for anything on the seven."

"Now, go." Rayne waved toward the door. "You should get ready if you're going to the Camp of the Forgotten tomorrow."

"I will. But first, someone's got to help you look like a prince when you speak."

Andrew already had a pair of dark gray breeches, a finely woven, cream-colored linen shirt and Rayne's black doe-skin boots set out. He topped off the lukewarm water in the bathtub with hot water from a kettle that had been sitting over the fire. Though Rayne tried to get Andrew to talk while Rayne bathed, the boy remained subdued.

Andrew held a warm towel up as Rayne stepped out of the tub, shivering in the chill morning air. Taking the towel from Andrew, Rayne dried his torso then wrapped the towel around his waist and padded into the adjoining room.

The suite Rayne had been given in Castle Inverness sat in one of the circular stone towers. Consisting of a bedroom and a sitting room, it was large and well furnished with heavy masculine furniture. Tapestries depicting famous scenery from around Inverness covered the walls, but the rooms always felt damp and never got quite warm enough to suit Rayne, especially now that the nights were turning colder.

Rayne reached his hands toward the fire Andrew had stoked moments before. Andrew followed him in, carrying his clothing. "You might as well get dressed in here since it's warmer than the bedroom."

Once Rayne was suitably attired and his hair combed, Andrew stepped back and nodded. "Now you look like a prince."

An awkward silence followed. "Well, I guess I should go now." Andrew turned, his shoulders slumped, and took two steps toward the door before Rayne stopped him.

"Andrew wait!" Rayne wrapped the boy in a tight bearhug.

"Everything's different now, isn't it, Rayne? When I come back you and Lexi will be married. We won't share your suite in Westvale.

"Mayda's gone and she's not coming back, ever."

"Life is filled with all kinds of changes, Andrew. It's going to happen whether we want it to or not. You have to decide for yourself how to face the changes when they come.

"Losing Mayda hurt. A lot. But I don't think she would want you to stay sad. For now, it's good and right to mourn. But at some point, there will come a time when it won't hurt so much. Remember all the good times you had with Mayda and they'll help you through the sorrow."

Andrew nodded, then called Boone to him. After giving the black dog a quick hug, he slipped out the door.

The weight of Andrew's sorrow pressed down on Rayne as he descended the grand staircase to the ground level of Castle Inverness. He entered the Great Hall and, looking up at the immense arches rising above his head, thought about his own mortality. The One had saved him from death twice. But, like Mayda and all the others who had lost their lives because of Sigmund, a day would come for Rayne when he would be released from the physical limitations of life here and be with the One.

He had begged to stay with the Son during the One's

challenge, but now the joy and peace he felt then seemed so far away and unreal. Yet he knew it had been real … and Mayda was there with the One and the Son even now.

"You look like you're a thousand miles away." Lexi's voice pulled Rayne from his thoughts.

He quirked a half smile. "I guess I was."

"Your parents should be down any time now. Are you ready?"

"I think so." A soft warm breeze filtered through him. *I am with you always.* "Yes. I am ready. This is my chance to reach out to those who sought my death and show them the power of the One's forgiveness."

"And this time I don't think they will try to poison you." Thorvin's voice echoed through the hall, like rocks grinding against each other. "Unless they're determined to start a war."

"Yes." Lexi nodded and her nose crinkled. "After losing the High Guardian, what you did, and all that has happened, they would be stupid to try to anything."

Rayne saw the conflict still written on her features. Though Mayda's death had touched Lexi on a deep level and she had pledged to release her hatred of scroll worshipers, she still struggled with her emotions. Rayne loved her even more for her struggle. It confirmed what he already knew; though her love for him turned her into an over-protective mother bear, her heart was too soft to cling to hatred for very long.

The words the One had spoken to Lexi and Rayne on Veres nearly five years ago surfaced in Rayne's mind. *My gift of love to you.*

Yes, he and Lexi were made for each other. And soon they would reinforce that commitment through the covenant of marriage. Once Rayne addressed the crowd today, his parents, Lexi, Thorvin, and Rayne planned to return to Westvale. Others would remain on Nemora to continue working with the ex-scroll worshipers; people like Gwyn and Mite. Captain Fontaine and a large contingent of soldiers would also remain until things settled down here.

Rowena and Theodor walked down the wide staircase. Rowena came to Rayne and gave him a motherly kiss. "Are you ready?"

Rayne huffed out a breath. "Why does everyone keep asking me that? Yes, I'm ready. I'm past ready. Though I look forward to sharing the One's words, I can't wait for this to all be over so I can head home and finally ... finally get married and live in peace."

"Finally," Lexi said under her breath.

"In peace?" Thorvin growled. "You've been a magnet for trouble since I first laid eyes on you. I doubt getting married is going to change that."

"It better." Lexi raised an eyebrow at Thorvin.

"Enough!" Theodor waved toward the door. "I believe horses are already saddled and waiting, as well as a guard. There will be plenty of time to discuss Rayne's aptitude for finding trouble later."

"It's not like I go looking for it," Rayne mumbled as he followed the others out the door.

50

Captain Ellis, Noah, Sashi, Stevie, and Benning waited in the inner courtyard of Castle Inverness with a dozen Arisimanian cavalry soldiers. Rayne had learned that Benning's friend Oliver lost his life in a clash with USO militia and before he mounted, he walked up to the soldier. "I'm sorry to hear about your loss. Her Majesty tells me you two were good friends."

Benning spoke with his eyes forward and a stiff posture. "Yes, Your Highness. Thank you."

Rayne nodded in response. There was nothing he could say to ease Benning's grief; only the One and time could do that.

Shalimar nickered as he approached, and Rayne delighted in greeting her as she nibbled at his shirt, looking for a treat. "Patience, girl. When we get back, I'll find you a nice, ripe apple."

Rayne relaxed into his saddle; riding the familiar Arisimanian mare felt like home. His parents rode in front and Lexi pulled in alongside him. She sent a grin in his direction and he winked back.

The smoke of hundreds of cookfires mixed with a dissipating layer of valley fog, coating tents and people with moisture and grit. Streamers of sunlight, blue-tinged and warm, broke through, looking like heavenly rays. As the party rode past groupings of tents and approached the platform Prime Shepherd Hamlin had used when addressing the scroll worshipers, Gwyn waved. Mite sprinted to Rayne and bouncing from foot to foot, said, "time, time, time. It is as the Creator-Father planned, it is, it is. Ray-ray will speak light into the dark again."

Rayne dismounted to walk with Mite the short distance to the raised stage. "So, Mite, from what I hear you and Gwyn have been doing a great job getting this crowd ready."

Mite nodded, his blue hair bouncing with the sharp movement. "Yes. Yes. Yes. Scroll people are dark lovers no longer. They are hungry, hungry for the Creator-Father's light."

"Thank you, Mite. Again, you have helped me."

Mite pulled to a stop and raised his large, gray eyes to Rayne's. "Always help Light Bringer, always."

Rayne's heart warmed at the ancient's open expression of delight. "Okay, Mite. Let's get this done." With energy to spare, the two jogged the final feet to the stage.

"Once you start speaking, Rayne, I'll amplify your voice," Rowena said as Rayne bent to give Mite a quick hug.

Gwyn approached Rayne, going down the three steps as Rayne ascended. In passing, Rayne reached out to the ex-scroll worshiper and shook his hand. "Thank you, Gwyn, for all you've done for me, my parents, and those who are leaving the USO behind."

Gwyn paused, his eyes misting. "No. I thank you. It is only by forgiveness, yours and the One's, that I have been released from the lies of darkness and come to know true light. I am honored to serve you, Light Bringer of the One. He used you mightily to change me and these people who have come to hear you speak today."

"He used us both." Rayne turned from Gwyn and bounded up the last step.

Rayne turned to face the crowd that had formed. The sun's light, now burning away the final tendrils of fog, warmed the air. He scanned the faces and realized Gwyn was right. These people were hungry. The One had done as he promised; prepared hearts and minds to receive his word. Rayne knelt, and closed his eyes.

As his lids lowered, Rayne sensed the coiled darkness within him stretch. *You think you are a worthy servant. Deception and lies. Your pride will be your undoing.*

Rayne shook his head. *No. These lies are not from the One. Depart from me. You can't touch me. The One is my rock and my fortress, my strong tower. Be gone!*

That Rayne still battled the dark thoughts from within, disturbed him. But no matter how many times they reared their deceitful heads, Rayne would not give in. Years ago, when he was still Sigmund's slave he had given in, yielded and surrendered to the demon. In that moment, the One called Rayne out of time and reignited the spark within him. *I belong to the One alone. By his strength I will always.*

The One's warmth flooded Rayne and he prayed. When he rose, he realized large numbers of those before him had knelt as well. He smiled then addressed the crowd of ex-scroll worshipers and soldiers.

"It is not by my power that I speak to you today. On Binding Day, I did not steal the power of the scrolls for myself. This is a lie. On that day, the One, working through me as the prophecies foretold, banished the demons who sought to bring darkness and enslave the worlds of Ochen.

"The being you called your High Guardian of the Scrolls was one of those demons. His goal was to use your faith in him to once again gain access to the worlds of Ochen and destroy faith in the One and his Church, not lead you to a new age of glory.

"Power still dwells within the scrolls. But not in the scrolls themselves. It resides in the Words they contain; that was always the strength of the scrolls—the Words. All power belongs to the One. I am but a poor reflection he has chosen to spread the truth of his power, his love, and his Son.

"Belief in the One, and belief in the Son, and their indwelling spirit are gifts. They can't be earned. Learning and reading the Words will help you to grasp the truth, but only a heart warmed by the One will bring you into his presence. You are blessed. Your hearts had been prepared while you yet worshiped the scrolls. When I challenged the High Guardian, you saw the truth. But not everyone who sees truth embraces it.

"There was a time in my life when I believed the High Guardian's lies. He went by the name Sigmund then and sought to defeat the One's prophecy and destroy me. He raised me to kill and I did. I'm not proud of what I did then. But I knew no way to escape my slavery. And yet the One sought me out, embraced me, set his spark of life within me, and drew me to himself.

"This is what he has done for you as well. The truth you are discovering now will grow as you mature in faith. Spend time with the One. Study his Words to the worlds of Ochen. Seek his will for your lives. You will be blessed in ways you never imagined. I know I could never have imagined the life I have now."

Rayne paused and a man's voice sounded. "We need to know. Is it true? You aren't going to punish us for what was done?"

Rayne rubbed fingers over his jaw, then traced the scar running up his cheek. "I do not hold what was done to me against you. Those responsible are either dead or imprisoned. But I wasn't the only one harmed. Innocent blood was spilled on that altar of evil. Though my father will not pursue this issue beyond those already in custody, you yourselves need to take responsibility for your actions.

"If you were involved in the sacrifices, pray to the One. Allow him to guide you. Trust him and ask his forgiveness. If you are truly sorry and ask for forgiveness, he will forgive you. He forgave me and chose me despite the evil I had done. If he convicts you, confess your involvement.

"Talk to Gwyn Thomas or Mite; they have agreed to accompany you to the Camp of the Forgotten. They want to help you adjust to your new faith. Listen to them.

"I'm leaving Nemora now. But I will come back in a few months. I hope by then, you will be settled in more stable circumstances. I will pray for you and I ask that you pray for me as well."

Rayne bowed his head. "Blessed One, please help those here before you now. Guide them. Help them deal with the guilt that will strive to draw them away from you. Help them to settle at the Camp of the Forgotten and find peace in your Words. Bring them to your truth and may they continue seeking your will for their lives.

"I also pray for those who lost their lives. The ones sacrificed as well as those who fought on both sides of the conflict. May this be a time of healing and peace for all Ochen. Thank you blessed Creator-Father."

Rayne descended the steps from the platform. Lexi waited until he stood in front of her before wrapping her arms around his waist. "Can we go now?"

He raised his eyes to meet his father's and Theodor said, "If you are ready, Son, I think it's time we left Nemora."

"I'm ready. Let's go home."

Lexi's face lit up and she attempted to drag Rayne to his horse as numerous people gathered and blocked the path. Rayne released Lexi's hand and began greeting people as they passed. Though most just bowed as he passed, several reached out to touch him and thank him. The look of adoration he saw on their faces unsettled him and he turned back to Rowena. "Mother?"

She stepped around a group of people in her path, Theodor at her back. "Yes, Rayne. What is it?"

"Could you amplify my voice again? From here?"

"Of course." Rowena's look of confusion morphed into one of understanding and she closed her eyes and pulled energy. After a few seconds, she opened her eyes and nodded.

Rayne's voice echoed back to him as he spoke. "Thank you for your support. I wish I could greet you all, but that is not possible. Perhaps I will have time to speak with you individually when I return.

"What I need you to understand before I leave now, though, is that I am not the One. I am but a servant. I have accomplished what the One asked of me only by his strength, not my own. Please don't honor me more than my position as prince dictates. Don't worship me. Save your worship for the One alone. Only the One and the Son are worthy of worship. Always remember that and never again venerate another person as a god.

"Thank you again. May the One bless you and keep you."

51

Nearly a month after Rayne spoke to those who had been part of the USO, end of summer heat and humidity called forth evening thunderstorms almost daily. They built up over the Cameron Sea and spent their fury on Westvale before rumbling off toward the plains east of the capital.

The sun's rays promised another hot and steamy day as Rayne sat on the floor of his balcony enjoying the early morning breeze. His knees were drawn up, supporting a copy of the Words of the One to Corylus, while his back rested against the cool stone wall next to the glass door to his rooms.

At Bishop Newson's suggestion, the Words had been copied from the scrolls into book format and Rayne appreciated the ability to turn pages wherever he sat rather than needing a table to unroll a bulky scroll.

Boone sat at the edge of the balcony, her head stuck between two banisters, her eyes closed and her tongue lolling as she panted.

Behind Rayne, the silence in his suite played havoc with his nerves. Today, of all days, Rayne needed the confidence Andrew's calming presence brought. And Rayne missed his cousin.

Giles and Rayne had spent many hours together since Rayne's return. Giles received the news that Marius's sentence included banishment to Arisima, and recruitment into the army there, with a stoic resignation. "It could have been worse," he said to Rayne as the two walked from the public hearing where Theodor had pronounced sentence. "Marius knows that. He could have been hung for murder and treason."

Rayne turned back to face Giles and nodded as they passed a knot of whispering courtiers. "Yes, that was a possibility. But Father and Mother talked to him several times before making a judgment. Their decision was wise; both just and compassionate. I think Mayda would approve. He'll be a fine scout for Captain Ellis, he knows Arisima well … and he'll live with the guilt of Mayda's death the rest of his life."

"Yes." A crease formed between Giles's brows. "In all the time I've known him, Marius has never taken anything so hard." His eyes shifted to Rayne as they strode the pathway toward the barracks. "Except betraying you to Sigmund."

"So." Rayne grappled with old memories of Marius from the days they spent together with Ponce and Mite before Rayne and Marius traveled to Corylus to face Sigmund. "He has created his own prison in his mind. Guilt forms the bars. Someday I pray he comes to know the One and learns to forgive himself. He's come a long way from the demon-possessed hunter he was when we first met."

"I haven't heard that story. Marius never wanted to talk about it."

Rayne swallowed hard. "Someday … maybe someday I'll tell you about that time."

Later that afternoon when Giles decided to skip to Arisima and join the army with Marius, Rayne wasn't surprised. Traveling together the past two years had solidified a friendship between the young men. Rayne chuckled at the idea of Giles as a soldier, but perhaps his cousin had matured enough since their time on Amathea to put in the effort. Rayne hoped so.

Rayne closed the book. Trying to read this morning was about as productive as trying to harvest blueberries in the dead of winter. He pushed to stand and raised his arms above his head, reaching, stretching the muscles of his back. A groan originating deep within his chest leaked through his teeth as he bent from side to side, working out the kinks that had formed as he sat.

Boone's ears pricked and she turned her dark, liquid eyes toward him.

"Sorry girl. I didn't mean to disturb you."

She voiced a soft whine.

"I know. You're waiting for Andrew too. He should have been here yesterday."

"I thought you would be waiting for me at the portal station."

Rayne's eyes widened and his mouth hung open for a second. He bounded into the sitting room, his face lighting up with a smile. "Andrew. I thought you'd never get here. I waited every time the skipping line switched to inbound from Nemora yesterday." Rayne huffed. "Where were you?"

Andrew shook his head in mock disgust and walked to one of the green leather loveseats where he dropped several packages before dumping a bag on the floor.

Boone yipped and charged to Andrew, her tail flapping in doggie delight as she circled him twice before planting her front paws on his waist. Her body trembled and she whined.

"Hey girl," Andrew said as he pushed her down then knelt to scratch behind her ears. She groaned, her eyes at half mast, then dropped to the floor and flipped onto her back for a belly rub. "Awe. Who's my girl? Who's my good girl," Andrew crooned as he rubbed her belly, eliciting a scratching reaction with her back paw.

Rayne chuckled. Joy bubbled up in him now that Andrew had arrived. "Have you eaten yet? If not, we can grab breakfast together and you can tell me why you weren't here yesterday. And ... fill me in on all that's happening on Nemora."

Andrew gave Boone a few more good scratches then stood. "I haven't eaten, and I do have a lot to tell you. Breakfast sounds good. I'm starving."

"I thank the One you're back Andrew. Deston, that page

from Arisima has been helping me. He means well, but he's as skittish as a newborn colt."

The two headed out the door and strode toward the kitchen at a good pace. "So," Rayne said. "Are you going to tell me why you didn't come yesterday? I was afraid something happened when you never showed up."

Andrew shrugged. "Nothing serious. I met with Mite and Gwyn when I got back to Inverness. They were skipping too so we decided to have dinner before we skipped. We started talking and before we realized it, it was too late to skip."

Rayne broached the subject he had debated avoiding. "How are you coping? You know ... without Mayda?"

Andrew walked in silence for a minute. The soft sigh he released spoke of ongoing sorrow. "I'm doing okay. Spending time with Vartan, Mr. Creedoff. He's been really good to me. He's nice and a hard worker. And the Camp of the Forgotten is great. Everyone is working to help the ex-scroll worshipers fit in. Vartan was a blacksmith before and now he's doing that again. He's got more work than he can handle so he's looking for an assistant."

Andrew got quiet again and Rayne pushed. "Did you want to stay there?"

Andrew's gaze shifted to Rayne then back to the hallway. "Part of me does. But ... I know it's not something I could do forever. No. I belong here. But, if it's okay with you, I'd like to visit again in a month or so."

The knot in Rayne's stomach released. He hadn't realized how much he counted on Andrew until the page was gone. "Of course. You can visit as often as you want. I'd like to join you sometimes. And I'm sure Lexi will too."

The two were greeted by Thorvin and Theodor at the door to the dining hall. "Come with us," Theodor said, wrapping an arm around Rayne's shoulders and propelling him away from the aromas of fresh bread and bacon.

"We were just heading toward your rooms when we saw the two of you," Theodor said. "Since you were heading toward the dining hall, can we assume you haven't eaten yet?" Theodor gave Rayne a quick sideways look.

"Well ..." Rayne started.

"Of course you haven't." Theodor ignored Rayne's attempted reply and continued moving forward.

"I was going to, but then ..." Rayne shrugged, but his eyes drifted back toward the dining hall. "Do you think Lexi's there? You know, eating?"

The two older men hooted. "Oh, no, my boy." Theodor choked then continued to chuckle. "Lexi, your mother, and Anne will not be seen outside the Queen's Suite until the wedding. This whole wedding thing is a big deal for women. And with your mother involved, well ... let's just say she's been looking forward to this day for a long, long time."

Rayne hunched his shoulders. "I can't imagine what they will be doing all day up there. I need to do something other than just sit around waiting for this evening."

"That's what we thought. And we were prepared to argue the point if you disagreed." Theodor's smile crinkled the skin around his eyes. "We have a whole day of activities planned, starting with breakfast at the church house with Shaw. Stevie and Noah arrived from Arisima yesterday. We also invited Mite and Gwyn, who skipped in from Nemora this morning.

"It just seemed right to have something for the men to do while the ladies were all busy with wedding preparations today. I suggested the activities and Thorvin agreed."

Rayne suppressed the urge to release a cheer and nodded, but his pace picked up and he bounded down the steps to the walkway linking the palace with the church grounds.

"What else?" he asked as he turned to walk backward, keeping his gaze on Theodor and Thorvin.

Thorvin scratched his chin and glared up at the sun brightened sky. "Well ... if it doesn't get too hot, we thought we could get in a good ride, maybe go up along the coast some. We also though everyone might enjoy a round of challenges in the practice ring."

"And lunch with Captain Fontaine and Captain Ellis at the barracks. They promised something special," Theodor added.

"That sounds great. Just what I need to keep the nerves at bay." Rayne turned to walk forward. His heart warmed along with the day. His day. Lexi's day. *Thank you, my Lord.*

52

꒕

Lexi yawned. She blinked and sighed. Her eyes popped wide open. "It's here. It's here. I can't believe I'm getting married today! I'm getting married *today?*"

Throwing off the light, summertime covers, she jumped from the massive four-poster, cherry bed and skipped to face the full-length mirror in the guest quarters she had been living in since her return from Nemora.

"This is it Lady Alexianndra Erland." She grimaced then wrinkled her nose at the other Lexi wrinkling its nose back at her. "Today you become Lady Alexianndra Erland Kierken-gaard."

An aborted laugh slipped out before the weight of the day pressed down on her. "Nemora's moons." Sashi's favorite phrase slipped from Lexi's lips. She groaned; her eyes locked on her reflection. "I'm not ready. How can I *not* be ready? Oh, no, no, no. I'm not ready!" She and Rayne had waited almost five years; both had grown and changed so much since meeting.

In some ways Rayne had become a stranger to her; he now carried a strength of faith and peace she wanted to match but couldn't … at least not yet. He had become the One's Light

Bringer in every way. Could she live up to his expectations? Would he find the woman gazing back at Lexi in the mirror beautiful—inside and outside?

Though she relinquished the craving for vengeance she had nurtured in her heart the last few years, she still struggled to dislodge tendrils of the well-anchored root. She wanted to be better for Rayne. Better for the One. But it wasn't easy.

A firm knock rattled her door. Before she could respond, Queen Rowena, dressed in a beautiful purple day dress covered in a print of tiny blue daisies, strode into the receiving room. The queen's long midnight black hair hung loose to her waist. She turned to talk to Anne who trailed her into the room and the deep black curls shimmered in the sunlight.

"We have much to do in a short amount of time, Anne.

"Come, come. Quickly now." Rowena's focus shifted and she spoke in a voice that brooked no disobedience as Anne stepped aside and four well-muscled servants wrestled a large copper tub through the doorway.

Lexi pulled in a breath as she walked out of the bedroom and the queen turned to her with a broad smile.

"My daughter," Rowena said. Her eyes widened. She stopped and pulled back her shoulders. "What? You look as if you just got up. What are you thinking, Lexi? At this rate you will never be ready in time for the wedding."

"Of course she will." Anne's quiet, soothing voice sent a wave of calm through Lexi. "She has us to help her."

"And me." Sashi stuck her head in the doorway as the servants retreated down the hallway.

"Sashi." Lexi's voice came out an octave higher than she expected and she clamped her mouth closed.

"All the way from Arisima." Sashi stepped between Rowena and Anne to lean in and wrap her long arms around Lexi. "You didn't think I'd miss this. Nemora's moons. Not for anything. Even though I did have to give up the chance to down some really fine ale with my husband, brother, Rayne, and those old scoundrels, Thorvin, Shaw, and His Majesty. Once again being the lone rose among the thorns." She sighed. "Oh, yes. I'm also supposed to let you know your father has arrived with several others from Veres. All those of male-persuasion were on their way to the stables when I left Noah to come here."

She shifted on her feet, her gaze taking in Rowena and Anne. She ducked her head toward Rowena. "Your Majesty. Excuse my lack of manners."

Rowena turned cold eyes on Sashi for a moment, then relented and the smile from earlier reappeared. "No offense, Sashi. You are family.

"Now. We need—" A soft sound at the door drew everyone's attention to three serving girls.

At a crisp nod from Rowena, the three entered. "Ah! Perfect timing."

One held a tray with steaming platters of eggs and bacon; the second balanced a tray with plates, silverware, and a dish of sliced bread along with stoneware bowls of honey and jams. The third brought in a coffee service, cups, and saucers, accompanied by a pitcher of cream and a bowl of sugar.

"Well, ladies, what's first?" Sashi asked with a twinkle in her eyes.

Anne chuckled and Rowena smacked Sashi in the arm. "Silly question, silly girl." The queen sent a sideways glance at Sashi. "Of course, we eat first; it takes energy to prepare for a wedding and for that we need nourishment. We will separate for baths, then return here for the meeting with the dressmaker and her seamstresses. By then it will be time for lunch. After lunch, things will get serious. We who have experience will pass our hard-won advice on to the bride."

Rowena's eyes took on an evil glint and Lexi wondered what kind of advice the queen had in mind.

Lexi's hopes for a quiet day evaporated as the three ladies took seats and began dishing out servings of food while chatting. Knowing things would only get more hectic as the day passed, Lexi relaxed into the activity. It was going to be a wonderful—if long—day.

Rayne emerged from the practice room, sweat dribbling down his torso, his shirt damp and sticky as he followed Shaw and Fallon, the two involved in a deep philosophical debate that had begun a couple hours earlier at lunch. Behind Rayne, Theodor, Thorvin, and the rest of the group laughed at the funny story Noah shared about a hopelessly clumsy thief he had arrested in Zoraya, the capital of Arisima.

The day had flown by as one activity led into the next. Good times with his father and their friends. Lexi's father, Justus Erland arrived from Veres soon after breakfast, bringing several friends with him. By the time they ended up at the practice ring, the crowd had grown to more than a dozen men.

Heat rose from the walkway as the sun beat down from a crystal-clear dome of blue. Rayne's thoughts churned as he wiped his face in the hem of his tunic.

"What next?" Stevie asked as he scooted past Shaw and Fallon and turned to face the others while walking backward.

Rayne stopped short. The vow he had made to himself two days earlier circled through his mind. It was time.

"Well everyone, this has been fun, and I want to thank you for spending this day with me but there's something I need to do before I get ready for the wedding. So ... I'll see you all later." He started to walk past Stevie.

"Wait," Stevie said. "What's so important you have to leave us on your wedding day? Is it something we can help with?"

"No. Thanks. This is something I have to do on my own." Rayne stopped and looked back at the others. "Father?"

Theodor's brow crinkled but he inclined his head. "Is everything all right?"

Rayne nodded.

"If that's what you want, we'll leave you to it, Son."

Andrew scooted past the others. "I'll head back to your suite now, then. Get things ready."

Rayne smiled at the teenager who so often acted like a wise older man. "I appreciate it. Thanks. I'll be there shortly."

With a wave, Rayne swerved away from the others. Stevie's question rose above the hum of voices again. "What next? We have a few hours before the wedding …"

Rayne lost the end of Stevie's words as he passed a stand of evergreens and picked up his pace. Not wanting anyone to know his destination, he ducked down behind some bushes, their spicy scent heavy in the steamy afternoon air. Once the noisy group was out of earshot, Rayne headed toward the far side of the palace.

53

ꝗ

The cool draft that greeted him chilled the sweat on Rayne's body as he entered the stone hallway beneath the palace. A shiver ran through him. The two guards he passed startled at his appearance, but both bowed and allowed him to proceed without saying a word.

Three other guards sat at a table playing cards in the small anteroom before the cells reserved for special prisoners.

"I need to see Duchess Cailyn." Rayne's words bounced around the stark room. All three guards jumped to their feet, one knocking his chair backward to the floor.

"Yes, Your Majesty," a guard with gray speckled hair said. He grabbed a ring of keys and opened the inner door.

Rayne took the keys from the bowing man, then closed the heavy wooden door behind him. The narrow passage stirred up memories of his time in the dark hole; moisture dripped in the distance. He paced to the third door on the left and rapped on Cailyn's cell door before unlocking it.

Her voice, subdued and soft, bade him enter. His eyes roamed the rough, uncut-stone room. Larger than the other cells, it was almost comfortable with a window that allowed in light. Set at ground level, it overlooked a broad, green, mani-cured lawn and a line of trees beyond.

Cailyn rose from her seat at the desk set within the window alcove and dropped into a deep curtsy. She wore a plain white shift and her unbound hair flowed in dark waves around her shoulders.

Dampness radiated up into the soles of Rayne's boots from the flag floor as he scanned the room. A simple cot and a second chair filled the remaining space. Uncertain why he felt the need to see Cailyn before his wedding, he scuffed the floor with the toe of a boot.

Cailyn lifted from her curtsy; a line of confusion set between her brows. "You wanted something?"

Rayne puffed out a breath. "No. Yes. I'm not certain." Rayne's eyes shifted around the room again.

Cailyn motioned toward the second chair. "Would you like to sit?"

Without a word, Rayne lowered into the seat, his sweat soaked pants pressed against his legs. A shiver ran through him and one question broke through his reserve. "Why?"

Cailyn dropped back into her chair and covered her face with her hands before running fingers through her tangled hair. "Why? You ask me why?" A soft, bitter laugh broke from her throat. She huffed. "Oh, my. That would be the question, wouldn't it?"

Her pale lavender eyes rose to meet Rayne's. "Vengeance, pure and simple. Oh, no, wait. There's nothing pure about ven-geance … nothing simple either."

She chewed the knuckle of her right hand and shook her head. "Nothing's pure and nothing's simple."

She shifted her gaze out the window, sadness tugging down the sides of her mouth. "When we were children, I looked up to your mother. She was the big sister who everyone admired and loved. I thought she would keep me safe always. But she couldn't; she married and left me.

"I lied to everyone, even myself. Said I was fine, I was happy for her. But beneath the surface this … this thing … this coil of dark resentment began to grow. Then you came along.

I was happy for Ro, happy that Brayden would have a friend. But the darkness birthed in me took new life in my son. I don't even know when I became bitter. It was just there one day."

She turned back to Rayne. "But you know all about that, don't you? After all you've done, all you've suffered, you still struggle to keep that beast down. I see it in your eyes. Tell me this, chosen Light Bringer; how do you live with it and yet not let it take control?"

Her eyes grew wide and she nodded her head several times, leaning forward, reaching out to Rayne. "Really, I want to know. Please explain this to me. Every time I think I've defeated the thing; it comes back stronger.

"I know how you tried to save Brayden on Binding Day. I've always known." A sob shook her. "And yet, the anger at how unfair the One had been wouldn't let go. Anger grew into fury ... a fury that demanded ... demanded retaliation. A great gulf of emptiness opened within me when Miles died. And I couldn't fight the anger any longer. Why did the One bless Ro with you and Theodor and curse me with such emptiness?"

She swallowed hard and her hands flitted around like flighty birds. "Beware the anger; beware the need for vengeance and self-proclaimed justice." Her voice rose until she was shouting. She dropped her hands to her knees, wheezing. "I wouldn't listen. Now I will face the consequences of my choices."

Her eyes lifted to impale Rayne's once again, pleading written in her lavender orbs. "Please. I want to be rid of the pain and anger. Help me?" Cailyn again dropped her face into her hands, soft sobs shaking her body.

Silence descended like a smothering blanket. Rayne sat unmoving. He didn't want to forgive his aunt, didn't want to help her. Didn't want to admit how much he still struggled with anger.

Every act of forgiveness he had offered over the years had been a gift of the One; every time he had preached the need for forgiveness and the incredible gift of the One's forgiveness had been a result of the One's love and guidance. There were moments when the cost threatened to overwhelm Rayne. But the One had held him close; the embers the One had planted within him as a child sustained him. And he had felt the loving embrace of the Son.

Despite Cailyn's actions, her need tugged at Rayne's heart. The One's warmth filled him. *I am with you. Help her.*

No words came, though inside Rayne committed himself to yet again respond to the One with a *yes. May my answer always be yes.*

He pushed onto his feet and crossed the gulf between him and his aunt in three steps, then pulled her to her feet and hugged her. Cailyn dissolved into hysterical crying. Rayne guided her to her cot. He pulled back the thin cover, helped her down where she curled in on herself. He pulled the cover up over her shoulders, turned, and left.

54

As the tailor's assistant finished the last few stiches on the hem of Lexi's bridal gown, Lexi stared at her reflection in the free-standing mirror the servants had set up before the final fitting began. The face staring back seemed a stranger. And yet she saw traces of herself. Her gold-flecked eyes. The light golden highlights that peeked out from her tawny locks now twisted and braided with white and silver flowers and left to cascade in flowing curls down her back, between her shoulder blades.

She ran her hands over the lace that formed tiny cap sleeves before running down the form-fitting front of the dress. She traced the pattern until it ended below her waist as the skirt streamed outward, bell-like, to the floor. She had never felt so beautiful.

"You look stunning." Rowena's voice held a hint of awe as the queen stepped in behind Lexi and set her hands on Lexi's shoulders.

"So do you." Lexi took in the beaded work that adorned the fitted bodice of Rowena's floor-length, dark blue silk gown. Rowena's hair had been pulled into a loose chignon and decorated with blue and silver flowers similar to the ones in Lexi's hair.

"Are you ready?" Rowena asked, her eyes twinkling.

Lexi shrugged. *I can do this. I can do this.* "As ready as I'll ever be. I just hope I don't trip going down the aisle."

"Not if I can help it." The deep voice sounded out of place to Lexi after spending the day with women. She squealed her delight as her father winked at her from his position at the open door. His eyes scanned her from head to toe and Lexi giggled. "What do you think? Will Rayne like it?"

Justus walked to Lexi and placing a hand on her arm, leaned in and kissed her cheek. "*Like* it?" He frowned. "He'll *love* it." He dropped his voice to a menacing tone. "Or he'll answer to me." He chuckled before continuing.

"Now, my dear, I'm here to do my fatherly duty and escort you to the cathedral. Your bridesmaids have already left, and your carriage awaits."

Rowena ran a calming hand down Lexi's back, a knowing look in her eyes. "You will do fine. Take a deep breath, relax, and enjoy yourself. This special day will not come again so delight in every moment. Rayne adores you. It's time you two celebrated your love." She placed a soft kiss on Lexi's cheek then winked at Justus. "You raised a lovely girl, Jus. Let's get her and my son married already."

The smile that curved Lexi's lips remained as she wrapped fingers around her father's elbow, and he escorted her through the palace toward the main doors. Servants gathered in the hallways and doors as they passed, waving and offering well wishes.

The late afternoon sun's rays hit Lexi in the face as the red, fiery disc dropped toward the Cameron Sea, still carrying the heat of the day. Lexi blinked as she lifted the hem of her dress and descended the four steps from the palace to the drive where a carriage and a team of matched white horses awaited.

Lexi swallowed and allowed the smile to dissolve as her father handed her up into the flower-bedecked, open landau. Delight filled her and she wanted to dance with the joy of it as she bounced around on the blue leather seat trying to look in every direction at once from the open carriage.

The driver climbed onto his seat. With a slap of the reins and a jolt they moved forward toward the open gate and the Great Square. The moment they left the palace grounds, the noise of the crowd assaulted Lexi's ears. The smile from earlier worked its way up from the tips of her toes to her face and she laughed. Her father reached over from where he sat opposite her and rested a hand on her knees. She met his eyes and they both laughed.

Well-wishers filled the square to overflowing. Hundreds of flags with the Kierkengaard insignia fluttered. The carriage moved at a snail's pace across the packed square to the front of the Westvale Cathedral. Lexi waved and laughed, caught up in the excitement.

When the landau stopped, Lexi hopped up and swayed, almost losing her balance.

"Steady now, daughter." Her father stood and took her elbow, stabilizing her. "You won't be able to walk up that aisle if you trip and break a leg."

He slipped past her as the driver opened the door and lowered the steps. When her father's feet hit the pavement, he and the driver turned to help Lexi descend. Under normal circumstances, she would snub the affront to her ability to jump from a coach, but with the dress hampering her movements, she gratefully placed her hands into the two waiting palms and using caution took dainty steps until her feet were planted on the ground and she stood smiling up at her father.

Reality bent as Lexi climbed the steps. She looked up to see the immense double doors leading into the narthex set wide open and her world spun. The crowd of people who had followed her to the cathedral now pressed in on her and taking a breath seemed impossible. Each step was a hurdle and once she was past them the large entry loomed like a dark cavity beckoning her to her doom.

Then her father's left hand touched her back and gently turned her to face him. "Look at me Lexi. His hands moved to rest on both her shoulders. "Breathe, Lexi. Just breathe." She locked eyes with him and breathed along with him, her out of control anxiety shrinking to manageable proportions. "You've got this Daughter. You and Rayne are meant for each other. Remember the One's words. Just breathe and take one step at a time." He rubbed her shoulders and her muscles relaxed under his warm, strong hands. "You okay?"

She nodded, forming words seemed an impossible task.

"Rayne's in there waiting for you. Now, let's get this wedding started."

The fear slipped from Lexi, her breathing evened out. "Daddy?"

Justus's eyes widened at the use of the term of endearment. "Yes?"

"I love you."

His face lit with a wide smile. "I love you too, Daughter."

Lexi turned to face the entryway and straightened her spine. Justus stepped in next to her and she wrapped her fingers around his elbow. "I'm ready."

Cool air caressed Lexi's face as she entered the darkened interior of the cathedral. The first thing she saw was the painting of Rayne defeating the Demon Master right here in this cathedral on Binding Day. It drew a smile of contentment to her lips. This was right. She and Rayne were meant for each other. Studying the painting, her heart beat a rapid rhythm. Rayne in all his glory, the lights of Ochen streaming up to meet the descending white light of the One. Memories of that moment stirred in her. *Thank you blessed One for bringing us through so much to come before you now and speak vows of commitment.*

Her attention shifted from the wall of the narthex to the sanctuary. Prismatic lanterns from Veres flickered along the main aisle setting the colors of the rainbow to dancing throughout the vast expanse. Other memories clamored for her attention; her first meeting with Rayne, meeting the elders of Carwyn Rill, the night she and Rayne spent singing with the people of the small village. She set them aside. Now was not the time to visit the past.

The faint fragrance of myriad blooms drifted on the air. Flowers set around the lanterns seemed to come alive as the flames tossed and wavered. Her eyes followed the glowing path and she saw Rayne.

Breathe. Just breathe. She thought her heart would break from the pain of so much joy flooding through her. As if he knew her gaze had fallen on him, Rayne's eyes locked on hers. Sparks flew between them as Lexi took in his raven-wing black hair, now trimmed to just hit the collar of his charcoal colored form-fitting jacket, before meeting his amazing amethyst eyes again. Her heart thumped harder. *O Blessed One. I love this man so much! Thank you!*

Voices called for Lexi's attention but the need to break eye contact with Rayne at this moment tore at her spirit. Sashi hurried to Lexi's side from a small room attached to the narthex, Anne following a few steps behind. Again, the question was asked, this time by Sashi. "Are you ready, Lexi?"

Lexi glanced back up at Rayne and he smiled.

"Yes." Lexi's answer came out strong and certain. "Yes, Sashi. Are you two ready?"

Anne handed Lexi her bouquet and a soft smile bloomed on her face.

"Nemora's moons," Sashi said. "We've been ready for the last three years."

Justus stepped next to Lexi and she once again circled her fingers around his arm. He signaled to the organist and the cathedral echoed with the strains of a wedding march.

55

Shaw shifted again and Rayne stifled a chuckle. The need to laugh juggled positions with the need to cry. He shook out his hands, his sweaty palms catching the slight movement of air that filtered through the cathedral from the doors set ajar to catch the evening breeze. He began to understand Mite's habit of hopping from foot to foot when excited and he scanned the packed benches hoping to catch sight of the ancient.

Shaw's voice sounded from next to Rayne's right shoulder. "Stop fidgeting; you're making me nervous."

Noah chimed in, standing like a statue on Shaw's right. "You've got this. Don't think; just breathe."

An unbidden memory from Rayne's past wormed its way into his thoughts. *Don't think; keep moving. Faster. Faster.* Rayne gritted his teeth against the unwelcome reminder of what he had been. But the visions of that day burned across his mind. *How could someone as beautiful as Lexi possibly want to marry a murderer? I should end this now; before it gets any further.*

The warm presence of the One permeated Rayne. The One didn't speak; Rayne understood. The accusations weren't from the One; they were from the Demon Master. Sent to attack Rayne especially at this moment.

They cannot stay if you bid them go. The One's words pressed into Rayne's spirit.

Rayne released a slow steady breath then drew in another. He closed his spirit to the spiteful words replacing them with quotes from the One's Words.

The warmth within Rayne strengthened and a vision opened before him: Lexi running on their favorite beach, three children pursuing her, the littlest one barely remaining upright as he toddled after her. Lexi turned back and, with an exclamation Rayne couldn't hear, sprinted for the little one, snatching him up and swinging him in a circle. They both laughed as waves crashed next to them and Lexi's loose hair whipped around her face in the wind.

The vision broadened and Rayne saw himself walking toward Lexi and the children, carrying a large picnic basket. The two older children, a girl and a boy, turned back and ran to embrace him. Such joy flooded through Rayne his legs went weak and his body threatened to drop him to his knees as the vision vanished.

Lexi stood alone in the narthex doorway just beyond the end of the aisle. *A vision. Another vision.* But she wasn't a vision. She was real … and staring right at Rayne.

Their eyes met and tears burned the backs of Rayne's eyes. *This is real!* He stifled the urge to run to Lexi. She looked like an angel in her white gown, her hair cascading down her back, flowers entwined in the tresses.

I … I … I'm going to breathe. Breathe. Breathe.

First Sashi then Anne moved into position, blocking Rayne's view of Lexi. The organ began the wedding march and Rayne went numb.

Lexi took her first step down the aisle. Time froze and Rayne's world shrank to a joy filled link of love uniting his spirit to Lexi's. A gift of love from the One.

Lexi's eyes met his and nothing else mattered. Their moment had arrived.

cswachter.com
Facebook page: C. S. Wachter
For more information about the worlds of
Ochen.
And updates on what's coming next.

REVIEW?

Reviews help others make informed decisions about
the books they choose to read.
If you enjoyed *A Weight of Reckoning*
please consider leaving a review on Amazon, Goo-
dreads, and/or any site of your choosing.

THANK YOU!

OTHER BOOKS BY C. S. WACHTER

THE SEVEN WORDS

The Sorcerer's Bane
The Light Arises
The Deceit of Darkness
The Light Unbound

Demon's Legacy: A Worlds of Ochen Short Story